I0775759

Fae Curses, Dark Kings,

and Other Things That Must Fall

The Leyward Stones, Book 3

Crystal Crawford

© 2022-2023 Crystal Crawford, first published in serial format as Part 3 (Episodes 66-128) of *Macchiatos, Faerie Princes, and Other Things That Happen at Midnight (The Leyward Stones, Season 1)*.

E-book and paperback formats published in 2023.

All Rights Reserved. No part of this publication may be reproduced, distributed, or transmitted in any form or by any means, including photocopying, recording, or other electronic or mechanical methods, without the prior written permission of the publisher, except in the case of brief quotations embodied in critical reviews and certain other noncommercial uses permitted by copyright law. For permission requests, contact ccrawford@ccrawfordwriting.com.

This is a work of fiction. Any resemblance to actual events or persons, living or dead, is entirely coincidental.

Cover art by Jason Crawford / Fierce, Inc.

Map of Faeside

before the first Dark War

Map of Faeside
Present Day

CONTENTS

CHAPTER 1

A WEE BIT OF SHOCK

Ayla

I never thought of myself as someone to charge into a conflict—much less a battle. But as I stand here, surrounded by people I love, I realize there's nowhere else I would choose to be. If the Dark King is coming for my friends and family, he'll have to face me first.

The ground quivers beneath my feet as Jordan and I stare toward the hilltop. Dark Fae soldiers, hundreds of them... all on the march, with a frenzied mass of darklings overhead.

Jordan tugs me deeper into the shelter of the trees.

My magic tingles at my fingertips, ready to protect him, because if I know one thing in all this craziness, it's that I _cannot_ lose him. Not again.

Behind us, our own small army waits hidden in the shadows, watching for Jordan's signal. Days of planning and preparation, and all the weeks of chaos and heartache beforehand, have brought us to this one moment. The Dark King's army is marching for Teionyr—and the fate of Upper Faeside depends on whether we've done enough to stop them.

One Week Earlier

I sat on the stone floor of what I'd heard them call the vault, still trying to get my bearings. Hadn't I just been in the middle of a battle in the market square? My memories from after Sevryn grabbed me were hazy—other than the terror, which I remembered too well.

But now, here I was with Jordan beside me, and with Grandpa, Callan, Madison, Reina, a Fae called Maxim Warwick, and a bunch of LeyGuards nearby. I could see it, now, the Fae in him. He was still my Jordan, but somehow even more gorgeous than before, with a new power rolling off of him... and a *dragon* peering down over his shoulder. I didn't even know how to process that.

Vyrthil was next to me, too—and Kaizyn, who was staring at me.

Kaizyn and I were now so entwined, my every tiny emotion was laid bare to him. He now knew how deeply I cared for him, but also how different it was from what I felt for Jordan. I was back with the guy I loved... and Kaizyn had just lost his kingdom.

Even if I couldn't *feel* his heart breaking, I would've seen it in his eyes.

"Kaizyn?" I stared helplessly at him, aching to soothe his pain.

His eyes locked on mine, and a wall of jealousy and despair slammed into me. This one man, this *Jordan*, now held the heart of the woman Kaizyn loved, *and* the throne of his kingdom. His whole world, shattered in a moment.

I couldn't change that reality for Kaizyn, even though my own heart was breaking for him. Any words I could think of to comfort him just felt like shallow platitudes.

Jordan leaned forward from beside me and held out his hand. "Kaizyn. It's an honor to meet you."

I glanced between them, feeling a glimmer of hope—they were *brothers,* now; maybe they could be friends—but a new wave of Kaizyn's anguish slammed into my chest.

He jumped to his feet. "I need a moment."

"Wait!" I stared up at him, desperate to help. "Maybe there's still a way, some magic that could undo this. So you—so we can both—be free."

The slice of pain that lanced out at me told me that had been the wrong thing to say.

I reached for him. "Kaizyn—"

He spun and hurried for the vault door, Vyrthil on his heels.

"Let them go," Jordan said softly from behind me.

The crowd of Teionyrians in the tunnel parted, and Kaizyn and Vyrthil rushed out.

As Kaizyn's boot-steps faded off into the tunnel, an awkward hush fell over the vault.

Kaizyn's grief still crushed in on my chest. I wanted to go after him, to fix things, but my emotions had partly *caused* his pain. He said he needed a moment, needed space... and chasing after him might have only made things worse.

Jordan knelt next to me and reached for my face. "Are you okay?"

His steady gaze grounded me, returning my focus to the vault—and the people around me—despite Kaizyn's pain still churning in my chest.

I stared at Jordan for a long moment. He was here—really *here,* and still alive.

I threw my arms around him.

He caught me against him, wrapping his arms tight around me and burying his face in my hair. "I missed you so much," he whispered near my ear.

Behind his shoulder, the massive red dragon watched me calmly with her head slightly angled to one side, as though trying to decide what to make of me.

I shivered.

Jordan pulled back to look at my face. "What's wrong?"

His gaze immediately followed mine to the enormous, shimmering-red snout hovering behind him.

"Oh." He relaxed. "Don't worry; she won't hurt you. She's safe."

"She?" I stared at the creature behind him.

Jordan's mouth quirked up into that half-smile that made my heart skip. "Would you like to meet her?"

Champ danced around the dragon's front feet, sniffing excitedly. Surely, the dragon couldn't be that dangerous if Champ wasn't worried, right?

But I froze as the dragon tilted her face so one of her enormous, dark eyes could stare more intently at me.

"I—"

Grandpa slapped his hands on his knees beside me. "Well, *I'd* like to meet her! It's not every day a dragon saves your granddaughter's life."

Jordan laughed, though his eyes never left mine. "You have nothing to worry about, Ayla. I promise." He squeezed my hand, then pulled back and stood, and tugged me to my feet beside him.

Grandpa moved up next to us, eager to see the dragon more closely.

A few feet away, Striker, Brone, Reina, Callan, Madison, Jordan's and Reina's parents, and Maxim Warwick all hovered, wearing expressions that ranged from curiosity to awe.

"The rest of you may as well come over and officially meet her, too," Jordan said, then turned back to me. His eyes lingered on my face, studying me with concern. "Are you feeling okay? You still look pale."

Honestly, I couldn't answer him. I *was* feeling strange—but between Kaizyn's churning emotions, the shock of almost dying, the relief of having Jordan with me again, and the startling terror of a *dragon* staring me down, my brain and body had a lot to process.

Grandpa stepped up next to me and squeezed my shoulder. His gaze swept over my face, and whatever he found there seemed to reassure him. He turned to Jordan with a spark of humor in his eyes. "She nearly died, she's bound to a Fae former-prince, and now her boyfriend is a Fae king *and* sear-bound to a dragon. You can hardly blame the girl for displaying a wee bit of shock, son."

Boyfriend. I glanced at Jordan in concern. We'd never discussed—

But Jordan only smiled warmly, without the least hint of pressure or judgment, and squeezed my hand. "I'm not her boyfriend... yet."

The mischievous glint in his eyes as he said it sent my heart racing.

Jordan grinned and turned back to the others. "I hope to remedy that soon, but first... Sorcha is demanding I introduce her." He gestured to the dragon.

"She's talking to you?" I gaped at him. "How?"

Jordan just smiled wider. "In my mind. I guess it's kind of like your mind-gift, though she says she can't speak to others, only me."

I glanced between Jordan and the massive red beast, who was still staring calmly at me with that one huge, dark eye. "What—what does she sound like?"

It was hard to imagine what it would be like to have a *dragon* speaking in my head.

A tiny puff of smoke escaped the dragon's nostrils.

Jordan grinned. "She finds you amusing."

I looked at the dragon. "That was a *laugh*?"

Jordan reached for my hand. "Yes. And to answer your previous question, her voice is rich and warm... kind of like a ball of light in my mind." He shrugged. "It's hard to explain. Sorcha doesn't really use words, but I can understand her."

"Her name is Sorcha?" I asked him, my heart pounding as I met her stare.

"Yes," Jordan said, squeezing my hand. "She said it means 'brightness.'"

I took a deep breath, then stepped around Jordan and planted myself in front of the dragon's enormous snout, fighting the urge to run.

Her head tipped to the side, like a puppy's, as she studied me.

"Thank you," I said, forcing myself to hold her gaze. "Thank you for saving my life."

Slowly, she shifted forward.

I held my breath as her nose came to rest against me.

She was so huge, I fit head-to-toe in the scaly, surprisingly warm surface between her nostrils. Warm puffs of air escaped on either side of me as she breathed out, wrapping me in a scent like charred wood.

Everything in me screamed to run, but before I could swing into full-blown panic, I felt Jordan grab my hand.

Sorcha pulled back, putting space between me and her snout again, and peered at me.

One glance at Jordan, and I could tell *something* had just been exchanged. "Wh—what did she say?" I asked him.

He gripped both my hands and pulled them to his chest, then looked straight into my eyes, his voice barely audible as he answered. "She said you owe her no thanks, because she and I are bound, and saving *you* was the same as saving *me*."

The world around me fell away as he stepped so close our faces were nearly touching. I didn't even care that the others must be staring.

He wrapped one hand around both of mine, still held to his chest. His eyes searched mine as he raised his other hand to tuck a strand of hair behind my ear.

My heart raced.

"Ayla, if you had died, I—"

A spear of pain lanced through my chest. My legs buckled.

"Ayla!" Jordan caught me before I hit the ground, then carefully lowered me to the floor. His eyes were panicked as he scanned my face. "What is it? What's wrong?"

Grandpa rushed to my side. "Ayla?"

Another stab of pain rushed through me.

Kaizyn.

I could feel him, his anguish, the sharp, piercing grief of loss and despair, so strong it was a physical pain. He was *hurting,* even worse than before. And I had caused it.

"Kaizyn," I rasped. The pain was so intense, I almost couldn't form the word.

"It's the bond," Grandpa said. "An entwinement like this—it can create a feedback loop. Her emotion and exhaustion compounds his, which in turn compounds hers, and—" His words blurred to vague sounds.

A fierce, icy rush shot through my veins, like being dunked in ice water from the inside out.

I gasped. My vision blacked. My body seized in shivers.

"What's *happening*?" I heard Jordan yell. He squeezed my hand. "Ayla?" His hand jerked back. "She's ice cold."

"That's her magic," Striker said, suddenly beside me. "Something's wrong."

"Her *magic*?" someone asked.

Puffs of breath swept over my face, carrying the scent of burnt wood.

I was so cold, the warmth felt like hot, stinging needles.

I cried out in pain.

"Ayla!" Grandpa called out, but he sounded far away.

"Sorcha says to get her outside." Jordan's voice was sharp with worry.

Arms wrapped around and lifted me. The familiar scent of Jordan enveloped me as he tucked me to his chest.

A new rush of shivers racked my body as memories of the day he'd rescued me in Grandpa's room flooded my senses. I clutched his shirt with both shaking hands.

"Hold on, Ayla," he whispered, then his voice hardened. "Do it. *Please!*"

A hot puff of burnt-wood breath flooded my nostrils, and everything dropped away into blackness.

CHAPTER 2

ALWAYS LIKED HONEYSUCKLES

Rory

By the time I made it to the archway at the east barrier of the Arcvale dome, the pain in my ribs was so bad I could hardly breathe. I kept running. If Keyja was right about this attack, I had to warn the Hub, and fast.

As I covered the last few steps, I shifted the satchel under my arm and shoved the stone Keyja had provided out in front of me.

The air inside the archway shimmered, then split open right ahead of me.

I stumbled through.

Darkness swallowed me.

I sucked in hitching breaths against the pain in my side and tried to look around. This Gate was supposed to take me to the Hub. Where was I? Everything was black.

Dread seeped in as I realized I must be back in the Void. But how? And how would I get *out*?

I turned around slowly, hoping to find the Gate behind me.

There was nothing, but in the darkness to my left, suddenly I heard low voices.

"Did anyone see you come through?" The voice was thin, reedy, and croaky, like how witches talk in movies. It could've been a woman's voice, or maybe an old man's.

"No." The answering voice was smooth as silk and definitely a woman, the kind of voice you'd hear from a sultry bombshell in an old black and white film—except that this woman's voice stirred a cold wrongness in my chest, though I wasn't sure why. The sultry voice laughed. "Why? Don't you trust me?"

"You know I don't, Miravel," the croaky voice answered.

"You don't trust *anyone*."

The voices were coming closer.

If there had been anything to hide behind, I might have. Instead, I clutched the stone and the satchel to my chest, quieted my heavy breathing as best I could, and listened.

A small, golden glow appeared in the direction of the voices. It was bobbing in mid-air. A lantern?

The light was getting closer—and fast.

Instinct told me I couldn't let these two catch me here, though I still wasn't sure why. I moved backward, but there was nowhere to hide. Maybe if I stood still, they would just pass right by me.

"Exactly," the croaking voice snapped, far too close for comfort. "I *don't* trust anyone. That's why I'm still ali—" Her words halted, and so did the bobbing glow. "Do you smell that?"

The glow swung my way, and the glare of a lantern was suddenly right in my face. Behind it, just barely as tall as my shoulders, was the *ugliest* old hag I'd ever seen, holding the lantern up in the air with a gnarled, clawed hand.

I froze.

The hag sniffed the air—*sniffed* it, like a dog—then stared right at my chest with a vacant expression. "Miravel, come here. Do you see anything?"

The most beautiful woman I'd ever seen stepped into the lantern's glow. Her hair fell in dark, glossy waves over the shoulders of her long, sweeping dress, and her face was gorgeous—full lips, the perfect cheekbones, eyes rimmed with dark lashes, skin that looked soft as silk. I couldn't have dreamed up a prettier woman if I'd tried, but when my gaze moved to her eyes, the strange glint in them immediately turned my stomach. She was pretty; no one could argue that... but there was a *wrongness* inside her, the same one I'd felt in my chest, and the longer I watched her the more I could see it.

Her mouth twisted in concentration.

I held my breath and stood absolutely still as she stared right at my face, but seemed not to see me at all.

She shrugged and turned away. "I see nothing. Let's go. You're wasting time."

I almost sighed in relief.

The hag huffed, still staring straight through my chest. "But I *smell* something." Her voice was whiny, like a begging child.

I could almost hear the other woman roll her eyes. "I said let's *go.*"

The lantern pulled away from my face as the pair turned the other direction.

Desperate to breathe, I slowly exhaled.

"Wait." The woman called Miravel turned back around, and this time her eyes locked right on mine. A chilling smile spread across her lips. "*There you are.*"

A cold, icy feeling spread in my chest, just as a blinding pain shot through my head.

"Gah!" I cried out, gripping my head with one hand.

The woman yanked at the satchel under the other arm.

"Stop it! Let go!" I yelled.

"Easy," I heard a very different voice say, and the dread and ice immediately faded. Hands were gripping my shoulders, gently steadying me. I heard a little gasp. "You're Rory Kane, right? How did you even open that Gate? It's been inactive for years. Rory—are you okay? Rory, look at me."

The pain in my head eased. I blinked my eyes open and found a pretty girl around my age, staring at me with large, dark, frightened eyes.

"Rory?" Her voice was bright and kind, even in her concern—almost musical. Compared to that thick, sultry voice threaded with evil still echoing in my mind, it was the most beautiful sound in the world.

With that voice, her strange clothes, and those big, dark eyes, I wondered for a second if I'd stumbled across some kind of magical woodland pixie. But then I noticed the surrounding room—polished floors, doors along the walls, bright overhead lights, stairs leading up to a second level. Was I in some kind of mall?

I glanced around. No, I must've reached the Hub. But everything felt so *bright*, still, like my eyes couldn't quite adjust.

The girl's delicate hands tightened on my shoulders. "Are you all right? What happened?"

I blinked at the ground beside her, where a massive cat stared up at me, twitching its tail.

I looked back at the girl. "I don't know. I—"

A strange ringing swelled in my ear, and the girl's face blurred.

"Rory, did something happen when you came through the Gate? Are you okay?"

Pain surged through my head again.

The girl's hands tightened on me as the room swayed. "Someone help!"

My knees gave out.

I felt the girl throw her weight against me to try to hold me up as I sank to the ground, and as the room faded from my vision, I had the strange realization that she smelled like honeysuckles.

I had always liked honeysuckles.

CHAPTER 3

CAN I HOLD HER AGAIN?

Jordan

Ayla sagged in my arms, unconscious. Her skin was rapidly growing colder, her lips turning blue. Panic seized my chest. I spun toward Sorcha. "What do I do?"

The sun will help me warm her, Sorcha said in my mind. *Hurry.*

I rushed out into the tunnels with Ayla still in my arms.

Sorcha followed me with her head ducked and her wings tucked in tight, barely fitting through the doorway.

The Teionyrians clustered at the cavern entrance jumped aside to let us through.

I neared a junction. Which way was the surface?

"Left!" Maddox yelled from behind us.

I took a sharp left, grateful for his sense of direction.

Maddox continued to call directions until finally I burst out into the open courtyard of the palace.

I rushed out the palace doors onto the hilltop and skidded to a stop in the blazing heat of the sun.

I'd scooped Ayla up on instinct, like I had that day at her house, but this was different—the thing harming her was *part* of her, that blasted bond, and I didn't know how to fix it. "What now?" I asked Sorcha.

Put her down.

I lowered Ayla to the dirt and paced anxiously next to her as Sorcha lowered her nose back to Ayla's chest. It was stiflingly hot outside, enough to start a trickle of sweat down my back.

Already, the color was returning to Ayla's lips.

"Are you doing that?" I asked Sorcha.

Not entirely, she answered, with something like a sigh of relief. *I am warming from within, with my magic. The sun is warming her skin. Only a little, but it helps. It is doing enough to give my magic time to work.*

Her voice carried a note of wariness.

Dread filled me as I wondered whether we might have lost Ayla, if the sun hadn't given that little extra sliver of time.

After a few more moments, Sorcha stepped back.

"Can I hold her again?" I didn't care how pathetic I sounded. I just needed to feel Ayla in my arms, to feel her skin warming and know she was safe.

Sorcha nodded her massive head, and I rushed forward to pull Ayla into my arms.

She felt almost normal again, with just a slight coolness to her skin, like she'd been sitting in an air-conditioned room.

Her magic is churning within her, Sorcha spoke in my mind. *I cannot prevent this from happening again when she wakes. I've only given her peace, for the moment. She will sleep for a time.*

My heart sank.

I repeated Sorcha's words to the others, then turned to Ayla's grandfather. "What do we do?"

His expression was grave. "We need to find Kaizyn."

Madison spoke softly, her wide, scared eyes locked on me. "Callan went to find him."

I glanced around, only then noticing that though everyone else had followed us outside from the cavern, Callan was gone.

I clutched Ayla against my chest where I knelt.

Her face was calm now, her breaths coming smoothly. But what would happen when she awoke?

The pain I'd seen in Ayla's eyes before Sorcha had sedated her had ripped my heart in two. I *hated* that she was bonded to Kaizyn, that his emotions could affect her this way, though I knew it wasn't really his fault. I'd have been heartbroken too, in his position... but *my* heartbreak wouldn't have nearly killed Ayla. I hated that she'd intertwined herself more deeply with him to save me. I hated the way he looked at her, like his heart belonged with hers. Knowing Ayla, even if she really did love me, it would hurt her to hurt Kaizyn. I hated that, too. And I hated that I was helpless to fix any of it.

There was nothing I could do to make this better for her.

Except, I realized suddenly, removing myself from the equation.

My chest clenched at the thought, but what if it was the only way to keep this from happening again? Kaizyn's broken heart over seeing Ayla and me together had set off this reaction, and my presence would only ensure this happened again and again. But if were to step away...

That would hurt Ayla too, but maybe not as much as being stuck in the middle, feeling Kaizyn's heartbreak every time she turned around. Maybe not as much as this.

I brushed Ayla's hair back from her forehead.

Could I do it? Could I walk away? *How* would I even do that? I had responsibilities in Teionyr, now. Ayla would know exactly where to find me, and if she stayed to try to change my mind, I'd fold in a heartbeat.

Wouldn't I?

You could be cruel to her, make her want to choose the other, Sorcha's voice sounded in my mind.

I spun toward her in shock.

Her warm voice chuckled in my mind. *But you would never, I know, because that would also hurt her. I am only helping to whittle down your choices.*

Her large, keen eyes studied me, and I could see a spark of mischief in them, one that rubbed me the wrong way.

"Is this a joke to you?" I whispered. "And how did you even know what I was thinking? You said you couldn't read my mind."

Her gaze softened. *I can't, King-of-mine, but I can feel your essence. There is a knowing, between a dragon and its bonded one. I know your heart, and I understand the situation. I simply put the two together with the expression on your face. It was not difficult. And no—I do not make light of this. I only wish to help you see the truth: that there is no way out of this without one or both of you getting hurt by it, even if only for a time.*

Only for a time. I could do that, right? Choose to be the one hurt by this, to remove myself from the equation, just long enough to find a way to break their bond? Because we *would* break their bond—of that, I was certain. I refused to believe otherwise, no matter what Maddox and Maxim said. I would break this bond, so long as Ayla still wished it to be broken, no matter *what* it took.

Callan rushed out of the palace, interrupting my thoughts. "The pri—I mean, *Kaizyn*, is leaving. When Ayla fell unconscious, the 'feedback loop' was severed, and he came to. He refuses to stay, knowing he caused her so much pain. He thinks distance may prevent another incident."

I glanced between Ayla's grandfather and Maxim Warwick. "Will it?"

Maxim shrugged. "Perhaps. I've not had much experience with entwinements like this. It's possible physical separation may lessen the effects."

That was a promising option.

"He can't just leave," Ayla's grandfather said, stepping toward me. "His life is still tied to Ayla's. He must be kept safe. Leaving the palace is too big a risk, especially now. Something dark is brewing; I can feel it."

His words sent a chill down my spine, but then Callan spoke again.

"Kaizyn is heading for Arcvale as a place to gather his thoughts. Sevryn's curse lifted the moment he died—Kaizyn just verified it himself with a runed sensing coin. Kaizyn is free now to move where he wishes. He's already on his way to the Gate that empties close to Arcvale. He will be safe there, with Keyja and Tofa. They're long-standing friends."

I studied Callan. I knew of Arcvale, though I'd never been myself. A strange and powerful Fae was said to live there, one usually spoken of as dangerous. "You are sure he'll be safe there?" I wished my concern were solely for the prince—he was my brother, of sorts—but though I did not wish him harmed, Ayla's safety was far more on my mind.

Callan nodded. "Yes. Keyja will protect him, plus I am going with him—if you will allow me." His eyes locked on mine.

Madison tensed. "What?"

Callan glanced at her with an expression of true regret.

At the same time, I asked, "Why in the world would you need my permission?"

A look of discomfort entered Callan's face as he turned back toward me. "I made a vow to protect Teionyr's *king*. My duty is to stay with you."

I swallowed. "You made that vow to Kaizyn, not to me. I understand there might be technicalities to that vow, but I want you to go where you feel you need to be, and right now, I can tell that's with Kaizyn."

"But—"

I waved away his protests. "Keeping him safe also protects Ayla, and I know that matters to you, too. Go with Kaizyn. Keep him safe. That's my official instruction... as your *king*." I couldn't believe I was saying that.

Callan studied my face. "Yes, my king." There was a hint of a smirk as he said it.

I smiled back. "Good. Now go. I don't know how much longer Ayla will sleep. If we really think distance will help, he needs to be gone before she wakes."

Callan nodded, then turned to Madison. "Can I speak with you inside?"

She followed him into the palace foyer.

Reina hurried over and knelt next to me and Ayla.

"How can I help?" Her eyes caught on Ayla, and she bit her lip. She looked nearly as concerned for Ayla as I was. "Should we wait and see if Kaizyn's distance helps? Or... is there a faespell we could try, maybe something to calm her when she wakes up?"

I turned to her. "Reina—go with Callan. Please. And your parents, too, if they're willing."

Her face paled. "What? Jordan, you're my *partner*. I can't leave you now, of all times. You're about to take over a whole kingdom, in the middle of a war!"

I met her stare, and I could see the loyalty there. She had been the best partner and friend I could've hoped for, even if I now suspected there had been something a bit *more* from her side that I never reciprocated.

"Reina." I reached for her shoulder. "Please. I trust you more than *anyone*, and keeping Kaizyn safe means Ayla is safe. *Please*."

She glanced at Ayla, and resolve solidified in her eyes. She looked back at me and nodded. "Okay."

I let out a relieved breath. "Thank you."

"Of course." Reina smiled, though it didn't quite reach her eyes, then hurried over to speak with her parents.

My parents came near, and Maddox scooted back as my mom knelt beside me.

"Jordan," my mom said softly, "Take a breath. You can't carry everything yourself, love. I know you care deeply for Ayla; we all do..."

She laughed at the look I gave her.

"Okay, maybe not the same way you do. But we *do* care about her, and you know Maddox does, too. This is *not* all on you." She placed her hand on my arm.

I stared down at it, glancing between her hand and Ayla's still face.

Beside her, my dad nodded. "She's right. You know we're here for you, but this—this might be something out of your power to solve. We'll call the Hub, see if they have any ideas. You don't have to figure this out alone."

As good as their support felt, something in me knew that part of this *was* mine to figure out. What if Kaizyn's distance wasn't enough? What if Ayla woke up, only to be racked with pain again? Maybe this wasn't all on me to fix, but there *was* a part of this that only I could do… the part where I stepped aside, if that was what it took to help her. Was I strong enough to do that?

I tightened my grip on Ayla, then stood and turned to Maddox. "You know this palace. Is there a room where we can take her? Somewhere she'll be comfortable until she wakes? But *not* in the prison wings." There were beds there, but the thought of returning to the prison wings now that I'd finally escaped them was unappealing.

Maddox nodded. "I haven't been here in years, but I'm sure there are still comfortable rooms in this palace. I'll help you find one."

"Actually," Maxim Warwick interrupted, "the prison wing might be just the place. Its wards against magic may dampen the girl's connection to the—to Kaizyn. It won't sever the bond, but she might not feel it as strongly, there. Between that and his distance, she may be able to wake with no ill effects."

I nodded slowly. I hated the idea, but he had a point. With both Kaizyn's distance and the prison wards, would that mean I wouldn't have to keep *my* distance, after all? My heart latched desperately onto that hope, at the same moment I fought to believe it. I had to be ready to walk away, if she needed me to, at least until we figured out a solution. I exhaled. "Okay… Yeah, that makes sense. We can try it."

Madison and Callan stepped back outside, Madison clinging to Callan's arm. She met my gaze with a startled stare. "You're going to put her in the *prison*?" She sighed. "I mean… I suppose our room with Etcher, whoever he really was, wasn't so bad. The bed was decent." Her mouth twisted. "I would offer to sit with her, but I—I'm going with Callan. To check on Rory. Callan said he's still in Arcvale."

From the look on Callan's face, that had been a reluctant concession on his part, though I could also tell he was partly relieved. I was sure it was a hard decision for him, trying to balance Madison's safety with his desire to be near her.

I huffed. Join the club.

"It's okay," I told Madison. "Ayla's grandfather can sit with her until she wakes. Right?"

"Of course I will," Maddox said, turning to me with a look of surprise, "but where are *you* going to be?" It was clear from his stare that he hadn't expected me to leave Ayla's side.

I felt a blush rise as everyone stared at me. I supposed I had made my feelings for Ayla pretty obvious, though I wondered how *she* would feel about this, were she awake. I didn't plan to leave her side unless I had to. But if, when she woke up, my nearness triggered some kind of pain loop between her and Kaizyn again... I needed to know someone would be with her, someone she trusted. Just in case.

I didn't want to explain all that, though. So, I shrugged. "I might have to handle kingdom business, right?" That was true, too—I had been Teionyr's new king for all of fifteen minutes. I wasn't sure yet what my daily duties entailed.

Maddox's shrewd gaze told me he knew it wasn't my real reason. "O... kay," he said.

My mind raced. Was I even doing the right thing by encouraging Kaizyn to leave? Would Ayla be unhappy about this when she woke? Would the bond make it painful for her to be away from him? Would *me* being with her be enough, or even helpful? I wasn't sure.

Maddox placed a hand on my arm, and his expression melted into something like compassion. "Ayla and I do need to get back to check on her parents, soon. With any good luck, Sevryn was the main conduit for that veilmist and now that he's dead, my son and his wife have woken, good as new. But if not—"

"Oh," I said. I was ashamed to admit I'd nearly forgotten about Ayla's parents. "Of course. Of course, you should check on them. Both of you. I'm sorry; I should've—I'm sure there's a LeyGate nearby you could—"

He chuckled. "It's okay, son. Let me worry about the logistics. But Maxim here has assured me he can work up a faespell that can help them, if they've still not woken. As soon as Ayla's stable, I need to head back to get it to them, though I hope they'll already be awake and waiting for me, ready to demand a full explanation of what happened to them and to scold me for letting their only daughter get bonded to a Fae." He grinned at me, then his grin slipped. "Ayla should come with me, to see her parents. They'll be worried sick. Besides, with this bond, and now with her new magic, the Hub is the best place for her right now. She'll be safe there while she learns how to control it."

I nodded, though my heart twisted when I glanced down at her. Ayla and I hadn't discussed where *we* stood yet, but she had her own life. I knew that. She was her own person, and she had a family, other friends, other people she cared about. She *needed* to go be with her parents... or even with her former prince, if that's where she was happiest. But I—I was king now. I had to stay here.

I wanted Ayla to be safe and happy, I truly did. It just sucked, really sucked, that somehow the place she'd be safest and happiest never ended up being *with me.* It was like I never had a chance.

Callan cleared his throat. "I know you'll need help, getting to know the kingdom, learning the ropes, especially with all the damage to the city. I'm sure the people will be frightened, and a familiar face might..." He trailed off. "Anyway, I'm happy to help you, if you'd like. Once I'm sure Kaizyn is safe and settled, I'll come back to help you however I can."

Right—because again, I was a *king*, now. Of a kingdom in the middle of a Dark Fae war.

I stared at him. "Thank you."

Callan took Madison's hand. "We're heading out. We'll check in as soon as we can."

They headed down the hill toward the city, probably to meet Kaizyn at whatever exterior LeyGate Callan had used to get here.

Maddox stood. "Let's get her to a room, then we'll figure out the rest."

He grabbed my arm and helped me stand too, since I was still holding Ayla.

Sorcha spoke in my mind. *Go with him. I will wait here.*

"Okay," I said, trying to keep my voice even as I turned to Maddox. "Lead the way."

My parents and Maxim moved behind us, ready to follow.

As we headed for the palace door, Maddox reached over and squeezed my arm.

When I looked at him, he smiled comfortingly.

"I know you don't want her to go back to the Hub without you," he said, "but you two will be together again quickly. I know you will. Trust me, I know my granddaughter, and she'll insist on returning to you the moment she's able, war or no war. She'll be back by your side before you know it."

I smiled back, my heart twisting... because though I hoped with everything in me that he was right, unless I could find a way to break this bond while *also* saving a whole kingdom from war, I really didn't know if she would.

CHAPTER 4

THE DISTRACTION IS MUTUAL

Callan

I tugged Madison's hand as we hurried toward the LeyGate tucked into the trees outside of Teionyr. The Gate was well concealed, and the short segment of the Void it emptied into before connecting with the Gate to Arcvale was most likely safe, but I still didn't want Kaizyn attempting to travel it alone.

Madison lagged behind. When I noticed her arm extended fully, her steps tripping as I dragged her along, I immediately felt guilty.

"I'm sorry." I slowed my steps. "I'm just eager to catch him before he leaves without us."

Madison's words were breathy as she answered, winded from the jog I'd put her through. "Do you think he would?"

"Yes." I had no doubt. Kaizyn hadn't wanted me to accompany him—he'd made that clear by leaving while I was still talking to the others.

Madison tightened her hand on mine. "We're going to the same place he is, right? If we miss him here, won't we just catch up to him there?"

There was logic to her words, but Madison didn't know the Void like I did. There were a thousand reasons Kaizyn could vanish between the Gate and our destination—but I didn't want to worry her. "Probably. Most likely."

She glanced over at me. "That's not a *yes*. What aren't you telling me?"

I stopped and turned to face her.

Voids, she was beautiful, even with dirt on her face from the battle in the square.

Her green eyes stared up at me, questioning.

I sighed. I couldn't lie to her. "What do you remember of the Void from when the hound brought you through?"

Her perfect lips twisted into a frown. "Not much."

I was glad for that. "There may be dangerous things, creatures I would not wish the prince to face alone. But you don't need to worry, not when you're with me."

She smiled. "I know."

I knew right then: *I would die for this woman.* Though I'd prefer it if I didn't need to.

I squeezed her hand, and we continued walking—quickly, but slow enough this time that she wasn't struggling.

She glanced at me again, her expression curious. "You still call him the prince. Isn't he... not?"

I shrugged. "He is still the king's son, adopted or not. He'll always be the prince, to me."

Her steps slowed. "Are you against it, then? Jordan being king?" Her voice sounded cautious, wary of my answer.

I smiled back at her. "Not in the least. It is his rightful place." The magic had made that clear. "Besides, I think he'll make a great king. But Kaizyn is..." I paused, searching for the right words. "He is family." I couldn't help the sadness that came with the words—I could only imagine how Kaizyn must've been feeling about everything.

Madison squeezed my hand. "You're a good man, Callan. A good guard, and a good friend."

I squeezed her hand back, then increased our pace slightly. "I try to be."

I'd spent my life serving Prince Kaizyn, protecting him, fighting by his side against every challenge he faced. But now his biggest challenge would be facing his own heart... and in that kind of fight, I had no clue how to protect him.

The edge of the forest came into sight in the distance.

"The Gate is just within those trees," I told Madison as she hurried along beside me.

"Will it hurt?"

I glanced at her in surprise, then realized she'd never properly traveled a LeyGate before. Of course, she would have questions.

"Not at all. Just keep hold of my hand; we'll briefly pass through the Void between this Gate and the one that opens to Arcvale."

Her grip on my hand tightened as we stepped through the row of trees. "Okay."

The Gate loomed in front of us, dark shadows pooling beneath the arch like an omen of what waited beyond.

When I glanced over, Madison looked far less worried than I expected.

She seemed to notice the shock in my gaze. She shrugged. "I trust you."

Those words, and the shy smile that accompanied them, made me wish we could have a few moments to spend together besides running from one place to the next. But duty always came first in my life. Always had, always would. It was the life of a guard, the life I'd been born to and trained for—protecting others, keeping them safe. I wasn't sure I could escape that urge to protect, even if I'd wanted to.

I loved Kaizyn, and I liked being a guard. I liked being useful. I just hoped that one day I could have a life of my own, too. Something of my *own* to protect.

Madison's soft fingers grazed my cheek, startling me. "Where do you go, when you stare off like that?"

I stared back at her. "To thoughts of you. Always."

Her smile could've lit the Void.

Yeah—that wasn't helping with my distraction.

"You must be thinking of me a lot, then." Her smile turned gentle. "You're quiet and thoughtful today. More than usual." She squeezed my hand, and her smile slipped. "I know you're worried about Kaizyn."

"I am. But—" A short laugh escaped me. "I'm usually very focused. You seem to be distracting me."

She gave me a teasing smirk, then stepped forward and threw her arms around my waist in a hug. "The distraction is mutual." She stared up at me, arms still around my waist. "But let's go check on our families."

In that moment, as I stared at her, I wanted nothing more than to offer her that life I'd begun to envision—a home, a family, safety and stability... together.

But that security, that steadfast togetherness—it wasn't something I could promise. Not now. Not with my kingdom in danger, Upper Faeside still at war, and my friend and prince in anguish. As always, my duty as a guard—as a Teionyrian, and as the prince's *friend*—came first. Maybe it always would.

Someone like Madison deserved better. She would want a family, safety, stability—a life I couldn't offer. And someday soon, she would realize that.

I pressed a gentle kiss to her forehead. "You drive me crazy, Madison Kane. But yes, we should go."

I stepped back and laced my fingers through hers, then we walked into the shadow of the Gate.

Chapter 5

I Don't Need a Babysitter

Kaizyn

I was ten steps from the Gate to Arcvale when the air split open behind me.

Callan and Madison stumbled out, clutching one another.

Madison's cheeks were flushed.

Vyrthil paused beside me, his tail twitching as he glanced up at me, waiting to see what I'd do.

I turned back toward the Gate. "Go back, Callan. Your duty is to the king, now."

He grabbed my shoulder.

Vyrthil let out a low growl at Callan's contact.

Callan quickly dropped his hand. "My first duty is to you, always, brother."

I glanced back at him. _Brother._ He hadn't used that term in years, not since we were children.

The sincerity in his eyes made my heart twist enough that I turned the rest of the way to face him.

He deserved that much, at least.

As I stared at him, I wondered how true the term _brother_ might be. We'd used it rarely, growing up, and only as a term for the closeness of our friendship. I would've willingly died for Callan, though my father would never have allowed it. Despite his fondness for Callan, Father would've said my duty was to the kingdom, my life too valuable. I would have done it, anyway. Callan had always been my best friend, as good as family to me. But now, knowing I wasn't *actually* a royal, I couldn't help but wonder how closely related Callan and I were. We truly could be family. Not brothers, given our similar ages and that my mother had died soon after my own birth, but perhaps cousins, even if distant ones. The thought arrested me for a moment, taking my mind elsewhere.

"My prince?"

Callan's hesitant voice brought me back to the present.

"I'm not a prince." I couldn't help the resentment seeping through my voice, though I tried to subdue it.

Callan huffed, eyes sparking with impatience. "You *are*. No more of this nonsense about royal lineages. The king *chose* you, he adopted you, and in the absence of his original heir, he made you next in line to be king. You're as much a royal as Jordan himself, so can you stop feeling sorry for yourself for a single moment and look at the truth? Our people *need* you, Kaizyn. As soon as this fiasco with your and Ayla's magic is figured out, you have to go back."

This fiasco with my and Ayla's magic. That was one way of putting it, I supposed, if by *fiasco* he meant absolute, gutting misery every time she looked at Jordan. How could I possibly explain that whenever she even glanced at Jordan, my whole chest burned like I'd swallowed acid?

"Go back and do what?" I snapped. "Follow the new king around?" The words came out venomous, but I was too exhausted to apologize for it.

I hadn't *asked* to become this, to feel all this. I hadn't asked to fall helplessly in love and then have my heart shredded, or to be bonded to someone who would never return my feelings. I hadn't asked to be trained my entire life to take a throne I no longer had a right to, or to watch the people I'd devoted my life to—*risked* my life for—bow and pledge loyalty to someone else. I hadn't asked to be forever alone.

"Just leave me alone, Callan."

Vyrthil bristled beside me at the pain in my tone.

I flicked a finger at him, signaling him to stand down.

I tried to ignore Madison's startled, green eyes gaping at me as she clutched Callan's arm, but they pierced something inside me, anyway.

I might not have asked for this, but I chose how I responded to it, and Callan didn't deserve my anger.

I sighed. "I'm sorry. I just... I can't go back. I'd only get in the way."

The truth was, I couldn't trust myself anymore, not while my magic was like this, while my *emotions* were like this, and I hated myself for that weakness.

Callan's voice softened. "He's going to need you too, Kaizyn. Jordan, I mean. He wasn't trained for ruling Teionyr. *You* were." He paused, studying me a moment. "I can't help but wonder if your father always intended for the two of you to work together."

My chest tightened. "I don't know what *our father* planned. I just know I need to get away."

"From Jordan, or from Ayla?" Madison asked.

She slapped a hand over her mouth as Callan turned to her in surprise.

"I'm sorry, I shouldn't have—"

I blinked at her, then sighed. "No. You're right." That familiar pain twisted in my chest.

The fury in me still roiled, eager to lash out. I was doing my best not to aim it at those who didn't deserve it.

But who *did* deserve it? Ayla? Jordan? Neither of them had chosen this, either.

The real answer, I'd had to admit more than once during the last few painful hours, was *myself.* I had been the one to bring the vial to the café, to trigger this bond. *I* had been the prince too weak to protect his kingdom. Everything that came after, whatever else had happened, was all on *me.*

I felt my walls lowering, for the first time in days.

Vyrthil relaxed, sensing the need for a fight had faded—though I wasn't entirely sure it had.

I ran a hand down my face. "I suppose I am running from her, as much as from anything."

Madison stepped closer. "I get it—I do. But will running really *fix* anything?"

I wasn't sure why I was baring my heart to a human I hardly knew... but Callan trusted Madison, and that was worth a lot to me.

"No." I sighed. "I *know* it won't fix anything, but I also don't know how to—"

The air split open again, and a red-haired girl in LeyGuard gear rushed out, one I'd seen in the vault.

"Reina?" Madison stared at her. "What are you doing here?"

"Jordan sent me," she said, her eyes settling on me.

My walls shot back up. "I don't need a babysitter."

Reina's eyes were cold and hard as they locked on me. "I never said you did."

"Then why are you here?"

She crossed her arms. "Believe me, I don't want to be."

I spoke through clenched teeth, my patience gone. "Then why *are* you?"

Callan glanced between us, then turned to face Reina. "I can protect Kaizyn. You don't have to stay."

Under his stare, Reina's coldness thawed a bit. "I know you can, but these are my orders."

To my shock, Callan acquiesced and nodded. "I see." They stared at each other a moment. An understanding seemed to pass between them.

I remembered, then, that Reina and Callan had been friends at school. He'd said she was a close friend to Jordan and Ayla, and that she had shown him kindness, had been warm and welcoming to him, even before she knew who he really was.

She crossed her arms and glared at me. "Well?"

Where was that warmness, now? From the moment this girl had arrived in Faeside, I'd seen nothing from her but bull-headed ferocity, a trait which it now seemed she'd decided to direct at *me*.

I bit back the sarcastic response I wanted to give and simply stared at her.

There was a flicker of something in her expression—sadness? Uncertainty?—as her gaze shifted to Callan, then to Madison, and back to me.

I decided not to press her further, since she was obviously as unhappy about her orders as I was. This was the LeyGuard girl Ayla said had fought off a mob of darklings while dangling by her fingertips from the side of a cliff. I hadn't seen much of her in the battle at Teionyr, but what I had seen was enough to make me wary of upsetting her. Between my battle skills and my magic, I could take her down if needed, but she would certainly get some jabs in with that sword or her dagger along the way, and I much preferred my abdomen *without* holes.

The Gate beside Reina crackled and split open again, and the mystery emotion I'd seen on her face vanished, replaced again by the icy glare.

"My parents are here," Reina said, and sure enough, two adult Ley-Guards who were obviously related to Reina stepped through the Gate into the Void.

The air snapped shut behind them.

"Good, we're all here," the man who must've been Reina's father said.

Reina nodded, then turned to me. Her tone was steely when she spoke. "Open the Gate to Arcvale. We're ready."

Callan put his arm around Madison, while Reina and her parents stared at me.

I sighed, then reached to open the Gate as they all moved closer behind me.

Apparently, I had *five* babysitters now. Fantastic.

CHAPTER 6

LIKE A THIRD WHEEL

Reina

I glared at the back of Kaizyn's head as he reached to open the Gate to Arcvale. How dare he be so snippy with me, when I was only here to protect him? So he didn't want a babysitter. Who would? I definitely didn't want to *be* one. But apparently Jordan and Callan both felt he needed one, otherwise he'd be heading for Arcvale alone.

"This Gate does not open directly into Arcvale," Kaizyn said in a grumpy tone that sounded as though he wished the rest of us would leave. "It empties at the edge of a village just beyond Arcvale. We'll have to walk the rest of the way, but it isn't far."

My parents nodded.

Callan grabbed Madison's hand then grunted his assent.

The gate shimmered to life, then the five of us followed Kaizyn through its opening, from the darkness of the Void out into a sunlit, grassy hilltop. To the left, visible at the base of our side of the hilltop, stood a small, abandoned-looking village.

No, *abandoned* wasn't the right word. It looked like it had been looted. Carts were overturned in the dirt paths between the tents of what had been the town's quaint marketplace, and even from the hilltop, I could see clouds of what looked like flies swarming over the spilled and spoiled fruits. The scattered cottages along the roads beyond the market had been assaulted as well—most of them looked like the doors had been kicked in, and others bore dark char marks, as though they'd been burned.

"What happened here?" I asked.

"Dark Fae." Kaizyn's tone was clipped. "Come on. This way." He led our group toward the other side of the hill.

I gave the back of his head another glare for good measure.

When we reached the opposite slope, a massive, transparent dome glimmered in a valley below, encasing what looked like fields of wheat and a small cottage, with another village behind the fields.

"Arcvale," Callan said, mostly to Madison, while pointing toward the dome. "That's where Rory is."

It wasn't far. Our group could easily cover the distance within a half hour.

Kaizyn glanced back, scanning the group. He didn't quite meet my eyes. "Let's go."

As we walked, I grew increasingly irritated with Kaizyn. He kept glancing back, waving us onward as if we weren't walking quickly enough, though what the hurry was, I had no clue. He didn't seem nervous, which I would have understood—in Faeside, dangers could hide even in an open field. Instead, he just seemed impatient, as though arriving in Arcvale would somehow alleviate his need for his guards.

Come to think of it, he wasn't even acting like we *were* his guards. He'd assumed control of the entire group, bossing us around. Didn't he realize we weren't his servants? Callan might be, and maybe Madison was cool playing along with that, but my parents and I weren't here as Kaizyn's slaves. We were here to protect him.

I clenched my fists at my sides, glaring daggers into the back of Kaizyn's pretentious head. If anyone should be giving the orders in this scenario, it should be the ones responsible for his safety. He had called me a babysitter. Well, since when did the *baby* boss the babysitter around? I had half a mind to—

"Reina." My father's hand settled on my shoulder as he moved up beside me. He spoke low, for only me to hear. "Something is bothering you."

My mom moved up to my other side.

It wasn't a question. They knew something was wrong, probably because my knuckles were turning white from me digging my fingernails into my palms. I forced my hands to release.

My dad glanced at me, but he seemed to know I wouldn't want to talk with the others nearby. Fae hearing was far too keen.

A few minutes later, we reached the dome.

Kaizyn thrust his hand against its shimmering surface. His face went pale, like it hurt him, though the only other sign he gave of pain was a clenched jaw.

A moment later, he yanked back his hand and shook it out at his side, and a doorway-sized entrance opened in the shimmering barrier.

Kaizyn rushed straight inside without even a glance at the rest of us.

Callan turned to me. "Keyja won't want to leave the doorway open. Come inside, but once you're in, you can linger here near the barrier for a bit. Join us as soon as you can. I'd rather we all stay together."

So he *had* heard, and knew my parents wanted to talk to me. Great.

Madison gave me a small smile, then followed Callan inside the dome.

My parents and I followed close behind them, and as soon as we had all stepped through, the dome sealed shut behind us.

From inside the dome, Arcvale was fairly unimpressive, just ordinary rows of some kind of grain crop next to a grassy field. A cottage stood on the opposite side of the field, with a large, odd-looking tree next to it.

I'd heard that the ArcFae who lived here were strange... and extremely powerful. I was curious to find out more, but my mother grabbed my arm.

"We should talk," she said.

Callan gave me a nod, then he and Madison headed after Kaizyn, who was already halfway across the open field.

I turned to face my parents.

They both stared at me—Mom chewing her lower lip in concern, Dad with his brows drawn together.

"Reina..." Dad began.

"Why am I being difficult?" I preempted his question; I could see it in his eyes, that same look he gave me as a younger teen whenever I'd talked back or disobeyed.

He sighed. "Well, yes. But this—"

Mom interrupted. "We can see you're upset, Reina. Talk to us. Heaven knows we've all been through a lot these past few days, but this isn't like you. You're usually bright and cheerful, a positive force, not..." She trailed off.

"Not *what?*" I crossed my arms, already rankled by her words.

"Not like *that*," Dad answered, gesturing to my crossed arms and stiff posture. He reached for my shoulder, and his expression softened. "Something's truly bothering you. We can see it. We just want to understand."

For a moment, I just stared at them, wrestling with my own stubbornness. I didn't *want* to talk about it. But it wasn't fair to them to keep snapping at them, or to shut them out. They just wanted to help.

My gaze fell to my parents' boots. For some reason, when I had something difficult to say, it was easier to talk to their footwear than their faces.

"It's just..." I sighed and dropped my arms. "It's Jordan. I mean, after everything I've done to protect him, all the years we've trained together, I just..." I drew a breath. "It just *stings* to be sent away like this, right when he's facing the most important moments of his life. I mean, he's becoming *king* for goodness' sake. Of a *Fae* kingdom."

I raised my gaze to find both my parents watching me intently.

"He could have sent *anyone* to guard Kaizyn," I said. "Why did he send me? We're supposed to be best friends! I mean, doesn't he *want* me there?" The words had just poured out, my hands gesturing for emphasis of their own accord, as they always did. I breathed deeply and dropped them to my sides again.

My mom studied me, then she said softly, "You mean, why doesn't he want you there, *too*? Instead of only Ayla?"

I blinked. "Wow, Mom. Ouch."

"Well, that's what you really meant, isn't it? For years, it's been you and Jordan in the thick of things, partnered up, training and fighting together, and Ayla was the *other* friend, the one you saw at school. Now, Ayla's slipped into this world, too, and suddenly things are different. He's clinging to Ayla, and you've been pushed aside."

Dad glanced nervously at Mom, as though wary where she was going with this. "I wouldn't say *pushed aside...*"

I interrupted. "No." I could feel the ache of a sob in my throat, the hot press of tears behind my eyes. "Mom is right. I *have* been pushed aside, and it—" The tears were rushing forward now, I couldn't stop them. "And it *hurts.*"

"Oh, Reina."

Both of my parents had their arms wrapped around me before I could even take another breath.

They held me like that, sandwiched between them, as the tears slipped out.

"Why is he acting like I don't even *matter* anymore?"

I pulled back to look at them.

Mom clasped my face and wiped at my tears with her thumb. "Have you considered that he sent *you* here with Kaizyn because *you* are the person he trusts most? Ayla's life is tied to Kaizyn's... and it's clear how he feels about Ayla."

A huff escaped me. "Yes. That part is clear."

"Oh." Mom studied my face. "Is this *because* of how he feels about Ayla?"

My shoulders sagged. "No. I mean—I don't know. I love Ayla, I really do. Aside from Jordan, she's my best friend in the world. I would never stand in the way of them being happy together. I just..."

"It doesn't feel good not to be someone's *first* choice," my mother said softly. "You feel like a third wheel."

I sighed. "*Yes*. And I don't know how to explain that to where they wouldn't just feel bad, or... *sorry* for me."

Dad gripped my shoulder. "Your mother's right, Reina. When you have a job that means everything to you, you send the person you can *trust* with everything. Jordan didn't send you here because he didn't care if you were with him for his important moments. He sent you because he trusts you with what matters to him most. With you here, he can focus on what needs to be done, because he knows you'll have his back—in every way. You *are* his first choice, just not in the same way as Ayla is. And... I'm sorry to say, you may just have to get used to that. It doesn't mean he no longer cares about you. Sometimes, things just change. It's not necessarily for better or worse, it's just... different."

I drew a deep breath, trying to process that.

I caught movement at the edge of the field.

I looked past Mom and Dad's shoulders to find Kaizyn standing a few yards away, staring at me.

Immediately, my guard went up. "Do you need something?"

My tone came out harsher than I'd meant it to.

Kaizyn glanced away. "No, I just—" He stiffened. "Keyja wants everyone in the cottage right away," he snapped, then turned and strode off.

Dad sighed. "Reina..."

I stared after Kaizyn, and immediately I regretted lashing out at him. His position was even worse than mine. He was in love with Ayla, and though it was clear Ayla cared about him, she certainly didn't feel for him the same way he felt for her, and now he'd lost the throne, as well.

Callan and Ayla had both spoken highly of the prince. Surely, he wasn't a bad person, and he didn't deserve to be treated like one. He was going through enough as it was.

I sighed. "Kaizyn, wait."

He glanced back, his eyes scanning my face in curiosity, but his expression shuttered at whatever he found there. His eyes turned hard. "*What*? You don't need a guide to find a cottage that's in plain sight, right? I'm sure you are capable of making it there without me."

I blinked, stunned.

"Keyja is waiting. Don't dally." He spun and stomped off toward the cottage.

Nevermind. It was probably *good* for the people of Teionyr that Jordan was their king now instead of this jerk.

My father stared after Kaizyn. "When Callan briefed us at the Hub, he never mentioned how *moody* his prince was."

I shook my head. "Whatever. Let's just go to the cottage."

Mom put her hand on my arm. "Are you sure you're okay?"

I drew a breath, then let it out slowly. "I will be. Let's just do what we came to do and make sure the moody prince doesn't get murdered."

My parents nodded and let me retreat into the comfort of duty—something with which we were all familiar. I'd figure out the rest later.

When we reached the yard of the cottage, Callan and Madison rushed out to meet us.

"Rory isn't here," Madison said, her eyes wide and a little panicked. "Keyja says she sent him to the Hub."

"Why would she have done that?" my father asked.

I opened my mouth to ask a follow-up question, but my train of thought careened off the rails as two insane things happened almost simultaneously:

First, an enormous, shimmering cow-creature emerged from the cottage, barely fitting through the doorway... then a Fae with dragon wings stepped out beside her, and the entire electrical cattle-creature crackled and folded in on itself, then zapped its way into a circular *hole* in the winged Fae's chest like a bolt of pocket-sized lightning.

"Sky and heavens," I heard my mother mutter, then she and my father tipped forward into half-bows.

"You must be the Madame ArcFae," my father said respectfully as he straightened.

"Yes." The Fae woman's voice was firm and clear. "You may call me 'Dame Keyja."

Father pointed at her chest with a slightly trembling finger. "And that was—"

I tensed, worried he'd offend the strange woman by pointing at the obtrusively odd crackling ball of lighting in her *chest*, but she smiled.

"Tofa," she said lightly. "The last living striniak of Arcvale."

I suddenly wished I'd paid a *lot* more attention in Fae Cultures classes at the Hub.

"I do not mean to be inhospitable," she continued, "but this is not a great time for visitors. None of you are safe here. I sent the human boy to the Hub to warn them. The—" 'Dame Keyja turned to the giant tree, which close up, resembled more of a building-sized stalk of celery.

"To warn them of *what*?" I asked her, but she was staring intently at the tree's trunk.

"Are you certain?" she asked tensely, as though addressing the tree.

The tree's upper leaves waved.

Talking to trees. Okay. Make that *three* insane things happening in Arcvale.

Keyja spun back toward us. "Mraugathal has lost sight of them. The Dark Fae armies are coming, but they're blocking his vinesight, somehow. We can't see them anymore. We won't know they're here until they're right upon us."

"How many Dark Fae?" Dad asked, immediately in LeyGuard mode.

"Hundreds, maybe more," Keyja said, a slight tremor in her voice. She pressed a hand to her stomach. "As of the last report, they were headed for the Hub... through Arcvale's Gates."

I stared. "What does that—"

Kaizyn stepped out from the doorway of the cottage, his eyes hard. "It means *we* are all that stands between them and the Hub. Rory has gone to warn the Hub that the Dark Fae are coming... but it's up to *us* to stop them."

Chapter 7

Like That Ridiculous Coyote

Madison

"It's up to *us* to stop the Dark Fae? Can we even *do* that?" The words flew out of me in a panic, though I regretted them when everyone turned to stare at me. A blush flooded my cheeks.

Callan stepped toward me. "Dame Keyja and Tofa are more than capable of defending Arcvale. Kaizyn and I will help where we can." He paused, and suddenly I knew what he was about to say.

"You're sending me away?" The way my tears immediately surged up only added to my embarrassment. I must've looked so pathetic to everyone else. But I couldn't help my fear at the thought of leaving Callan again. Did he really have to send me away? Sure, I wasn't trained in battle like the rest of them, and I didn't have magic. I was human, through and through... and as Callan stared at me, chewing his lower lip in concerned thought, I realized that yet again, I was the weak link, the one who would inevitably need saving.

I sighed. "Of course you are. I understand. I'll go." It sounded poutier than I'd intended, but I meant it genuinely. If I stayed here, he'd have to split his focus between protecting me and protecting Kaizyn, which was the real reason he'd come.

I was a liability.

Callan grabbed my hand. His expression and voice were gentle. "I just need you safe. You understand that, right? If something were to happen to you…"

I stared down at our clasped hands. "Where are you sending me? Back to Ayla and Jordan?"

Callan tucked some loose hair behind my ear.

When I looked up at him, his brown eyes held a warm expression.

"I think that would be safest, especially since the Hub—"

"The Hub," I blurted, startling him. "Please. My brother. Let me go to the Hub. They'll be able to protect us, right? I need to make sure Rory's okay. And my parents…"

Callan's mouth twisted into a frown. "Madison, the Hub is where the Dark Fae are headed next. If we don't—"

He stopped, but not before I caught his meaning.

I could feel the weight of everyone else pointedly *not* staring at us, pretending not to hear our private exchange.

"Callan, what if you *can't* stop them here? I can't lose you, either."

His mouth curved up into that grin that always made my heart skip. "You won't lose me. Just let me get you to safety and leave me to worry about the rest."

His expression seemed utterly confident, but I couldn't help the lump of anxiety in my chest.

"Okay," I said softly. What else could I do? If my experience getting attacked by Sevryn and then kidnapped by the Fadehound and imprisoned had proven anything to me, it was how weak and scared I really was. Compared to Callan and the others, I was a coward. What help could I possibly be in the middle of a Fae war? I had nothing to offer any of them. I was just one more responsibility. I couldn't stay with Callan and put everyone more at risk by distracting him.

To my surprise, Reina came over and put a hand on Callan's shoulder. "Let her go to the Hub, Callan," she said calmly. "Traveling back through the Void to Teionyr would be too dangerous right now, anyway, and even if the Hub is the Dark Fae's target, the LeyGuard have wards and Guards all over the city, not to mention the dozens at the Hub itself. There really *is* no safer place to be if Fae attack."

Callan glanced back at her, then sighed. "You're right. As usual."

I mouthed Reina a silent *thank you*, and she smiled.

Callan turned back to me. "I'll help you get to the Hub so you can be with Rory. But please, promise me you'll stay there. I'm not pretending to hold any kind of authority over you, but for the sake of my sanity, *please* don't roam around the town." He pulled me into a hug. "I may look smart, but I promise you, I don't have enough brain cells to fight off Dark Fae and worry whether you're out getting kidnapped by them all at the same time."

I nodded against his chest. "I won't wander. If I need to leave the Hub, I'll be sure to ask someone to go with me."

Callan tensed, then pulled back to look at me. "I was mostly joking. Why would you need to leave the Hub? Rory's already there."

"My parents aren't, and I haven't checked on them since all this happened. I don't even know if that magic coin you gave me to fix my dad's mind worked."

Callan clenched his jaw, then he sighed. "Okay. But please, don't just take Rory. Take a LeyGuard, or something. I don't mean to disparage your brother, but—"

"No, I get it." I sighed, too. "He's only a human, like me."

Callan lifted my chin and stared into my eyes. "You aren't *only* anything. You're my everything. I love you, Madison."

My heart melted a little. I knew he loved me, though he'd never said it so boldly—or in front of others.

But I also knew that I couldn't truly be his *everything*, and I didn't expect to be. As much as he may have meant that phrase, he had other people he cared about, too. He had duties and responsibilities, people relying on him other than just me. I'd known that from the beginning, and I would never ask him to choose me over that. As much as I dreaded it, I had already decided that the day Callan felt he had to choose between me and his duties would be the day our relationship had to end—because I loved him, too, and I could never ask that of him.

As his dark eyes studied me, I wondered whether I should just end things between us now. It would happen eventually. I could feel it hanging over me, an anvil about to drop and flatten me like that ridiculous coyote in the cartoons. I was standing right under it, just *asking* to be crushed. We both were. I knew I should be the strong one, for once... but I just couldn't bring myself to do it. Not yet. It would hurt too much, and I just wasn't ready—which was further proof how weak I was.

My heart twisted painfully as I wrapped my arms around Callan and rested my face against his muscled chest. "I love you, too."

I truly did. More than anything.

I just also knew that one day—maybe sooner than either of us realized—that love would require walking away.

CHAPTER 8

A Pixie and a Moody Cat

Madison

Callan walked me to the Gate that Rory had taken, the one that led to the Hub.

The others hung back, giving us our moment to say goodbye without eavesdroppers.

There wasn't much left to say.

Callan pressed a kiss to my forehead. "I'll come for you as soon as it's safe."

I nodded.

He stepped back and squeezed my hand. "I love you, Madison. I truly mean that."

I smiled at him. "I know. I love you, too."

He watched me wordlessly, a world of things communicated in the intensity of his gaze.

I lingered on his expression a moment, memorizing it, then with a heavy feeling in my chest, I stepped through the LeyGate.

The cold, salt-scented air and bright lights which greeted me on the other side were immediately disorienting.

A smiling face popped up next to me. "Madison Kane!"

I blinked at the girl. "Do I—do we know each other?"

She seemed to be about my age, although her eclectic, flowing clothes had a youthful feel and she was dainty in a pixie-like way. Her dark hair flowed down almost to her waist.

"I know *you*," she said, good-naturedly waving her hand in the air as though brushing away my words. "Don't worry, it's not mutual... or it wasn't until now. I'm Dove." She grinned at me, then grabbed my hand. "Come with me. I'll take you to your brother."

"You know Rory?" Anxiety set in as she dragged me by my hand into the bustle of official-looking people crossing the courtyard in front of us. "Wait. I don't—who are you, again?"

She glanced back at me with a giggle, like she found me amusing. "Dove. Now, come. Rory's upstairs."

Dove led me through the mass of busy-looking people hurrying in all directions, to a polished staircase at the other end of the courtyard.

The adults rushing around us seemed not to notice the strange girl dragging me helplessly behind her, or maybe they just weren't concerned about it.

About halfway up the flight of stairs with Dove, I noticed a large cat staring down at us from the landing. I wasn't sure if cats could be judgmental, but if they could, this one definitely was. The way he glared at me gave me goosebumps.

"Wait, I have a message," I said as reality caught up to me. "'Dame Keyja said they've lost sight of the Dark Fae. They don't know where they are anymore, or when they might attack."

Dove looked back at me over her shoulder with an expression of concern, then nodded. "Thank you. I'll let the council know as soon as I show you to your brother."

When we reached the landing, the cat slid aside to let us pass, then swung into step behind us.

I glanced back at it. "Is that normal?"

"Don't mind him; he's always like that." The girl smiled, then tugged me to the right, toward a row of doors. "We're almost there. Here, it's this one." She placed her hand against a panel on the wall, and the opaque door slid open.

"Madison!"

I breathed a sigh of relief as Rory smiled at me, propped up by pillows in a cot against the far wall of what looked like a medical exam room.

"Rory, thank goodness!" I rushed toward him just in time for him to push to his feet and wrap me in a hug.

"I was so worried," he murmured into my hair.

"Me too. I heard you came here to warn the Hub, but the last I'd heard before that, you were injured."

"I'm okay now, I promise." He squeezed me tighter.

"I already told this to Dove, but... 'Dame Keyja lost sight of the army. They don't know when they might attack."

I felt him draw a breath then nod against my hair. "It'll be okay," he said simply.

At his words, some of the tightness released from my chest—even though I knew he couldn't *know* that it would be okay. Neither of us could.

We stood like that for a long moment, then Rory pulled back to examine me. "No offense, Mads, but... you've smelled better." His eyes widened. "Is that dirt on your face?"

I laughed. "Probably. I did almost die, you know."

He pulled me back into a hug, his humor vanished. "Yeah. I know."

Dove's lilting voice spoke from near the doorway. "Quinn and I have a shower in our room, if you want to borrow it. Quinn's clothes might fit you, too. She's my roommate."

I glanced at her. "No, thanks. I mean, I wouldn't want to intrude—"

She grinned at me. "No intrusion. I invited you, and Quinn won't mind. Come on, I'll show you where."

Rory stepped back. "Go ahead, Mads." His gaze lingered on Dove in a way that made me do a double-take. "You can trust her."

I raised my eyebrows and leaned near him. "It seems *you* certainly do." That wasn't a light statement. Rory hadn't dated much since high school, and he didn't trust easily. I wasn't sure he'd ever brought a girlfriend home or let them very far into his life, even back then.

He gave my shoulder a playful shove. "I just met her. But she's nice. She'll take care of you."

"Oh, I'm not a caretaker," Dove said sweetly from the doorway. "You'll have to shower and dress *yourself*, but I'll show you where before I go talk to the council."

I laughed, despite my discomfort that she'd obviously overheard everything. "A shower sounds wonderful." I squeezed Rory's hand. "See you soon?"

He nodded. "I'll be right here."

Dove led me across the landing to her room, which was more like an apartment than the dorm room or hotel room I'd expected.

"You live here?" I asked her.

She smiled and shrugged. "For now."

The apartment was strangely furnished, but somehow it suited her.

"You said your roommate's name is Quinn?"

"Yes," Dove said, leading me past a plush couch where that same glaring cat now perched—still glaring at me—and down a hallway to a restroom. "She's away right now. She won't mind if you borrow some clothes, though. I think hers will fit you better than mine." She pointed across the hall to an open door, what looked like a bedroom. "They're in her closet."

I bit my lip. "You're sure she won't mind?"

Dove smiled. "Positive. Quinny knows what it's like to be on the run. She'd never turn away someone who needed fresh clothes."

That was oddly comforting, though it didn't bode very well for Quinn's lifestyle, and opened a *lot* of questions I decided not to ask. I smiled back. "Thank you."

Dove shoved a giant, fluffy purple towel into my arms and skipped off down the hallway. "You're welcome! Shampoo's in the shower!"

The apartment door swung shut behind her.

I stood in the hallway for a moment, the judgy cat still staring at me from the sofa in the living room.

"Well. Okay." I took a deep breath and slipped into the bathroom.

The moment the hot water hit my shoulders, I forgot all about feeling awkward in a stranger's bathroom. The shower felt amazing. Dove's shampoo and body wash both smelled like some kind of flower, and the showerhead was one of those massaging kinds, even better than I'd expected. Rivulets of dirty water ran down as I washed my hair, but I was just thrilled to be getting *clean*.

By the time I stepped out of the bathroom, wrapped in that fluffy towel, I didn't even care that the cat was still glaring at me.

I crossed the hallway, then picked out the simplest outfit I could find from the back of Quinn's closet in hopes she wouldn't be needing it soon: a plain grey t-shirt and jeans that looked like they might be a little tight on me but should fit well enough. I turned to lay them out on the bed, wishing I could swap out my sweaty underthings, too. But I drew the line at borrowing some girl's underwear without permission.

To my surprise, though, there was a sealed package of fresh undergarments in my size sitting on the bed, tagged with a heart-shaped, hot pink sticky note: *Brand new, from the Hub supply shop! I hope they fit. XOXO—Dove.*

Okay, Rory was right. This girl was a gem.

I got dressed as quickly as I could, ran my fingers through my wet hair, and exited the apartment.

I pulled up short when I saw Striker leaning against the wall, chewing on a match.

"Oh! It's you."

He barked a deep laugh, then nodded. "It is. Came to report in and heard you were here. Thought I'd check on you."

I smiled at him. "Thanks. I'm okay."

Striker had been one of the guards who checked in on me in the hospital. Callan had told me he was a LeyGuard... and that I could trust him.

He grunted, then pushed off the wall and moved toward the stairs. "That's all I needed to know. If you need anything, I'll be around."

A thought occurred to me. "Wait. Striker?"

He turned back, still chewing that match. "Yeah?"

"Have you heard anything about my parents? I haven't had a chance to check on them."

Striker studied me. "Last I heard, they were back home. Reports say your father's got no recollection of what happened with the Selkbloods. The Hub *may* have led your parents to believe you and Rory were on a brother-sister vacation with some friends."

I gaped. "They lied to my parents?"

Striker nodded. "Until you and Rory were both back and ready to go home, the council thought it best not to panic them."

An ache settled into my chest. "Can I go see them?"

Striker held my gaze. "They don't know about the Fae world, and the council wants to keep it that way." He stepped closer, lowering his voice. "Though, as far as I'm concerned, that should be *your* decision to make. Not that they'll be fond of you leaving when we're on high alert like this."

He glanced around, then slid a coin etched with markings from his pocket.

"Here. This will open the Gate in the service corridor downstairs. Take this staircase down to the lobby, then go to the end and use the first double-door on your left. It's supposed to be for LeyGuards only, but everyone here is in such a tizzy making preparations, I doubt they'll even notice you. Follow it to the end, then take another left. You'll dead-end right into it. The Gate will drop you at the north edge of Havenridge. You can make your way from there, right?"

It was a short walk to my house from the north edge of town, maybe twenty minutes. I pocketed the coin, then stared up at him. "You're just... letting me go see them?"

He nodded. "Tell them whatever you think is best, even if it's the truth." He grinned. "Actually, I'd *suggest* it be the truth. World has enough lies."

I exhaled. "Yeah." The question was whether they'd even *believe* me. Suddenly, the promise I'd made to Callan popped into my mind. "Wait, Striker—I can't go alone. I promised Callan I wouldn't leave the Hub without protection."

Striker tilted his head, amusement glinting in his eyes. "Well, we can't have an angry Fae guard. That boy is far too good at throwing knives." He scratched at the stubble on his cheek. "I'd go with you, but I'm due for a meeting with the council in ten minutes. I'll see if I can find someone to—"

"We'll go." A voice from behind me made me jump.

I turned around to find Dove smiling at me. That unsettling cat sat beside her leg, glaring up at me. How had he even gotten out of the apartment?

I didn't want to offend Dove, but she looked all of five feet and a hundred pounds. I wasn't exactly sure a pixie and a moody cat were the type of protection Callan would approve. I opened my mouth, searching for words to let her down politely. "I—"

But Striker clapped my shoulder, nearly knocking me over. "Perfect!" He pulled his hand back and grinned at me. "Don't worry, she's fiercer than she looks." He leaned near. "But it's the *cat* you'll wanna watch out for."

Somehow, I believed him.

Striker winked, then strode off.

Dove turned to me with a cheerful grin. "Rory's just been cleared by Doctor Harlowe. We can all go together. This will be fun!" She grabbed my hand, tugging me back toward Rory's medical room.

"Yeah—fun." I stumbled along behind her, wondering how my parents would feel about Rory finally bringing a girl home to meet them... but I supposed, by the time we were done telling them where we'd really been, that would be the least of their concerns.

CHAPTER 9

SURVIVAL

Etcher (Varias Burgild)

I landed at the southern edge of Vinewood Forest and stretched my aching wings. Teionyr was in the far distance behind me, now—four hours of flying's worth of distance—and I still wasn't sure how I felt about it, other than *sore*. My muscles were protesting this much flight all at once, that was certain. Four hours of flying would've been negligible to me before, but after nearly two decades trapped as "Etcher" in Teionyr, I was feeling the strain.

I was also feeling the pull of *him*, that sharp tug against my rib cage which my agreement with Maddox and its accompanying tattooed runes had protected me from for the past seventeen years. Now that my vow to Maddox was released and the runes had faded, *he* could sense me again.

The Dark King demanded my return.

I reached my arms up over my head and rolled my neck, working out the kinks in my back as the overhead sun warmed my muscles.

The ache in my ribs remained, steadily intensifying.

I sighed and dropped my arms, swallowing back a lump of disappointment.

I'd almost forgotten what it felt like for the Dark King to control me. After so long in Teionyr, it had been easy to entertain the fantasy that when I was finally released from my vow to Maddox, I might actually be *free* for the first time in my adult life. I'd been foolish to hope a decade or so was long enough for the Dark King to forget his favorite slave. I should've known better. No matter how hard I tried to change, no matter how much good I added to the tally of my life, in the end, I would still be *his.*

If Maddox had known how deeply the Dark King held me, he may never have made the deal with me. Then again, perhaps Maddox had suspected. His reaction when he saw me in the market in Teionyr hadn't exactly been trusting. Maddox had used me, willing as I was, to hold his secret all those years ago—and I'd used him to keep my master at bay. I'd fulfilled my vow to Maddox, perhaps even above what was asked of me. A small part of me was proud of that. But Maddox had his secrets back now... and I'd been returned to my shackles. It didn't serve me, anymore, to pretend otherwise.

I turned toward the range of steep cliffs beyond the trees. This was the barrier to Lower Faeside—two steep mountain ranges with a bottomless cavern between them, topped with a thick ridge of magical fog. The fog created a supposedly impenetrable barrier, created in the wake of the last war. That war had ended with the establishment of Upper Faeside and Lower Faeside as two independent realms: Upper Faeside ruled by the Courts of Order, and Lower by the Courts of Chaos, now controlled by the Dark King himself.

For decades, that division—keeping the kingdoms of Morrowen and the Mountain Fae separate from Teionyr and Veylden and the Eldervines—had been enough to prevent further bloodshed. Travel between the two realms was strictly monitored, and travel to Earthside by those from Lower Faeside had been all but forbidden, a consequence of the brutality of the Selkbloods and the Mountain Fae's use of dark magic—chaos magic—in the previous war. But that's the thing about chaos. It doesn't like to be contained. In recent years, the attacks had resumed.

Now, the Eldervines were all but extinct, dozens of villages of various Fae cultures across Upper Faeside had been razed, and the kingdom of Veylden was reduced to rubble, still struggling to rebuild. Teionyr, with its strong ancestral magic, was the last remaining bastion of Upper Faeside's strength. If it fell, the whole realm would fall. The Dark King would rule all.

The rocky surface of the cliff in front of me shimmered as the sun hit it, the only sign that the hidden Gate was still there. It was one of several, and though Upper Faeside knew the Selkbloods had some way of breaching unmonitored into their realm, and the Teionyrians had discovered and sealed up several unauthorized Gates over the past decade, they'd missed a few—including this one.

I considered just walking away... but I knew from experience that if I ignored that tug against my ribs, the Dark King would not be merciful. Even from a realm away, he held sway over me. If I resisted too long, that tug would become crippling pain. If I defied him entirely, he would simply stop my heart from beating. *It would be a waste*, he'd told me once. *You're so useful, you see.* But he would do it, I had no doubt, if I ever reached the end of my usefulness.

Useful. That was to be my legacy. Not good, not honorable. *Useful.* As a young ArcFae looking to carve a place in the world, the power the Dark King offered me had been intoxicating, as had... other things. His promises had quickly soured, but not before I'd gone in too deep.

Try as I might, I could never go back—not to Arcvale, and not to the man I'd once been. I had killed Teionyrians in the assault on the palace all those years ago, and not even the rash vow I later made to Maddox could undo that—or the guilt I carried for my *own* people's lives. Because of *me*, the Dark King had attacked Arcvale when it was at its most vulnerable. Our leaders had been slain, the striniak's birth interrupted, our people's power severed, all survivors forced to flee our home. And in the wake, while I was playing a fake LeyGuard in Teionyr in an attempt to atone for my sins, the striniak *herself* had disappeared, and Arcvale had well and truly fallen. Any honor I'd felt in upholding my vow to Maddox was undone by the cost of that attack on Arcvale. The Dark King's forces had breached our dome because of what he had learned from *me*. I was a traitor, with my own people's blood on my hands. That sort of blood would never wash off, no matter how much good I tried to scrub it with.

My soul, at this point, was a lost cause. All I had left was survival.

The Gate on the cliff shimmered again, then split open. A beautiful woman stepped through, accompanied by a Veil-witch even uglier than most.

My heart sank. "Miravel." Of all the minions the Dark King could have sent, he sent the one who'd first lured me to serve him. I supposed he found humor in that, though I did not. My relationship with Miravel had lasted only as long as it took her to convince me to pledge my loyalty to the Dark King, but I'd believed I loved her, once.

Miravel's lips curled in a smile as she spotted me. "Hello, Varias. How lovely to see you again. Have you been well?"

Her voice was sweet as honey, but the glint in her eyes revealed the trap behind it. Her ploy was the same as always, though the memory of her lips pressed to mine now elicited more revulsion than longing.

I spoke through clenched teeth. "I've been better."

Her laugh rang through the air between us. "That much is obvious." Her keen eyes swept over me, no longer feigning politeness. "Can you even still fly? You already look spent."

I glared at her. "I'll manage."

The hag beside her huffed in impatience. "I'm not getting any younger, out here. That sun burns my eyes."

That hideous Veil-witch had been Miravel's sidekick since before we'd met. Once I'd seen the truth of who Miravel was, I partly wondered if the old hag wasn't just a physical manifestation of what Miravel was like on the inside. They were certainly both revolting enough.

Miravel glanced down at the Veil-witch, then turned back to me. "He's sent me with your next task."

I'd been expecting that. "Get on with it, then."

"You're to gather information, pretend to ally with the targets—find out what you can. Collect your report for the Dark King. Gain their trust, Varias. You're deceptive enough for that. Then remain in place until you receive further orders."

So it was to be my old job again. Had he not found anyone else in all these years to be his pet spy?

I sighed. "And where am I to insert myself this time? My cover in Teionyr is ruined."

She turned back toward the Gate, ushering the Veil-witch into the darkness, then glanced back at me over her shoulder. "Arcvale."

My chest went cold. "Arcvale is deserted."

Miravel's lips curved up into a sinister smile. "You might be surprised." She stepped through the Gate. "Lovely to see you as always, my dear."

The Gate snapped shut, leaving me alone by the cliff.

I drew a deep breath, then stretched my wings. *Arcvale.* Were there truly still survivors there? Did the domed village still stand? It was almost too much to hope for.

The curiosity of what I might find there pulled at me, but I hesitated. I could accomplish nothing good by returning. After my change of heart in Teionyr, I'd fed the Dark King just enough info to keep him appeased until I had the protection of Maddox's vow. The Dark King would never fall for such a thing again. He'd be watching me closely.

A sharp pain shot through my ribs, accompanied by a firm tug to the west. It faded swiftly, but left an ache behind—a promise of more to come, if I didn't obey.

I sighed.

Survival was the game, these days. And it seemed, for now at least, I had to play it.

CHAPTER 10

WE CAN'T JUST LEAVE

Ayla

I woke up in a soft bed next to a wooden armoire in an unfamiliar room. I was still fully dressed, and the bed's thick quilt was pulled nearly up to my chin. An overhead light was on, but dim. Beyond it were two doors, one that looked like a room door and another, narrower one I assumed was a closet. Before I could panic at not knowing where I was, I noticed a soft breathing and turned to find Jordan in a chair squeezed between the wall and the other side of my bed, sound asleep with his head and arms slumped against the bed's edge.

His presence relaxed me immediately.

I considered letting him sleep, but I had no idea where we were—and I sort of needed to use the bathroom. I slid my arms out from under the quilt and nudged him. "Jordan?"

He popped up, blinking as his eyes focused, then threw his arms around me. "I'm so glad you're awake." He pulled back, studying my face. "Are you okay? How do you feel? "

His golden eyes peered at me with concern. His hair stuck up on one side from where his head had rested against his arms, but it was kind of adorable.

I smiled. "Yes. I feel fine." And I did. The pain, the cold of my magic, and the overwhelming tide of emotion I'd gotten from Kaizyn earlier felt like a distant dream, now.

Suddenly I realized I couldn't feel Kaizyn *at all*. My chest tightened as that reality sank in.

"Where's Kaizyn? Did something happen? I can't feel—"

"Ayla." Jordan interrupted me, his voice gentle. "It's okay. He's okay. You're in the prison wing of the palace. It's warded to prevent magic. You won't be able to feel your bond right now. It's why we brought you here... to stop the feedback loop."

"Feedback loop?" I vaguely remembered hearing my grandfather use that term before I lost consciousness, but I didn't really need a full explanation. I had heard the term used about microphones and speakers. I could piece together what it meant when it came to the bond. I sucked in a deep breath. "Will it happen again?"

Jordan shook his head. "We're not sure. But Kaizyn's gone away, for now—to Arcvale. We all thought it best to put some distance between the two of you until the magic is under control."

I nodded. I cared deeply for Kaizyn, in a familial sort of way—but it was a relief not to have his emotions in my head, right now.

"Callan and Reina and her parents all went with him, to make sure he'll be safe." Jordan smiled. "Madison went too, though she didn't exactly go for Kaizyn's protection."

I chuckled, remembering how worried Callan had been about Madison. "No, I imagine not."

Callan obviously felt a strong connection to Madison, and now that we had her back, I doubted he'd want to let her out of his sight.

The thought of Callan and Madison together was heartwarming, but I still had to pee.

I bit my lip, feeling a bit awkward. "Um, is there a bathroom here?" I had no idea why it always made me uncomfortable to tell someone I needed to use the bathroom when it was literally a universal human function, but then again, I was also the kind of awkward human who couldn't figure out where to put my hands when I was having a conversation.

Jordan, however, was a pro at making me feel like he didn't notice my awkwardness. "Oh, right, of course. Yeah, this room has its own bathroom, over there." He pointed to a door on the other side of the room, the one I'd assumed to be a closet.

"Great." I sat up and swung my legs out from under the quilt.

A soft knock sounded on the door. "Jordan?" My grandfather's voice.

I glanced between the room door and the bathroom door, torn between which to handle first.

"He's been checking on you every half hour." Jordan smiled at me. "Go ahead. I'll let him in." He placed a gentle kiss on my forehead, then went to open the outer door.

I hurried over to the bathroom. It was surprisingly similar to a typical Earthside bathroom, but with a strange pull-chain contraption suspended from the ceiling for flushing the toilet and activating the water in the sink. By the time I finished up, Grandpa and Jordan were already deep in conversation by the bed.

"I know you're wary," my grandfather was saying, "but we can't put it off much longer. She needs to—"

They both turned toward me as I opened the bathroom door.

"Ayla!" Grandpa rushed toward me, throwing his arms around me in a tight hug.

I hugged him back, and when he pulled away, I stared at him in astonishment. He was steadier than before, his eyes clearer and sharper than I'd seen them in years. "Grandpa," I breathed. "You look—" I stopped, unable to find the right words.

Grandpa smiled and gently squeezed my arm. "I look like *myself*. For the first time in a long time."

His simple statement brought tears to my eyes. I nodded. "Yes. That's it exactly. It's like before, you had a layer of fog around you we'd all just gotten used to, and now it's been cleared away."

His eyes sparkled, then he placed a hand on my face. "My good girl. You've been through quite a lot. But it's time, finally, for me to take you home."

"Home?"

Grandpa nodded. "Well, to the Hub first, but home to Earthside, at least."

I stared at him. "But Jordan is king of Teionyr, now." I glanced at Jordan over his shoulder. "Aren't you? We can't just leave."

Jordan's face fell, and for the first time since I'd woken, he wouldn't meet my eyes.

Grandpa's touch on my cheek brought my gaze back to his. "Jordan isn't coming, Ayla. Just you and me. But now that you're stable, we should leave right away. With Sevryn gone, there's a chance the veilmist is broken and your parents are awake."

My parents. "You really think so?" A surge of guilt washed over me as I remembered we'd abandoned them at the Hub.

Grandpa smiled. "There's a good chance. And if not, Maxim has given me a faespell to try on them. Either way, we need to go back to the Hub, to check on them—"

I was nodding, even as I glanced at Jordan, feeling torn.

"—and to see about getting you trained in how to use your magic, so that it won't be as big a danger for you in the future, even if the bond does trigger it," Grandpa finished.

"The Hub can do that?" I asked.

Grandpa nodded. "That's the hope. Your magic is unusual, but you're LeyGuard. I'm sure there must've been a similar manifestation of magic somewhere in the history of the LeyGuard House families. There's bound to be someone at the Hub who would know where to point us in helping you learn to wield it."

I glanced at Jordan again. "But—"

Finally, Jordan met my eyes, and the look I saw there made my heart ache.

"I can't go with you, Ayla," he said. "Not this time. But Maddox is right, you need to go. You'll be much safer once you understand how your magic works. Plus, your parents could be awake now, and I'm sure they're anxious to see both of you."

I stared at him. "I want to see my parents, but..." My mouth twisted, like it always did when I fought the urge to cry. "I just got you back. I don't want to leave you." Ugh, stupid tears. Why did I have to sound so pathetic?

Jordan shoved his hands in his pockets and dropped his gaze to his boots.

Grandpa squeezed my shoulder gently. "You two need a moment to talk. I'll be out in the hall when you're ready."

Chapter 11

Magic Phone Stone

Ayla

Grandpa slipped back out into the hall and shut the door.

When I looked back at Jordan, he was watching me with anguish in his eyes.

I drew a steadying breath, forcing back the urge to cry. I had faced down monsters and Selkbloods and nearly died *twice*. Surely I could have one mature conversation about my concerns without bursting into tears.

"How long will I have to be gone?" I asked him. "Learning to use my magic, that could take..." I trailed off. How long *would* it take? Days? Weeks? *Months*?

His silence confirmed my worry—he didn't know how long it might take, either.

I opened my mouth to ask him to go with me, but he'd already given me that answer. He couldn't. He was *king* now. His responsibilities were here, in Teionyr.

Another knock sounded at the door, firmer than Grandpa's had been. "Your Highness?"

The unfamiliar, deep voice was followed by an annoyed announcement from my grandfather. "Give them a moment! They're talking!"

Jordan stared at me, then crossed the room in a few quick strides and pulled me to his chest. "I don't want you to leave, either. I swear, if I could, I would leave all of this. I never wanted *this*, I just—"

Another shout from Grandpa. "Hey! Don't you understand what a *closed door* means?"

Jordan pulled back and sighed. "Our meeting to discuss the logistics of me assuming rule of Teionyr is scheduled for tonight, but the palace staff have been bothering me all day for all kinds of *vital* business like deciding what type of food I want at my official coronation ceremony, and whether my dragon expects housing inside the palace..."

"I'm going to miss your coronation," I said, the realization just settling in. "Jordan, I'm so sorry. Maybe we can wait to leave for the Hub, or I can—"

His eyes locked on mine. "No. *I'm* sorry, Ayla. I never asked for this. I didn't want to be king. I only wanted—"

Another firm knock on the door. "Your Highness, you're needed downstairs."

I stared up at him, ignoring the knock. "You only wanted what?"

His gaze locked on mine. "I only wanted *you*."

I grabbed his face and pulled him down into a kiss.

He returned it eagerly.

The knocking on the door turned into a firm banging. "Your *Highness*."

Jordan groaned, then pulled away and yelled, "One second!" He turned back to me and cupped my face with one hand. "I love you, Ayla. I mean that. Somehow, there or here, I'll find a way for us to be together again soon. Okay?"

The sincerity in his eyes was so pure, I believed him. A small part of the knot in my chest relaxed as I nodded. "Okay."

Jordan pulled two flat, runed stones from his pocket. He pressed one into my hand. "Here."

"A summoning stone?" I asked, because it was similar to the stone Striker had given me before.

Jordan shook his head. "Not as good as that. It's for communicating. The stones are tied together by magic and runed with ten charges, and they work literally *anywhere*. Even across the Veil." He pointed to the stone.

There were ten identical symbols etched in a line across the stone's surface. "You just press your thumb against a symbol, and say the word to activate the rune. A rune on the paired stone will glow, and when the other person activates it on their end, you can hear each other. Each charge only gives a few minutes of communication time, and when it's used up, the rune vanishes. Once all the runes have been used up, the magic is spent—it won't work anymore. They're meant for short-term missions, and usually used only when there's a vital message to communicate."

I turned the stone, studying the symbols. "So... it's like a prepaid magic phone stone, but we can only talk ten times?"

He let out a soft chuckle. "Basically, yes. You can call me anytime you need to, even just to talk... at least until it's used up."

I looked up at him. "And what about after that?"

He leaned down and pressed a gentle, lingering kiss against my lips, then placed another on my forehead. "I fully plan for us to be back together by then," he mumbled against my forehead, then pulled back to smirk at me. "We just probably shouldn't use them all in one day."

I smiled up at him, though my heart was partly breaking. He wasn't just someone I was hopelessly falling for—although he certainly was that—he was also my *best friend*. The thought of returning to the Hub without him left a hollow ache in my chest.

"Your *Highness*," the voice said again.

Jordan winced. "I should probably go."

I threw my arms around him again. "I'm going to miss you so much."

He sighed and held me tight. "So am I."

I gave him one last squeeze, then pulled back and grinned at him. "You'd better go, before whoever that is out there blows a gasket."

He laughed, placed one final kiss on my forehead, then strode over and pulled the door open.

Grandpa stood just outside the door, casting an annoyed sideways glance at an anxious-looking Teionyrian guard.

"Your *Highness*," the guard sighed, a note of relief in the word this time. He gave a deep bow, then popped right back up. "Your dragon has set fire to the great hall. We managed to extinguish most of it, but now the servants are all terrified to go downstairs."

Jordan tensed. "*What*?" He tilted his head as though focusing on something in the distance, then sighed and rolled his eyes. "She says it was an accident. She was trying to entertain the children and didn't realize how flammable the curtains were."

The guard looked skeptical.

Jordan turned back toward me with a look of regret. "I'm sorry. I wanted to walk you to the Gate, but I—"

I smiled at him. "No, it's okay. Go be king. We'll be together again soon, right?"

He nodded. "As soon as humanly possible." The intensity in his gaze sent my heart racing.

"Fae-ly possible," my grandfather muttered.

We both turned to stare at him.

He shrugged. "Fae-ly possible, because he's a Fae."

I stared back at Jordan. He *was* a Fae.

A look of uncertainty crossed Jordan's face, but I smiled at him.

"Fae-ly possible, then," I said. "Whatever is fastest."

Fae or not, king or not, to me he would always be Jordan.

He strode toward me and pulled me into a kiss, to the absolute horror of the guard, whose face I could see over Jordan's shoulder before I closed my eyes.

The kiss was tender but short, then Jordan pulled away and grinned. "As you wish." He winked at me, bowed, then strode away.

The guard hurried along behind him.

I stared after them for a moment. Becoming king seemed to have unlocked a new, somewhat cheeky side of Jordan's personality, a side that reminded me oddly of Callan.

Grandpa chuckled. "Royalty suits him. I always knew it would." His voice softened on the final words.

When I looked at him, his eyes were misty.

I took his hand. "Come on, Grandpa. Let's go home." I glanced over at him. "You do know where the Gate is, don't you? Because I don't."

Grandpa laughed, a full belly laugh this time. "Yes. I do." He smiled at me. "Let's go see your parents."

A realization hit me. "Wait—Grandpa, Jordan gave me a stone to communicate with him, but he never told me the word to activate the runes on it."

Grandpa's eyes widened, and he lowered his voice. "Don't let anyone know you have that. Those were all destroyed after the Gates between the realms were sealed. They aren't supposed to exist anymore."

I blinked at him. "Oh."

He leaned close. "But the word to activate it is *vragal.*"

I raised my eyebrows. "You've used stones like these before?"

He smirked. "I *created* them." He pulled back, then offered his hand. "I'll tell you more some day, but right now, we've got a royal chamber to break into."

I gaped at him. "What?" Grandpa been pulling me into his shenanigans my whole life, but usually it was things like sneaking me candy after dinner or ordering pizza instead of eating Mom's leftovers, not breaking and entering in a palace.

He shrugged. "You didn't think we were going to hike a mile outside the palace to the Gate the others used, did you? I'm *far* too old for that. My bunions would revolt." He pulled a key from his pocket. "'Breaking in' is a loose term, anyway, since it seems they still keep the key in the same place they did seventeen years ago."

I shook my head and bit back a smile. Apparently, getting his memories back hadn't removed my grandpa's signature mischievous streak. "Okay, Grandpa. But if we get caught, I'm blaming you."

He grinned, then led me down the hall. "Of course, Peanut. I wouldn't have it any other way."

CHAPTER 12

Magic That Baffles the Great Maddox Rogers

Ayla

When Grandpa and I stepped through the Gate into the Hub, we were met with quite the commotion.

Chairman Hart ran out to greet us as soon as word reached her we had arrived.

"How are things in Teionyr?" she asked. "And the prince?" The look she and Grandpa exchanged made it plain she knew exactly who the true prince had been.

"All is well, and the true king is on the throne," Grandpa said.

Chairman Hart relaxed. "Good. Then I assume the others won't be returning yet?"

Grandpa shook his head. "They'll be staying a while. Reina and her parents have gone to protect Kaizyn in Arcvale. Callan is with them. Jordan and his parents remain in Teionyr preparing for his coronation."

Hart nodded, but then her face grew tense again. "I have news, and it's not good. Come, let's talk in my office."

I swallowed down my anxiety as she led us down the hall.

When we reached her office, she gestured for us both to sit in the chairs in front of her desk. She shut the door behind us and when she turned to us, she gave a brief smile. "I do have some good news, first. Maddox, your son and his wife are awake."

I perked up. "My parents are really awake?"

Chairman Hart nodded. "Yes. I heard from Striker that Sevryn is dead. We assumed that's what broke the veilmist. Your parents are still recovering. It was a strong spell, but it seems they'll be okay."

Grandpa's shoulders sagged with relief. "I wasn't sure. I knew he had others help him. Sometimes it can be trickier than just destroying the main conduit."

Hart nodded. "Seems we were lucky in that regard. But our luck elsewhere isn't as good." She leaned forward. "Now for the bad news: Rory Kane arrived an hour ago. He collapsed as soon as he came through the Gate."

I shot forward in my chair. "Why? Is he okay?"

Hart nodded. "He's fine. Seems he had some sort of incident on his way here; we're still not sure what happened. It might have been a hallucination, maybe a reaction to the dark magic in the Void since his body was still recovering from the attack he'd had before. He's okay—Doctor Harlowe attended to him. The important thing is the message he brought with him. 'Dame Keyja sent him from Arcvale to warn us."

Grandpa tensed. He leaned his hands on Hart's desk. "To warn you of what?"

Chairman Hart met his gaze. "The Dark King is coming, with his whole Selkblood army. Commanders, darklings... dozens of them, maybe hundreds. 'Dame Keyja said her Eldervine ally was able to see them briefly before all traces of them vanished. We don't know the exact timing of the planned attack and of course by this point, our intel might be outdated, but it's all we have to go on. Rory said the message he was told to bring is that they're coming for the Hub."

"The *Hub*?" Grandpa's voice raised an octave.

"They plan to use us as an access point, to use our Gates to breach the Fae villages. We're to be their portal into Upper Faeside, their linchpin for turning the tide of the war."

Grandpa had gone pale. "We can't let that happen. We've got to get a warning to Teionyr just in case. If they breach here, then use the Gate we just came through to enter the palace…"

My heart lurched. I hadn't even thought of that possibility, yet.

Chairman Hart placed her hand on Grandpa's. "We're taking every precaution. We sent word back to Arcvale to inform us of any further information, but we're already in the process of recalling all non-essential teams. You made it through to the Hub just in time. We're about to lock down all the Gates."

"Still…" Grandpa glanced at me. "We must warn Jordan. Teionyr is their target, I'm certain of it. It's the only thing left standing in Upper Faeside still worth sieging. The Dark Fae are probably planning to gather supplies from the other villages and take out any of our allies they encounter along the way, but Teionyr has to be their true target. If they can get control of the palace, they'll have all the most powerful resources of Upper Faeside at their command."

Hart nodded. "That's why we can't let this happen. We've worked too hard for the past few decades. Too many lives have been given for peace, both from our side and from the Upper Fae. We cannot let Teionyr fall." Chairman Hart met Grandpa's eyes. "I know we need to get word through, but it's imperative we shut the gates down immediately, before anyone else has a chance to breach. If you go to warn Teionyr now, you won't be able to get back."

Grandpa glanced at me. "I know a way to get word to them without the Gates."

Hart studied him a moment, but didn't ask questions. "Do it. And if you think of anything else that might be relevant, anything at all, the council and I will be meeting upstairs this evening. In the meantime, we need all able-bodied LeyGuards armed and ready to fight, just in case. Even if we don't need to make a stand here, we may have to send forces elsewhere to support our allies once we learn where the Dark King is headed next."

Grandpa nodded again.

Hart stood, dismissing us. "The council and I have this under control for now. Go see your family. They've been eager for your return."

She gave us directions to a recovery room on the second floor.

Grandpa and I headed upstairs, but he pulled me aside before we reached the room.

"That door in the corner there is a restroom," he said. "Slip in and make your call to Jordan. Try to keep it quick—none of that 'You hang up—No, *you* hang up' stuff." Despite his serious expression, mischief glinted behind it.

I rolled my eyes. "We've never done that, Grandpa."

He shrugged. "You were in that room at the palace for a long time. How was I supposed to know what was happening in there?"

I huffed, but Grandpa waved me off. "Go on. No time to waste."

I hurried to the door Grandpa had indicated, then slipped inside the small, single-stall bathroom and pressed my thumb to one of the runes on the stone. "Vragal," I whispered. The rune surged to life with a bright blue glow. I waited a few moments, but nothing happened. I even tried softly saying, "Hello?" a few times, but with no response. I sighed and slipped the stone back into my pocket, then went back out into the hall.

Grandpa was waiting for me outside the bathroom. "Well?"

I shook my head. "It didn't work," I whispered. "It lit up, but then nothing happened."

Grandpa nodded. "That means he didn't activate the lit rune from his side, yet. You won't be able to hear each other until he does."

At my nervous expression, he waved his hand.

"He's probably just in a meeting or something. He can't let others know he has the stone."

"Oh. Right."

"The stone will warm when he activates his side, and he knows enough to wait for you to speak first once he does. Just keep it in your pocket, so you can feel it when it activates. Then slip away somewhere to talk to him. I'll help you find a reason to slip out, if I can. Just get my attention."

I nodded. "Okay."

We headed to the recovery room Hart had told us.

The moment the door slid open, Doctor Harlowe turned around. He grinned when he saw who had entered. "Ayla. Maddox. It's a pleasure to see you both back here."

He stepped aside, and for the first time in weeks, I met my parents' eyes.

Mom's face lit up. She jumped up from where she sat on the edge of one bed and hurried toward us. "Ayla!" She threw herself at me, wrapping me in a tight hug.

"Easy," Doctor Harlowe cautioned. "You're still recovering. No swift movements, remember?"

I pulled back. "Are you still not well?"

Mom shook her head, then smoothed my hair. "Just a little dizziness. The doctor says it will pass."

I bit my lip, concerned, but nodded. I glanced past her shoulder at Dad, who had stood up from the other bed in the room.

He grinned at me, then headed toward us. "Hey, Peanut. So good to see you."

He and Grandpa had both called me that same nickname since I was a baby because I'd been born so small. They didn't always use it, but I always felt a warmth in my chest when they did.

"Hey, Dad." I slid past Mom and threw my arms around his solid chest.

Despite how much I missed Jordan, and all the things still going wrong around us, having my parents awake and well made me feel like a massive piece of my life was suddenly *right* again.

My dad hugged me tight. "You gave us quite the scare," he said, pulling back to look at my face.

"Are you kidding? You guys had me terrified!" I blurted.

Dad chuckled. "Well, to be fair, we don't remember most of what happened. But when we woke here and were told you had gone into some other realm—" He paused, looking pensive. "I have to admit, we didn't believe them at first. But we've seen quite a few things while here and have now amended our understanding of the scope of reality."

My mom chuckled. "That's an understatement." She glanced at my grandfather. "We always thought you were in a cult."

Grandpa guffawed. "Well, can't say you were far off. A cult probably would have been a little less dangerous. Maybe even more exciting."

Doctor Harlowe laughed. "Hardly."

Mom eyed Grandpa, her face growing serious. "You're a hero, Maddox. They showed us the records. Your name is written down in their textbooks here, like some kind of legend."

Grandpa blushed and averted his eyes. "Yeah, well, it doesn't feel quite so heroic when you're the one doing it. I made a lot of mistakes. I tried my hardest to protect my family from them." He glanced at me. "Seems I failed at that."

I hurried to him and put my arm around him. "You didn't fail at anything, Grandpa. You came exactly when I needed you most. I'd probably be dead if it weren't for you."

Mom and Dad both let out a little gasp, and Mom's hand fluttered to her mouth.

Grandpa's eyes grew teary. "I would never let that happen, Ayla. You're too good. The world needs you."

For a moment, we all just stared at each other.

Then Doctor Harlowe cleared his throat and glanced up from a small screen on his wrist. "I'm sorry to intrude, but Chairman Hart sent a message that Ayla may need some tests run. It seems Striker's report contained some... concerns?"

I glanced at Grandpa.

"Yes." He nodded. "About her magic. It manifested when she was Faeside, and we're still not sure what to make of it."

Mom and Dad both stared at me in shock.

Curiosity sparked in Doctor Harlowe's eyes. "Magic that baffles the great Maddox Rogers?" He raised an eyebrow. "I have to admit, I'm intrigued."

I laughed nervously. "Don't get your hopes up. There's not much I can do with it yet. It kind of has a mind of its own."

Doctor Harlowe smiled reassuringly. "That's exactly the sort of thing I specialize in. I'll get a bed cleared off and get the sensors set up. I promise it won't hurt a bit."

Grandpa squeezed my shoulder. "He's the best at what he does," he murmured near my ear. "If anybody can identify what's going on with your magic, it'll be him. Once we know what we're dealing with, we can find someone to help you train it."

Doctor Harlowe ushered us out into the hall so he could get things ready.

The stone warmed against my leg. I shoved my hand into my pocket and gripped it. "I, uh, need to go to the bathroom for a moment."

Grandpa glanced at me, then nodded. "We'll be here." He turned back, talking to Mom and Dad.

I hurried back to the bathroom and slid the stone from my pocket. "Jordan?" I said softly.

"Ayla."

I sagged against the sink with relief. "You're there." It was *so* good to hear his voice, even though it hadn't been long since I'd seen him.

"Are you okay?" His voice carried a hint of distraction. "Is something wrong?"

"No. Well—yes." I told him quickly about Rory's warning.

I could picture him nodding in thought as he replied calmly. "Okay. Thank you, Ayla. I'll tell the guards here, and we'll try to get word to Callan, too. There may be updates from Arcvale, by now." The weight of kingship carried in his voice, but then his tone shifted to tender concern. "How are your parents? Did they wake up?"

"Yes. They're fine."

I heard him sigh in relief. "I'm so glad to hear that."

I stared at the stone. His disembodied voice was a poor substitute for his presence, but I was still thankful to have it. "Doctor Harlowe wants to run some tests on me, to study my magic."

Jordan was quiet for a moment, but when he spoke, his voice was confident. "You can trust him. He's a good doctor, and he knows a lot about magic." He hesitated, and when he spoke again, his voice carried a note of humor. "Just don't let him test out any technology prototypes on you. His safety protocols might be a smidge lacking."

I laughed. "Do I want to know the story behind that?"

He chuckled. "I'll explain sometime."

The blue glow of the rune flickered.

"It looks like our time is running out," he said with a note of regret.

I swallowed. "Yeah."

"I love you, Ayla," he said.

"I love you, too."

The light winked out. He was gone.

I sighed, then slid the stone into my pocket and slipped back out into the hall.

Grandpa met my eyes, and I gave him a quick nod. The warning of the impending attack had gone out—in Arcvale, here at the Hub, and in Teionyr.

Now we just had to pray we'd all survive it.

CHAPTER 13

CAN'T EXPECT PEOPLE TO KNOW WHAT THEY DON'T KNOW

Rory

"You're free to go, Rory, though we highly suggest you remain at the Hub until we're sure things are safe. Help yourself to some food from the cafeteria downstairs, if you'd like. Dove can show you where." Doctor Harlowe smiled, then slipped out of the room again. It seemed he was a busy guy around here. The door slid shut behind him.

I opened my hand to examine the small, flat stone he'd given me. Strange symbols he'd called *runes* were etched on the stone's surface. *Just in case,* he'd said. That sort of statement was enough to give a man anxiety. I dropped the stone into my pants pocket.

The door slid open again and Dove stepped in, beside a much-cleaner looking Madison than I'd seen thirty minutes ago.

Just the sight of Dove created a light, pleasant feeling in my lungs, like the air became fresher from her presence. I blinked. What was *wrong* with me? I peeled my eyes from Dove to check on Madison. "You look better."

Madison nodded. "It's amazing what a shower can do. I almost feel human." She gave a short, dry laugh that twisted something in my chest.

I opened my arms. "Come here."

Madison hurried forward, and I wrapped her in another hug.

I might be a mess, but I was still her big brother. We hadn't always gotten along over the years, but we always had each other's backs when it mattered.

I allowed myself a small glance in Dove's direction. "Thanks for helping her."

Dove's bright smile sent a warm jolt through my chest. "No worries!" Her words were gentle and bright, just like the rest of her. "Doctor Harlowe asked me to show you where to find food, but we might not have time right now since they're about to seal the LeyGates." She glanced at Madison.

"What do you mean?" I asked.

Madison pulled away and stepped back. "Rory... have you heard anything about Mom or Dad?"

The mention of our parents dropped a cold stone of unease into my stomach. "Only that Dad seems okay and doesn't remember what happened."

"They think we're on a trip." Madison chewed her lip, one of her few tells for when she was nervous.

Most people seemed to think Madison was ultra confident and invincible, but if so, they didn't look closely enough.

"I want to go see them," she said.

I tensed. "Is that a good idea?" Visions of the woman and the old hag I'd seen in the Void resurfaced, and I fought back a shiver.

What could I tell Madison? That some imaginary women I'd hallucinated were giving me ominous vibes? Doctor Harlowe said I'd probably just reacted poorly to traveling the Veil since I was still weak, and that the women were probably the magical equivalent of a vivid fever dream. But I could still hear that gorgeous-but-evil woman's smooth voice in my head, still feel the chill that shot down my spine when she'd seen me.

I met Madison's gaze. "It might not be safe for us, out there."

Madison stared at me. "No one's after *us*, Rory. Not now that Sevryn's gone. It's not like we're LeyGuards or Fae. Besides, I promised Callan that if I left the Hub, I'd take protection. We won't go alone."

Madison had already discussed this with Callan?

"You've obviously made up your mind." I tried to keep the irritation out of my voice. Madison had been through even worse things than I had these last few days. I couldn't begrudge her the desire to return to the familiar—even if our home life wasn't exactly peaceful in the best of times.

Madison frowned. "Do you not want to go with me?"

I bit back a sigh. "No, of course I do." I still couldn't shake the feeling something bad was coming. There was no way I was letting Madison go out there alone.

Besides, we probably *should* check in with Mom and Dad. They had no clue what was really going on, but if we didn't show up for days on end, they'd eventually question our absence.

"So who's going as our protection?" I asked Madison.

Dove bounced on her toes. "We are."

I looked at her. "We?"

She tipped her head to the side like my question confused her. "Myself and Fogarty, of course." She gestured toward the ground—to her cat.

I blinked, then inhaled sharply. "Right. Okay."

The girl was adorable, but I was beginning to wonder if she was entirely sane.

Madison shrugged. "I had the same reaction, but Striker insisted Dove and her cat are more than capable of protecting us if we need it."

I glanced at Dove, who watched me patiently like a teacher waiting for a student to arrive at the correct answer.

I cleared my throat. "Are you sure? I mean... I'm certain you're very capable of—of—"

I felt myself grow red. I actually had *no idea* what Dove might be capable of. An awkward laugh escaped me, and I groaned inside. This was *not* coming out right.

I tried again. "I'm sorry; I didn't mean—" Words failed me, and I blurted the first thing that came to mind. "It's just—that's a *cat*. Shouldn't you leave it here so it doesn't run off or something?"

The cat let out a disgruntled-sounding mewl.

Dove reached down to pat its head. "You just have to let it go, Foge. You can't expect people to know what they don't know."

I raised my eyebrows. "Um..."

Dove glanced up at me and shrugged. "You offended him, but don't feel too bad. He's sensitive these days." She smiled sweetly.

The cat glared at me.

"Uh, sorry." I scratched the back of my neck and averted my stare back to Dove.

If I were honest with myself, the thought of taking this beautiful, kind, gentle girl to my house was at least half my hesitation. My family wasn't the most functional. What would Dove witness once we got there?

Mom and Dad had argued constantly, even *before* Dad began acting strangely. As kids, I'd taken Madison outside and distracted her so she wouldn't hear the growing shouts. The only thing that changed as we got older was that we each found our own ways of dealing with it. Madison became our parents' perfect little princess, while I became a constant disappointment. When I lost my football scholarship, Dad had seethed for *months*. I'd found peace in my new path, my new plans, but up until Dad had seemingly lost his mind—which I now knew to be the Selkblood control—he was still so angry he could barely look at me. I wasn't sure what I'd find waiting for me at home, now that Dad was back to himself.

Dove might be able to handle a potential Fae attacker just fine, but baring my family's disappointment in me to a girl I'd just met felt like an entirely different kind of threat. Not that I could *say* that to her.

"Rory? Are you okay?" Madison asked.

I shook my head, realizing I'd gone quiet and they were both staring. "I'm sorry. I just—" I forced myself to meet Dove's gaze. "Are you sure you want to go with us? You've already been so kind, and... I just don't want to put you in any danger." It was the truth, just not the *whole* truth.

Dove's lips quirked up into a mischievous smirk. "Oh, I wouldn't worry about *that*."

The foreboding in my gut intensified, but I forced a stiff smile. "Okay... great. Then I guess we should go."

We made it through the LeyGate Striker had told Madison about without any issues, then walked the twenty minutes toward home. The houses on our side of town were spread out, each on its own parcel of land. Most were set back enough from the road that there wasn't much to see beyond the fancy, iron gates and privacy hedges.

When we reached the entrance to our own driveway, Madison typed in the code and the gate swung open with a creak.

That was strange. Dad had people for everything, even for oiling the gates. I'd never heard it creak before.

But with how Dad had basically ruined the family business these past few months, we were fortunate this family estate had already been paid off with his inheritance... and Mom had dipped deep into savings to make sure all our groundsworkers kept their jobs. She hadn't wanted anyone to lose income while we figured out our mess. Maybe she'd cut back on oiling the gates, though. It wasn't exactly a priority.

The sprawling yard was empty, which wasn't that odd since it was getting toward evening. The gardener and any other workers would have already headed home.

Still, something felt off. It was probably just my nerves.

Dove's eyes widened as we approached the circular driveway in front of my house.

I glanced up, realizing for the first time what our home must look like to new visitors. With its expansive green lawn, pristine white columns, and rows of windows with ornamental facades, it was practically a miniature White House.

"You live *here*?" she asked, her voice breathy with awe as we traveled the stone walkway between the perfectly manicured rose bushes.

Dusk had set in, and the timed lights for the front garden were already turning on, illuminating our path with knee-high white lanterns while colored spotlights burst to life around the hedges in other parts of the yard.

Nervous, I scratched the back of my head. "Uh—yeah. I mean... it's..."

It was basically a mansion. What else could I say? That didn't mean what was *in* it was all that great.

Madison glanced sideways at me.

I was sure she noticed my discomfort, but she kept her comments to herself.

She smiled at Dove and pointed at one of our downstairs front windows. "It looks like a light's on in the parlor. Mom or Dad must be in there." She took Dove's hand and tugged her toward our front steps.

Fogarty glanced back at me with silent disdain, then trotted after them at Dove's heels.

It seemed this was happening, whether I wanted it to or not. I drew a long breath, then let it out in a sigh. "Wait up, Mads. I'm coming."

I joined her on the top step, then gave a reassuring smile to Dove, who stood just behind me with her cat on the step below us. Whatever was about to happen, I'd feel better if I faced it head-on and ran interference. Dove didn't deserve to be pulled into my mess.

Madison tried the door handle, but it was locked. She pressed the doorbell, then glanced past me at Dove. "Gladys will probably answer the door. She's our housekeeper. She's amazing, actually. She—"

The door swung inward, and at the sight of my mother, my heart plunged into my stomach. Her eyes were ringed with dark circles, her hair a mess, her clothes disheveled. I'd never seen her look worse.

"Mom?" I stepped up next to Madison.

Mom let out an anguished little yelp, then threw her arms around us both at the same time and broke down in sobs.

CHAPTER 14

GOT A BIT OF FAE IN IT

Ayla

Ten minutes after ending my brief stone-conversation with Jordan, I was reclining on stiff pillows in a hospital bed in a room down the hall, with a bunch of electrodes stuck to my chest and forehead.

Doctor Harlowe stood in front of me, holding a tablet that apparently controlled some kind of testing program my electrodes fed into. A large monitor full of colorful, blipping lines hung on the wall to my left.

"Okay, Ayla," Doctor Harlowe said. "I want to explain this fully before we begin. We're dealing with magic here, which means, like most everything at the Hub, there will be a good bit of science and technology needed, along with a bit of something extra."

"Something extra?"

He nodded. "Just some passive magic for observation. No need to be nervous."

Mom and Dad glanced at each other from the corner of the room.

Grandpa sat in a chair in the opposite corner, looking completely unconcerned.

Doctor Harlowe pointed to the screen on the wall. "Those charts will monitor fluctuations in your brain waves, and in the energy surrounding you. Some of those lines are set to monitor different types of LeyGuard magic. Others are set to monitor things like spikes in emotion or sudden increases in various other types of brain activity. You don't need to worry about what they mean; I'll interpret the results here." He gestured to his tablet. "All you need to do is try to clear your mind, and follow my instructions. I'm going to give you some words or phrases, and I want you to picture what I say in your mind. I may also ask you to follow some simple commands. Okay?"

It sounded easy enough. I nodded. "Okay."

Doctor Harlowe gave a curt nod and stepped back, assuming what I could only describe as a game face. "All right, Ayla. Here we go. *Badger.*"

The abrupt shift in conversation jarred me, but almost immediately, an image of the animal flicked into my mind, followed by the realization that *badger* could also be a verb. I pictured two people arguing, one of them nagging at the other.

Doctor Harlowe eyed his tablet and nodded. "Good. *Extreme.*"

I saw a girl cold and shivering in my mind, icicles dangling from her nose.

"Okay," Doctor Harlowe said, "now picture the opposite extreme."

I imagined the girl standing in a sweltering desert, her face red with sweat dripping down it.

Doctor Harlowe nodded again. "Good. Now, *near.*"

I saw a Void-snake lunging at me.

The monitor erupted in a flurry of beeps.

Doctor Harlowe glanced up at me, slight concern in his eyes. "Okay, let's try another one. *Far.*"

I saw the blackness of the Void, and in the distance, Jordan running away from me, his back disappearing into the shadows.

Doctor Harlowe peered at me over the top of his tablet. "Good, Ayla. One more and then we'll take a break. *Flames.*"

I saw a flurry of images: Jordan, toying with a dancing flame across his knuckles when I first learned he was LeyGuard. Kaizyn and his flaming fire-cat, his hands glowing amber as his magic faded. Jordan, shooting columns of flame in the courtyard—this was a scene I hadn't witnessed, just one I'd overheard the others discussing, that he'd lost control when he thought I'd died. Then I saw Sorcha, a funny image of the story from the palace worker, her flames setting the curtains on fire while children squealed with delight nearby. The last one made me chuckle under my breath.

Doctor Harlowe looked up at me from his monitor and smiled. "Excellent, Ayla. Great job. Let's take a break. Why don't you get some water while I analyze these results?"

I looked at him. "That's it? You aren't going to ask me to cast my magic or try to do anything with it?"

"I don't need to. I can already see what we're working with."

I stared at him. "You can?"

He grinned. "I see more than most, Ayla. I'm a Selkblood, remember?"

Sudden dread clenched my chest, slowly fading as I reminded myself that Harlowe was a friend. *Selkblood* didn't always mean *enemy*.

Doctor Harlowe smiled warmly at me. "I saw that, too. I read emotions, Ayla, and more often than not when it comes to magic, there's an emotional component driving it. Most LeyGuards are trained how to channel theirs, or how to separate the magic from their emotions so they can keep it steady even when their emotions are not. But Fae are naturally more emotional in their magic use, and in how it manifests."

He tilted his head, studying me, then pointed at the chart on the wall. The lines now showed spikes and dips I hadn't really noticed while we were testing.

"The curious thing about yours is that it almost seems to be more Fae than LeyGuard... at least in how it responds," he said.

I stared. "What are you saying?"

My parents watched me from the corner, expressions wary.

Grandpa, on the other hand, didn't look very surprised.

"My guess," Doctor Harlowe said, "is that your bond with Kaizyn is augmenting your normal LeyGuard magic. Whatever your magic would have been, it's not purely LeyGuard anymore. It's got a bit of Fae in it."

My pulse quickened. "What does that mean?"

He shrugged. "Well, ice magic is unusual for LeyGuards to begin with. Your family comes from Fortis. Usually, Fortis Guards manifest some variation of wind ability."

I glanced at Grandpa. I hadn't seen his magic in the courtyard, but I'd heard it had been spectacular. I turned back to Doctor Harlowe as he continued.

"Power over wind is essentially power over air and its movement. That can manifest in lots of different ways, anywhere from wind storms"—he glanced significantly at Grandpa—"to even changing the temperature of the air by controlling the movement of its molecules."

"Is that what I'm doing?" I asked.

"Partly," Doctor Harlowe said with a shrug, "but that wouldn't account for the rapidity or intensity of temperature changes Striker described in his report. It seems you've also received a touch of the inverse of your Fae prince's magic."

I stiffened at the term, and Harlowe was quick to apologize.

"I'm sorry. I realize that phrase is muddled now, given that Kaizyn wasn't truly the heir prince, and the true prince is a LeyGuard-trained Fae." He chuckled. "In any case, Kaizyn is a fire-Fae, and you're bound to him... but it seems the magic shared through the bond, perhaps triggered by dark magic from the time you spent in the Void as your LeyGuard magic manifested, has decided to invert itself. So while you're receiving the brunt of Kaizyn's emotions exactly as they are, you're receiving a trickle of the *opposite* of his magic. Where he has fire, you get ice."

I chewed my lip, considering. "Okay. Then, without my bond to Kaizyn, I'd lose this magic?"

Doctor Harlowe shook his head. "It's not as simple as that. Think of your LeyGuard magic as a growing tree. When a seed sprouts, it's already encoded with everything it needs to grow into whatever kind of plant the seed came from. However, the soil quality, the amount of water, sunlight, and even other plants growing around it can all impact how that tree grows. You can plant the same seed in twenty different locations, and while you may get roughly the same tree, some of them will grow stronger than others, and some may not grow at all. Meanwhile, one might sprout up right next to a towering oak and have to bend itself to grow around the tree that's already there."

He stared at me as if I should understand his implications.

"You're saying my magic bent itself around Kaizyn's?"

He nodded. "Yes. Once a tree is bent, it doesn't ever unbend. You can try to force it to turn back the other way as it continues to grow, but unless you catch it while it's happening, the part of it that curved in that initial growth will already be established. It will always be curved in that direction, even if the rest of the tree bends the other way."

At this, my dad spoke up. "So she'll always have ice magic?"

Doctor Harlowe nodded. "Yes, or at least that's my best guess." There was a spark of excitement in his eyes. "It's a fascinating addition to our LeyGuard repertoire, actually. I can't say we've ever experimented with the impact of Fae magic on a developing LeyGuard's abilities. This opens a whole new realm of experimentation and study. It could change quite a lot."

Grandpa leaned forward, tense. "My granddaughter will not be a lab rat."

Doctor Harlowe's eyes widened. "Of course not. I have no intention of keeping her anywhere or running tests against her will. I simply meant to say that as she grows, observation of her magic, even from a distance, could provide a lot of insight into the potential for future LeyGuard abilities."

Grandpa nodded, seeming mollified.

I turned back to Doctor Harlowe. "I still don't know how to control it."

His face lit up. "That's because we didn't get to that part yet. Your magic, being somewhat Fae, seems almost entirely dependent on your emotional state, particularly when it comes to your fear response. I would wager that the original manifestation of your magic happened at a moment when you experienced an adrenaline spike of some kind, yes?"

I thought back and nodded. "Striker had thrown a fireball at me."

Doctor Harlowe's eyes widened.

"Not on purpose," I added quickly. "He was trying to take down some kind of Void monster and overshot."

Harlowe relaxed. "I see."

"Although he did do it on purpose the *next* time."

Harlowe's eyes widened again.

Grandpa raised an eyebrow. "I'm sure he had his reasons?"

I chuckled. "Yeah. He wanted to make my magic happen again."

Grandpa laughed.

Harlowe nodded thoughtfully. "Was it *always* at a moment of fear that your magic emerged?"

As I thought back through it, I realized there really hadn't been any moments I *wasn't* afraid, the entire time I was Faeside. "I suppose so."

Doctor Harlowe smiled. "That's excellent news. That means my diagnosis is correct, which gives us a plan for proceeding."

I met his eyes cautiously. "Please don't say you're going to just terrify me again and again until I get control of it."

Doctor Harlowe blinked at me. "Well, it's not the *only* thing I plan to do."

Grandpa chuckled. "It's okay, Ayla. The sooner you get this over with, the sooner you'll have control of your magic, which will mean you *won't* have to be as afraid in the future."

Mom and Dad looked warily at each other.

Doctor Harlowe noticed and nodded to them. "You have a concern?" he asked.

My mother cleared her throat. "It's just... she's always been anxious." She glanced at me apologetically. "I'm sure I haven't helped much with that. I used to be the same way. But I'm just not sure that she... I mean, this could be very hard on her."

Beside her, Dad met my gaze. He gave me a firm nod. "She can do it," he said with confidence. "She's stronger than she knows."

Tears prickled behind my eyes.

Doctor Harlowe turned, appraising me. "I think we've all seen evidence of that." He offered me his hand to shake. "Ayla, I would be honored to help you master your magic. Will you trust me to do so?"

I glanced at Grandpa over his shoulder.

He gave me a quick nod.

I turned back to Doctor Harlowe and placed my hand in his and shook. "Yes."

He grinned, then dropped my hand and rubbed his hands together. "Excellent. I'll have a training room set up for you. Meet me downstairs in an hour."

CHAPTER 15

TIME TO COME OUT AND PLAY

Rory

Madison and I sat stiffly on the sofa in our parlor, across from where Mom sat wiping her swollen eyes with a tissue in the armchair on the other side of the coffee table.

A moment after wrapping us in her sobbing hug, Mom had sucked in a deep breath, then ushered us inside with a perky, "Well, come in! And shut the door, you'll let in the mosquitoes," as though her sobs had never happened.

She hadn't said anything since.

Dove perched politely on the edge of a loveseat to my left, scanning the room with cheerful curiosity while her cat glowered at me from the cushion next to her.

The clink of porcelain dishes announced my father's arrival as he brought a tray of tea things into the room.

"I'm afraid I couldn't find the cream." He set the tea tray on the coffee table, then handed my mom a steaming cup of tea.

Mom sniffed and dabbed at her eyes again, then took the cup by its handle and looked up at him. "We might be out. Gladys always took care of that. It's all right; I can do without cream."

Dad settled into the armchair next to Mom's and reached over to place a hand on her free one.

Mom squeezed his fingers and offered him a teary smile, which he returned.

I hadn't seen my parents being this nice to each other in... well, ever.

Madison glanced at me with wide eyes, then grabbed a cup of tea from the tray and sipped it.

I knew it had to be hot enough to burn her mouth, but it left me to be the one to talk. She'd always been clever like that.

"Would you like—" I began, turning to Dove, but she shook her head.

"I'll wait til it's cooled." Her smile was relaxed and friendly.

"Okay," I said, then turned back forward.

Dad turned to Dove. "It's so nice to meet one of my children's friends." He smiled politely. "So, how do you know one another?"

Dove gave him a bright smile, completely at ease. "We met where I work."

Mom nodded, her eyes not quite meeting Dove's. "Oh, how lovely."

Neither of them asked any follow-up questions—not about which one of us Dove was friends with, or where she worked; not even about the cat, though Madison and I had never been allowed to have pets and I was certain nothing fur-covered had ever stepped foot into this house before. Even my mother's fur stoles were imitation.

The awkward silence in the room was beginning to feel suffocating.

I reached for a steaming cup, then decided against it and rubbed my hands on my thighs. "Um, Mom?"

She glanced at me over the tea cup she held, her eyes still red and puffy. "Yes?"

I looked at Madison, whose full attention suddenly seemed to be on her tea.

I sighed, turning back to Mom. "Are we not going to talk about why you were crying?"

Mom's posture stiffened. "What's there to cry about? My children are home."

She and my dad exchanged a glance that only heightened my unease.

Madison clanged her tea cup down on the coffee table. "Okay. *What* is going on right now? You two are being so weird!"

Mom and Dad both glanced at Dove simultaneously.

"Wait." I stiffened. "Are you afraid to talk to us because Dove's here?"

My father's eyes hardened while Mom's face flushed red.

"Rory!" Mom scolded. "That's incredibly impolite of you. Of course we are *happy* to have a guest, anytime you may choose to bring—"

Dove popped to her feet like the pleasant pixie version of a Jack-in-the-box. "I will step outside."

"No!" Madison and I both shouted in unison, then stared at each other.

I grabbed Madison's arm and pulled her from the couch. "We just—um... I'm sorry, Dove, can you wait here one moment? Please don't go anywhere."

I dragged Madison out of the parlor and into the hallway.

"Why don't *you* want Dove to leave?" I asked in a whisper. "It's clear Mom and Dad have something they don't want to say in front of her."

"She's supposed to stay *with* us. She's our protection," she whispered back, "Besides, it's already dark out. Wouldn't it be rude of us to make her wait outside?"

I sighed and scrubbed a hand down my face. "Yes. It would be."

Madison planted her hands on her hips. "Why don't *you* want her to leave?" Her eyes bored into me.

"I—" I really didn't have an answer for that, only that I wanted her here. "I mean, like you said, it would be rude."

Madison rolled her eyes. "That was a weak answer, Rory, and you know it."

Yes, I did. But I wasn't about to admit it.

"You *like* her." Madison jabbed a finger at my chest. "I can tell."

I opened my mouth to respond, but my father's voice from the parlor interrupted me.

"So *where* did you say you work, again?"

"Oh! The Hub," Dove answered sweetly, and there was a clatter of something crashing to the floor.

Madison and I locked stares, then dashed back toward the living room.

Dad stood, fists clenched, legs wide, his armchair toppled over behind him. "You work *where*?" His voice raised with each word, until the last one was a shout.

Mom shot to her feet, gripping his arm. "Darren, honey, this isn't the time," she hissed, glancing nervously at Dove.

Madison stared on with wide eyes, seemingly frozen to the spot.

I stepped around and planted myself between my father and Dove. "What is this about?"

Dad clenched his jaw. "Get out of the way, Rory. You don't understand what's happening here."

I met his steely gaze with a glare of my own. "Then explain it to me."

Mom turned pleading eyes on me. "Please, Rory. Your father—he's... not well. He thinks..."

"I don't *think* it, Raquel, I *know* it!" Dad yelled. He turned to me, eyes blazing and expression desperate. "They did something to my mind. Those people, the Hub. They came here, they said they were parents of your friends but I knew. I *knew*. They're not right, those people. They hide secrets. They—they say it's not real, but it is, I *know* it is, I remember!"

The room fell silent.

Madison stepped forward. "Dad," she said gently.

He turned a glare on her. "Don't try to tell me I'm crazy. I'm not. I'm *not*, Madison. I know it doesn't make sense, but I—I'm telling you, I saw... I saw..."

He drifted off, as though uncertain what to say.

Mom looked nervously at Madison and me. "Maybe you should take your friend outside, just for a moment. So your father and I can—"

I stepped forward. "You're not crazy, Dad." Had the Hub really tried to alter his memories? Was that something they would do?

Mom's hand fluttered to her chest. "Rory, please. You don't have to—"

"No," Madison said quietly. "He's right."

Dad stared at us both in alarm, and a bit of relief. "Then you—you know?"

"Know *what*, Darren?" Mom burst out, but there was something strange about the desperate way she said it. "There is nothing to know!"

"You know, too," I said carefully as realization set in. "You know, but you aren't supposed to admit it."

Mom went still, her swollen eyes wide. "I don't know what you're talking about."

Dad drew a sharp breath and ran a hand over his face. "A woman came. She said our best chance for keeping you safe was to pretend none of it happened, that I never saw a thing. That my *delusions* had put you both in danger, and if I kept talking about it, it could make things worse for you. She said there were people who, if they knew about my delusions, might come after our family. After the two of you. I think she thought that we wouldn't remember that she came here, but I do. I *do* remember. And I know what I saw at that warehouse..."

The Hub *had* tried to erase his memory, somehow... but it hadn't worked. Had that runed coin Madison gave Dad prevented whatever the Hub tried to do to his mind, too?

"But after what happened with Madison's bodyguard," Dad whispered, "we couldn't risk—"

He raised his gaze again, and my heart lurched at the tears I saw there.

Madison rushed forward and threw her arms around him. "We're safe, Daddy. It's okay. We're right here."

He hugged her to his chest as my mom looked on, tearing up again.

"Madison, what happened to you, to Gerard—" He looked down at her, his eyes full of tears. "I'm so sorry I wasn't there. I never even came to the hospital. I should've been there. I'm so, so sorry."

Madison clung to him. "It's okay, Dad. It wasn't you. I know that. It wasn't you."

"It *wasn't* me," he said. "It was... it was that voice in my head. It said I shouldn't go, that you wouldn't want to see me. And the men at the warehouse, they could... their eyes weren't right, and they could do things..." He shook his head, his eyes clearing. "I know it sounds crazy. And maybe—maybe I am crazy." His voice trailed off in a way that made my heart lurch. "Your mother believes I am."

"Mom?" Madison asked, pulling back. "You really think Dad's crazy?"

"I don't know what to believe, anymore." Mom's voice sounded utterly exhausted. "Those people from the Hub, they said they were doctors. I thought maybe the hospital had sent them, because of your attack. They said he'd imagined it all, and that we shouldn't even speak about it." She shook her head. "I want to believe your father. I *did* believe him at first, as crazy as it sounded, but..."

Dad sighed. "It's okay, Raquel." He looked up at me over Madison's head, then reached for me. "I'm sorry, son. My mind—I don't even know what's real, anymore. Some days I even question if I really did see what I—" He cleared this throat. "Anyway, I'm just glad you're both here. Did you have a good trip?"

I stared at him, shocked by his casual change of topic, then grabbed his hand and let him pull me into the family hug. "Dad—" I didn't know what to say. Maybe it *was* better for him to think he had imagined it all, for him not to know the danger we had been in—the danger that the irrational foreboding in my chest told me we might *still* be in.

"But you did really see it," a soft voice said from behind me.

"What?" I spun to look at Dove, but her eyes were locked on my father.

"You aren't crazy, Mr. Kane," she said gently. "It's all true."

My father pulled back and laughed, wiping at his eyes. "That's kind of you, but—"

"I can prove it," Dove said.

Dad froze, panic sparking on his face.

Dove hurried on in that soothing, lilting voice. "I would never hurt your family. I'm not part of the enemy you faced, and I had nothing to do with the attempt to block your memories. But I can prove you didn't imagine those strange things. I can prove you aren't crazy, Mr. Kane... if it's okay with you?"

At those last words, she looked right at me.

The wild hope in my dad's expression was answer enough for me. I glanced at my sister. "Mads?"

Her eyes were locked on my dad's face, seeing the same thing as me. She nodded. "Yes, do it."

I turned back to Dove. I had no idea what she was about to do, but as her steady, gentle gaze met mine, I realized I trusted her completely. "Go ahead."

A glint of mischief sparked in her eyes. "All right, then. Step back."

I nudged my parents and Madison back a few steps.

Dove reached into a small pouch at her waist and pulled out what looked like a dark pink, dried flower petal. "Time to come out and play, Foge," she said cheerfully to her cat.

Then she crushed the petal between her fingers and blew the dust in his direction.

Chapter 16

They Know My Name

Rory

The cat on the loveseat pillow exploded into a full-sized bear.

Madison screamed.

Mom sagged back into her armchair.

Dad cried out in alarm.

Dove blew more petal dust in the bear's direction and he popped back down to cat-size and settled onto the loveseat once more, licking his paws like he'd never moved.

I gaped at Dove. "What just happened?"

Dad hurried over to check on Mom.

Dove smiled and shrugged. "You saw Fogarty. As he really is, I mean. The cat suit is just a glamour."

I stared at the cat with fresh alarm. "*What*?"

Dove giggled. "Well, there aren't a lot of bears walking around next to people here Earthside, are there? He needed to blend in."

"Lands alive," I heard Dad mutter behind me.

"You have a pet *bear*?" My voice came out an octave higher than I'd meant for it to.

Dove's eyes widened. "No! He's not my pet. He's my... well, there's not really a word for it in this language. He and I are bonded. He protects me."

"Like a bodyguard?" I asked.

"No," Madison said, her tone carrying awe. "Like Jordan's dragon."

I turned to stare at her as my mom shrieked, "Like Jordan's *what*?"

Dad patted Mom's arm, then stepped toward us. "Rory. Madison. What is really going on here? Tell us the truth. We're ready."

One glance at Mom's pale face and I wondered if Dad should just speak for himself.

But then Mom took a shaky breath. A calm resolve seemed to pass over her as she tore her stare from Fogarty and turned to Madison and me. "Yes, please tell us the truth. I want to know what's really happening."

Dove moved toward the door. "Foge and I will wait out—"

I grabbed her hand. "No, stay. Please."

Her face flicked up to me, and my heart lurched as her gaze searched mine. Something shifted between us in the exchange, though I couldn't explain exactly why or what.

"If you want me here, Rory Kane, I will stay," she said softly.

I slid my fingers between hers. "I want you here."

She smiled and tightened her hand around mine. "Then I will stay."

It was well into the night by the time Madison and I finished explaining to my parents everything that had happened.

Mom and Dad listened mostly in silence, asking questions only to clarify details.

All in all, they took it *much* better than I'd expected.

When we finished, they processed our words in silence for a few moments, then Mom shifted forward in her seat. "Are you still in danger now?"

I shook my head. "Not directly. But our friends are." I swallowed. "I'm sorry, but I don't think I can stay here. I need to help, in whatever way I can."

Madison reached for my hand. "I need to go back, too. Callan is there, and I..."

She drifted off, leaving me to wonder exactly how serious her relationship with him had become.

"Not that there's much I can do to help," she said finally, "but I at least want to be at the Hub, where I'll know what's going on."

Dad sighed and rubbed a hand down his face. "You realize, as a parent, letting your kids get wrapped up in a war against deadly monsters is *not* the same as sending them off to college, right?" He huffed a dry laugh. "I mean—I can't exactly just sit here and condone you marching back into danger."

Madison stiffened. "What are you going to do, then? Ground me? Dad, please—give me a bodyguard again or whatever you have to do, but *please* don't ask me to sit at home while my friends are in danger. I can't. I... I won't."

"I've half a mind just to pack our bags, throw you both into the car, and drive as far away as we can get." Dad stared her down for a moment, then sighed. His shoulders slumped. "You're growing up, you know that?" He gave her a sad smile, then looked at me. "You've become so brave. Both of you. I know I can't protect you forever. And it seems you already *have* a bodyguard," he added, glancing at Dove and Foge.

Madison relaxed minutely, though her guard was still up. "Yes. And when we're with Callan and Reina and the others, we'll have *several*," she said.

Dad nodded, thinking. "You're convicted that you need to do this? That it's what is right?"

Madison and I both nodded.

"Yes," I said. "We can't abandon our friends."

Mom drew a sharp breath, then straightened in her chair. "Then take us to the Hub, too. We want to help."

Dad stared at her. "What? Are you sure?"

"Yes, of course." She nodded, insistent. "We should all go." She looked back at Madison and me. "There has to be some way your father and I can help you or your friends."

Dad turned to Dove, who still sat on the loveseat next to Fogarty. "Can we do that?"

Dove shrugged. "Theoretically, yes. Your knowledge of the Fae and the war could put you in danger now, too, so the Hub should agree to offer you protection and let you in." She said it so calmly, like the most normal thing in the world.

I gaped at Mom and Dad. "Do you even know what the Hub is? What exactly will you *do* there with a bunch of trained LeyGuards?"

"Anything." Mom shrugged. "Whatever is needed. But there's a war to be fought, right? Am I going to send my children into a battle while I sit home and do crossword puzzles? You have to be out of your mind."

Dad grabbed her hand.

Their eyes met, and something wordless but tender passed between them that made my heart squeeze. Maybe things really *had* finally changed in their relationship.

Dad turned to Madison and me. "We'll all go. Just let your Mom and I pack a couple bags, and we'll head out immediately."

"Um—" Dove's gentle voice made us all turn to stare. "It may not be that easy. The Hub LeyGates were locking down as we left," she said with an apologetic smile. "I'm not sure we *can* get back in, at the moment."

Madison turned to her. "There has to be a way, right? Maybe if we contact Striker?"

"I can get through to someone, but it may take me a bit," Dove answered. "The Hub is chaotic right now, and I'm sure they're prioritizing emergency calls. But you two need to sleep and eat, anyway. Why don't you eat something while we're here and rest a bit, while I try to get a message through to—"

Her words blurred as a dull ringing started in my ears, swelling into a full-out, resounding gong.

"Rory?" Madison's voice was sharp with panic.

I felt the room tilt sideways.

Strong arms caught me—my dad's?—and lowered me to the floor. "What's happening to him? Rory?"

I smell you, another voice said—a croaky voice, like an old witch.

"Rory?" I smelled honeysuckles, felt Dove's cool, slender fingers on my face. "Rory, can you hear me?"

I feeeeel you, a voice said, smooth as silk this time.

A wrongness settled in my chest.

There you are.

A chill shot down my spine.

"Something's wrong. His skin is like fire," Dove said. I felt her peel open my eyelids, heard a little gasp. "Dark magic. His eyes—they're solid black."

Either Madison or my mom let out a stifled sob.

Dark magic? I began to panic, but then I remembered the stone the doctor had given me.

"P–pocket." I forced the word out, though my jaw felt clenched tight.

Someone patted down my shirt, then my pants, then dug into my pocket. A moment later, a cool stone pressed into my hand.

"Deep breaths, Rory," Dove's gentle voice said. "Focus on my voice. Deep breath. In... out."

I forced a breath, but it felt like fire in my lungs.

The smell of honeysuckles swept over me as she brushed hair back from my forehead. "Good, Rory. Again, okay? With me. In—"

The stone stung my palm like an electric jolt. My fingers jerked open.

"Don't let go of it," Dove said, closing my fingers back around it. "Now, breathe."

I sucked in a shaky breath.

The wrongness clamped hard around me, like an oily black fist crushing my lungs.

I see you, the silky voice said with a hint of triumph. *I see you, Rory Kane.*

"Out," Dove said, squeezing my hand around the stone. "Rory, breathe out!"

I forced the breath out, though it felt like my lungs were spasming.

The fire began to fade.

The dark, oily fist let go.

Slowly, the room came back into focus.

Dove's wide, dark eyes hovered over me, full of concern.

When my gaze met hers, she exhaled a breath of relief.

"Rory, you scared me to death." She helped me sit up, then threw her arms around me. Her honeysuckle smell enveloped me, then she pulled back to look at me. "What happened?"

The sound of that cold, wrong voice lingered in my head as I met her stare. "The women from the Void—they know my name."

CHAPTER 17

It Is Your Council, Your Highness

Jordan

Maxim Warwick led me down a hall off the palace common area, and into a large meeting room with high, stone pillars and a long, polished wooden table surrounded by high-backed chairs.

Though there were at least a dozen chairs at the table, all but four were empty.

I tried to ignore the stares of the Fae men sitting in those four chairs—already wearing their deep blue officiation robes—as Maxim pointed me to the ornate, padded chair at the table's end.

"The king's seat." He gestured to it with a small bow, then backed away.

All eyes turned on me as I scooted the chair out and settled into it.

Maxim moved over against the wall, away from the table, and clasped his hands in front of his waist.

"Why aren't you sitting with us?" I asked him.

His eyes widened. "I am not on the royal council, Your Highness."

"Why not? You were loyal to the true king, right?"

Maxim nodded as his cheeks flushed. "Yes, but I have not served in the palace in some time. I was dismissed long ago, and even then, I was the royal apothecarist, not a council member."

The Fae men at the table glanced at one another uncomfortably.

I turned to them. I wasn't even sure who they *were*—Maxim had rounded them up from their homes in the city. These men had been fired from the council during Beirthyr's brief reign, for their loyalty to my father and to Kaizyn. The other council members, those who had opposed Kaizyn and stayed to serve under Beirthyr and Sevryn, had apparently fled after the battle.

"Can I *add* him to the council?" I asked the men sitting at the table. "I trust him, and I would like to hear his advice on our discussion."

One of the older Fae men seemed to be the implicit ringleader; the others cut their gazes in his direction, waiting for him to speak.

He looked at me. "You may add whomever to the council you wish. It is your council, Your Highness."

I studied him for a moment. He was sturdily built and about Ayla's grandfather's age, with grey-flecked dark hair, deep blue eyes, and a tanned, lined face that evidenced his years. His expression was polite, but he also looked mildly concerned—not that I could blame him, since he was now saddled with a king who didn't even understand how his own council worked.

"What is your name?" I asked him.

"Kurrum, Your Highness."

"How long have you served on the royal council?"

"Since King Veilar took the throne, Your Highness—not counting Sevryn's banishment of me during Beirthyr's illegitimate reign, of course."

I leaned forward. "You were appointed by King Veilar himself?"

He nodded. "Yes. Most of us were." He gestured to the other council members.

They were all middle-aged or older, though some were still young enough that they must have been around Callan's age when they originally were appointed.

Something tightened in my chest. These men had been appointed by my *father*—and I had a sudden longing to have known him. I knew he had been a good man. An honorable man. He had been a worthy king, and I would have loved to have his advice or even some wise, remembered words to fall back on at this moment, because I had no clue what I was doing.

I extended my hand across the table. "I am grateful to have you on this council, then, Kurrum."

He startled, then tentatively shook my hand.

From his reaction, royal handshakes were not a usual custom in Teionyr.

I turned to the others. "And what are your names?"

They introduced themselves. The middle-aged man with thinning brown hair to Kurrum's right was named Thorim, the balding older man beside him was Orvyx, and the dark-haired, thick-bearded middle-aged man to Kurrum's left was Arval.

I smiled at each of them. "I am grateful for all of you."

They all nodded their thanks with small smiles, and the mood in the room relaxed.

I turned to Maxim. "Please, join us." I gestured to the empty chair to my left.

He hesitated, but when the others gave no objection, he made his way to the table.

The others nodded at him in greeting as he sat beside me.

Now, with all five men staring at me, I placed my hands on the table. "I have news. We have reliable word that a Dark Fae army is marching toward Arcvale, with intent to breach the Hub and use its LeyGates to ambush key cities and villages in Upper Faeside. At least, that's our best guess as to their intentions." I glanced at each of the council members in turn. "I need your help. I'm a fighter, I can wield runes, and I'm good with strategy, but I'm still learning Teionyrian customs and I know little about what resources the palace has at its disposal. What are our options, here?"

The men exchanged startled glances.

Kurrum leaned forward. "Do we know the size of this army, your highness?"

I shook my head. "Nothing exact, but I believe it to be large—several collectives of darklings, each with a Selkblood commander at the helm, with the Dark King himself in the lead. Overall, perhaps a few hundred strong? Fewer, if we're lucky."

All five council members paled.

"A few *hundred* darklings?" Thorim whispered.

Maxim leaned toward me, his voice low. "This may be the time to inform the council of the darkling attack in the tunnels earlier."

I nodded, then turned to face the others. "It may have been a remnant of Sevryn's control, and not an attack from the Dark King himself, but—there was an incident earlier with some darklings in the tunnel outside the vault."

Kurrum stiffened. "Dark Fae breached the tunnels of the palace? *When*?" His eyes were wide with fright, and his panic was mirrored in the other three men's faces as well.

"While His Highness was summoning his sear-bind," Maxim answered.

The other four men stared at me.

I nodded. "Darklings appeared in the tunnel suddenly—dozens of them. The other LeyGuards with us fought them back. It seemed the darklings were trying to breach the vault."

Kurrum and the others stared at me with horrified expressions.

"The palace magic should not have allowed that," Arval said in a shaky voice.

Maxim leaned forward. "While we did want you informed, I do not believe the darklings' breach is as strong a cause for alarm as you might think. In the absence of its proper heir, the magic of the palace was weakening. King Jordan's summoning of his sear-bind has not only re-stabilized that magic, his power has made it stronger than ever. It has been ages since a dragon has been bound to Teionyr's monarch, and once he is properly coronated, that effect will only increase. We are in our *best* position now to protect our kingdom. I would not fear for another breach within the tunnels, though outside the palace is another story."

King Jordan. I wasn't sure I would ever get used to that.

The others relaxed slightly at Maxim's explanation.

I turned to Maxim. "Is there a way to verify that the protective magic on the tunnels is reestablished and there are no possible breaches or access points?"

He nodded. "A simple probing faespell would suffice. I can conduct it myself, but it will take some time. I will have to test the tunnels section by section."

"Are there others who can also conduct the spell? Would a team help?" I still wasn't sure which fire-Fae abilities were common and which were more specialized. My textbook studies of Teionyrian magic at the Hub had not been extensive, and I realized more each hour just how many gaps I had in my knowledge.

Maxim met my gaze. "Yes—there are several others in the city capable of conducting the spell. At least a few of them I know personally, and they are trustworthy. Having a team would certainly speed the process, and I believe those few would help if I requested it."

"Good. How do we get word to them?" I asked.

"If Maxim can write down the names, I'll summon a messenger to fetch them," Orvyx said.

Maxim nodded, then reached inside his cloak and pulled out a small notepad and charcoal pencil.

I wondered what other handy things he carried on him, but now wasn't the time to ask.

Maxim scratched down a few names, then tore off the sheet and passed it to Orvyx before tucking the notepad and pencil back inside his cloak.

Orvyx scanned the list of names, then looked back up at me. "Shall I do it now?"

"Yes, please do," I said. "Ask them to meet here at the palace as soon as possible, and to report to Maxim for instructions."

"Yes, Your Highness." He gave a quick bow, then exited the room.

I turned to the remaining council. "So with its magic restored, Teionyr is well-fortified against attack... but some of the allied villages outside our walls do not have protection. Can we bring those people to Teionyr?"

Arval shook his head. "I fear many of them would not come. Trust of Teionyr's royals will take time to rebuild, after Sevryn and Beirthyr's rule, plus they may not want to abandon their homes."

"They deserve to be warned, though," I said, "and to have shelter offered to them. Do they not?"

A nervous expression overtook his face. "Of course, Your Highness! I was not suggesting we shouldn't offer shelter—only commenting that they may refuse."

I studied him for a moment. Did the council members trust me so little that they thought I would take offense at honest input or a difference of opinion?

Then again, they didn't know me... and they had just witnessed an unstable tyrant wreaking havoc on their kingdom. Arval said the villages' trust of the royals would take time to rebuild, but the truth was, my own council had difficulty trusting me, too. And how could I blame them? I was stumbling around like a rookie LeyGuard.

I didn't even know my own kingdom's resources: Did Teionyr have a standing army? What magic was at our disposal for defense?

As a king, these questions were humiliating to ask, but I shoved down my pride and asked them, anyway.

"An army?" Thorim stared back at me. "No, Your Highness, not for decades. Teionyr has been a symbol of our kingdom's peace—at least until Beirthyr and Sevryn took over."

"And the royal magic that protects the city, what are its parameters?" Heat entered my cheeks at admitting I didn't even know what my *own* royal magic encompassed. This level of ignorance in a LeyGuard trainee would be grounds for discipline or even dismissal, but as a king, it was an even worse offense. How could the Teionyrian people depend on me like this? Why *should* they trust me?

Suddenly—and much to my own surprise—I wished Kaizyn were here. He and I had a massive conflict of interest where Ayla was concerned, but he had trained all his life for this role, and the people had loved and trusted him. I could've used his advice.

Maxim ignored my embarrassing ignorance and answered my question patiently. "The royal magic forbids entrance to the vault by anyone but the seated heir, and it also fortifies the magical barriers around our city. Those barriers can be activated at the king's will and can also be adjusted, using specialized faespells infused with a drop of royal blood, to block all access in and out of the city, or to allow access for Teionyrians only, or even to forbid access by those with certain types of magic, provided you have a drop of their blood as well to target the spell. Or the barriers can be spelled to do any combination of the above. Those barriers are our city's best defense, particularly now with the strength of your own magic. The strength of the barriers is directly correlated to the strength of the seated royal and his or her sear-bind. With a dragon as a sear-bind..." He drifted off slightly, glancing at the others, then huffed a short laugh. "Well, so long as you command your dragon's assistance, those inside Teionyr's walls will have all the protection we could need."

"Command her?" I asked. "So her power does not automatically augment my own?"

"The sear-bind is a complicated relationship," Maxim answered, looking suddenly uncomfortable. "With a dragon, in particular, it is even more complicated."

"Complicated how? Is there something different about the sear-bind relationship when it's with a dragon?"

Maxim glanced away. "Perhaps you should ask her yourself, Your Highness. I am not a dragon; it is not my information to share."

I studied him for a moment, unease churning in my stomach. What was he not telling me? I trusted him—but he was obviously hiding something. Was it really that he didn't want to meddle in dragon affairs? Or did he just not want to talk about this in front of the council?

From the confusion on the other council members' faces, it seemed they were as clueless as I was.

I started to ask Maxim to convene with me outside in the hall, but then I felt the warm tickle at the edge of my consciousness that I was coming to recognize as my bond with Sorcha. Maybe Maxim was right—it would be better to go to the source.

Sorcha? I channeled my thoughts toward the distant, familiar presence.

Her voice answered back in my mind, though muted as from a distance. *Yes?*

A flickering glimpse of blue sky and clouds appeared in my mind, then a glimpse of rolling green hills and the sturdy walls of Teionyr visible far below. It seemed she was stretching her wings above the palace.

Can you come meet me? I asked her. *On the hill outside the palace.*

I pictured the hill where Sorcha had saved Ayla the second time, warming her when her magic had gone haywire. A flash of longing pierced my chest at the thought of Ayla. I missed her.

On my way.

I turned to Maxim and the other council members. "Would you excuse me for a few moments? Feel free to take a break; I'll find you when I'm ready to reconvene."

Thorim looked at me with concern. "Is everything all right, Your Highness? We still need to discuss your coronation ceremony. It's taking place in a few hours."

I nodded, my jaw clenched. "Yes—I believe so. I won't be long. I just need to speak with my dragon."

CHAPTER 18

WHAT I MIGHT LOSE

Ayla

Doctor Harlowe's boots clanged ahead of me as he led me down a long, metal-walled corridor topped with white fluorescent lights. Rows of identical, opaque glass doors lined both sides of the hall, each door labeled by a metal plate on the wall next to it, etched with *S-* and a room number. I assumed *S* stood for *sub-level*, because the special elevator Doctor Harlowe unlocked to take us here had plunged us well past the basement and down into some unmarked floor in the bowels of the Hub.

I tried not to think about being so far below ground. I wasn't claustrophobic, at least not diagnosably, but that didn't prevent panic from simmering in my chest at the thought of getting trapped down here.

I hurried to follow Doctor Harlowe as he strode briskly down the hall.

Being *alone* down here with Doctor Harlowe also wasn't helping the creepiness factor. It wasn't that I didn't trust him, but this was exactly the type of setting I had screamed at horror-movie characters not to walk into, right before they inevitably got murdered.

Doctor Harlowe tucked his tablet under his arm and glanced back at me, seeming to sense my discomfort.

Then I realized, *of course* he sensed my discomfort. He was a Selkblood.

He slowed his pace until he was walking beside me, then gave me a friendly smile. "I know you would be more comfortable if your family were here with you. We just need to run a few simulations and basic training modules with you alone to get a baseline, before we move to anything more complex. But I'll do my best to move through this part quickly, and your family can join us for your next session."

His too-blue eyes were kind, though their unbelievable similarity to Sevryn's still unsettled me.

I swallowed down my discomfort and offered him a smile. "Thank you."

Doctor Harlowe didn't deserve to be compared to Sevryn; he had been nothing but kind to me from the start. This creepy corridor was just getting to me—and so were my nerves about whatever training might entail. Would it be like an exam? Could I *fail* it? Doctor Harlowe had evaded most of the questions I asked on the elevator ride down here. He said the first session would be more beneficial for me if I reacted to the training exercises as they were presented. He didn't want me to overthink the process—which I absolutely would have, if I'd had any info to go on. I was doing a pretty good job of overthinking it even *without* information.

Doctor Harlowe glanced at me again. His smile was kind. "Your grandfather and your parents will be watching from monitors upstairs, able to see and hear everything that goes on in your training room. You'll be able to talk to them through the monitors between training modules, if you want to, though of course the fewer interruptions we have, the more quickly we can complete this component of your training."

I stared at him in surprise, and a genuine smile broke through all my nerves. "Thank you." Knowing my family was watching to make sure everything went safely, and that their voices were just a button-push away, would definitely be a comfort—if I ever *made* it to the training room in the first place.

This creepy murder corridor was starting to feel like the hallway that never ended.

Finally, Doctor Harlowe stopped in front of a door labeled *S-58* and swiped his fancy watch over the metal plate.

There was a soft click.

"Welcome to Training Room 58," he said, nudging open the door. "Come on in."

Training Room 58. Did that mean *all* the rooms in this corridor were training rooms?

I opened my mouth to ask, but as soon as I entered, my question was forgotten, swallowed up by the sheer overwhelm of what looked like a high-tech virtual reality gaming cave.

Flat-screened monitors lined every wall, floor to ceiling and even *on* the ceiling. Five soundwave-like ripples of color zinged across the walls and ceiling in rows, making a rapid circuit of the entire room before starting in unison at the other side again. It took me a moment to realize the waves of color were actually a synchronized loop of video, like a screensaver, moving over the monitors like a crowd-wave moving through a stadium.

The floor was the room's only solid, non-screen-covered surface, and it seemed to be made of some kind of color-shifting metal—until I realized the changing colors were actually colored lights, coming from an assortment of tiny projectors tucked between the monitors overhead and reflecting on the floor's metal surface.

A small table stood near the door, stacked with what looked like plastic 3D glasses.

"What *is* all this?" I asked.

"An immersion suite. With the monitors and projectors, I can create extremely realistic simulations—especially if you wear these." Doctor Harlowe shifted his tablet to one hand, then grabbed a pair of glasses from the table and handed them to me. "They're VR glasses, more or less. There are also some built-in olfactory ports in the nosepiece, and speakers in the glasses' frames, though I'll have you wear earbuds instead, to enhance the simulation."

"These glasses make *smells*?" I turned them over, examining them, but aside from tiny pin-holes on the earpieces and nose piece, they looked completely ordinary.

Doctor Harlowe laughed. "Only a few scents, preloaded and pro-grammed to deploy if I trigger them. Things like burning wood, fresh-cut grass, ozone, pine trees, a sea breeze, and newly fallen snow—smells I've found tied to many people's most intense memories. I can also program combinations specific to the individual I'm training, like a loved one's perfume or hand lotion, a favorite baked treat, or—less pleasant but also powerful—a specific revulsion, like sour body odor or the scent of a rotting animal."

"Wow," I said, still examining the glasses.

"In your case..."

Doctor Harlowe tapped something on his tablet, and a tangy-sweet smell swept over me, hitting me straight in the chest with a fierce wave of nostalgia.

He smiled at me. "Among other things, I've programmed pomegranate jam."

And it was—that *exact* smell, one I hadn't even realized was tucked so deeply into my memories until an image of Grandpa appeared in my mind: him sitting at the breakfast table, early morning light filtering in on him from the window. The moment reappeared so vividly I could hear the *scrape-scrape* from my butter knife on the still-warm toast I held as I spread the jam on for Grandpa then handed him the plate. The memory faded a moment later, dispersing with the scent.

I stared up at him. "How did you do that?"

"Memories attach to our sense of smell, often on a deeply emotional level. Sometimes, a scent can trigger vivid memories, almost as though we are reliving a moment. In other cases, it may just evoke a very specific feeling. The right scent can unlock *many* things."

A strange tension pooled in my stomach. Doctor Harlowe had said my magic was tied to emotion, especially to fear. Was that what he was planning to unlock? I'd been through a *lot* in the past two weeks, but I'd been anxious, even before all this. I'd lived pretty much my whole *life* in fear, and I never really knew why. What would the right scents unlock, for me? Did I *want* those things unlocked? I stared down at the glasses.

Doctor Harlowe set his tablet on the table and moved around to face me. When I glanced up at him, his expression was pure compassion.

He rested a hand lightly on my shoulder. "You have nothing to fear from the past, Ayla. Everything that has happened, no matter the pain it brought you, cannot be changed by re-experiencing it. But it also does no good to bury such things. You must feel them, embrace them—so that you can release them. Until we release the past, we cannot yet understand how much it controls our future."

I stared at him, fidgeting with the glasses I held. "I don't have anything super traumatic in my past. At least, not until all this Fae and LeyGuard stuff." I let out an awkward laugh, but as his chilling blue eyes met mine, I felt I could trust him. "I don't *know* why I'm always so anxious. People have been through far worse things than I have, but even before all this I was just... always nervous. Like—like I'm afraid of what might happen, or... what I might lose."

There it was. *What I might lose.* I felt the tears press hot in my throat, even as I said it. That had always been my fear, deep down, and it had only worsened with Grandpa's illness. I had never cared about popularity at school, or fancy clothes, or sports, or cars, or any of the things other kids seemed to care about. I had my mom and my dad, my grandpa, and my small handful of friends—but they were *all* I had. Or at least all that mattered to me. And the thought that I might lose any of them, for *any* reason, completely terrified me. What happened these past few weeks had intensified those feelings—with Jordan, and with my family, of course, but also with everyone else. I'd gained new friendships, and deepened old ones. But if anything, it had only shown me how *much* they all really meant to me.

Doctor Harlowe moved beside me, leaning against the table. His voice was gentle as he continued. "Your blend of magic is unique, Ayla. I have suspicions that it could be very important in the coming conflict against the Dark King and his army—if you can figure out how to channel it.”

I cut a sideways glance at him. “Important how?”

He shrugged. “We don’t know much about the Dark King, but we do know he’s Fae. We know he rules the Courts of Chaos from a palace inside the Mountain Kingdom, in the southern section of Lower Faeside between Morrowen and the Wilds. Access to the Mountain Kingdom is strictly guarded by the Dark King’s armies—and to my knowledge, no one outside the Courts of Chaos has actually *seen* him since he was banished back to Lower Faeside in the first war decades ago. Accounts from the previous war only describe him as shadowed and very, very powerful. Not many saw him up close and lived to tell of it. However, our best guess is that he’s a very powerful Fae *from* the Mountain Kingdom who has dabbled in dark Void magic to augment his powers.”

It seemed like he thought that should mean something to me.

I shook my head. “I don’t understand.”

He turned to face me. “Forgive me. At times, I forget you were not raised LeyGuard. Ayla, the LeyGuard Houses were created to *balance* the Fae kingdoms’ powers—infused with the same root powers sourced from Aeden, each crafted as the mirror and answer of their Fae counterparts. For each of the four major types of Fae magic—wind, fire, earth, and water—there is a corresponding LeyGuard House, a bloodline bred and honed and trained to fight magic *with* magic, should the need ever arise. The Mountain Kingdom is a *wind-Fae* kingdom, Ayla. Wind, like Fortis.”

Fortis was my grandpa’s LeyGuard House. *My* LeyGuard House.

I stared at him. “I—I still don’t understand.”

His expression was patient as he continued. “The LeyGuard has no answer to Void magic. That is why the Dark King and his armies are such a threat. Even Fae struggle to face down Void magic, but we Fae are at least equipped with an instinct for sensing it. That gives us an edge, however small, in fighting it. Of all the forms of Fae magic, the fire-Fae magic seems to be most effective against Void magic. It is part of why Teionyr still stands, when so many other Upper Faeside kingdoms and villages have fallen. But the Dark King's core magic, if we are correct, is Mountain Fae magic—*wind-Fae* magic. That means you—as a wind-wielding Fortis LeyGuard who also happens to be infused with a touch of inverse fire-Fae magic due to your bond with Kaizyn—*you* might be one of our *best* weapons against the Dark King."

I blinked, processing that. But if *I* was the Hub's best weapon, then we all were surely doomed.

I huffed and tucked my arms tight around my stomach. "I don't know how to control my magic. I can't be a weapon. I can't even protect *myself*."

An eager glint came into his eyes. "Not *yet*."

The thought of being a weapon honestly terrified me. But if I could use my magic to defend those I loved, to protect them...

Doctor Harlowe's gaze softened. "I can feel your fear, Ayla. But no one will ask you to do anything beyond what you *choose* to do. Your magic is yours to use. No one will force you."

I unfolded my arms from around my stomach, still holding the glasses in one hand, and stared up at him. "They're all in danger, everyone I care about. They've all *been* in danger, and we've just barely survived it so far. Now, the Dark King is coming, and I—" Tears pooled in my eyes, and I glanced away, clenching my jaw against them.

The Dark King had always been coming for Teionyr, and my grandpa had long been tangled up in it. I hadn't started this mess, but I *had* stumbled into the center of it. The moment I broke that vial in the café, I set off a chain of events that put everyone in danger... and yet, that mistake also *saved* Kaizyn's life and put us all—even Jordan—exactly where we needed to be.

There's no way I could attribute that all to coincidence.

For weeks, I'd been praying just that my loved ones and I would survive—but perhaps part of God's answer to those prayers *was* all of this, everything that led to this moment.

Losing the people I loved was my greatest fear. But if Doctor Harlowe was right, then letting that fear paralyze me might be the very thing that guaranteed it would happen.

I hadn't known about the Fae world when this all began. I'd been helpless and running for my life. I wasn't to blame for that, but I had a choice in what happened from here, because now I had my own magic. It had been fairly useless so far... but what if Doctor Harlowe was right, and my magic could make a difference in this war, if I learned to control it? No one would force me... but could I live with myself if something bad happened to my friends or family, or even to an entire kingdom—*Jordan's* kingdom—and I hadn't even *tried*?

I clenched my fists at my sides and drew a deep, shaky breath.

I had started this chain of events by accident, but I wasn't helpless anymore. I'd been given the ability to fight back.

My fingernails dug into my palms as I said another, desperate prayer. *Please, God—help me to be brave.*

A hot resolve pooled in my chest as I turned back to Doctor Harlowe. "I can't lose them. Not any of them. I *won't*. Show me how to use my magic."

Doctor Harlowe picked up his tablet, then grinned as his eyes locked on mine. "That, my dear one, is *exactly* why we're here—and I think you're finally ready."

CHAPTER 19

NOT SURE HE DIDN'T DESERVE IT

Callan

I slid my freshly polished dagger back into its sheath, dropped the soiled rag on Keyja's kitchen table, and leaned back in my chair. Only a few hours had passed since I'd said goodbye to Madison at the Gate, but I missed her already—not that I would admit that aloud to anyone but her. I shoved away the distractions of my feelings once more and turned to Kaizyn instead.

He had been jabbing his wooden spoon into his bowl of stew for nearly fifteen minutes, and he still hadn't taken a bite.

I leaned toward him across the table. "You should eat something, brother. You'll need your strength."

Kaizyn glared at me, then stuffed a spoonful of cold stew into his mouth.

Apparently, his bad attitude was now also directed at me. He'd been snapping at me and giving one-word responses all day.

But I bit my tongue—now wasn't the right time to confront him on it, not with Reina and her parents sitting together on the cottage bed a few feet away.

Reina glanced over at us, then went back to her task of weaving straw-ropes with her parents.

Keyja had given us all tasks—all things she claimed were to help defend Arcvale, but which I highly suspected were to keep us busy while she and Tofa made their own preparations. ArcFae magic was mysterious but powerful, and I doubted some rope-nets for capturing darklings would do much in comparison to the strength of Keyja and Tofa's magic. But at least it was something we *could* do. The anxious tension of waiting around for an attack was starting to get to everyone, myself included.

Kaizyn shoved back his chair. "It's time for another patrol."

"But you haven't eaten your—"

I silenced my argument when he gave me another glare.

I stood. "Fine. I'm coming with you."

Kaizyn narrowed his eyes at me, but didn't argue. He knew he wouldn't win. It was my job to protect him, after all, even if he no longer thought he needed it. He grabbed his own dagger from the table and stormed outside.

Vyrthil, who never strayed far from Kaizyn, was waiting just outside the doorway. He swung into step beside Kaizyn as he strode across the grassy field, toward the dome's northern barrier.

The cottage door swung shut behind them.

I grabbed my small sack of provisions from the table and hurried after them, holding back my words until we were halfway across the grassy field and well away from the cottage.

"Since when do you not even wait for me? I said I was coming." I couldn't help the annoyance in my tone. Kaizyn had always treated me as a close friend—as a brother—even though I was his guard, but his behavior the past few hours had been outright hostile.

I knew he was going through a lot, but pushing away the people closest to him wasn't the right way to handle things. And I hadn't even received the worst of it. He would barely even acknowledge that Reina *existed*, even when she was sitting a few feet away.

Kaizyn glanced at me over his shoulder. When he caught the annoyance on my face, the hardness in his glare cracked. He stopped walking.

"I'm sorry, Callan. I—" He turned to face me, but looked away as a wave of emotions cascaded over his expression: guilt, pain, sorrow, fear, all in a wave, landing on a wide-eyed desperation. "Everything I knew, everything I thought I was, is *gone*. What am I going to do?"

He dropped his gaze to his boots.

Vyrthil nosed Kaizyn's hand and chuffed nervously at Kaizyn's side, sensing his anguish.

I stepped toward him. "Nothing about who you are is gone, Kaizyn. You are still the prince, a son *chosen* by the king and loved deeply by him. You are still a leader, someone your people respected and loved, someone Sevryn feared so much he tried to kill you, then banished you with a curse, because he knew the people would rally around you—that they would follow you."

He forced his eyes up to mine. "I am not the heir. I am not the king the people thought I was, back then."

"No," I said, holding his gaze. "You are not the king. But you *are* the one raised and trained to lead Teionyr. You *are* the one your people know and trust. They need you, Kaizyn. Jordan is going to need you. The people need stability, to see their prince serving side-by-side with their new king—not absent or, worse, glaring at him from the shadows."

Kaizyn narrowed his eyes. "I never glared at him."

I huffed. "You did."

Kaizyn's frown slowly melted into a half-smile. "Okay. Maybe I did. But I'm not sure he didn't deserve it."

I laughed. "For what? Stealing a girl who was already in love with him?" As soon as the words left my mouth I tensed, wondering if I'd gone too far.

But Kaizyn only sighed. "You have a point. I may not have been able to help how I feel about her, but she never asked for this bond—and neither did he. Perhaps, even without the bond, I may have fallen for her, may have been heartbroken that she didn't choose me. But the bond has made everything... unbearable."

I placed a hand on his shoulder. "I know. I'm sorry."

Kaizyn grabbed me in a sudden hug. "No, brother. *I'm* sorry." He pulled back, clasping both of my shoulders as his eyes locked on mine. "Please forgive me for how I've acted toward you. I was not in my right mind."

I smiled at him. "Is any man in love ever in his right mind?"

He laughed, and for a moment, he looked like himself again. "You tell me." He raised an eyebrow.

I felt my cheeks flush. "We are talking about *you*, at the moment."

He chuckled. "So we are. We'll return to you later."

But then his face grew serious.

"I need to find a way to break this bond, Callan. I cannot imagine living all my years like this, not at peace even when I'm a world away from her, yet also afraid I might run across her somewhere and set off the bond's magic. It would torment us *both*. I need it gone."

My heart ached for him. "I know. I promise, we will figure it out. Perhaps there is information in the palace archives—Maxim knows them well. I'm sure he's already searching, but I'll send a message reiterating the urgency and letting him know where to find us."

Kaizyn nodded. "Thank you. And thank you for staying by my side... even when I was intolerable. I could not have hoped for a more loyal guard—or a more loyal friend."

"*D'lenyi merture iyn Kaizyn*—'My life in protection of Kaizyn.' Always."

Discomfort flitted over his face at my repetition of the royal guard's motto. "Your actual vow was to the royal heir, not to me."

"I know, and I intend to fulfill it. But my loyalty to you has not changed, my prince. I would still die for you, as I would have before all this."

Kaizyn's lower lip quivered slightly. "And I would die for you, brother." A small chuckle escaped him, as though he'd just thought of something. "Perhaps, now, I would even be allowed to—now that I am no longer the heir-king."

"You *are* the heir-king, should anything happen to Jordan."

He tensed. "It won't." Horror crossed his face. "It cannot. For all my own pain, I do not wish him ill. He is—he is Father's true son. And he is the *king*. Our people need him."

I nodded, my pride for him—and for his unselfish heart, even now—swelling up into a smile. "Then you understand what we must do."

He drew a breath, then resolve settled on his face. "Yes. As soon as this bond is broken and I know I am no threat to Ayla, I will return. Even if Jordan will not have me by his side, I owe it to my people to show him support, to ease their minds in trusting him. What little influence I still have may be leveraged for some good. I will bow alongside my people, and publicly acknowledge Jordan as the true king."

I gripped his shoulder. "And I will be by your side. As always."

He studied my face for a moment. "Callan, I want you to promise me something."

I dropped my hand from his shoulder. "Anything. You know that."

The thoughtful expression in his eyes made my stomach tense, but I trusted him—and I had already vowed my life for his. What could he ask that I wouldn't have done, anyway?

His expression turned somber. "When the time comes, I want you to leave me—to stop being my guard."

"What?" I gaped at him. "Anything but *that*. You know I will not."

He held up one hand. "Hear me out, Callan. One day, you will want a life of your own. You will *want* it. And when that time comes—when you reach the day where your vows to me stand in opposition to your own heart—I release you. Do you understand? I release you in advance. You don't even have to ask. Just tell me, and I will joyfully accept your resignation. I'll even throw you a wedding feast."

I wanted to argue that day would never come, but I already felt my heart shifting—felt, for the first time in my life, that *home* was no longer here with Kaizyn but a world away.

I would never abandon him, but if the circumstances were right, and if he gave his blessing... No. I couldn't even entertain that thought. My duty was to be by his side.

I forced an awkward laugh. "Are you so eager to be rid of me?"

His expression softened. "I will never be rid of you, brother. We both know that."

I chuckled but his eyes were serious.

"I mean it, Callan. I can get other guards—not that any will be as good as you—but one day, I want to stand beside you at your wedding, and live life alongside you as your *friend*. Not as your royal duty."

Was the future he described really possible? I tucked away that tiny spark of hope he offered and swallowed, my throat suddenly tight. "You know you have always been both."

"And *you* deserve happiness, when this war is over. And it will be over soon. I can feel it."

I nodded. "So can I."

His sober expression split into a grin. "Then it's a promise. You will marry what's-her-name and live happily ever after, or whatever those human fairy tales say."

I narrowed my eyes, though I knew he was joking. "You know her name."

He smirked. "Of course I do. But the expression on your face is so much more amusing this way."

I smiled, relieved to see him back to his normal self again. But there was still one thing to discuss. I sighed. "Kaizyn..."

His smirk vanished. "I know that look. I've done something grievous again."

Vyrthil's tail twitched as he glanced between us, trying to read the situation.

I shook my head. "It's about Reina. I couldn't help but notice—"

He ran a hand down his face and groaned. "She's insufferable. She's annoyed by everything I do! Did you hear her ask me if I was going to continue to sigh in self-pity all afternoon? I was *breathing*, Callan. I can't even *breathe* correctly for her."

I laughed. "I heard... but you *were* kind of sighing."

Kaizyn's eyes widened. "I was not."

"Fine—a misunderstanding, then. But Kaizyn..." The grin slipped from my face. "She's hurting too, you know. This thing with Ayla and Jordan hasn't been easy for her, either. Them being together, I mean."

Kaizyn's brow furrowed. "Why not? Isn't Jordan her LeyGuard partner? And Ayla is her friend. I'd expect her to be happy for them."

"Everyone would *expect* her to be happy for them, that's the point. But you, of all people, should know the sting of what might run beneath that."

He stared at me. "Oh... *Oh.* Does he know? Does Ayla?"

I shook my head. "I think Jordan might suspect, and Ayla might now, too, after how Reina has acted. But I'm not sure Reina has admitted the depth of it, even to herself. She and Jordan have a very close bond as LeyGuard partners, but it was always more, for her—I could see it the moment I watched them interact. She's hurting, but unlike you, she cannot let anyone know her reasons. Admitting what she feels—or felt—for Jordan would only make things more awkward and push him further away. She already feels cast aside by him, because he sent her here instead of wanting her present for his coronation."

Kaizyn's expression melted into compassion. "I knew she resented getting sent here to guard me, but the rest... I had no idea." He paused. "I should have seen it, though. I am usually more observant. Aren't I?"

"You are. But you are hurting, too," I said, clasping his shoulder. "When one's own pain screams loudly enough, it can be hard to hear anyone else's."

He glanced away and nodded.

"Reina is going to be here for a while. Some kindness might go a long way." I said, then grinned. "Besides, I'm getting a headache from all the tension and bickering."

He laughed, then met my eyes. "Thank you, Callan. For everything."

I tipped my head. "Of course, my prince."

Kaizyn squinted at me. "You aren't ever going to stop calling me that, are you?"

I smirked back. "Only if you become *truly* intolerable."

He grinned. "Come on. Let's finish the patrol we never started."

We both turned north, in the direction of the barrier—and froze. A dark spot, large enough to be visible at a distance, shimmered on the barrier's surface.

"A breach," Kaizyn breathed, then we both yanked out our daggers.

"Keyja!" Kaizyn yelled as he sprinted back to warn the others.

Vyrthil dashed out in a wide circle around him, doing a sweep of the area near the cottage.

I settled into ready stance, my gaze locked on the dark blotch... which was rapidly widening into a shadowed doorway.

"Kaizyn?" I called back over my shoulder. "Hurry!"

Someone—or some*thing*—was about to come through.

CHAPTER 20

SLEEP, MY PRINCE

Rory

Dove glanced at me over the breakfast bar in my parents' kitchen, then returned the phone receiver to its holder. "Still nothing." She had been attempting to contact the Hub via my parents' landline for over an hour, with no answer.

Madison and I sat on the stools on the other side of the bar, while Mom and Dad busied themselves upstairs packing for their unexpected departure to the Hub. The breakfast plates of scrambled eggs, toast, and fruit Mom had fixed us were still sitting on the counter in front of us, barely eaten—even Dove, as calm as she seemed, had only managed to eat a few bites of toast and some fruit.

Madison was trying not to look nervous and failing. She'd already bitten her thumbnail down to the quick, and she only ever bit her nails when she was in a complete panic. "Is there another number you could try? Isn't there any other way to get through?" she asked Dove for the second time in the last half hour.

Dove smiled sweetly and shook her head. "I'm afraid not. When the Hub's on lockdown, they only take calls through the emergency number." She glanced at the phone. "It is strange no one's answering, though. There's usually someone on duty taking messages."

Fogarty paced the countertop in front of Dove, still in cat form.

My mom would have a fit if she knew an animal were on her kitchen counters, but I wasn't about to rat him out.

Madison dropped her hands into her lap, fidgeting with her fingers instead of chewing on them, and glanced at me. "Are you feeling okay? Any more... visions?"

I was trying to *forget* the sound of those women in my mind, the fear in Dove's voice when she said my eyes were black with dark magic, and the way that woman had said my name. But Madison was making it kind of hard to forget, since she kept asking about it every ten minutes.

I pivoted the stool to face her. "Madison—I told you I would let you and Dove *both* know the moment anything else weird happens. If it happens." I suppressed a shudder. "I'm kind of hoping that was a one-time thing."

Dove rested her arms on the counter and leaned toward me. "You really should rest, Rory." She glanced at Madison. "You both should. It's been a while since either of you have slept."

Madison's shoulders slumped a bit.

I could tell she was trying to act like she wasn't tired, but she clearly was. Her eyes had that bleary, sunken look.

She glanced at me, fear cutting through her exhaustion. "What if it happens again while you're sleeping? How will we know to help you?"

A thread of panic shot through my chest. If I were being honest, I was terrified of that possibility, too. I laced my fingers together on the counter. "I don't know. But Dove's right—we both should sleep. I can't just stay awake forever."

I jumped as Dove's cool fingers rested on mine, then I immediately relaxed. Her touch had a way of calming me, even when it took me by surprise.

Dove leaned toward me, and her large, dark eyes met mine. "I will sit with you and watch over you as you sleep, Rory—if you'd like." Her rosebud lips curved up at one corner in a shy half-smile.

I would've *liked* lots of things—foremost at the moment, to kiss her—but we were nowhere near that stage of our relationship, yet. I wasn't even sure what our relationship *was*.

I shoved the thought away and cleared my throat. "That would actually make me feel a lot better... if you don't mind."

Her face lit with a smile that made my heart race. "Of course, I do not mind. Otherwise, I wouldn't have offered."

Madison glanced between us, and I could see her fighting back a smile of her own. "O-kay, well, I'm just gonna go to my room for a nap. I'll leave the two of you to figure out the rest." She stood and headed for the kitchen door, then turned back and nodded to Dove. "Thank you. I may actually be able to sleep, knowing you're watching over him."

"You're welcome," Dove said cheerfully.

Madison gave me one last glance over her shoulder, fighting a grin, then headed upstairs.

I turned back to Dove, and because I was still a gentleman who had boundaries—one of which was not inviting a girl I was extremely attracted to into my room to nap alone with me—I blurted, "I'll rest on the couch in the living room. You can sit nearby on the loveseat or one of the chairs. Will you be comfortable there?"

She smiled at me. "I can be comfortable with you anywhere."

Foge stopped pacing and stared at her.

I wasn't sure how to take Dove's statement—or Foge's odd behavior—so I chose not to read more into it than she may have meant. "Okay, good. If you need anything while I'm asleep, like food or anything, please feel free to help yourself. My parents won't mind."

It didn't take me long to realize that sleeping with someone watching over me was a bit more difficult than it sounded. I settled down under a thick blanket on the couch, and did my best to nap... but that partially healed wound near my shoulder blade from the attack in the Void kept aching, and although I was happy to have Dove sitting a few feet away from me, I could feel her gaze on me every time I closed my eyes.

"Dove?" I said, peeling one eye open.

She leaned forward on the edge of her chair. "Yes?"

Foge peeked at me from where he lay curled up next to her, then closed his eyes again.

"You don't literally have to *watch* me every second," I told her. "You can relax, if you want."

She smiled. "I enjoy watching you, though. You look so peaceful." She tilted her head. "Is it making it hard for you to sleep?"

I sighed. "A little."

I watched for her expression to turn hurt or offended, but to my surprise, her smile just softened into one of compassion. "Would it help if I sang for you?"

I opened my eyes fully. "You sing?"

She shrugged. "Of course! All women in my village did, though some better than others." She let out a little chuckle. "I was never the best in my age group—that honor went to Delia Riverthrush every single year—but I believe I am fairly skilled. Would you like a lullaby?"

I couldn't help my grin. "I would love one."

Her face lit up with pleasure. "Then close your eyes, Rory Kane. Just breathe deeply, relax, and listen."

I closed my eyes. The moment she began to sing, a deep peace washed over me.

Her voice was like nothing I'd ever heard—gentle and beautiful and breathtaking and gut-wrenching all at once, like all the emotions I'd ever buried inside me had been cracked wide open. The words began in a language I didn't understand, but within moments she was singing in

English—or perhaps she was just singing so directly to my soul that I understood her. I honestly wasn't sure.

Sleep, my prince,
As daylight falls,
Sleep and take your rest.
I'll carry away
The cares of your day
And the strain you feel crushing your chest.
I'll bind them in gold
With the songs from of old,
And they'll all drift away on the wind,
But my heart you will keep
As you drift through your sleep—
The heart of a love and a friend.

I felt a tear slip out of my closed eye, but before I could brush it off in embarrassment or even open my eyes, her soft finger gently wiped it away.

"Sleep, Rory," she whispered, her face close to mine. "You are safe."

I drifted off a moment later into the most restful sleep I'd ever had, filled with dreams of an enchanted woodland faerie who looked exactly like Dove, singing colorful flowers up from the ground in a forest clearing while the golden rays of sunset cast down through the leaves onto her dark, flowing hair.

CHAPTER 21

THE TRUTH IS THE TRUTH

Jordan

Sorcha's large shadow crossed over me as she circled above the hill outside the palace, angling down to land.

For as big as she was, she landed gently, though I didn't miss the wide eyes of a palace worker staring out through a crack in the doorway before he scurried away.

I couldn't blame him—my own pulse sped as Sorcha sailed toward me, then landed with a heavy thud on the grass and stumbled to a stop right in front of me like an oversized, red-scaled, flighted elephant. If the Teionyrians had realized that a dragon was just as new and strange for *me* as for them, they might have felt less embarrassed about gawking. Perhaps I should've made a point to tell them.

Every time Sorcha came near, I experienced the shock of her size all over again.

She towered over me, until she craned her neck down to get closer to my face. Tiny puffs of smoke escaped her nostrils as she tilted her head to look at me. *King-of-mine. Did you need something?*

The greeting slid through my mind with affection, warmth, and a sooth-ing glow—like sipping hot chocolate by the fireplace on a cool night. It was pleasant, but it couldn't overpower the wariness caused by Maxim's statements about dragons and the sear-bond. A needle of concern had embedded itself in my chest during that conversation, and Maxim's refusal to elaborate had only made it worse.

I forced a smile at Sorcha. "Thank you for coming."

Her massive head tipped in a gentle nod. *Of course.* She continued to stare at me, and I could feel her curiosity through the bond. *Why did you summon me?*

I ran a hand down my face, trying to figure out how to word my questions.

Sorcha's eyes narrowed at my stressed gesture, but she said nothing. I felt no judgment through the bond, only concern and further curiosity.

I took a breath, opened my mouth, then exhaled and closed it again.

Sorcha wasn't likely to be offended by me probing into dragon culture, despite Maxim's obvious reluctance—but I was also embarrassed. Sorcha seemed to understand me instinctively, but though I trusted her, I had to admit I knew very little about her, or about dragons in general. I wasn't even sure how to ask what I needed to know.

Speak, my bonded one. There need be no secrets or pretense between you and me.

I looked at her cautiously. "No secrets?"

Of course not. You may tell me anything.

I steeled my nerves. "Tell me about dragonkind and the sear-bond, Sorcha. What does it mean for you to be bonded to me?"

A flash of surprise crossed her dark eyes, echoed by a thread of alarm through the bond. She angled her head to peer more closely at me with one massive eye. *Why must you know that? All that matters for you is how the bond affects you. How it affects me is my own to carry.*

I forced myself to meet her stare. "You just said no secrets. Did you not mean that?" I narrowed my eyes. "Or does it only apply one-way?"

After a long, tense moment, her surprise melted into compassion. *Some secrets are for protection, my little king.*

I held her gaze. "The truth is the truth, Sorcha. We will both be better protected by facing it... especially if we face it *together*."

Her breath escaped in a small huff of smoke. Wary resolve mingled with the compassion I felt from her through the bond. *Very well. Ask what you want to know, King-of-mine. I will answer you honestly.*

I nodded my appreciation, keeping my eyes locked on the large, dark one she still had tilted toward me, then tried to voice the questions stirring in my heart. "Why are there so few dragon sear-binds?"

The dark eye she held angled toward me glinted as she studied me. *We are rare in the Wilds where the summons occur, and we are also very powerful. Only an equally powerful Fae may summon us.*

I blinked back at her. "*Equally* powerful?" There was no way I held as much power as a dragon.

Amusement warmed the sensation of the bond. *Did you believe it is common to do what you did in the marketplace? There has not been a fire-Fae with such magic in a long time. You, King-of-mine, are as rare as I.*

I just stared at her, processing that, then shook my head. "I didn't know what I was doing in the marketplace—or when I conducted the sear-bind ceremony. I didn't know who or what would answer my call; I only hoped it would be something that could save Ayla." I paused, thinking of how Maxim had said I could *command* my dragon to augment my power. "Did you come by choice, or were you forced?"

She studied me for a moment. *I was forced... once the magic caught me.* A hint of cold fury slid through the bond.

Horror flooded me. "Is that the way with *all* sear-binds?"

Yes.

I stiffened. "I'm so sorry," I whispered.

Sorcha's fury melted. The expression in her eye softened as she peered at me. *I would have come even by choice, Jordan of the LeyGuard. I cared not whether you were the true king. Your heart called through the magic—pure. I could feel your need, your love for that girl.* She turned her head forward again, then lowered herself closer to me. Tiny puffs of warm, charred-wood breath danced around my face. *King or not, I would not have refused you.* I felt her smile through the bond, though on her dragon-mouth it appeared a terrifying grimace. *It seems I am somewhat of a romantic, in these recent years.*

I stared at her. "How old *are* you?" The question just slipped out.

She pulled away slightly. *Old, to you. But we do not measure age the same as you do. I am grown, for a dragon, but still strong and with much time yet to live. I am at the age I might have mated and born young.*

Might have. My heart sank as she said it. "Can you not, now? Because of me?"

Her gaze locked onto me again. *I could, still. Nothing in the magic of the bond prevents it.* A sliver of hesitation entered the bond.

"What are you not saying?" I asked her.

She paused a moment, as though arranging her words, but to my relief, she didn't refuse to answer me. *There is one other reason dragon sear-binds are so rare—why dragons are so rarely seen in the Wilds, at all.* She let out a small huff of smoke breath. *We avoid the Wilds, to prevent being called by the bond. We have not frequented that part of Lower Faeside in decades.*

My curiosity swelled. "Then why were you there?"

Her dark eyes locked on me. *I came for you, Cathal-Reigar, son of Veilar, once known as Jordan of the LeyGuard. Even before you summoned me, I came.*

I stared at her. "What?"

Her emotions turned somber. *Though we were once allies, dragons are now forbidden to meddle in Fae affairs. It's an ancient law, since the Old War few remember. But that does not mean we do not watch. What happens among the Fae affects us all.*

"I still don't understand."

A trickle of fond respect drifted through the bond. *I felt your flame, son of Veilar. Dragons are attuned to magic. When you called yours in the marketplace to avenge your love, it answered tenfold. I felt that call straight down to the barrier of the Lower Void. I don't think there's a dragon within a hundred lengths who didn't feel it.* She paused briefly, studying me. *I was already on my way to aid you, no matter the others' disagreement, when the bond-magic you activated in the vault caught me. I was too close to the Wilds to escape its pull.*

"I'm sorry," I said again. "I never meant—"

A thread of warm affection seeped into my mind through the bond. *As I said, King-of-mine, I was coming anyway.*

Suddenly her words sank in. "What did you mean by 'the others' disagreement'? Did the other dragons not want you to come help me?"

As I said, there are laws... and I had to fly over the Wilds to get here, which my synod highly opposed, for the reasons I've already explained.

I started to ask what a synod was, but she anticipated my question.

My council, I believe you would call it. They advised me on important decisions.

"Does that synod advise all the dragons?" I asked, trying to understand. "How many of you are there?"

Smoke escaped her in a small chuckle. *You have many questions, little king.*

"Forgive me," I said quickly. I hadn't meant to pry.

That terrifying, toothy smirk slipped back onto her snout. *I do not mind. I trust you, and we seldom get to speak of ourselves to outsiders. As for how many, our clan is the last, but we are about two dozen strong—as strong as any clan could hope to be, these days.* Her mood darkened; I could feel it in my mind. *The Dark King has done much to harm the balance of magic in Faeside, especially in Lower Faeside. It is harder for us to grow strong than it once was. Magic is so deeply a part of our beings. And no—not every dragon has a group of advisors.* She hesitated. *Only me.*

My chest clenched as I anticipated her next answer. "Why only you?"

She sighed, a heavy huff of smoke. *Because I was next in line to lead the clan.*

I blinked. "You're a royal?" The word seemed insufficient for the majestic creature standing before me. "Like a princess? A queen?"

Something like that, yes, she answered, studying me carefully. *I was to rule over my clan when I came of age—at the next harvest season.*

Was. "But then I bound you to *me.*" The weight of that hit me gradually but heavily, like a steamroller slowly crushing me.

You did not intend to do so, she said gently.

I gasped as more realizations hit. "Your clan must be furious with me."

Her scaly lips flinched in what almost seemed like a wince. *They are displeased, yes, but mostly with me. For decades we had carefully avoided any chance of the sear-binding—it is seen as enslavement.*

Enslavement. The word dropped on me like an anvil. "I'm so sorry." No matter how many times I said that phrase, it felt wholly inadequate.

That warm affection flooded the bond again. *Do not be sorry, my little king. We all face the consequences of our own rash choices, and I will not blame you for mine. I would have helped you, either way, but now I have a chance to help you more fully. It is not what I planned, but I do not completely regret it. With me, your magic can be stronger. Teionyr can be stronger. Together, we might even withstand the Dark King's armies—though I cannot promise victory. Even I am only one dragon. But whatever magic I have within me, it is yours to use, now. You need only call me, and I will come.*

I didn't miss the sliver of pain that slipped through with her words. "Thank you," I whispered. "I appreciate that more than I can say. You said you don't *completely* regret it, but you do regret it some."

She sighed. *Yes—how could I not? I have displeased and disappointed my clan. They will not trust me to serve them, so long as I am bound to you. They will scarcely trust me even to be given a mate, if at all. At present, I am not even allowed back inside our clan's borders. They say they cannot trust me while I am bonded to a Fae.*

My alarm at that statement must've been plain to her, because she quickly shifted her gaze back to me.

Do not carry my sorrows, my little king. I will be fine. And no dragon of my clan will harm you or your people, for my sake, regardless of their displeasure at our situation.

I stepped forward and threw my arms around the end of her snout, or as far around it as I could reach. "I'm so sorry, Sorcha. I didn't know."

Sorcha flinched, then settled into my awkward hug, huffing warm puffs of charred-wood breath over my shoulders. Her voice slipped warm into my mind, bright as a golden summer sun. *Do not dwell in regrets, King-of-mine. We are together now, so let us face what comes... together.*

I pulled back to look at her. "I will find a way to undo this bond and set you free."

A hint of sadness slipped in through the bond with her smile. *I believe you will try. But no matter what happens, I will not abandon you in the fight to come. Whether by magic or by choice, I am with you now, King-of-mine. Come what may.*

I placed my hand on her warm, scaled snout. "And I'm with you, too—come what may."

I returned to the council meeting room a few minutes later, to find all five of them seated and waiting for me.

They rose to their feet as I entered.

I gestured for them to sit. "That's not necessary."

"I beg your pardon, Your Highness, but it is," Thorim said. "It is a recognition of your rank. With how new you are to our people, such ceremonies will be of even greater importance in establishing your authority and commanding the people's respect. We will sit when you sit, Your Highness."

I met his gaze, then nodded. "Very well. Thank you." I walked swiftly to my chair and settled into it, and the five men all sank into their own seats again—much to my relief.

Maxim studied me from the chair to my left. "Did you find the information you sought, my king?"

I sighed. "Yes, plus more that I didn't ask for but needed to know."

He held my eyes for a moment, and I wondered how much *he* knew. I planned to ask him later. Maybe he even knew a way to free Sorcha from the bond, so she could return to her clan once this was all over.

A silence fell over the room, then Orvyx cleared his throat. "The messenger I sent is gathering the chosen faespell Wielders as we speak, Your Highness. They will report here in a group as soon as he has collected all of them. They will be ready to begin the assessment of the tunnels immediately, provided Maxim is ready to guide them."

Maxim tipped his head. "I am."

Orvyx nodded at him, then looked back at me. "We have also taken the liberty to dispatch messengers to the nearest villages to warn them of an impending attack and to offer refuge to any who wish to accept it. I believe some will. Thorim and I both signed our personal guarantee on the missives, vouching for the trustworthiness of our new king. We do not have great influence among the villages, but since our families both descended from respected lineages among the villagers, we do have some."

I let out a small sigh of relief. "Thank you." I glanced around at my five advisors. "My dragon, Sorcha, has agreed to lend her power in defense of our city. She will not withhold any of her magic from our bond, so Teionyr's magic will be at full strength. She will also lend whatever additional protection we need during the coming battle, so long as it's within her power, though I do not intend to abuse that generous offer."

The men met my gaze, nodding their assent.

"What more can we do to prepare for the Dark King's attack?" I asked. "What else needs to be done?"

Kurrum steepled his fingers and leaned toward me. "The most important part, Your Highness—your coronation. Without that, your royal magic will not be at full strength even *with* Sorcha's aid, and the city will not have its full defense." He glanced at the others. "We have made all the preparations, already—everything that did not require your direct involvement, that is. But there is still the robe to be fitted, and it is traditional for the royal aides to perform a cleansing ritual on the new king—"

I gaped at him. "A cleansing ritual?"

At my widened eyes, Maxim interjected. "A bath, Your Highness," he said with a chuckle. "Just a very elaborate bath, with scented oils that represent the virtues of our kingdom."

"Oh." I relaxed.

"You have already activated the heir-magic and stated your vow to serve as king, at the pool in the vault," Kurrum said. "The public coronation this evening will simply finalize that process. However, there are many small rituals, traditions of our people, which a new monarch is expected to perform before the main event." His gaze held concern, as though I might refuse.

I gave him a warm smile. "Forgive me. My reaction was from confusion, not refusal. This is all new to me, and I am still learning your—*our*—people's ways. I am grateful for your patience with me."

His gaze softened. "Of course, Your Highness."

The three other men on his side of the table relaxed, too.

"We have everything prepared for you, Your Highness, if you are ready to begin, though we must hurry to get everything completed in time for tonight's coronation," Arval said. "The palace staff are all on standby, awaiting your arrival in the royal suites."

I shoved away my nerves and smiled, pushing back my chair. "I'm ready. Just show me what I need to do."

CHAPTER 22

You're Never Fighting Alone

Ayla

My sneakers, even with their rubber soles, clanked far more noisily against the training room's metal floor than I'd expected as I walked out into the darkened room. It almost seemed like the floor was hollow beneath, though I didn't really want to dwell on that thought.

Doctor Harlowe stood in a shadowed corner behind me, out of my line of sight, as I took my position in the center of the training room floor.

I was all hooked up with remote sensors—tiny electrodes he'd stuck to my collarbone, the base of my skull, and a few places on my head beneath my hair. Wireless earbuds were tucked into my ears. The glasses with their olfactory nozzles were perched on my nose, feeling like plastic safety goggles.

"Ready, Ayla?" Doctor Harlowe asked from behind me.

A crackling came through the earbuds. "Ayla? Can you hear me?" It was Grandpa's voice—staticky, but clearing toward the end.

I glanced back at Doctor Harlowe, visible just as a silhouette in the shadows, and held up a hand. "Wait! It's my grandpa."

Doctor Harlowe nodded and lowered his tablet.

"I'm here," I said, hoping Grandpa could hear me.

His voice came back clear and strong. "You're never alone, Ayla. And I don't just mean me talking into your ear. *Trust,* Ayla. Trust yourself, trust those around you, and when you hit the end of your own strength, trust

God and pray with everything you've got, just like I did at that pool in the vault. Just like Jordan did. You hear me, Ayla? You're never fighting alone."

Tears pressed at my eyes. "I hear you, Grandpa."

My parents' voices came through next. "You can do this, Ayla," my dad said, followed by my mom: "We love you, Sweetheart."

I nodded, though I wasn't sure if they could see me or not. "I love you, too. All of you."

Trust—and when I hit the end of my own strength, pray with all I've got. I could do that—I hoped—though I was planning to pray from the start of things, too, because I didn't *want* to be doing this on my own. God had always been my comfort when I felt lost, like how singing and praying to Him had comforted me after that first time I saw Kaizyn in the café. In the panic of all the last few weeks, I'd kind of lost sight of that.

Grandpa's reminder had brought a sense of peace I sorely needed.

I turned back to Doctor Harlowe. "I'm ready."

He nodded and raised his tablet. "Beginning simulation in three... two... one."

The room plunged into absolute darkness.

I pivoted slowly, heart racing, suddenly disoriented. I whispered a frenzied prayer for courage as my fear began to mount. Then I heard it, a subtle hiss.

The Void-snakes? Was I back in the Void?

I smelled the lavender oil-diffuser in Grandpa's bedroom, and my back pressed against something hard and uneven. I reached one hand behind me, but then the bookshelf snapped into view, and suddenly I was inside Grandpa's room again.

Sevryn immediately lunged at me, slamming my back against the shelves. His hands crushed my throat.

I scrambled to claw him off, but I was too weak—his hands were like steel, cutting off my air. I couldn't make a sound. I could barely even breathe. My heart raced in panic.

His glowing blue eyes locked on mine, full of hatred. "This time, you won't escape," he growled.

He was dead; I *knew* he was dead. But it felt so real, and my body had a mind of its own, its panic drowning out my logic.

He's not real, I told myself. *Not real, a simulation.*

I forced one very labored breath and the fact that I could breathe, even slightly, helped me regain my senses. I raised a shaky hand and attempted to call my magic. A puff of ice burst out from my fingertips but fizzled.

Sevryn narrowed his eyes and laughed. "Pathetic." He pressed into my throat, squeezing it tighter.

I tried to grasp that pool of cold magic I felt building in my stomach—the power triggered by my fear. Could I use it? Could I control it, if I stayed calm enough? I tried, but it slipped through my mental grasp.

I adjusted my feet, shut my eyes to block out Sevryn's terrifying glare, and tried again.

"Ayla!" a rasping voice cried in terror. "Ayla—help!"

My eyes flew open. "*Jordan?*"

Grandpa's room had vanished. I was in the Void.

A giant lizard monster, like the one Kaizyn had killed, had Jordan pinned against the trunk of a dark tree.

My heart lurched.

Jordan's body hung limp, his forehead gashed and bleeding. He was groaning in pain.

Not real, I told myself. *It's not real.* But a dark splotch of blood covered the front of Jordan's shirt, and was spreading. I could *smell* the iron tang of his blood from here, could smell the beast's swampy sweat and feel the tremors in the ground as it stomped and snarled and rammed its horned head into Jordan again, slamming him into the tree.

I jumped to run toward him, and yanked back hard, sharp pain shooting through my wrists.

I glanced up.

Metal cuffs held my wrists, bolted to a stone wall, like the outside of a cave.

It's not real, I told myself again. *Not real, not real.*

"Ayla!" Jordan's voice broke as the monster rammed him against the tree again. More blood sprouted from his stomach. His head lolled to his chest.

The monster pulled back and Jordan dropped, slumping to the ground.

"Jordan!" I screamed for him. All the logic in the world couldn't keep my panic from erupting at what was happening right in front of my eyes. "Jordan!" I yanked and felt the cuffs cutting into my wrists. *It's not real. It's not real.* I squeezed my eyes shut and forced a breath. *Get it together, Ayla. Focus. This is a test—a simulation.*

But what was I supposed to *do*?

The moment I opened my eyes, I could see Jordan's blood pooling around him on the dark ground.

A wave of fresh panic and nausea washed over me. *Not real, not real, not real.*

The hisses sounded again. I looked down.

A massive Void-viper, huge as an anaconda, slithered in front of me then curled back around to face me. It locked its eyes on me, then it raised its undulating body and coiled to strike.

My magic. That was the whole point of this—to train my magic. "Focus, Ayla," I whispered to myself. "None of this is real." I grasped for my magic and felt it raging inside me, but it was too chaotic to grasp. My pulse was racing, my heart pounding crazily, my breaths panicked and shallow. But all of that was only fear—fear, triggering my magic, controlling everything. Fear was just an emotion, a physiological response. I could feel it, ride through it... use it to my advantage. Couldn't I?

I forced a deep breath. Fear triggered my magic—but that didn't mean the fear had to *control* my magic.

"You can do this," I told myself. I shifted my hands up in the cuffs, turning my palms to face the snake, then focused on the churning pool of fear and magic inside of me, and tried to channel it toward my hands.

The viper lunged, and I jerked my body to the side, just barely missing its bite on my left hip.

Cold vapor spurted from my fingertips where my hands were still cuffed to the stone, then fizzled.

"Come on!" I tried again.

The snake lunged once more.

This time, a shard of ice shot out from one of my bound hands—but it missed.

The snake crashed into me. Searing pain shot through my thigh as it sank its fangs into me.

I screamed.

The venom shot through my veins like fire.

My leg seized up, muscles spasming. My panic skyrocketed again. "No, no, no, no!"

In the distance, Jordan cried out in pain as the lizard-beast planted one of its giant, clawed feet on his chest. It was going to crush him.

"Jordan!" I screamed, but my vision blurred as the searing fire-pain of the viper's venom raced up my leg and torso, toward my chest.

It's not real. I told myself that again, but I was losing. If this *were* real, I would be dying. Though I knew this was just a simulation, horror flooded me at that thought. If this were real, I wouldn't get any other chances beyond this one, so I had to act as if this *wasn't* a simulation. I had to figure this out.

The venom had reached my lungs. My breath was coming in gasps. I reached deep inside me, past all the fear and pain and panic, past the pool of my churning magic too chaotic to control or grasp.

I dug as deep as I could, envisioning myself rolling all of it into one, churning mass, then channeled it up through my chest and into my quivering, clamp-bound hands. I focused on my Grandpa's words—*You're never fighting alone*—then strained my trembling fingers outward, clamps digging into my wrists, and cried out inside my mind with everything I had—*Help me! Please!*—as I forced it all out through my palms.

The viper exploded into an icy mist.

I screamed again, forcing out another burst of magic, and the clamps fell loose from my wrists, clanking to the hard ground.

I gasped heavy breaths as the searing fire dropped away from my lungs, then drained quickly from my leg.

A few feet away, the lizard beast turned toward me with glinting eyes, then leaned its weight deeper onto Jordan's chest. A challenge.

Jordan let out an agonizing groan that sent my pulse racing.

It's not real, I reminded myself, but the fear I felt very much was.

I clenched my teeth and took a limping step forward, thigh still cramping from the recent spasms. "Get off of him. Now," I growled.

The beast narrowed its eyes at me, then reared up—and slung its weight down toward Jordan.

"No!" I screamed, slamming my power toward it.

Spears of ice shot from my palms, impaling the beast from the side. The force knocked it off course, and its front feet slammed into the ground, hard, just shy of Jordan's body. It staggered, reeling from the injuries and impact.

I stared in shock—I hadn't even known I could *do* that.

The beast staggered again and let out a rasping squeal of pain, then toppled sideways to the ground with a heavy *thunk*, just missing Jordan's unconscious body.

I ran toward him—

The Void winked away, and I staggered, blinded by colored lights.

"Excellent, Ayla! Incredible!" Doctor Harlowe rushed up next to me, steadying me with one hand. "You harnessed your power! Did you feel it?"

Through my earbuds, I heard Grandpa shout out. "You did it, Ayla. You did it!"

The room swam, all the lights blending together as I tried to get my bearings. I tore the glasses from my face and stared up at Doctor Harlowe. "Could you *see* all of that?"

He nodded and angled his tablet toward me, which contained a digital, silhouette version of me, currently standing in an empty space. "Yes, I could see everything. Whatever you're experiencing in the simulation is projected here, in a three-dimensional model, so I can compare the stimuli to your responses. A copy of everything I'm seeing here, along with some direct camera views of this training room, are also being transmitted to the handheld monitor I provided to your family."

"Oh." I glanced around. Bits of melting ice littered the floor. One of the monitors was covered in a thin layer of frost, and another screen was ruined, impaled by an ice-shard. I really *had* harnessed my magic and used it. For *real.*

"Would you prefer your family not watch?" Doctor Harlowe asked, his brow drawing down in concern.

"No—no, that part is fine." Usually, the pressure of someone watching would have amplified my nerves, but the simulation had been so intense I'd nearly forgotten anyone else was there. I glanced around the room again and winced. "I'm sorry about the damage."

Doctor Harlowe smiled. "Don't worry about that. It's expected with trainings like this." He studied me for a moment. "Are you all right? Do you wish to continue? I would like to run a few more scenarios, if you're up to it. The more you practice here, the better your control will be when real danger strikes."

My disorientation was finally fading as reality settled back in around me. I blinked up at the screens.

A large monitor at the front of the room now held a scoreboard: *Simulation: 0. Ayla: 1.*

A tiny prickle of satisfaction blossomed in my chest.

I thought of the *real* danger I'd faced in the past and how terrified and helpless I'd felt—and then of how I'd managed to pool my fear and panic during the simulation, stepping outside of it to let it fuel me rather than control me. Once I'd prayed and re-centered myself, control of my magic had become almost instinctual. It had done exactly what I needed without much of a conscious thought.

Fear had become my tool, *not* my master.

Suddenly, I was eager to go through the simulator again... and again... as many times and as many different scenarios as it took for that instinctive control to become second nature.

Doctor Harlowe's mouth pulled up into a grin as he sensed the change in my emotions. "Are you ready for another round?"

I slid the glasses back on. "Let's do this."

CHAPTER 23

ALWAYS READY

Reina

Kaizyn's panicked shouts of Keyja's name broke through the silence of the cottage.

My parents dropped the straw-ropes we were weaving and ran for the door.

I took only long enough to snatch my sheathed sword from the table, buckling it on as I rushed outside after them.

Mraugathal's branches were waving erratically beside a frantic, pacing Vyrthil, but the moody prince we'd just heard shouting was nowhere in sight.

"Where's Kaizyn?" I asked Mraugathal and Vyrthil, not that either of them could answer me.

Then I saw him—bolting through the fields of wheat toward the distant barrier of the dome.

Callan was right on his heels, and Keyja and Tofa were running toward them from another direction, all converging toward the barrier.

"What the—" There was a dark spot on the distant dome. A breach. I yanked my sword from its sheath and spun toward my parents. "Something's coming through. Let's go!"

As soon as we took off for the barrier, Vyrthil swung into a fast lope beside me, keeping a steady pace with me as I ran.

Had he been waiting outside the cottage for *me*? That didn't make any sense. It also didn't make sense that Vyrthil would let Kaizyn run off toward a possible attack without him, but we had a breach to deal with—I couldn't waste energy worrying about the fire-cat's weird behavior right now.

"It could be darklings, or worse," Mom said as we ran. She glanced over at me. "Be ready for anything."

"I always am," I grinned back.

Dad glanced at me from Mom's other side, matching my grin—but there was a thread of tension beneath *all* of our expressions. We were used to fighting, and had trained for it, but that didn't mean we weren't wary... especially when we had no clue what we were running toward.

The last time my parents and I had run into danger together like this was the battle at Teionyr, and before that, the time Jordan got himself kidnapped by Selkbloods at the docks. My parents had barely survived that one. Jordan was lucky he had survived *either* of those times.

I couldn't help the knot of fear tightening in my stomach, even as I raced toward danger. Because the truth was, there was no guarantee, *ever*. Anything could happen, any time we rushed in to fight Dark Fae. But if this really *was* the start of the Dark King's attack, this could turn from bad to worse in a heartbeat. And if anything happened to my parents...

I didn't finish that thought. It would have paralyzed me. I just shoved it down, like I'd been trained to do, and kept running.

My parents and I reached Kaizyn and Callan just as Keyja and Tofa reached them from the other direction.

"What's happening?" I asked. "What's coming through?"

Callan drew his dagger and planted himself to the right of Kaizyn, who was already in a defensive stance just a few feet from the dome's barrier, watching the black splotch on its transparent surface.

The developing breach was already almost big enough for a person to walk through, and steadily expanding. Something would be coming through at any moment—maybe *lots* of somethings.

Callan glanced over at me, but to my surprise, it was Kaizyn who spoke.

"We aren't sure—no sign of anything, yet. Just the breach itself." Kaizyn's eyes met mine with a look of concern. "Be ready."

His doubt in me rankled. "I'm *always* ready," I snapped as I stepped into position on Kaizyn's left.

I'd probably said it more harshly than I needed to, but I was on edge. Jordan had sent me to protect Kaizyn—to protect Ayla *by* protecting Kaizyn—and I would. With my life, if I had to. The least he could do was have some faith in my competence.

Mom and Dad nodded at me and took positions on my other side, while Keyja and Tofa took position next to Callan.

"A breach like this should not even be possible," Keyja said softly. "Whatever or whoever is coming through, they are not opening a door from the outside of the barrier as I did to let you in. They are tearing a rift straight through the dome, most likely from somewhere in the Void, based on the darkness, though I cannot tell for sure." She glanced at the rest of us. "You must be ready for anything, but this village belongs to Tofa and me. It is *our* duty to protect it. If there is an attack, Tofa and I will take the lead. If the rest of you see a chance to get to safety, take it."

There was a strain in her voice, as though she were in pain, though she looked normal.

Kaizyn tensed. "We will not abandon you."

"We cannot," Callan agreed. "This may be the last defense for the Hub as well. The Dark King's army could breach it from here."

"They will not," Keyja said. "I have shut down the Gates. Until I personally reopen them, nothing can breach to the Hub through Arcvale. Nothing should be breaching through at *all*."

"Does that mean we are trapped here if anything happens to Keyja?" my dad whispered.

That was an unsettling thought.

But before we could ask her, Kaizyn interjected.

"Then what *is* breaching through?" The alarm in Kaizyn's words was plain—because whatever was making this rift, it had overpowered Keyja's blocks.

Keyja's eyes narrowed. "I do not know, but whatever it is, it will have used up enormous energy breaking through. There is a reason the rift is opening so slowly." She gave a grin so menacing that it sent a chill down my spine. "Whatever is opening this rift is experiencing *excruciating* pain while doing so. I made sure of that." Her wings snapped open, spreading out wide behind her, as she turned toward the barrier and raised her hands. Sparks crackled from the space beneath her collarbone and danced between her fingers. "Once they have breached, they will find even *more* pain. Tofa and I have already faced one Dark Fae invasion of our home. We do not intend to allow another."

And I didn't intend to let my parents, Kaizyn, or Callan be harmed.

Hopefully, Keyja and Tofa could defend themselves, especially if they were our only way out of this place. Tofa was already glowing white hot, her skin sparking with arcs of energy. I pitied whatever creature tried to attack *her*. She could probably take down a dozen or more with one touch... but if there were hundreds, like Mraugathal had initially reported, even Tofa's power might not be enough.

I said a quick prayer: *Please, don't let anyone die today*. Myself included.

"Do you have a plan?" I asked the group of them. Mom and Dad and I could fight together instinctively; we knew each other's fighting styles well. But the rest of these people were wild cards. I'd only seen Callan in action a few times, Kaizyn had been slap-unconscious most of the battle in the square, and I had no *clue* what Tofa and Keyja usually did in a battle. I was good at improvising, but this many unknowns was nearly enough to glitch my brain.

"Stand behind me, all of you," Keyja commanded. "You do not want to be within reach of what Tofa and I are about to unleash. Once they are through—if they survive—you may engage."

Callan and Kaizyn shared a glance, then moved behind her.

My parents and I followed their lead. I flanked Kaizyn, opposite Callan as I had before, with my parents beside me—but *behind* the crackling ArcFae and her electro-bison, this time.

It wasn't exactly a *plan*, but as Keyja had said, this was *her* home—and I, for one, was not eager to get barbecued by magical lightning powers.

As the dark splotch's spread slowed, my fear mounted, and I ran through my breathing exercises to keep it at bay. Fear was natural for LeyGuard warriors, but the key was not letting it control you. When fear took control, people did crazy things.

We weren't here to do crazy things, today. We were here to survive.

The splotch's expansion halted. The breach was now the size and shape of an arched doorway, its opening as black as the Void but swirling slightly, like a whirlpool of darkness.

"Steady," Keyja whispered.

The whirlpool slowed.

I stared at the sluggishly rotating splotch of darkness. It seemed to be growing denser, like the whirlpool was thickening into sludge.

Then a shadow shot through it—and right out onto the ground.

"*Virthas!*" It yelled in a deep voice, human-sounding, then collapsed in a heap just as a massive bolt of energy from Tofa hurled toward it.

"No!" Keyja shouted and threw herself in front of the bolt.

The bolt struck her straight in the chest—and absorbed right in.

She shook her head slightly, the last crackles of electricity escaping into the surrounding air, then patted Tofa's nose before spinning to the crumpled body on the ground.

A dark cloak covered the man's body and face, and his back was to us. I wasn't even sure he was still conscious.

"The ArcFae word for mercy," Kaizyn whispered—I assumed as the explanation for what the stranger had yelled.

"Who are you?" Keyja asked, holding out one crackling hand as she stared down at him. "Speak!"

The figure pushed up on trembling arms and turned to face us.

"*Varias?*" Keyja's mouth dropped open in shock. "I thought you were dead!"

I gasped. He was the same ArcFae I'd seen at the battle in Teionyr.

He stood on shaky legs, one hand pressed to his side as if in pain, and met Keyja's stare. "I could say the same about you, little Keyja."

CHAPTER 24
SECOND CHANCE

Etcher/Varias

I scarcely believed my eyes. "Keyja Alrendak, is that really you?"

She was far more grown than I remembered her, but no other female ArcFae had ever been missing an archeart before—at least, not any female who survived infancy.

I was a child when Keyja was born, and our mothers worked closely as village healers, so we had known each other well. But truthfully, not a child in Arcvale hadn't known Keyja's name. Keyja Alrendak, the deformed child the Elders had tried to banish—the child the striniak had then chosen as its protector, despite the flaw for which the others shunned her.

My mother's final moments, crying out in pain from an illness not even Keyja's mother could cure, still visited my nightmares often—but my mother's death had been no one's fault. I couldn't say the same about the woman standing before me. I'd *watched* Keyja die in the battle against Arcvale, seen it with my own eyes. Her death had *absolutely* been my fault. And now that she was standing in front of me again—alive—I couldn't decide whether to be overcome with joy or terrified.

I glanced at the striniak behind her, then dropped into a bow. "Forgive me."

Striniaks were sacred to our people, and as the chosen protector, Keyja was akin to a priestess. The striniak could kill me with a single touch, and would have a right to, if I dishonored either of them.

And I had—even if they didn't yet know it.

Keyja rested a gentle hand on my shoulder. "Rise, Varias. You have nothing to fear here."

Keyja really *had* grown. When I raised my face and straightened, I was only a few inches taller than her, though we were *both* taller than the humans and other Fae nearby... all of whom were staring at us. I couldn't bring myself to care.

"Are you truly alive?"

She smiled. "If I were dead, wouldn't I know?"

She was beautiful now. I'd never been appalled by her lack of archeart the way some others had been. To me, she'd simply been Keyja. She grew pretty as she got older—she was just becoming a young woman when I left—but I'd seen her like a younger cousin, a friend. Now, she was fully a woman... and a rather intimidating one, at that.

Keyja's death had been my *biggest* regret for nearly two decades... not that I could tell her that, the same way I couldn't tell her that *I* had brought the Dark Fae to our dome.

And now, she was standing in front of me—very much not dead.

If I weren't a cursed man, I would've thought I'd been graced with a miracle. Though, perhaps, the miracle had been for *her* sake, and not for mine.

"How did you—" I started to ask, but she spoke at the same time.

"How are you even alive, Varias? I saw the darklings drag you away."

"Yes... they did." They *had* dragged me away, a few years before the assault on the dome, right into Miravel's waiting arms and my supposedly bright new future. Apparently, the ruse had been believable to those here in Arcvale. "I survived. I—" I swallowed. I wanted to tell her the truth. I'd been carrying the guilt of it for far too long. Perhaps her survival was my sign that I *should* tell her—

"Gah!" Pain sliced through my ribs, and I buckled forward, gasping.

Keyja rushed forward. "Are you all right? Is it the magic? I'm sorry! I didn't know you would be coming when I set those wards."

I glanced up at her, still heaving from the pain. "No, no it's fine. I—I mean, yes, it's from magic, but—" The pain receded and I sucked a deep breath. My muscles slowly relaxed, though my hands still trembled.

That had been a warning. If I said anymore, the punishment would be even worse.

I crossed my arms and tucked my hands into my armpits to hide the shaking. "I'll be okay."

"I'm so sorry, Varias," Keyja said softly. "I intended to drain and harm whoever attempted to enter, but I never would've dreamed it was *you*."

"I will live," I said, offering her a weak smile. "But you—I believed you had been killed in the attack on Arcvale."

She'd been cornered by a Dark Fae Commander and his darklings. I nearly ran to help her, but Miravel grabbed my arm. The next thing I knew, half the courtyard had exploded into ash—including Keyja. I'd *seen* it. She was there one moment, and the next... gone, nothing but flames and ash left behind. How had she survived?

She smiled up at me, then gestured to the striniak behind her. "Tofa saved me."

"Tofa?" I stared at the striniak, who had let go of her power and now stood covered in dull brown fur, though she was still massive and a sight to behold.

The striniak watched me with dark, knowing eyes.

I glanced away, turning back to Keyja. "This is not Dahlia?"

Keyja's smile fell away. "No—Dahlia birthed her youngling as expected, despite the attack. Dahlia is gone." Her smile returned as she gazed fondly at Tofa. "Tofa chose me as her protector—and more. We are... one. As a team."

I studied her. To be chosen by *one* striniak was a once-in-a-lifetime honor. To be chosen a second time, even by the offspring of the former one, was unheard of. "A team? What do you mean?"

Tofa flared into blinding light. Her whole body snapped inward into a ball of pure electricity, then shot out in a sizzling bolt right at Keyja.

I cried out—but before I could push her out of the way, the bolt surged right into the hole where Keyja's archeart would have been and settled like a crackling, white-hot orb in her chest.

"An archeart," I breathed.

Since Keyja had been born without one... Tofa had *become* one for her.

I stared at the crackling orb in shock, but when I looked up at Keyja's face, she was grinning at me.

"I almost did die that day, but Tofa saved me with her magic. For a moment, I was pure magic—just as she is—and then I returned... stronger than ever, thanks to her," she said proudly. "She and I, we are stronger together. As I said, we are a team."

"As though made for each other," I said, still breathless in awe. This was a power I'd never even *heard* of—power that, I realized with fresh panic, the Dark King now knew about... because of me. I had no doubts he could hear and see everything that passed through my mind. Perhaps even everything *I* saw and heard. I should never have come here. I staggered backward. "I have to go."

Hurt flashed behind Keyja's eyes. "So soon? But you've just gotten here. Varias... everyone else fled that day. I don't even know if they're still alive. You may be all the family I have."

Her words were like daggers in my chest. "Keyja, I—"

Even if I could've spoken truth against the Dark King's hold—which was doubtful, since he'd punished me the moment I even *thought* about it — I wouldn't have had the heart to do so now, with her staring at me like a brother returned from the dead. The truth would crush her.

Instead, I reached for her, and pulled her into a hug.

She threw her arms around me, returning it.

In that moment, I promised myself: no matter *what* it cost me, Keyja would not be harmed. The Dark King could rip my heart out himself, if he wanted, but I would never hurt Keyja. She was as good as family—my *only* remaining family—and her standing there alive, right in front of me, felt like the second chance I never thought I'd have.

CHAPTER 25

RARELY EVER SUCH COINCIDENCES

Ayla

The monitor read *Simulation: 0, Ayla: 5* by the time Doctor Harlowe flipped on the lights in the training room. After so long in the dark simulation room, the fluorescents overhead made my eyes water. Strange, how the monitors looked just like boring monitors, now that I could see everything—though they were all the worse for wear from my ice-shards and showers of frost.

Over the past three hours, I'd faced down Sevryn, Void-monsters, darklings, and more. I'd watched my friends and family being attacked, maimed, and held hostage, all while various monsters and threats came after me, too. During those attacks, I'd learned I could shoot ice spears, encase a creature in ice by freezing the moisture in the air around them, vaporize any living thing in close range by freezing and imploding it, and even shatter metal or other solid objects by plunging their temperature low enough to turn them brittle. Once, I was even dropped over the edge of a cliff and dangled only by a creaky branch—not my favorite, but easy enough to get out of, once I realized I could use my magic to drive ice picks into the side of the cliff to make handholds for climbing back up.

Doctor Harlowe set his tablet on the back table and turned to face me. "You've done remarkably well, Ayla. Better than I'd even hoped. You seem to have full control of your magic, now."

I sighed. "Yes. At least, enough to protect myself... and hopefully others."

He smiled. "More than enough for that. And I'd wager your magic will only get stronger with use. You may be capable of far more than we've discovered here."

That thought was both exciting and sobering. "I just hope I can use it when it matters."

His smile turned gentle, and he placed a hand on my shoulder. "You will, Ayla. I believe in you."

"As do we!" my grandpa's voice shouted through my earbuds.

I winced at the piercing sound, but chuckled. I'd forgotten they were still there. "Thank you, Grandpa."

A chirping alert sounded from the ceiling, followed by a series of fluttering blue lights, like a signal.

"What's that?"

Doctor Harlowe turned toward the training room door. "The visitor bell." His mouth twisted. "I wasn't expecting anyone." He tapped a few things on his tablet.

A girl's face came into view on his screen.

I recognized her—Quinn, the LeyGuard girl who'd helped Reina, Callan, and me plan our great escape when we busted out of the Hub to go save Jordan. That felt like so long ago, now. Had it really only been a couple weeks?

Doctor Harlowe's brow furrowed as he stared down at the screen. "Quinn? What—"

"I'm sorry, Doctor Harlowe. I know you requested no interruptions," she rattled off, "but I—I've had a vision. About Ayla."

The doctor's eyes widened. "Hurry. Come in." He tapped a button on the screen, and the training room door slid open.

Quinn hurried inside, and it shut behind her.

She wasted no time rushing over to us. She glanced between Doctor Harlowe and me as she spoke, her eyes with wide concern. "I saw an Arc-

Fae, maybe in Arcvale? It looked like Arcvale. But it was a guy ArcFae, not Madame Keyja. I've never seen him before, but he seemed... dangerous."

Doctor Harlowe gestured for her to keep going. "What did he look like?"

"Tall, muscular. Dark wings. A typical male ArcFae, I guess? He was muttering something about tattoos, though he didn't have any. Honestly, he seemed kind of out of his head. Maybe crazy."

I wanted to ask what this had to do with me, but Doctor Harlowe beat me to it.

"You said this is related to Ayla?"

Quinn's face paled, and she glanced at me. "Yes. He was—he was hurting her. Her *and* Kaizyn. He had them tied to each other by their hands, like this." She held up her wrists as though bound. "And he had straps over their foreheads and torsos and legs, too, holding them to the table. They couldn't move. Their heads were near each other, but they were both lying on their backs with their wrists up over their heads, tied together. They were screaming in pain as he cast some kind of magic. It flowed out of his hands and then up and over them, faster and faster in a ring around them both." She swallowed. "It was like—like he was sacrificing them, or something."

My heart plunged into my stomach.

Doctor Harlowe glanced at me, then back to Quinn. "Thank you, Quinn," he said. "Have you told anyone else?"

She shook her head. "No. I know I should've told Chairman Hart, but—well, you're the one who taught me how to channel my visions more clearly. I thought maybe you could help me make sense of this one, before I told anyone else." She glanced at me. "Except you, of course. Since you were in it."

I nodded my thanks, but I was still too scared to form words.

Doctor Harlowe turned back to Quinn. "I heard you were leaving on assignment."

"Yes, I'm on my way out just now. It's an info mission, to gather updates." She paused. "From Arcvale."

Doctor Harlowe stilled. "You know there are rarely ever such coincidences with your visions."

"Yes," Quinn said, her voice somber. "I'm aware."

He placed a hand on her shoulder. "I'll tell Chairman Hart myself—after you've gone. We both know she would just try to reassign you. She's too cautious, when it comes to you."

Quinn nodded, resolve settling onto her face. "Yes, Doctor Harlowe." Her eyes met mine. "Don't worry, Ayla. I'll see what I can find out about this vision while I'm there."

Doctor Harlowe tapped a button on his tablet, and the training room door slid back open. "If you have any other visions about this, message me right away."

She nodded, already on her way to the door. "Of course."

"But Quinn—be careful," he added.

She glanced back over her shoulder with a grin. "I always am."

She slipped out, and the door slid shut behind her.

I turned toward Doctor Harlowe, my stomach still churning with the news of the vision. "You said Chairman Hart is too cautious with Quinn. Why?"

He glanced at me. "Quinn's ability is rare. Chairman Hart only gives Quinn the simplest of assignments, just to keep her from getting restless. Even when Quinn's ability could reap vital information, Hart often considers Quinn too valuable to place at risk."

"But you don't?"

He met my gaze. "I don't like risking her, either—but I've seen firsthand what Quinn can do. I trust her ability to look out for herself." He tapped a few more things on his tablet, and I saw part of a message with Quinn's name, then the name *Brone* flashed up before Doctor Harlowe tapped *Send* and tucked his tablet away under his arm.

Brone was Striker's partner—and from what I'd heard, they were the best LeyGuard team the Hub had.

I narrowed my eyes at Doctor Harlowe. "Did you just tell Brone and Striker to follow Quinn to Arcvale?"

His eyebrows shot up, then he smirked. "I said I trusted her—not that I wanted to send her alone into danger."

I laughed. "That's a relief."

Doctor Harlowe's smile slipped. "Her vision does make me wary though, Ayla. Sometimes she's only seeing part of the picture, but she seldom sees wrongly. The outcome of her visions *can* be altered, but without intentional intervention, they usually occur just as she has foreseen."

My chest clenched. "Then how do we intervene?"

Grandpa's voice cut through the overhead speakers as his face appeared on one of the front monitors. "I've got a bad feeling that I know who that ArcFae is, Ayla."

Mom and Dad sat behind him, looking worried.

Doctor Harlowe glanced up at the screen in shock, as though he'd forgotten they were listening.

Grandpa continued. "If it's Varias, him coming after you is a *world* of trouble. I'm betting he's returned to serving the Dark King. And if he had both you and Kaizyn tied up like that in the vision, it has to have something to do with your bond. Varias may have found some way to use your bond to weaken Teionyr's magic... or worse."

His words sent a tremor of fear through me. "What do we do?"

"We have to break the bond," Grandpa and Doctor Harlowe said at the same time.

"As quickly as possible," Doctor Harlowe added.

I glanced between them. "How?"

Grandpa sighed. "I thought for sure the answer would be somewhere in my journals, but I've come up empty. And last I spoke with Maxim before we left, he hadn't found anything in Teionyr's records, either."

Doctor Harlowe bit his lower lip, then turned to my grandpa's face on the monitor. "You know where to find Archive Room Five?"

Grandpa nodded. "Of course, but I've never had access."

Doctor Harlowe held up his fancy wristwatch. "I do. Meet us there in ten minutes. The Hub has hundreds of old Fae records stored in the digital archives, everything from apothecarists' journals to royal records to Dark Fae sympathizer missives, gathered from the remnants of Veylden and the other Upper Faeside villages destroyed in the last war. At least *one* of them has to have information about breaking a faespell bond."

Doctor Harlowe tapped some more buttons on his tablet, and my family's faces winked out.

"Come on, Ayla." Doctor Harlowe hurried out of the training room.

I followed, but as I jogged behind him down the corridor, I couldn't shake the anxiety building in my stomach. While I wanted Doctor Harlowe to be right about the archives holding our answer, I was afraid to get my hopes up. If this turned up another dead end and Quinn's vision came true, the feedback loop of Kaizyn's and my emotions might be the *least* of our troubles.

CHAPTER 26

TRAINED IN HOW TO BE CHARMING

Reina

A reunion with 'Dame Keyja's long-lost whatever-he-was had not been a possibility in my mind for what might've come through the breach in the dome, but it was a fair sight better than anything I *had* imagined.

The tension slowly bled from my shoulders, and I saw Kaizyn, Callan, and my parents relax, too.

"I'm sorry for startling you," the ArcFae told Keyja as he took in our small, armed resistance near the barrier.

Keyja smiled at him. "We were not expecting *you*, that's for certain."

I watched him for a moment before I worked up the courage to speak. "I recognize you. From the battle in the market at Teionyr."

The ArcFae's dark eyes flicked to me with interest, but his gaze held a shrewd edge. I had no doubt he'd sized me up in a single glance.

He turned to face me. "Yes. Your friend Jordan knew me as Etcher." His words were measured. And it was not lost on me that he knew I was friends with Jordan—and presumably, knew who I was—without me ever stating it.

Keyja looked at him, confusion darkening her expression. "Etcher?"

He drew a quick breath. "Yes. I ended up in Teionyr, almost eighteen years ago..." He paused, apprehension crossing his face as though waiting for something bad to happen. But after a moment, his face relaxed, and he continued. "I was there when the Dark Fae attacked, and I made an alliance with Maddox Rogers, to help him protect the young king's identity so Maddox could get him to safety, and to secure safe passage from the palace during the attack for the king and for the infant who would remain in the king's care." He glanced at Kaizyn.

Keyja studied them both, then nodded. "I see."

There was a lot more to that story, I was sure, but it seemed Varias had come on other business.

"I regret to say, I'm not here only to catch up." He winced, then sucked in a breath. "I—I was unaware there was anyone still living here. I came for… safety." He pressed a shaky hand against his side, then glanced pointedly at our weapons. "Were you expecting an attack?"

Whatever Keyja's barrier magic had done to him, he seemed to still be feeling its effects.

Keyja grabbed his hand. "We were, yes. We've had word of a Dark Fae army heading our direction. But come, you're unwell. Let's get you in—"

He froze, her hand still gripping his. "You're expecting a Dark Fae attack *here*? Why?"

Keyja started to answer, but then Varias leaped forward, covering her mouth with his hand.

"No! Don't tell me! Don't—" Varias gasped, then dropped his hand and pressed it back to his side. "Don't say anything more of how you know."

Keyja gaped at him with wide, frightened eyes.

A chill snaked down my spine. If she was frightened, the rest of us certainly had reason to be.

Small snaps of lightning crackled from Keyja's chest—a warning from Tofa, if I had to guess.

But Keyja seemed to be afraid *for* Varias, not *of* him. She stepped toward him and touched his arm. "Come. You need rest. Let's get you inside."

He took one more shaky breath, then let her lead him toward the cottage without another word, the rest of us casting confused glances at one another as we followed.

Keyja insisted Varias lie down on the bed inside the cottage, then she led the rest of us across the fields to the village in the distance.

The village was small, just a dozen or so rows of modest-sized homes with an open courtyard in the center that must've once been used as a market square or common area for gatherings. The entire place had a dusty, abandoned feel, though it looked tidy otherwise.

Keyja led the way toward the courtyard, Tofa at her side.

My parents and I took up the rear, with Callan, Kaizyn, and Vyrthil walking behind Keyja... though Kaizyn kept glancing back at me, for some reason I couldn't fathom.

Keyja directed us to a large barn at the far end of the courtyard, then hauled open the barn's two large doors.

Inside, the barn was dirt-floored and mostly empty. There was a mound of straw to one side with a divot in it, like a large animal might have used it for bedding, and a table over to the other side, lined with rows of tiny, colorful bottles. Other than that, the only other thing in the barn was a massive, metal bin in one corner—similar in size and shape to the dumpsters we had behind our high school.

"This was the barn where the striniaks gave birth when the time came," Keyja said, "and also where my mother and the other apothecarists practiced their craft." She turned to face us. "But today, it will be our command center. I trust Varias, but I suspect there is more wrong than he is letting on. I would like to give him some privacy while he rests, so we will move the rest of our preparations here." She strode over to the table, tracing a finger along the colored vials. "There is still an attack coming, and we need to be ready."

Kaizyn's hand rested on his dagger. "Vyrthil and I can continue to patrol the barrier—"

"Tofa and I will take the next shift of patrols," Keyja interrupted. "My ward should alert me if anything else comes through, but I would like to inspect the barrier myself."

Kaizyn lowered his hand and nodded. "Very well. What other preparations would you like us to make?"

Keyja walked over to the big dumpster-shaped thing and pulled a metal lever on its side. The front wrenched open, and hundreds of arm-sized bales of dried straw toppled out. "More rope nets," Keyja said with a smile, then hurried toward the barn entrance. "I'll be on patrol if anyone needs me." She stepped out and shut the barn doors.

Kaizyn dropped his head back with a groan. "More ropes!"

"This feels like busywork in high school all over again," my dad said as he walked over and lifted a small bundle of straw from the pile. "Are rope nets the most useful thing we could be doing, right now? We've already made dozens of them."

Callan chuckled. "I think she's trying to distract us."

Anxiety prickled in my chest. "From what?"

Kaizyn raised his head and sighed. "Probably just from being in her way. As much as I hate feeling useless, she and Tofa have been defending Arcvale *without* our help for nearly two decades."

That made sense—though I couldn't help staring at Kaizyn in shock that he'd said a whole cluster of civil words to me. Two whole sentences of them. At once!

Kaizyn noticed me staring at him and glanced away.

"Do you think she'll *use* all these nets we've been making?" my mother asked.

Callan shrugged. "Perhaps. Eventually. I mean, they might come in handy in battle—if darklings *do* manage to breach through her wards."

I shivered. "I'd rather us have no use for them."

Callan met my gaze. "Me too."

Kaizyn moved over toward my dad and nudged the pile of straw bundles with his boot. "Well, I guess we should get to work." He grabbed two bundles, then walked past Callan, right up to me, and handed me one. "Here you go." His eyes locked on mine as he pressed the straw bundle into my hands.

I took it by instinct, but froze as his gaze held mine, his fingers pressed against my hand. My heart fluttered strangely in my chest.

Kaizyn slipped his hand from mine and smiled, leaving the straw bundle in my grasp, then walked away.

Callan grinned at me from across the room, then grabbed some straw of his own and followed Kaizyn over to the far wall, where they both settled down to unwrap their bundles.

Vyrthil sauntered over and sank down onto the dirt at Kaizyn's side.

I stared after Kaizyn, clutching the bundle he'd shoved at me, then jumped as my mom nudged my shoulder.

"I do believe that boy was attempting to flirt with you," she whispered.

I gaped at her. "*What?*"

Kaizyn glanced up at my louder-than-intended response, then went back to unwrapping his bunch of straw.

I dropped my straw on the floor and grabbed my mom's arm. "I—uh—"

I didn't even bother to finish the rest of my excuse, I just dragged her out through the front doors of the barn.

My dad followed, shutting the barn doors behind him.

I made sure we were out of Fae-hearing range, on the other side of the courtyard, before I spun back to face my mom.

"Flirting? *What* are you talking about?" I whisper-hissed at her.

She shrugged, fighting back a smirk. "He's not very good at it, but I've witnessed my share of bumbling flirtations."

My dad gave Mom a playful glare, but she just laughed.

"Bumbling flirtations are adorable, in their own way," Mom continued.

Dad chuckled. "Well, that's a relief."

I felt a flurry of strange emotions as I replayed Kaizyn's latest interactions with me—the glances back at me earlier, and now the way his eyes had held mine when our hands touched...

Mom smiled at Dad, then turned a more serious gaze on me. "I know things didn't start off well between the two of you, but he's trying, Reina. Surely even you could see that."

I sighed. "Yeah..." It *was* clear that Kaizyn was trying to be more friendly toward me, and I'd wondered about the subtle glances in my direction, but... *flirting*? It had to be a miscommunication or something. I shoved thoughts of his handsome face and winning smile out of my mind. "He's not flirting, he's a *prince*. He's *trained* in how to be charming. He's been moody this whole time, and he's probably just feeling guilty about it and trying to be nice. Besides, we all know he likes Ayla."

She stared at me, then tilted her head. "And if he *is* flirting?"

"I really think he might be," my dad chimed in with a grin. "I should know. I'm the champion of awkward flirtations."

I thought back to the expression in Kaizyn's eyes when they'd locked on mine... and my heart did a tiny little flutter. I froze. I wasn't sure if I was more shocked that my parents might be right, or that the idea of Kaizyn flirting with me actually sent a little thrill of excitement through my chest. I hadn't felt that sensation in *ages*... which was why I immediately shoved it as deep-down as I could, while simultaneously rolling my eyes at myself.

I crossed my arms. "He's not."

What was wrong with me? The *last* thing I needed was to entertain feelings for yet another guy who was head-over-heels in love with my friend.

I strode back to the barn, and my parents followed. I could *feel* their worried stares on the back of my head. When we reached the barn doors, I turned to face them. "Not another word about it. *Please*," I whispered. "We're here to do a job—to keep him from dying. And that's *it*, okay?"

They both studied my face and seemed to realize I was serious.

My mom glanced at my dad, then sighed. "All right."

Dad nodded his agreement. "You can't avoid talking about your feelings forever, but... okay. For now."

I breathed an inward sigh of relief. "Good." I was still trying to sort through all my feelings about Jordan, and that was complicated enough. With any luck, whatever interest Kaizyn had suddenly taken in me would pass quickly, and my parents could get any ridiculous notions about him trying to *flirt* with me out of their heads.

I pulled open the doors, making sure not even to glance in Kaizyn's direction, then grabbed my straw from the floor and sat as far across the barn from Kaizyn as I could get.

Mom and Dad picked out their own bundles of straw from the pile, then sat beside me, and all three of us got to work unwrapping our straw bundles and arranging the strands to make ropes.

I kept my head down, staying busy—and pretended I didn't notice Kaizyn watching me in concern.

Chapter 27

Probable Futures

Kaizyn

Well, that was a disaster. Why had I ever listened to Callan? It didn't take much astute observation to realize my interaction with Reina had only made things *worse* between us. She'd been staring so intently at her bundle of straw the past ten minutes, I was shocked she hadn't burned a hole into it.

I dropped my straw on the floor and rubbed my hands on my thighs. "I need some air. I'm going outside."

Callan glanced at me but didn't question—for which I was glad.

I jumped to my feet and hurried outside with Vyrthil close behind.

The barn door swung shut behind us, but I paced across the courtyard to the row of small houses, still feeling the need to put some distance between myself and my humiliation. Ever since Callan had pointed out how unfair I'd been to Reina, something had shifted in my mind. My own pain had blinded me to her before, but the more I watched her, the more I realized how keenly she observed, how she stayed alert, how she relentlessly served everyone around her, taking so little care for her own needs. There was a reason Jordan had sent her to protect me, and as much as it hurt my ego to need that protection, I'd been a fool not to be more grateful that she'd agreed to come.

And then, in the barn...

I wasn't sure what had come over me. For a moment, I'd allowed myself to entertain the possibility that a pretty, brave, selfless, intelligent, strong, capable girl my age might be an actual option for me—for my future. But I'd only made a fool of myself. She was shocked and confused by my attention, possibly even affronted. Not that I could blame her. No woman would want to be with me with the mess I was in.

I sank to the ground, resting my arms on my knees.

Vyrthil bumped my leg with his head and chuffed.

I looked up at him. "I'm all right." But was I? I sighed. The truth was, bonded to Ayla, I probably *couldn't* ever be with anyone else—

It suddenly occurred to me that I'd hardly thought of Ayla *all day*. Since the moment the bond had activated weeks earlier, she had been a constant presence in my mind, every hour... but somehow, even without the bond broken, today I had nearly forgotten about her.

I processed that for a moment, searching through my feelings, and I realized—the moment things began to change for me was when Ayla and I awoke to Jordan in the vault. It had been agony, seeing the way she looked at him... but I knew then, without a doubt, that Ayla would *never* want to be with me. That part wasn't a surprise—I'd felt her feelings for Jordan before that. But somehow, seeing it, and seeing how obviously it was reciprocated, made it even more real. In the moment, that realization had caused a meltdown that unintentionally harmed Ayla. I was still ashamed of that. But when that loop had broken and I awoke, something deep inside me had shifted. Until that moment, I'd been holding on to a sliver of hope that Ayla might one day change her mind, and now that hope was gone. She would never change her mind.

The shocking part was that I was feeling more and more *okay* with that truth. I still cared for Ayla, but picturing her with Jordan no longer felt like pouring acid into a chest wound. It just felt... lonely. Because I knew, so long as I was bonded to Ayla, I could never be with anyone else. Ayla had never been as emotionally impacted by our bond as I had, but even if I did get over Ayla and tried to move on, I would have Ayla's emotions flooding my mind anytime we were in proximity. That level of distraction and entanglement with another female would not be fair to any other romantic partner. I could never ask a woman to put up with that, *especially* not one I truly cared about. And I wouldn't want to be with someone I *didn't* care about.

Unless I figured out a way to break this bond, I was destined to be alone forever.

I was just about to sink further into my own self-pity—contemplating just lying down right there in the dirt—when Keyja appeared at the other end of the courtyard, startling me out of my thoughts.

"There's someone attempting to activate the Hub Gate—from the *Hub* side." If she had noticed my moping session, she said nothing about it. She strode toward me, holding my gaze. "It feels like one person, and they're using an authorized runestone for access. Do you wish for me to allow them in?"

I was the person Keyja knew best from the group here visiting Arcvale—aside from Varias, of course. It was natural she would come speak with me first about Faeside matters... but this was about the Hub.

She seemed to notice my confusion. "I do not know the LeyGuard girl and her family as well as I know you. I will defer to *your* judgment on how to handle this."

I paused. "Is there a way to see who it is, first?"

Keyja shrugged. "We can *ask* them who they are."

I glanced back at the barn, wondering if I should consult the others—but even if the visitor wasn't friendly, Keyja and I could easily handle one person, especially with Vyrthil and Tofa helping us. And I didn't wish to startle the others unnecessarily.

"Okay." I nodded. "Let's go see who it is." Once we had determined who was at the Gate, we could alert everyone else.

When Keyja, Vyrthil, and I arrived at the barrier, the sealed Gate was shimmering.

"It's the attempted activation," Keyja said. "Stand back; I'll ask our visitor to identify herself."

"*Her*self?" I asked.

Keyja glanced at me. "From what I've seen, I believe it is a female." Electricity crackled from her chest as she reached toward the barrier.

I stepped back readily.

After a moment, the barrier grew almost translucent. I could see a blurred silhouette on the other side—the form was slim, feminine.

"Hello?" a female voice said. She sounded young—maybe a teenager.

Keyja nodded toward the barrier, obviously expecting me to do the talking.

"Uh—who are you?" Not my most eloquent moment, but it served its purpose.

"I—I'm Quinn," the voice said. "I've... come to speak with the Ley-Guards who are here, to get a report for the Hub." She pressed her hand to the barrier. "Hello?"

Vyrthil moved up next to me, ready for anything, as always.

Quinn. I recognized that name. Callan had mentioned her as one of the teens from the Hub.

"We can trust her," I told Keyja. "Are you certain she's the only one there?"

"Yes," Keyja said without hesitation.

"You can let her in."

Keyja nodded. "Very well."

The shimmering divider vanished, and Quinn toppled inward.

I jumped forward to catch her by instinct, steadying her in my arms.

She flicked her face up at me in surprise. "Oh!"

As soon as I realized what I'd done, I dropped my arms and stepped back. "Forgive me. You seemed like you might fall."

She was just a few inches shorter than me—just the height to have stared up into my eyes in my embrace. Her hair was long and dark, swept back in a high ponytail, and she wore black LeyGuard battle leathers with knee-high black combat boots. Her large, brown eyes locked on mine, and she smiled. "That's all right. I probably would have." Her smile was warm, genuine, and it instantly put me at ease.

But before I could even respond, the expression on her face shifted.

"Wait, you're Prince Kaizyn!" she said, her gaze suddenly intense. "I've seen you in my visions."

She glanced at Vyrthil as though having just noticed him, but I was still stuck on what she'd just said.

"You've—your what?" I stared at her.

Keyja tensed beside me. "What visions?"

"I had one, of a male ArcFae," Quinn said, looking at me. "He had you and Ayla bound to a table, and he was..." She winced. "To be honest, I think he may have been torturing you with some kind of magic. I've already warned Ayla about it."

I flicked my gaze to Keyja in alarm.

Keyja drew a shallow breath. "I'll look into that. Do not trouble over it."

I trusted her—even if I now trusted Varias even *less*. I tore my gaze away and turned back to Quinn. "What else did you see?"

"Well, that was the major one, but... I did see something else. Something I haven't told anyone, yet." She glanced at Keyja warily, then looked back at me. "Something specifically about you—about your future."

I started to say that she could speak in front of Keyja, but Keyja placed a hand on my shoulder.

"I will wait for you at the edge of the village," Keyja said. "Some truths are for only *one* pair of ears to hear."

She walked away before I could reply.

Vyrthil stayed at my side, of course, but I supposed since we were bonded his ears were as good as my own.

Quinn watched Keyja go, then shrugged and turned to me. "Well, do you want to know?" Her face turned serious. "Not everyone does... want to know, I mean. It's your choice, whichever you prefer."

I studied her for a moment. *Did* I want to know? She could be about to tell me how and when I would die, or... well, anything. But *not* knowing what she'd seen, for the rest of my days, would drive me mad. Now that I knew there was something to know, I was too far in to turn back. I drew a steadying breath, then nodded. "Yes. I want to know."

Quinn smiled and clapped her hands together. "Excellent! You do not end up with Ayla."

I stared at her. "That's it?" A huff of frustration escaped me. "I did not need a vision to tell me that."

But Quinn only grinned wider. "I'm not done. You don't end up alone, either."

My heart stuttered. "What?"

Quinn glanced to the side and shrugged. "I can't help with much more than that. I couldn't see much of what the person looked like—I was seeing it from an angle, kind of shadowed. But you were definitely in a committed, romantic relationship with a young woman who *wasn't* Ayla; her height and build were different. She was taller than Ayla, and... I don't know, just shaped differently." She grinned at me. "I'm pretty sure she was hot."

A desperate, flailing thread of hope tried to fight its way into my chest, but I beat it back down. "How can you be sure? The committed, romantic relationship, I mean. What did you see that makes you so certain?"

Quinn stepped toward me, her gaze gentle. "My visions are choppy—but I heard her knock on your door. She asked, 'Are you decent?' I guess it was your room or something, because you let her in... The vision jumped a bit, from there, but I saw you kiss her forehead and hold her close, and you smiled. You looked content. Happy... and hopeful."

The thread of hope morphed into a gnawing ache in my chest. Was it possible? Was there a future where I ended up happy—*in love*—and not utterly alone? It was almost too painful to hope.

Vyrthil nudged my leg with his head, sensing my emotions as always.

Quinn rested a hand on my upper arm. "I know how lonely it must be, knowing Ayla doesn't return your feelings. Especially with everything augmented by the bond. But please, believe me—there *is* a future where you end up happy, and in that future, you are not alone."

"How do I make sure it happens, this future?" The words came out almost as a whisper, dragged from the depths of my chest.

Quinn's warm smile returned. "That, I can't say for sure. My visions usually happen, unless we intentionally do something to change them, but no vision is ever *guaranteed.* They're more like probable futures. But... for this one, I don't think you need to worry. Just be who you truly are—and your future will find you. I can't say how I'm so certain, but I am."

I stared at her for a long moment, letting her words sink in and warm me. "Thank you, Quinn. You've given me a lot of peace, more than you could possibly know."

Her smile turned into a grin. "You're welcome! Do you mind if I hug you? I'm a hugger, and this seems like a moment that needs a hug."

"I—uh—sure?"

Her arms were around me before I finished my answer.

It was a quick hug, then she stepped back and gave me another smile. "You're a good person, Kaizyn. I can tell. Good things will come for you—just you wait."

I'd never wanted so deeply for a vision to be true.

Quinn gestured at Vyrthil. "He's adorable. Can I pat his head?"

Vyrthil flicked his startled eyes up to mine.

"I... um..." I stammered.

"Nevermind, he seems hesitant," Quinn stepped back, seeming unbothered. "We'll just save that for another time."

A few moments of semi-awkward silence passed, but before I could figure out what to say next, Quinn bounced on her toes.

"Well, I'm off to talk to the others. Gotta report back to the Hub with all the latest news." She paused. "Wait—could you show me where they are?"

I laughed. "Of course. I'll take you to them."

"Great!" She smiled again. "Lead the way."

CHAPTER 28

TAKES ONE TO KNOW ONE

Kaizyn

Quinn, Vyrthil, and I met Keyja at the edge of the village, and she walked with us back to the courtyard.

"I'll come by in a bit," Keyja said when we were almost to the barn. "I need to go check on Varias."

I nodded, though there was a strange tension between us at the mention of his name, now.

Keyja seemed to notice. "I am sure all is well, but I do want to speak with him about Quinn's vision, unless you prefer I didn't?"

I relaxed a bit. "Yes, speak with him. Perhaps the ArcFae that Quinn saw wasn't him, or perhaps there is an explanation."

Beside me, Quinn kept silent, though her presence was comforting.

Keyja nodded once, then strode away.

I turned to Quinn. "Everyone else is in here." I led her toward the barn, but when we reached the barn doors, I hesitated. My interaction with Reina flooded back into my mind, along with its accompanying mortification.

Quinn glanced over at me. "Everything okay?"

I ran a hand through my hair. "Yeah—fine. It's just..." I sighed. "Yes, it's fine." I pulled open the doors.

Everyone turned from their positions around the barn floor to look at us.

As soon as Reina saw Quinn, her face lit up. "Quinn!" She jumped to her feet and rushed forward, wrapping Quinn in a hug. "It's so good to see a familiar face."

I blanched. "You—you two know—" I stopped halfway through my statement. Of *course* they knew each other; they both trained at the Hub, I'd already known that. I swallowed my words and turned to shut the barn doors before I could make a bigger fool of myself, but when I turned back around, they were both staring at me, waiting for me to finish.

Thankfully, Callan came to my rescue.

"Quinn," he said, hurrying over. "It's good to see you." He offered her a handshake, which she took with a smile.

"Thank you," she said. "I'm glad to see you all, too."

Reina's parents joined us, and Reina's mom wrapped an arm around Quinn's shoulders. "We are glad to see you, Sweetheart, but did you travel here alone? I'm surprised Hart would've allowed that." The concern in her tone was unmistakable.

Quinn glanced up at her. "Well, yes, but I—"

Reina's mom pulled back to look at Quinn. "Quinn, honey, did you come here *without permission?*"

"What? No, of course not! I'm here for a report, but it was just supposed to be a quick in-and-out. It's just... well... the Gate into Arcvale was blocked and it took much longer than I expected. They're probably getting worried about me by now. And I bet the Hub's already on full lockdown by now, too. I'm not sure I'll be able to get back."

Reina's dad tensed. "They've put the Hub on full lockdown?" He looked thoughtful. "I suppose that's good. Cautious. Smart, given the circumstances." He smiled at Quinn. "No worries. If it is already locked down, you can stay here with us until this all blows over."

The way he said *blows over* made it sound like nothing but a summer storm—but I was sure it was only for reassurance. We *all* knew how serious this situation could become.

Callan eyed Quinn. "How *did* you get through the Gate? Keyja said she sealed them all."

Quinn shrugged. "She and Kaizyn let me in."

Everyone turned to stare at me.

I nodded. "Keyja told me someone was at the Gate, and I—*we*—went to see who it was. When we realized it was Quinn, we let her in."

Callan's brows lowered. "You didn't think you might need backup, in case it *wasn't* someone friendly? Or in case it was a trick?"

I *had* thought about that, I'd just decided against it, so I had no answer. I shrugged. "Um... no?"

Callan and Reina both rolled their eyes and gave a deep, exasperated sigh—in unison, almost like they'd rehearsed it.

"How am I supposed to *protect* you if you keep doing stupid things like that?" Reina snapped. Her green eyes held a flash of anger.

"I–I'm sorry. I didn't want to worry anyone," I said, feeling a bit sheepish. I hadn't been thinking at my best when Keyja had told me someone was at the Gate, but the last thing I wanted, at this moment, was to explain why.

Quinn stepped up to my side and placed her hand on my arm. "He was just trying to help, I think. Right, Kaizyn?"

I blinked down at her. "Yes... I didn't want to cause a stir if it wasn't something to worry about." Though I'd also just wanted to get away from the barn. I looked back up at the others. "I thought I'd come get you all if it turned out to be dangerous."

Callan and Reina both glared at me.

"Kaizyn," Callan sighed, clearly annoyed. "*Really*?"

Well, I supposed when I said it like that, it *did* sound foolish. I shrugged. "I had Keyja."

Callan relaxed a bit, pondering that, but it only seemed to make Reina *more* angry.

She crossed her arms and glowered at me. "And if it had been the Dark Fae army?"

"I—" What *would* I have done? I stiffened, but when Reina's scowl only deepened, my patience snapped. "Then I would have *dealt* with it, like the soldier I am. Like the *prince* I was raised to be. I am not a *child*, and I don't need to be treated like one just because *you* didn't want to be sent on this mission."

Callan stepped forward, his eyes wide. "Kaizyn..."

For the briefest of moments, the steel in Reina's expression vanished, and I saw the pain behind her eyes. Then the steel wall slammed back up. "You're *worse* than a child," she said, stomping toward me. "Children are innocent. But *you* are an unbearable, arrogant, idiotic *jerk*!"

There was a collective gasp from the others in the barn.

"Reina!" her dad's voice chided, but my attention was on the furious redhead staring death-daggers at me.

She was right in front of me now, nearly in my face, and the longer I held her glare, the more the condescension in it angered me.

I clenched my fists as fury rushed through me, and closed the distance between us. "Well, you're—*ow!*"

I glanced down where Quinn's fingernails had dug into my forearm... but that tiny break was all I needed to regain my senses. I snapped my mouth shut.

"I'm *what*?" Reina said, seething. Her face was tilted up at me, just inches from mine.

Despite the absolute fury in her eyes, it was weirdly intimate, and... disorienting.

I averted my eyes and cleared my throat. "Nevermind." What *had* I been about to say? Probably something insanely childish, like *You're a jerk, too,* which would have only proven her point.

Reina gave a frustrated groan and stepped back, still glaring at me in challenge as she crossed her arms over her chest.

Quinn leaned close. "At least you didn't say 'It takes one to know one,'" she whispered up at me with a smirk, then dropped her hand from my arm and stepped back. "I didn't mean to cause all this trouble," she said to the others.

Reina's glare flicked to her before returning to me. "Oh, you didn't. *He* did."

Reina's mom stepped forward, eyes still wide from the shock of what she'd just witnessed. "Okay, that's enough. What's done is done, and I'm sure we'll all be more cautious in the future." She gave us all a smile that was a mix of exasperation and warning. Then she turned to Quinn. "So you're here for a report, Sweetheart? What did you need to know?"

"Oh!" Quinn said, as though just returning to herself from watching the engrossing drama produced by the rest of us. "I'm just here to find out if there is any further information on the impending Dark Fae attack, anything the Hub might need to know. Although..." Her words slowed as her thoughts changed direction. "I suppose that information is kind of pointless, now, since I probably can't get back into the Hub to give it to them."

It *was* odd that the Hub would send someone to gather information, then not arrange a way for that person to bring the information back.

Reina's dad put a hand on Quinn's shoulder. "They know you've come. I'm sure they're working out a way to get you back home. They may even be planning to make an exception to the lockdown for you, when they see you attempt to re-enter." He stepped back, gesturing for her and Reina's mom to follow him. "There's not a lot of information to give—the darklings have gone silent—but why don't you come sit with us, and we'll tell you what we know, and then we can ask Keyja to re-open the Gate and we'll see if the Hub will let you back in. If not, we'll find another way to get the information to them, even if you can't go in person. I'm sure we can think of something."

Quinn brightened. "Yeah, okay. That sounds good."

Reina's parents both glanced at Reina and me in concern, then led Quinn over to where they'd been sitting against the wall.

Reina spun her glare back on me the moment they were out of earshot. "You and Quinn seem *friendly*."

I tensed. "What is that supposed to mean?"

Reina narrowed her eyes. "That's what *I'm* wondering." She stormed off toward the pile of straw bundles, violently snatched one from the mound, and sank down by herself against the far wall of the barn.

I turned to Callan. "What... was..."

He stared at me, eyes wide. "I have *no* idea." His gaze tracked Reina, then he glanced at me. He leaned near, keeping his voice low enough for only me to hear. "If I didn't know better, I'd say she was jealous."

He walked back over to his spot along the opposite wall, leaving me to ponder his words in silence.

CHAPTER 29

THE RIGHT COURSES OF ACTION

Kaizyn

As soon as we sat down, I whispered an explanation of Quinn's vision to Callan—the one about the ArcFae torturing Ayla and me, not the other one. That one I kept to myself.

Callan listened, then asked me, "Do we tell the others?"

I glanced across at Reina, then at her parents, and shook my head _no_. "It may not be him."

Callan nodded his agreement. There was no need to spread distrust of Varias—Etcher—unnecessarily. Besides, Ayla and I would have to be in the same location for the events in the vision to take place, and Ayla was nowhere near Arcvale. Though Quinn obviously knew about the vision, we wouldn't mention it to the others. Not when there were still so many unknowns.

We went back to making straw ropes for the nets.

The tension inside the barn was palpable for the next few minutes, until Quinn popped to her feet. "Kaizyn, can I speak with you outside?"

I could _feel_ the glare Reina gave me, though I didn't dare look in her direction.

I set down my straw bundle and stood. "Yes. Sure."

I followed Quinn outside and shut the barn doors. As soon as we stepped outside, Quinn's face took on an unsettling expression of concern.

I led her across the courtyard so we could speak freely. "What is it?"

The way Quinn was wringing her hands wasn't making me feel any better. "I, um..." She drew a breath, as though steeling herself, then her words came out in a rush. "The girl from my vision of you in love is Reina."

I stared at her. "What?"

She gave a nervous laugh. "I'm sorry, I said it too quickly. Um... the girl from my vision with you in it, the one where you were in love—it was Reina."

I blinked. "No, I heard you the first time, just—*what*?"

Quinn stepped closer, peering up at me. "I told you I couldn't see her clearly, like it was kind of shadowed. And her voice, it had sounded familiar, but I couldn't place it..." She sucked in a quick breath. "Then in the barn, I had another flash." She put her hand on my arm. "It's her, Kaizyn. It's *definitely* her."

I pulled back. "Then your vision must be wrong."

Quinn tensed.

I backtracked. "I just mean, you must not have seen all of it, or... or there's some other explanation." Or perhaps what she'd seen wasn't right, at all. The thought that Quinn's entire vision might have been mistaken was devastating—maybe I *didn't* end up in love and happy.

Whatever the vision was, it couldn't have been what Quinn thought she had seen.

Quinn shook her head. "It was the same scene as before, with you kissing her forehead, but this time I saw her red hair, Kaizyn," she said gently. "And the side of her face. I'm *sure* it was her."

"No, it was probably—" I had no way to finish that sentence. It clearly wasn't *this* redhead Quinn had seen in her vision. This one hated me. The Reina I knew would never let me kiss her forehead. I'd be insane to even try. A hug, perhaps, I could envision in the right circumstances, but a kiss on the forehead seemed like an intimate gesture... yet Quinn said her visions were never wrong. *Something* was not adding up.

Quinn placed a hand on my arm. "Kaizyn."

She waited until I looked at her.

"I know it's hard to let yourself hope, with the way things seem now. But I *know* what I saw—both in my vision and today in the barn. There *is* a spark between you two, it's just… it's a bit explosive right now. And not the good kind." She smiled. "Give it time, Kaizyn. I don't know Reina more than casually, but I know she's a good person. She's brave, and bright, and *very* talented, and usually also very kind. The Reina I saw today… that's not how she usually is. She's been through a lot, these past few weeks. Please, just give her time."

Quinn was beginning to sound a lot like Callan.

I dropped my gaze to my boots and sighed. "I'll work on being more patient with Reina—more kind. I know she's been through a lot. But I'm *not* planning to do that because I expect to fall in love with her." I tore my gaze from my boots and locked eyes with Quinn to emphasize my point. "I'm doing it because I've *also* been through a lot, and I know how it feels. I'm doing it because it's the right thing to do."

Quinn grinned. "And that is *exactly* why she's going to fall in love with you."

"What? No." I sighed. "I'm still not sure that you—"

"Pardon our interruption," Keyja's voice said.

Quinn and I both spun to find Keyja standing between two buildings at the edge of the courtyard.

Etcher stood right next to her, still looking exhausted.

Quinn sucked in a little breath. "That's him," she whispered.

I didn't need to ask for clarification.

Etcher stepped toward me, noticing my reaction. "I have no intention of harming you—of harming anyone. You need not fear me."

So Keyja *had* spoken with him. I didn't know whether I could trust Etcher's word, but I was willing to give him the benefit of the doubt… for now. For all I knew, Quinn's vision about Etcher was as misconstrued as her vision about Reina and me. I was beginning to question whether Quinn's visions were reliable, at all.

Then Etcher stepped forward, glancing between Quinn and me. "I may know what I was *doing* in the vision, though. I know how it must have looked, but I don't believe I was harming you." His gaze held mine, his face serious. "I believe I was breaking your bond."

Before I could process that, Keyja stiffened. "The Hub Gate. There's someone there—more than one. I can feel their attempts to open it." Sparks crackled from her chest as she turned to me. "Should we tell the others?"

I wasn't about to suffer a repeat of what had just happened in the barn, so I nodded. "Yes. Quinn, can you—"

"On it!" Quinn said, then sprinted toward the barn to get the others.

I turned back to Etcher. "What do you mean, you were breaking my bond?"

Etcher held my gaze. "I know you may not trust me, and I cannot blame you. But what Keyja described to me from the vision could very well be a severing ritual." He glanced at Keyja, and she nodded her agreement. "I'll need to get more details from the young seer, of course, to verify—but Keyja and I suspect that was the case."

"Quinn said you were *torturing* us."

He winced. "Yes, well, it is not a gentle spell. It can be painful. Then again, the right courses of action often are." His expression shifted, and his gaze drifted ever-so-subtly in Keyja's direction.

Quinn burst back out from the barn with Callan, Reina, and Reina's parents in her wake, all strapping on their weapons. Vyrthil appeared too, roused from his nap behind the barn by all the commotion.

"I'm glad you included us this time," Reina said with a hint of venom, but I chose to ignore it.

Callan moved up beside me, casting an uneasy glance at Etcher. "I'm with you, whatever happens," he murmured near my ear.

Keyja nodded at all of us. "Follow me."

To *all* of our relief, once we arrived at the Hub Gate at the barrier, the people on the other side were Striker and his LeyGuard partner, Brone.

Keyja opened the Gate and let them through.

Striker was as towering as I remembered him, and he gave me a warm smile. "Prince Kaizyn. It's good to see you well."

"The same to you." I smiled back.

Brone nodded his greeting to the rest of us, then turned his attention on Quinn. "Doctor Harlowe sent us to check on you. You okay?"

"Yes." Quinn nodded. "I'm fine. I've got the information I needed, though it isn't much. The Eldervine can no longer see the darkling armies, so we're *all* operating blindly at this point."

Brone's expression darkened. "Well, not the best news we could've gotten, but it doesn't change much. I've got some not-so-great news, myself... or maybe good news, depending on how you look at it," he said, glancing at the rest of us.

I tensed. "What is it?"

Striker stepped next to him, focusing on Quinn. "Seems we're stuck here for a bit, including you, Quinn. Brone and I have been tasked to help defend Arcvale, and the Hub's last open Gate was the one they used to send us."

Quinn nodded, eyes distant with thought. "Okay... but how will we get information to them if anything changes here?"

Striker held up a runed stone. "Hart had Maddox Rogers take care of that for us." He winked. "Just don't tell Doctor Harlowe. He'll want one of his own."

Quinn chuckled. "Noted."

The LeyGuards—even Reina and her parents—all seemed to relax a bit. Apparently, safety in numbers *was* a thing for them, and having a whole group here made them all less worried. Or maybe it was just having Brone and Striker here that made them feel more safe. I'd heard those two were a force of nature when they fought together. They'd probably give any breaching Dark Fae a memorable welcome.

After another moment, Brone cleared his throat. "We do have another bit of news." He turned to Reina and her parents. "Since Reina is his partner, we thought you would all want to know—we received a report from Teionyr that Jordan and the others there are preparing for a potential attack. Jordan's coronation is scheduled for tonight, in just a few hours." He glanced at Reina. "His parents were the ones who sent the message. They say he's holding up well, but seems pretty stressed—especially tonight, as it nears time for his public coronation. It's hard for him, doing all this so quickly, and with everything else that's going on."

My heart tensed for Jordan. Though he and I were not close—for obvious reasons, including that the throne he was about to take had not long ago been *mine*—I wouldn't envy anyone the stress that accompanied kingdom-wide ceremonies, particularly in a wartime situation like this. And for Jordan, with this all so new... It was no wonder he was feeling the strain.

"I should be there," I said, before I even realized I'd uttered the words out loud.

Everyone turned to stare at me.

"What?" Reina said... but it was the tears pooled in her eyes that shocked me.

Had she started crying because of what Brone said about Jordan?

She sniffed and scrubbed at her eyes with the back of a hand, realizing I'd noticed. "Why would you go, Kaizyn? He doesn't even *know* you."

I froze with everyone gaping at me, but Callan gave me an encouraging nod from the other side of the group.

"I—" I drew a breath. "It's hard, becoming a new king, but I imagine it's even harder for someone who doesn't know our customs. And my absence will be noticed by the people. It will look as though I don't support his ascension to the throne." With every word, I grew more confident in my decision. "I should be there for the coronation."

But then, as Reina's tortured eyes met mine with what seemed like grudging respect, I remembered Callan's words about her feeling cast aside.

The next words just burst from my mouth before I could stop them. "We *both* should."

Reina stiffened. "What? No. He... I'm not even sure he *wants* me there."

"Of course he does," I said, more sure of it by the moment. "Why would he *not* want his best friend and partner by his side at a moment like this?"

Brone nodded. "I think Prince Kaizyn is right. Jordan's parents said it's been hard on him, with Ayla at the Hub and with you *here*. You two are his closest friends, and he could use friends, right now. From what they've said, he's kind of struggling."

"He *sent* me here," Reina said, somewhat pathetically.

"That doesn't mean he *wanted* to," I said gently, turning to her. "He just had to make a hard choice—as kings often do. But Ayla isn't in Teionyr right now, and I'm far more stable than I was when I fled. I can return, to be where I'm needed... and so can you."

Reina and her parents all stared at me. I could see the hope building in Reina's eyes. It was almost intoxicating.

"How will we get there?" her father asked, startling my focus away from Reina. "Brone said the coronation happens in a few hours. We'll never make it in time."

I glanced at Callan, considering my next move, but when he gave a subtle nod of his head, I decided to go for it.

"I cannot take Reina there instantaneously as the bond allowed me to do with Ayla, but there is a secret access Gate near Arcvale that only a royal can open. Callan and I and the other guards used to travel it often. I can take her through there. We can be in Teionyr within an hour, maybe a little more."

"You—you don't mind me joining you?" Reina asked me.

"Of course not." I smiled. "Though, perhaps..." I looked at Keyja, worried about abandoning her with a possible attack coming.

"We will be fine here, Kaizyn," Keyja said. "The barrier is secure, and if the Dark Fae *do* attack here, we have Varias and now these LeyGuards to help, should Tofa and I need it." She smiled at me as more sparks crackled out of her chest. "Which I can almost guarantee we will not."

"She's right; the Madame ArcFae is known for her power," Brone said, earning a glance of respect from Keyja. "But should she need us, Striker and I are no weaklings, either." He rested a hand on a pistol at his waist.

I drew a breath, then nodded. "All right." I turned back to Reina. "Then I will happily take you with me to Teionyr, if you want to go."

"We'll be going, too," her father said, almost like a question.

I stared at him. "Yes, of course. Reina does not know me that well. I would never expect her to travel with me unaccompanied. I can take all three of you."

Callan cleared his throat. "All *four*, you meant, because obviously I'm going, too. I am your guard, after all."

I rolled my eyes. "Yes, I am aware."

Reina sucked in a small breath. "So—when can we leave?"

The hope in her voice did strange things to my heart. "Right away, if you'd like."

"Yes." She nodded. "We'll just go grab our things."

As we all headed back to Keyja's cottage for our supplies, I replayed the past few minutes in my mind. For the first time, Reina had looked at me like someone she *wanted* to be near—like someone she could respect. Of course, then I had to remind myself that it was the hope of seeing *Jordan* again which had made her so happy. It had nothing to do with me.

Reina, Callan, Reina's parents, and I all grabbed our travel bags, then Keyja, Etcher, and the LeyGuards walked the whole group of us to the northeastern barrier of the dome.

I gave Etcher an uneasy glance as Keyja prepared to open the barrier. I still didn't trust him, but I supposed I would have to hope for the best.

"Be careful," I leaned near Quinn to whisper.

She smiled up at me. "I will be. But don't worry; Brone and Striker are here. I'll be safe."

The barrier split open, and Keyja gestured toward it.

Callan led Reina and her parents out through the rift in the barrier, then Vyrthil moved up beside me as I prepared to step through.

"Goodbye for now, my friend," Keyja told me with a smile. "May you find everything your heart desires."

Though it was a customary farewell for Arcvale, it hit me differently this time—not the least reason for which was Quinn's exaggerated wink I could see past Keyja's shoulder.

I swallowed and returned Keyja's smile. "And may you do the same."

I stepped through into the dark Void, and the barrier snapped shut behind me.

I turned to find my small traveling group watching me, but it was Reina's intensely curious glare—almost like I was a puzzle she was trying to figure out—that sent my heart racing.

I cleared my throat. "This way," I said, then hurried in the direction of the Gate to Teionyr. I had a new mission to fulfill, now: helping put the new king of Teionyr safely on his throne.

The rest of this mess, I would have to figure out another time.

CHAPTER 30

ON A SCALE OF ONE TO TWENTY

Jordan

My parents were waiting for me in the hall when Kurrum led me out of the council meeting room. The sight of them brought an instant wave of relief—I hadn't realized how badly I'd needed a familiar face until that moment.

The other council members took their leave, heading off to complete various preparations for tonight's ceremony, but Kurrum lingered nearby.

"We've just sent a report to the Hub," my mother said as she and my father walked toward me. "They're locking down, and I wanted to let them know how things were going here. How are you holding up?" she asked, smoothing my hair.

The gesture made me feel like a child, which probably wasn't good for my king image, but I couldn't bring myself to pull away. I gave her a shaky smile. "Good. Fine. Well—I mean, okay, considering."

She studied my face with an expression of understanding. "It's a lot to take on at your age, but you're doing great, Jordan."

My father stepped up behind her, nodding. "You're doing amazingly well. I'm proud of you, son."

Tears pressed behind my eyes. Did kings cry? I supposed they did, but crying on my coronation day would not be the best start toward inspiring my people's trust. I blinked the tears back and forced a smile. "Thank you. I'm trying."

Kurrum cleared his throat. "Forgive me, Your Highness, but time is of the essence right now."

"Yes, of course." I turned to him, smoothing my shirt. I was still wearing the spare clothes my parents had brought for me in their travel bag, which I'd changed into during the hours Ayla had been unconscious. They were the long-sleeved fitted shirt, leather pants, and leather vest of a LeyGuard in training—not the clothes of a king—but at least my parents hadn't insisted I wear the protective armor plating over them.

The thought of walking through the palace, dressed as I was, made me question how my people would view me. They already knew I was only seventeen, but if they knew I wasn't even a full LeyGuard, just a trainee, would that undermine their confidence in me? Then again, I couldn't be other than what I was, and how would the Teionyrians know what the LeyGuard clothes meant? I was starting to second-guess *everything*. I drew a shaky breath. "Lead the way."

Kurrum led us through several increasingly ornate palace corridors, until we finally rounded the corner into a lavishly furnished hall which dead-ended into massive, arched, double doors made of a dark wood that had been polished until it shone. An intricate carving of a forest scene with some antlered animals that resembled deer covered both doors. Two uniformed palace workers, wearing matching hunter-green tunics and dark breeches with polished brown boots, stood on either side of the entrance to the hall, and two more stood on either side of the doorway.

"The king's private chambers," Kurrum said, leading us down the hall. "Beirthyr chose to use the easy-access royal suites on a lower floor rather than these, thank goodness."

In other words, these were the chambers which had last belonged to my father. The weight of that settled over me as I followed behind Kurrum.

The uniformed workers pulled open the doors when we reached them.

My jaw nearly dropped open at what awaited me inside. The chambers were every bit as fancy as I had expected the king's personal chambers to be, with polished wood floors accented with thick, colorful rugs; an ornate, four-poster bed covered in lavish curtains; a sitting area with plush furniture next to a crackling fireplace; and a massive, bronze-framed window that covered almost an entire wall, revealing a breathtaking view of the sunlit, rolling hills of Teionyr below. A large, claw-footed bronze tub was planted to one side of the room, full of steaming water and giving off vapors that smelled like an entire herb garden in bloom. But the truly shocking feature was the *people*—more than a dozen of them, all stationed in various places around the room, and all staring at me.

"So many..." I whispered. Were they all here to *watch me take a bath*? Any other words I might have said in soon-to-be-kingly greeting escaped from my head. I just stood, gaping at them, like a deer in headlights.

"Is the room not to your liking, Your Highness?" Kurrum asked, staring at me in concern. "Would you prefer—"

I waved my hands frantically. "No, no, it's... it's lovely." My face flooded with heat, but at least my words were working again. I glanced at my parents in desperation, though what they could do to help me at this point was anyone's guess.

My father stepped up next to me, then looked at Kurrum. "Is there something he's meant to do next?"

"Oh, right, of course!" Kurrum's discomfort melted. "Right this way, Your Highness. Your dressing chambers are just through that door." He gestured to a door on the far wall that I hadn't even noticed... because there had been at least five people standing in front of it. "There is a ceremonial robe inside," he continued. "You'll know the one; it's set out for you. You can leave your current clothes on the floor. You won't be needing them again tonight. One of your attendants will take them to the laundress after you've bathed."

I had that same feeling of massive discomfort I got when the LeyGuard doctors sent me for a massage and I was put in a room with only a robe and a sheet-covered massage table, unsure how much of my clothes I was expected to take off or leave on before the masseuse arrived.

I turned to Kurrum, trying to keep my voice low, though with how intently the palace workers were watching us, they were sure to hear, anyway. "Do I just... undress, then come out in a robe and get into the bath? With all of them here?"

Kurrum's eyes widened. "Oh! No, Your Highness—they are all here for you to instruct, in case there are any comforts you wish them to retrieve or tasks you wish done. They await your commands, but if there is nothing you need, they will leave before you bathe. I mean, unless you wish for some of them to remain in case you need something, though they will avert their eyes if so."

I breathed a sigh of relief. "Oh. All right."

I glanced around, but decided I'd made things awkward enough and it was time I just address the people in the room directly.

I raised my voice. "Thank you all for coming. I'm... not sure what I might need. Honestly, I'm relying on all of you to help me get through this." A nervous laugh escaped me. "But if all I need to do right now is take a bath, I believe I can manage that."

The mood in the room was intensely awkward, all of them staring at me like they were hanging on every word.

I forged ahead. "I... uh, I mean... I'll need someone here to tell me what I need to do *after* the bath. So maybe one or two of you could stay outside the room? You can decide who. But the rest of you can lea—I mean, thank you very much for being here, for being willing to help me, but you're... you're free to go."

It was probably the most awkward speech in the history of new king speeches, but it had its desired effect. The palace workers all hurried from the room, some with rushed curtsies or bows but all avoiding eye contact with me.

As the last one slipped out and shut the door, I groaned. I imagined they'd be talking about *that* disaster for a while to come.

Kurrum turned toward me, biting his lip in a way that almost looked like he was attempting not to laugh. "Very well, Your Highness. Now, if you don't need me for anything else?"

I glanced at the tub. "How long should I—I mean, you said this is a ceremonial bath. Is there a certain period of time I'm meant to stay in it?" The bath looked relaxing, and I could use a moment alone to think, but he'd also said we were in a time crunch.

"Until the water cools, Your Highness," he said with a kind smile. "At least, that's customary. When you're finished, just put the robe back on and call for one of the attendants. They'll bring in your clothes for the ceremony."

I nodded. "Thank you."

He headed for the door, then turned back as though remembering something. "After you're bathed and dressed, you'll be expected to give a brief greeting to the palace workers in the great hall. No formal speech is expected, just an official introduction of yourself to your closest staff, before you're presented to the public. You can keep it casual. It will be the same attendees who were in here today, along with the rest of the core palace staff. Perhaps four dozen people?"

Right. Just the same people I'd humiliated myself in front of, plus three dozen of their coworkers who were sure to have heard about it by then. Perfect. I swallowed. "Okay."

Kurrum met my nervous gaze. "You need not fear your own people, my king. We all understand you are new to our customs. It is strange for *all* of us, but... the Teionyrian people are a good-hearted people, and kinder than you might think."

Something tightened deep in my chest. "Thank you, Kurrum."

He smiled warmly, then slipped out and shut the doors behind him.

I turned to my parents. "On a scale of one to twenty, how disastrous was that?"

They both chuckled.

"A five, perhaps?" my dad said, grinning. "But don't let it bother you. You're learning. No one expects you to act like a seasoned king on your first day."

That was the problem, though—the Teionyrians *deserved* a seasoned king. I had no clue what I was doing.

I felt a hot ache in the back of my throat again, but I swallowed it down. "I'm going to put on the robe."

I headed for the dressing room door before my parents could notice how much I was struggling. It would only make them worry, and there wasn't anything they could do about it. They couldn't be king *for* me, and they couldn't help with much else, either, other than just being there for me, for which I was immensely grateful. But *none* of us knew Teionyrian customs well enough to get through this without me feeling like an idiot.

I was adrift, a lone plank from a shipwreck, bobbing in a sea of Teionyrian expectations and kingly responsibilities. How was I ever going to do this on my own? With everything familiar hundreds of miles or even *worlds* away? Even with my parents here, I still just felt so... alone.

I had a sudden, intense, aching need to speak to Ayla. Just to hear her voice, to know that she was still there—even if she wasn't *here*.

My parents were still watching me, where I'd stopped just outside the dressing room door.

"Are you okay, son?" Dad asked.

I turned to face them. "Yeah, I'm—well, I mean, I will be." My parents knew I had the runestone Maddox had given me, but no one else was supposed to know and for all I knew, a palace worker might walk in at any minute. I pulled the stone out of my pocket, then backed toward the changing room door. "I'm just going to..."

My mom smiled when she noticed the stone. "Oh, that's a wonderful idea. You'll need to keep it brief, but I'm sure speaking with her will make you feel better." She grabbed my dad's arm.

He nodded. "You'll want your privacy for the bath, anyway. We'll wait out in the corridor, but we're just on the other side of that door if you need us."

They slipped out, and I sank against the changing room door in relief, then opened it and stepped into the room itself for good measure. No sense standing out in the open where anyone might walk in.

The changing room was lit by sconces and was about the size of a large walk-in closet, with plush carpet, a rod hung with clothes at one end, and a large, gold-framed, full-length mirror on the wall. A cushioned bench stood in the center of the room, with a dark red, gold-embroidered, velvety looking robe laid out on it. A robe fit for a king.

I sighed, then pressed my thumb to the stone. It lit with a warm hum. "Please answer," I whispered, then I waited.

CHAPTER 31

THE KING THEY DESERVED

Jordan

I didn't have to wait long.

"Jordan?"

I clutched the runestone, heart racing at the sound of her voice. "Ayla."

"I'm so glad to hear your voice," she said.

That was definitely mutual.

She continued, her tone threaded with concern. "Is everything okay?"

"Yes. I just... I needed to talk to you."

There was a little pause, then she said, "I'm glad you called me. You can *always* call me. You know that, right?"

There was that burning, thick feeling in my throat again. I swallowed it down. "Yes. And the same for you."

"I know. Jordan, you're upset. I can hear it. Did something happen?"

I sighed. She knew me too well. "No. I just—" I drew a heavy breath. "The coronation is in a few hours, and I don't know the customs, and everything here is different. I feel this massive pressure not to let them down, to be the king they need, but I don't—" I paused, and the last few words came out thick from that ache I was still fighting in my throat. "I just don't know if I can."

"You can." She said it immediately, as though there wasn't a doubt in her mind. "You can, and you will. You were *born* to do this, Jordan. Literally. There is *no one* better suited for this than you. You just... have to learn, a bit. So what? We all do. Everyone who ever started a new job had to learn things. Every CEO, every school principal, every president or royal, even every LeyGuard. *I'm* learning new things every day. Every expert had to train and learn at some point, Jordan."

I exhaled. "I suppose you're right. I just feel so far behind where I need to be, like I'll never catch up."

"You aren't expected to know it all right away," she answered. "But your heart—*that's* what will set you apart, what will make it all okay. Because you care. You *always* care. And you always do the right thing, no matter how hard it is. The Teionyrians are *lucky* to have you as their king... and if they don't know that yet, they will."

I let her words wash over me, trying to *believe* them, as I stood staring at the stone, wishing more than anything that I could see her face. "I love you, Ayla."

"I love you, too." She paused. "Is Reina there, at least? I hate to think of you doing this alone."

"No. She and her parents are still in Arcvale with Callan, protecting Kaizyn." My words came out sounding more strained than I'd meant them to. It had been a hard choice to send Reina away. I did want her here. We'd been friends my whole life. There hadn't been a single milestone or ceremony, school or LeyGuard or otherwise, that one of us wasn't there to cheer the other on.

"You sent them away for me—to protect Kaizyn, because of me," Ayla said softly. "I'm sorry."

"It's not your fault," I whispered back.

She sighed. "I wish I could be there for your coronation."

I drew a breath. "So do I." A tiny spark of hope tickled in my mind. "Maybe... I mean... how's your magic coming? Have you made any progress?" It was foolish to think she'd have mastered her magic so soon. But if she had, maybe she could come—

"I figured it out," she said, excitement taking over her voice. "Doctor Harlowe put me in a simulation, and I can *use* my magic now, Jordan. I can control it."

"Are you serious? That's amazing!" I tried to visualize what her magic looked like, but I didn't know enough. "Tell me what it was like. What can you do?"

The stone's bright glow blinked rapidly—the warning that the charged rune which powered our call was about to run out.

"Oh," I said, unable to keep the disappointment from my tone. "We don't have much longer."

"It's okay," she said. "I can tell you about my magic later. Jordan, I want to come to you, but... the Hub's on lockdown. They say *no one* can come in or out until they're certain where the Dark Fae army is and whether the Hub is a target."

Oh. Right. I could hear the disappointment in her tone as well. "It's okay, Ayla. At least you're safe there. And now that you've mastered your magic, you can come once this is all over, right? I mean, we still have to figure out the bond, but—"

"I will be there the moment I'm able to, Jordan. I promise." She paused, and her next words were full of regret. "I hate that you and your parents are there all alone."

"It's not your fault. But so do I." I sighed. "I miss everyone... even Callan and Madison. I even kind of miss Kaizyn."

Ayla laughed. "Really?"

"Yeah. I know things are ridiculously complicated, but he was my father's son. He *knew* my father, he knows what he was like, and he also knows all about Teionyr and what's expected of the king. If I'm honest, I've kind of wished he could be here to help me. Or at least so I could get to know him a little."

"Wow, Jordan." Ayla's voice was gentle as she responded—affectionate. "I'd love for the two of you to get to know each other. Once this bond is broken, I mean. I actually think you'd get along. I have a feeling he and I will always be close, after what we've been through… or at least I'd like to be. I know the bond is *beyond* weird, but I've come to think of him kind of like family. Is that crazy?"

I pondered that for a moment, the unexpected future in which Ayla, Kaizyn, and I could all be friends. Family, even. I wasn't sure if that future was possible, but I *hoped* it was. "It's not crazy," I said softly. "I want that, too."

The stone gave a rapid warning flash, then began to dim.

"We have to go. I love you, Ayla. I miss you so much."

"Please call me if you need me, even if it uses another charge from the stone. I love you, Jordan! I miss—"

The stone's glow winked out.

I stared at it, tempted to call her again… but there were only ten runes on the stone, and we had already used two of them. I didn't know how much longer we'd be apart or what else we might need them for.

I pocketed the stone, suddenly feeling very, *very* lonely.

The robe stared at me from its fancy, cushioned bench.

I sighed. "Okay. Guess it's time."

I hoped the water from the bath hadn't gone cold, though I could warm it with my fire magic if it had—so long as that didn't violate some kind of ceremonial rules. If it did, hopefully Kurrum would have mercy on my ignorance.

I had just unfastened the third button on the side of my leather Ley-Guard vest when a heavy knock sounded on the outer door.

I left the changing room and hurried to open it.

Kurrum stared at me in shock, surrounded by a cluster of attendants. "Your Highness! Have you still not bathed?"

But the redhead standing behind him was all I could focus on. "*Reina?*"

She blushed and bit her lip. "I'm sorry. I know you may not want me here, but I—"

It was then that I noticed Callan, Kaizyn, Reina's parents, and Kaizyn's strange fire-cat, all standing behind the cluster of palace workers.

I shoved forward, servants jumping out of my way, and threw my arms around Reina.

She stiffened, then wrapped her arms around me and returned my hug.

"I'm *so* glad you came." I pulled back, staring her in the eyes. "I mean it." Then I turned to the others. "I'm so glad *all* of you are here." I made sure to make eye contact with Kaizyn as my gaze slid over the group, so he would know he was included in that statement.

Kaizyn stared at me in shock—not that I could blame him.

There was a brief, tense silence as all the palace workers gaped at us, then Reina broke into a grin. "Maybe we should—"

"Right! Yes, of course. Come in, though I can't talk for long because they're expecting me to bathe." I hurried back into my chambers, gesturing for Reina, Callan, Kaizyn, his fire-cat, and both my and Reina's parents all to join me inside.

"We can give you only a small while longer, Your Highness, then you're needed in the great hall!" Kurrum called out as I shut the doors.

I turned to face my unexpected visitors, and as I stared at the group of them, my aching heart was almost full again. I must've been more of an emotional mess than I'd realized, because I was even happy to see Kaizyn's weird, flaming cat. I was still missing Ayla, but having them all here... "Thank you. Thank you all so much for coming for this. I thought..." I trailed off.

There was a hint of tears in Reina's eyes as she smiled back at me. "That I'd miss watching my best friend become *king* after he sat through my annual, three-hour piano-recital-slash-Christmas-concert every single year since we were seven?" Her smile spread into a grin. "Not on my life."

The awkwardness there had been between us in the past few weeks, that tension I hadn't been able to figure out, was gone now. I had my best friend back... and she'd brought an entire chunk of my family and friend circle with her.

As I swept my gaze over them, Callan nodded his support—and Kaizyn shifted minutely closer to Reina, which didn't escape my notice, but I decided I'd explore that curiosity later.

"We're here for you, Jordan," Reina's mother said, drawing my attention to her. "And we'll all be right there, front row or wherever you want us to be, to support you during your coronation."

"Thank you," I said again, meaning it, then I turned to Kaizyn. "I know things have been strange between us, but I—I would love it if you..." I didn't quite know how to ask what I wanted.

But he smiled. "Whatever you need, Jordan, I will do. I've come to support you, as our king, and... as my brother. I hope one day we can use that term in its fullness, as Father would have wished."

I smiled back as relief flooded me. "I would like that, too. And I am *so* grateful you've come, because I do not have a clue what I'm doing."

He laughed. "I will help you. Whatever you want to know, just ask."

I looked back over the group of them again, and as I met my parents' proud gaze, my world felt infinitely less overwhelming than it had just minutes earlier.

Kaizyn glanced at the tub, which was no longer steaming, then winced. "Your water is cold." He sent a stream of fire into it from his hand and set it steaming again. "There. You should complete your bath before Kurrum begins pounding on the door again. And don't forget the robe. He's sure to ask whether you put it on before bathing." He smiled at me. "If you need anything, we will all be waiting for you out in the hall."

The rest of the group deferred to Kaizyn's wise advice—I think no one wanted to see a truly angry Kurrum—and followed him out into the hall.

As soon as the door closed again, I hurried to the changing room and donned the soft robe. I shed it a few steps later when I reached the tub—whatever the point of even wearing it was, I'd never under-stand—and sank down into the wonderfully hot water.

"Until it gets cold," I muttered to myself, though I suspected Kurrum would be calling an end to my bath in a few minutes, whether my water was cold or not. Right now, though, it was steaming hot... and exactly what my tense, battle-sore muscles had needed. Perhaps there was something to this "cleansing ritual," after all... especially since Teionyr's royals were known for working hard and going into battle alongside their people.

I reclined against the sloped back of the tub and tried to relax, which was a lot easier than it might have been twenty minutes earlier.

I would be crowned king of a *Fae kingdom* in a few hours. I still couldn't wrap my mind around that. But at least now I had people here to support me, people I knew and trusted. And Ayla, even though she wasn't here, was here in spirit, and only a stone's call away.

This would be okay. *I* would be okay. Somehow, I would figure out how to be king. And what I didn't know, I would learn. I would become the king my people needed.

The king they deserved.

With that thought on my mind, and a full garden's worth of soothing, herbal vapors in my nose, I lay my head back against the tub's edge and let myself drift into a shallow slumber.

CHAPTER 32

IMPLICATIONS

Jordan

A firm knock on the chamber door woke me from my doze, and I found myself sitting in lukewarm bath water.

"Your Highness?" Kurrum called out. "Have you completed your bath? It is time for your official introduction to your palace staff."

"One moment!" I groaned and hauled myself out of the water, grabbing a shockingly soft towel the previous attendants had laid out on a ledge near the tub. I'd have to ask someone what these towels were made of... and whether it was possible to smuggle some Earthside as future Christmas gifts for my friends at the Hub. I'd never given anyone a towel as a gift, but then I'd never felt a towel like this before—I was sure once they felt *these* towels, they'd thank me.

After quickly toweling off, I slipped the robe from earlier back on and cracked open the door to peer out.

Kurrum shoved a small stack of folded garments at me. "Put this on. There was no time for your official fitting, so the seamstresses adjusted it to their best estimate. They're waiting here in case it doesn't fit, but you need to hurry, my king. I allowed you as long in the bath as I could, but we are behind schedule."

"Schedule. Right. Um—the introduction, and then... when am I sup-posed to be where, again?" I had no idea how I was supposed to plan my activities around the invisible itinerary inside Kurrum's head, but apparently he expected me to try.

Kurrum's eyebrows raised. "Your coronation, Your Highness! Did you forget?"

"No, I just wasn't sure when I—" I decided to just bite my tongue, and nodded. "Right. Of course." Didn't these people have cell phones with schedule alarms, or at least watches or something? Even a piece of paper with a basic agenda would help. But maybe the king usually just waited for someone to tell him he was supposed to be somewhere.

Kurrum stared at me, looking something between bewildered and skeptical.

"I—I'll be there," I stammered. "I mean, of course, I'll be there; it wouldn't be a coronation without—um—"

I halted my rambling.

The small cluster of my family and friends was visible over Kurrum's shoulder, standing near the opposite wall behind him.

Reina was watching our interaction from near the back of the group with an amused smirk.

I grabbed the bundle from Kurrum. "I'll be as quick as I can." But before I could shut the door, Reina called out for me.

"Jordan! Wait a sec."

She ran toward me—and my face split in a grin as I saw who else slipped out from the group, bounding along on a leash beside her.

"Champ!" I dropped to my knees as he shoved his hard head right through the crack of the door and forced his way through.

Kurrum nearly toppled over when Champ pushed past him, but at the moment I didn't care. I was just so freaking *happy* to see this goofy furball.

"I missed you, buddy!" I rubbed his head and ears as he pressed his wiggling body into me, then I looked up at Reina. "Thank you! I'd thought Striker and Brone took him back to the Hub after everything that happened in the vault."

Reina smiled at me. "I asked them to leave him here. I thought you'd want him with you—but I guess no one actually *told* you." She laughed. "I found him down in the kitchens, worming his way into the cook's heart with those sad puppy eyes."

"I absolutely want him here." I pulled Champ close as I stared up at her. "Thank you. Seriously. You always know me so well." Our eyes locked for a long moment.

Reina blushed slightly. "Of course, I do. You're my best friend."

Something tender but also slightly awkward passed between us as I held her gaze.

"And you're mine." I stood.

Champ instantly sat on my foot, wanting to be as near me as possible.

I kept my eyes locked on Reina. "I haven't even had a chance yet to thank you for saving Champ's life. I heard what you did. *Thank you*, Reina. Every time I feel like hope is lost, you're right there, having my back."

"You're welcome." She smiled at me, but it didn't quite reach her eyes.

I held her stare. "I'm serious, Reina. You *are* my best friend, and there's no one I trust more. You and Ayla—"

She glanced away and laughed, and I immediately sensed tension.

"I mean, Ayla is... it's different, with her, of course," I blurted.

"Of course." Reina watched me with a guarded look.

I stepped toward her. "But no one can ever replace what *you* are to me. You know that, right? You've been my best friend my whole life. I think of you as family. I *love* you like family. Like a sister. And I always will." I needed her to understand that, to understand what she meant to me—but also what we *weren't*, and what I *couldn't* offer her... especially now, when so many things were changing.

I just hoped it wouldn't mean I'd lose her.

I could feel the weight of the rest of the group watching from across the hall.

Reina was silent for a moment as her gaze studied mine, then she sighed. "I know. I think I'm finally understanding that." She glanced down at

Champ, avoiding my eyes. "I love you too, Jordan. I always have. Get dressed, okay? We'll all be waiting out here." She walked back toward the others.

She hadn't said she loved me *like family*—and the implications of that left me wildly uncomfortable.

I gestured Champ inside, then shut the door, unsettled by that exchange but unsure what to do about it. I couldn't bear to lose Reina—she meant *so much* to me. But I also couldn't bear to hurt her, which now seemed inevitable. I sank my head back against the door. "How in the world do I fix this?" Maybe things would get easier between Reina and me with time? I had to hope so, because right now, there was nothing else I knew to do.

Champ's tail thumped against the wall beside me.

I glanced down at him, and his mouth dropped open into a tongue-lolling grin. I laughed. "You always know how to make me feel better, don't you?" I sighed and ruffled Champ's fur. "I'd better get dressed. Think they'd agree to make you a royal canine outfit? They said the attendants were here to fulfill any of my requests..."

I smiled down at him one more time, then carried my stack of folded garments to the changing room.

Once inside the room, I set the stack of new clothes Kurrum had given me on the bench, then grabbed my LeyGuard clothes from the floor, carefully folded them, and stacked them on the bench, too.

I glanced between the two piles, then grabbed the new clothes. When I unfolded them, I discovered they contained a finely woven, deep blue tunic with dark blue breeches, and a satiny, crimson, gold-embroidered thing, kind of like an open-fronted ceremonial robe, to wear over the outfit.

I exchanged the bathing robe for the new clothes.

They seemed to fit well enough. Kurrum had even included a clean pair of dark, very comfortable socks. He had provided no other special footwear, so I slid my trusty LeyGuard boots on over the socks and secured my dagger in its sheath over my new outfit, then hung the discarded bathing robe on an empty hanger on the clothing rack.

When I finally turned to look at myself in the mirror, my breath caught. I looked like a king.

"I'm not ready for this," I whispered. My reflection stared back at me like a complete stranger.

I hesitated, wanting to call Ayla, craving her calm encouragement—but I couldn't afford the time *or* another use of the stone. Instead, I crossed back to the bench where I'd left my clothes. My LeyGuard pants' pockets had the stone and a couple other personal items in them—including my favorite ink pen and my cell phone. The phone was practically useless here in Faeside, but I still didn't want to lose it, and I definitely didn't want to lose the stone. I wasn't sure folding my clothes on the bench would be enough to prevent the laundress from taking them, so I grabbed an empty hanger and hung my entire outfit up on the end of the clothes rack. I would ask Kurrum to make sure no one came to wash my clothes until I'd found a safer place to store my personal items, but for now, hanging them up would have to do.

I could come back to the room to call Ayla after the coronation, when I had an update to report. Hopefully, by then she'd also have time to tell me more about her magic. The anticipation of talking to her later calmed my nerves a bit. I could do this. I could get through this coronation—and afterward, my friends and family would all still be there. Even if I made a fool of myself, I still had what mattered... not that I *wanted* to make a fool of myself. But still, the thought helped.

I forced myself to look back at the mirror. Was this what my father had looked like on his coronation day? Had he worn this same outfit, or one like it? What would he think of me now if he were here? And my mother—she had given her *life* to protect mine, to make it possible for me to one day take this throne. What would she think of me?

Suddenly, although I'd never met them, I desperately wanted to make them both proud.

I drew a long breath and forced myself to stare my reflection in the eyes. "*You* are the king, now," I told myself. "You can't run from it. You can't avoid it. You just have to step up and figure it out—step up and be the king they deserve."

But I had no delusions. I was going to need all the help I could get.

Sorcha's warm voice drifted into our bond. *King-of-mine? They are gathering your attendants into the great hall—and the stage they have assembled for your coronation is already amassing a crowd. Where would you like me to wait for you?*

Her words sent a tremor of panic through my chest, but I forced away the image of a massive crowd awaiting me outside and focused on my response to her question. *Can you wait on the other side of the palace? Away from the crowds. I don't want to startle anyone.*

A faint tinge of amusement drifted through the bond. *I believe it is too late for that… There are already many staring at me, even though I'm flying far above. Dragons are not good at hiding.*

I chuckled. *All the same, I want this to go smoothly. I'm not sure how the people will react to a dragon up-close. I would like to be with you when you officially approach the crowd, so I can try to avoid unnecessary panic.*

Very well, King-of-mine, she answered. *I will wait on the far side of the hill, away from the crowd—though they will still be able to see me.*

That's fine, Sorcha. I'm sure they all know about you already, anyway, I told her with a smile in my thoughts. *But we'll make our official introductions together. I'll see you soon.*

My focus returned to my image in the mirror—me, yet so *not* me.

The King of Teionyr. Was I really ready for this?

I most definitely wasn't ready, but I was doing it, anyway.

I said a quick prayer that my ineptitude wouldn't spiral the entire kingdom into a panic, then I stared myself back in the eyes. "You can do this. You have no clue what you're doing, but—you have help. So… it's going to be fine." I glanced down at Champ. "It's going to be fine, right?"

Champ's tail thumped against the bench as he stared up at me.

"Right, sure, we're fine. It's all fine." I drew a shaky breath, and as I smoothed my fancy robe, I felt a strange peace settle over me. I really *was* doing this.

There was no backing out of it now, so I might as well embrace it.

"Okay," I said, looking down at Champ. "Let's go meet my royal attendants."

Chapter 33

On a Tight Schedule

Jordan

Kurrum was waiting for me right outside my room with a small group of seamstresses on standby, as promised.

I mentioned I didn't want my LeyGuard clothes washed yet, and he immediately sent someone to convey my message to the laundress.

Then, after a 360-degree scan to make sure my clothes fit properly, Kurrum dismissed the waiting seamstresses and ushered me—and my entourage of family and friends and one dog—back through several corridors and into the great hall.

The great hall was a large, open, rectangular room with rows of doorways down both long walls—all currently propped open. We entered from a door on one of the shorter walls of the rectangle, with the full length of the room spreading out before us. The floors were polished wood, and rows of sparkling, glass chandeliers cast bright light on the room from above—electric lighting, or some magical variation of it, rather than candlelight. The entire room smelled bright and citrusy, like they had polished the floors with lemons.

Our boots all clicked on the hardwood as we entered, and the murmur of voices I'd heard a moment earlier immediately hushed.

A few dozen people stood in neat rows near the other side of the room, wearing various shades of green tunics, dresses, and robes—my attendants, I assumed, though I'd yet to decipher the color coding system for various types of staff. They all turned politely patient faces in my direction, watching me enter the grand hall.

A small stage loomed against the wall opposite where we'd entered, just in front of a broad window which let in a swath of bright daylight through the charred remnants of what must've been the curtains Sorcha torched. Through the window, I could see another stage set up on the grassy hillside outside the palace. Teionyrian people covered that hillside, what looked like *hundreds* of them, standing in loose rows that reached almost back down to the road into the city—the crowd Sorcha had mentioned. I tried not to focus on that as Kurrum led our group toward the stage.

"Your friends and family can wait there." Kurrum stopped us a few feet away from the stage and gestured to an empty area next to it, then to the stage itself. "And you'll be on the platform, of course, Your Highness. Say what you would like, but please keep it somewhat brief—we are on a tight schedule."

My mouth instantly went dry.

"You'll be fine," a male voice said calmly near my ear, and I glanced back to find that Kaizyn and Vyrthil had moved up behind me.

"Come with me," I asked Kaizyn before I could second-guess myself. "I want them to see us both. To know that I'm not... that I'm—"

"That you're not stealing my throne from me?"

I glanced back at him with alarm.

He smiled. "Don't worry. *You* are the rightful king, and I'm here to make sure they all know that. If you want me by your side, I'm there."

I nodded. "Yes."

His smile widened. "Then lead the way."

I caught Reina and both our sets of parents watching our exchange from behind Kaizyn, with Callan hanging just behind them... though Reina was mostly watching Kaizyn. She looked pensive—almost confused.

My mom and dad's gazes, though, locked on mine. Dad gave me a firm, confident nod. Mom looked like she was about to burst into proud tears.

I drew a breath and turned back to Kaizyn. "Okay. Let's go."

Champ trotted along beside me. I didn't stop him, even though Vyrthil hung back with the rest of the group instead of joining us.

Wide eyes followed Kaizyn and me as we approached the stage, and more than a few people cast a shocked glance at Champ. I wondered if they didn't have the same kinds of dogs here that we had Earthside—I hadn't thought to ask.

Kurrum thrust a glowing red stone into my hand, then gestured me toward the steps to the platform.

"That's for amplifying your voice," Kaizyn said quietly, leaning near me. "Like a microphone, I believe you call it. Just close your fist around it when you're ready to speak."

"Thank you," I whispered to him.

We climbed the shallow steps, and suddenly I was staring down at four dozen expectant faces.

Kaizyn stepped up next to me, close but angled just behind me so it was clear I was in front.

Champ flanked my other side.

Kaizyn glanced at me with a reassuring smile. "Whenever you're ready."

I closed my hand around the stone—and I spoke.

I couldn't even remember later exactly what I'd said. It included a bumbling introduction of myself, and of Champ—and then of Kaizyn as my adopted brother, who I said was still officially a prince, of course, even though they all already knew that. I followed that up with a rambling monologue about how grateful I was to have his support and help, how grateful I was for *all* of them here to help me, and how I vowed to do my very best to be the king my father would've wanted me to be—the king they deserved. My mouth basically went on autopilot halfway through my speech while the rest of me floated in a state of semi-coherent panic.

When I finally regained my senses, I stopped. "Um—" I glanced at Kaizyn as panic crept back in. "Do you want to say anything?"

He smiled at me—a genuine smile. "No, my king. You've said everything as well as I could have myself."

To my surprise, when I looked down at the attendants' faces, they all seemed relaxed and welcoming.

Well. Perhaps I wasn't entirely failing at this, yet. Speaking from my heart—or the strange blacked-out, rambling place my heart apparently retreated to when forty-eight people were staring at me—seemed to have done the trick. I drew a deep breath, then turned back toward the attendants watching me.

"Those people over there," I said, gesturing to my cluster of friends and family, "along with Prince Kaizyn, are my closest and most trusted allies I have here in Teionyr. You will see them here in the palace often, and I want you to know who they are, and that you can trust them as I do. They are here to help me serve you better—to help strengthen and defend our people and our kingdom. And, well, I think that's all I had to say." I opened my hand, and the stone's glow faded.

Kaizyn clapped me on the shoulder and leaned close. "Well done," he whispered as Kurrum hurried up onto the stage.

"Before we dismiss," Kurrum said with a voice obviously also augmented by a stone, "I would like to present our new king with his personal palace staff."

A line of attendees broke off from the crowd and filed into a row, facing me, at the base of the stage.

I stared at him. "Aren't these *all* my palace staff?" I whispered, glancing down at the rest of the crowd.

Kurrum released his grip on the glowing stone and leaned near me. "Yes, of course, but the king always has an inner circle, the ones who serve him directly as guards and attendants in his private chambers. I've taken the liberty of choosing them for you from our finest staff, but of course, if any displease you, they can be replaced."

I drew a breath and nodded. "Right—okay."

Kaizyn gave me a reassuring smile.

I turned forward to face the row of special attendants staring up at me. There were four broad-shouldered men in dark green guard uniforms, all looking to be in their mid-twenties or early thirties; another, thinner man in an olive green tunic who looked about the same age; and one slim, kind-faced woman in a light green dress who looked close to forty—though I knew some Teionyrians aged *very* well, by human standards, so some of them could have been older than they seemed.

"Pacha, Ferim, Melor, and Vymus will be your personal guards," Kurrum said, gesturing to the broad-shouldered men. "They will rotate shifts outside your chambers, and one of them will accompany you any time you must leave the palace—though you may also bring your own allies as additional protection, should you wish." He added the last part quickly, glancing at the cluster of LeyGuards, Callan, and Vyrthil waiting at the side of the stage.

I nodded to each of the guards in turn. "I'm glad to meet you all. Thank you for your protection."

They nodded back at me. "Of course, my king," they said almost in unison.

I wondered if they'd rehearsed that.

"Barthas is your personal assistant," Kurrum continued, gesturing at the thinner man next to them, then turning to face me. "His chambers will be assigned near yours, so he will always be available should you need something."

I glanced down at Barthas, feeling guilty that *anyone* would have to build their life around being on call for my requests—but he was staring with open-mouthed wonder at Champ, who had inched near him, sniffing his face.

"Champ!" I laughed, bending down to grab his collar. "I'm sorry. He's curious, but he's friendly. Please don't let him alarm you." I paused. "Would you like to pet him?"

Barthas stared up at me, eyes wide with surprise. "You mean *touch* him, Your Highness?"

"Yes, but only if you want to," I said, readying to pull Champ back, but then the man's face split into a grin.

"I would love to, Your Highness." He reached a shaky hand forward, letting Champ sniff it—and Champ immediately shoved his head into the man's hand.

The man stroked Champ's head, grinning with delight as Champ's tail wagged up a storm.

Something about that simple exchange cracked open the tight ball of anxiety I'd been carrying in my chest.

I chuckled as I stood. "He seems to like you, Barthas, and he has a great sense for people. Anyone Champ likes that much is someone I'm happy to have in my inner circle."

Champ rejoined me at my side, but not before getting one last scratch on the head from Barthas.

The man grinned widely as he stared up at me. "Thank you, Your Highness!"

Kurrum cleared his throat, but when I glanced at him, he was smiling. "And lastly, my king, is Millia," he said, gesturing to the kind-faced woman. "She leads the team that will prepare your room—making sure you have clean sheets, clean clothes, and any other items you need or comforts you may desire. If you need anything at all for your room, let her know, or you can send Barthas to relay the message if she isn't nearby. She is also your personal apothecarist. If ever you have an ache, a pain, trouble sleeping, or any ailment at all, let her know right away. She is extremely skilled with faespells and tinctures."

I studied the woman's face. I was wary about taking *any* kind of substance from someone I didn't know, but I knew Maxim would also be nearby. I could ask him later whether this woman was trustworthy—though I imagined she was, if Kurrum had personally chosen her, and I certainly didn't want her to feel unappreciated. I met her gaze and nodded. "Nice to meet you, as well, Millia."

She blushed and smiled back at me. "It's my pleasure to serve you, Your Highness."

My pleasure to serve you—Yeah, that felt weird. I wondered if that was something a king eventually got used to.

Kurrum smiled at her, then looked up at the crowd at large. "You are all dismissed—you know your assignments!"

They scattered like a flock of startled birds, literally *running* out the great hall's many doors.

Kurrum turned to me. "Well done, Your Highness." He smiled. "Now, it's time for your coronation."

CHAPTER 34

A Way to Keep the Darkness at Bay

Ayla

The archives were held in a secured wing on the main floor of the Hub. Doctor Harlowe and I had taken the elevator from the training rooms' sub-level to the main floor to meet up with my family, then Doctor Harlowe led us all through the secured door and into Archive Room Five.

We'd been scouring records ever since—Doctor Harlowe included.

Now, five hours into our search, my eyes were blurry from scanning the computer screen in the cubicle I'd claimed, my backside had gone numb from sitting, and I was wishing someone had thought to bring food.

I leaned back in my padded office chair and rolled the kinks out of my neck. "Any luck?"

Mom flopped back in her chair in the cubicle next to me and rubbed her weary eyes. "Not so far." She peered over the divider at my dad, who was in the cubicle across from her.

He shook his head. "Nothing here, either."

I turned to my other side to ask Grandpa, but chuckled when I found him asleep with his head on his arms. When I leaned closer, I could hear him softly snoring.

"Nothing there either, I'm guessing," I said to Mom.

She laughed. "Doctor Harlowe?"

We all glanced around, but the doctor was nowhere in sight. He had been in the cubicle beside my dad the last I checked.

I stood up. The four other cubicles in the small archive room were empty, as was the small table by the door. "Where did he go?" I hadn't seen or heard him leave.

The door slid open and Doctor Harlowe rushed inside, looking frenzied. "Here!" he said, then plopped a thick, dusty book down on the table, holding his hand between the pages to save his place in the book. "Come look. Hurry."

Mom, Dad, and I all rushed over.

"What is it?" my dad asked.

"I found a mention of a bond-spell in one journal from Veylden—it told of a ceremony to sever the bond, but referenced an obscure ArcFae ritual as the means of doing so. When I cross-referenced that ritual, I got a result from an old Mountain Fae historical text, smuggled out of Lower Faeside by Upper Faeside operatives during the ending of the last war. *This* book." He gestured to the one on the table. "Stored in the physical archives, down in Room Nine." With a dramatic flourish, he flopped the dusty book open. "Inside, I found *this.*"

When the plume of dust settled, I fought the urge to sneeze and leaned in to look. My breath caught. "It's Quinn's vision."

There, in an ancient-looking, hand-drawn illustration in colored ink, was the exact scene Quinn had described, down to a shirtless male ArcFae standing over two people bound to a table with their wrists tied together—only it was two sallow-looking Fae tied together on the table, rather than myself and Kaizyn. Rings of magic were shown flowing between their chests and the ArcFae's, and the bound Fae's mouths were contorted in what looked like horrified screams.

Mom gasped as she peered at the drawing over my shoulder.

"Wha—" Grandpa sat up, rubbed his eyes, then stumbled over to see what the commotion was. "What's the—*Oh.*" He stopped as he took in the drawing.

Dad slid up behind me, grasping my shoulder. "It'll be okay, Ayla. Take a breath."

I hadn't even realized how close I was to passing out from shallow, rapid breathing until he said that. I forced a slow, deep breath, letting his voice calm me. It *would* be all right—we would figure this out. Wouldn't we?

Mom pressed her hand to her chest. "How do we stop this?" she asked Doctor Harlowe.

He shook his head. "I don't think we can... and I don't think we *should*."

I gaped at him. "What?"

He tilted the book toward me and pointed at etched symbols in the bottom-right corner. Some kind of Fae writing.

Grandpa leaned in, peering closer, as I glanced up at Doctor Harlowe.

"What does it say?" I asked.

Grandpa straightened, his eyes wide and excited as they locked on mine. "It's not a sacrifice, Ayla—it's a cure! This is the ceremony to break the bond! But—"

At his sudden pause, my heart plunged from soaring down to my feet in an instant. "But *what*, Grandpa?"

He glanced at Doctor Harlowe. "That's a complicated rune."

Only then did I notice the intricate symbol charred into the wood of the table the two people were bound to.

"I know," Doctor Harlowe replied.

"There's no living Runist here at the Hub talented enough to pull that off."

"I know," Doctor Harlowe said again.

The two men met gazes for a moment, then Grandpa turned to me. "I know now why Varias was in Quinn's vision. He—*Etcher*—may be the only living Runist skilled enough to pull this off."

I stared at him for a moment. "He's actually a Runist? I thought that was just his cover, and he was really an ArcFae."

"He's both," Doctor Harlowe said. "The LeyGuard skill in Runing was *learned* from ArcFae, centuries ago. Runing, and its companion skill, the Wielding of runes, were established as two of our core LeyGuard aptitudes after decades of studying under ArcFae allies and tutors. For LeyGuards, they are two separate skills, but not so for ArcFae. A talented ArcFae like Varias could craft *and* channel runes that even the best LeyGuard Runists and Wielders could only dream of pulling off."

Grandpa turned to me. "Jordan told me Etcher had him wield a rune to sense into Beirthyr's mind and free Beirthyr's sear-bind from Sevryn's trap. But Etcher—Varias—would have been fully capable of wielding those runes himself. His use of Jordan was likely to maintain his LeyGuard cover—and also because Jordan is indeed a powerful Wielder, especially with his innate Fae magic added to the mix. Varias was already expending much energy maintaining the glamour that made him appear as an old LeyGuard. Wielding a powerful rune might have made his glamour slip, even momentarily—a risk he wouldn't have wanted to take." He gripped my hand. "Ayla, Varias really *is* our best hope of breaking this bond. There's no Runist alive who is more skilled."

My heart lurched. "But you said we couldn't trust him. You said he might have gone back to serving the Dark King!"

Grandpa gave my hand a squeeze. "I know. But this new information changes things. If you want to break your bond to Kaizyn *before* the Dark King finds a way to use it for evil, Varias might be our only chance."

Silence fell over us.

Grandpa glanced down and traced a finger over the picture with his free hand. "Varias *was* evil, once—he betrayed his own people for the promise of power at the Dark King's side. But then he saw the blood spilled for it and had a change of heart. He asked me for a way to keep the darkness at bay, a chance to do some good to redeem himself. I obliged, and in exchange, he kept my secrets. We had an agreement—and I trusted him, so long as that vow held." He looked up at me with concern. "The Dark King won't be happy that Varias betrayed him, much less eluded him for so many years. Now that Varias is freed from the vow to me, the Dark King will try to get his claws in him again, I'm certain of it. I wish we had a better option for you, Ayla. I just don't believe we do."

My heart sank, for multiple reasons. As much as I didn't trust Etcher—Varias—the thought that someone had tried to escape the Dark King and turn their life around for good, only to be trapped by the Dark King again in the end, was unbearably sad. "Whether he's willing to help us or not, he already helped Jordan and Madison... and you. He at least deserves a chance for freedom, doesn't he? Can't we do anything to help him?"

Grandpa sighed. "Unfortunately, I don't think so. It was a miracle he escaped the Dark King's clutches enough for us to work the vow the first time. I don't envy Varias the punishment that's sure to find him now, if it hasn't already. We'll just have to hope we can trust him to do the ceremony as things stand."

I glanced between Doctor Harlowe and Grandpa. "So we're all just accepting that his fate is sealed? If we find him, and he wants to be free of the Dark King again, couldn't we at least *try* to find a way?"

Grandpa smiled at me. "A minute ago, you didn't trust him. Now you want to save him?"

I felt my face heat, but I didn't care. "Yes, if we can. You said he wants to be free."

Grandpa's face turned serious. "His vow to me was the only thing that protected him from the vow he had *already* made to the Dark King. He can't be freed without being bound to someone, Ayla. And while I'd like to think that a vow to me was a fair sight better than a vow to the Dark King, the truth is... neither one was freedom. I'm not sure what more we can do."

I glanced between him and Doctor Harlowe. "There has to be *something* we can do."

"Yes," said Doctor Harlowe. "We can kill the Dark King."

The weight of that settled on the room.

"Doctor Harlowe is right, Ayla," Grandpa said softly. "Until the Dark King is dead, there's no way to guarantee Varias can truly be free—if the Varias I knew is even still in there." His gaze met mine. "But we can't wait for the Dark King to be killed to do this ceremony."

I stared at him. "But if we can't free Etcher first, then how do we know we can trust him?" As much as I wanted to help free Etcher of the Dark King's hold, I also couldn't forget the image of the horrified, screaming faces tied to the table in the drawing in front of me... and I did *not* want to live out my own version of that image.

Grandpa sighed. "Every day that you are bound to Kaizyn is another day you're *both* at risk, Ayla—from the feedback-loop of the magic itself, and as targets. The way the new king of Teionyr feels about you is no secret to anyone... and until Jordan has children, Kaizyn is second in line for the throne."

That realization took me by surprise. Kaizyn *was* still an heir to the throne, just no longer the primary one. My life *was* still tied to a prince... and to the stability of the Teionyrian throne.

"Killing either you *or* Kaizyn would kill you both, devastate Jordan, and possibly incapacitate the entire kingdom of Teionyr," Grandpa continued. "The Dark King will quickly realize that, if he hasn't already. Delaying the removal of your bond to Kaizyn is just too big of a risk... despite the concerns with Varias."

I stared at him, my conviction for helping Etcher wavering under the weight of my fear. "So I just have to hope that an ArcFae who may or may not be under the control of the Dark King will actually use this torture ceremony to *help* Kaizyn and me, rather than betraying and killing us?"

"I don't love the risk either, Peanut." Grandpa dropped his hand from the book, then looked up at me. "But keeping you in the Dark King's bullseye is an even bigger risk. Varias did once make the choice to *be* good, even while under the grip of evil—it's how we were able to bind the vow in the first place. I've trusted him before, and now I'll have to trust him with something even more precious to me... but we won't proceed unless I'm sure he's on our side." He squeezed my hand again. "Once we find him, if he seems like himself and I feel I can trust him, we can ask him to do the ceremony. Of course, we'll also have to convince Kaizyn to agree. The ceremony requires you both."

My parents and Doctor Harlowe were all staring at me with concern.

I turned away from everyone's watching eyes and took a deep breath.

Knowing we couldn't free Varias from the Dark King's hold before asking his help made this feel wildly reckless. I had *just* figured out how to control my magic, and now I was being asked to surrender control—to trust someone I barely knew, and to let him perform a ceremony on me that looked shockingly akin to torture in this drawing. Trust had never been my strong point, anyway, *especially* when it required surrendering my control of a situation.

Already, I could feel the fear mounting inside me, awakening my ice magic. My fingers itched with a cold tingle, eager to protect me from a threat I wasn't even facing yet. I wasn't even sure I *could* do this. What if I panicked the moment they put me on the table? What if the feedback loop sent Kaizyn and I both into a cataclysmic shutdown, or my magic freaked out and hurt someone?

But then I thought of Jordan, and how *I* would feel in his position, if the person I loved *and* my adopted-brother-slash-heir-to-my-throne were both killed in one fell swoop. Every day I left this bond in place, I was risking that outcome—and now that I knew a way to undo the bond, I would be risking that by *choice*. I couldn't do that to Jordan... and somehow that was an even stronger motivator than my concern for my own life. Varias had risked himself to help Jordan when they were both prisoners—and he had risked everything when he bound myself in his vow to my grandpa, too. That good part of him *had* to still be in there somewhere. If we found Varias and he was willing to help us, maybe we could eventually find a way to help *him*.

I drew a deep breath, my magic quieting and the warmth returning to my fingertips as my fear morphed into resolve. I turned to face the others. "Okay. As long as Kaizyn is okay with it, I'll do it."

Grandpa pulled me into a hug. "You're braver than you give yourself credit for, Ayla." He pulled back and smoothed my hair. "This will all be over before you know it—the war, all of it. It's all coming to an end soon, I can feel it."

He smiled at me, but his words settled like rocks in my stomach. I could feel that it would all soon be ending, too—I just hoped that end was the happy kind, and not the kind where people I cared about ended up dead.

I looked at Doctor Harlowe. "The Hub's on lockdown. Does that mean we can't go right now?"

He nodded. "Once the imminent threat is past, the Hub will return to a semi-lockdown state, a typical post-crisis security measure. When that happens, I'll inform Chairman Hart what we've discovered and let her know that you need special clearance to travel to Arcvale."

"Could we train my magic some more while we're waiting?" I asked him. "I want to make sure I—"

The archive room plunged into darkness. Piercing sirens split the air.

"Code Five," a recording of Chairman Hart's voice blared through the speakers above. "All personnel, activate your designated security protocols. I repeat: Code Five. All personnel, activate your designated security protocols."

"What's happening?" my mom's voice shouted over the sirens as I blinked, struggling to see in the sudden darkness. "What's a Code Five?"

A blue glow erupted from a runestone Doctor Harlowe had pulled from somewhere, illuminating a small area around us—along with Doctor Harlowe's panicked face. "Code Five means the Hub is under attack." He rushed to the door of the archive room and pressed his hand to the wall panel. "It's not responding." His eyes widened.

"Did someone cut the power?" I asked.

"The Hub has multiple layers of backup systems," Grandpa said. "That shouldn't be possible."

Doctor Harlowe, meanwhile, ran back to the table where he'd set his tablet and frantically tapped a few things on the screen. An image of his face appeared on it as he held it up, like he was using a front-facing camera. "Hello, this is Doctor Harlowe down in Archive Room Five. We—Hello?"

He spun slowly to us, still holding the tablet with wide, frightened eyes. "It's not going through. The signal's blocked."

My mom pulled out her cell phone. "No service. I swear I had a signal just moments ago." She glanced up at my dad, and their eyes met with an expression that sent a chill down my spine.

Grandpa turned to me. "Ayla can send a message."

Everyone stared at me.

"What?" I said, still struggling to think clearly over the blaring sirens and the internal panic.

"Ayla, maybe Jordan can get through from the outside and find out what's happening," Grandpa said.

It took me a second to realize what he meant. "Oh!" I pulled the stone from my pocket, pressed my thumb to it, and spoke the word to activate it.

"Please answer, Jordan," I whispered. "Please."

The others stared at me as the rune lit blue—then they all huddled around me as we waited for him to answer.

CHAPTER 35

Long Live the True King of Teionyr

Jordan

There are people who can speak to an audience of hundreds with full confidence, there are those who panic and freeze, and then there are those who just flat pass out. When I finally made it up onto the hilltop stage, with the full population of Teionyr staring up at me in expectation, I worried I was about to become one of the latter.

Kurrum's amplified voice echoed against the backdrop of palace and mountains as he faced the massive crowd from the stage. "The royal council is pleased to present the true heir of our late king Veilar, may he rest in peace, the new and rightful king of Teionyr and thereupon also the High King of Upper Faeside—Cathal-Reigar, son of Veilar!" He swung his arm wide, gesturing for me to take center stage as he hurried off the stairs on the opposite side.

Thankfully, Kaizyn had joined me again at my request, and his steady hand landed on my shoulder. "Breathe, Jordan. You'll be okay. Our people want to know you. The real you. Don't overthink it. Just say what's on your heart."

In his other hand, tucked out of sight behind his cloak, he held a golden crown etched with intricate vines—the king's crown—ready to present it to me when I completed my speech. It had been his idea that he present the crown rather than the council, to communicate solidarity to our people, and I couldn't have been more grateful.

I loosely held the glowing stone Kurrum had given me, not wanting to activate it too soon, and forced my steps toward the center of the stage, then drew a deep breath as I truly took in the Teionyrian people for the first time.

They were... ordinary. All ages, all shapes and sizes, just like I would've found at a crowd back home, and even though their garb was different, their faces looked *human*. They weren't actually human... they were Fae. But then, as it turned out, so was I.

They weren't some scary, foreign obstacle to face like my fear had tried to shape them. They were *people*. My father's people. Kaizyn and Callan's people. *My* people. People with wives and husbands and children and families, with jobs and roles in their community; with dreams and goals and causes for which they cared deeply—all waiting with expressions of wary hope to see what kind of ruler fate had delivered them.

In that moment, I knew exactly what I needed to say.

I clutched the stone, and my voice echoed out over the crowd.

"I was not raised to be a king. I never knew I was royalty. But I wasn't quite a normal human teenager, either. While my friends were playing games after school, I was training to defend myself. To protect others. To observe my surroundings. To work closely with a team." I glanced at my parents and the others, standing off to the side of the stage, and my eyes caught on Reina. "To always have my partners' backs."

I looked back at the crowd. "I was raised to be a LeyGuard—to put honor and duty first. To be a warrior, smart and skilled. To protect my town, even when it didn't know it needed protecting. To help and serve my people, even when I did it without thanks. Even when I did it in secret. I am still learning how to be a king. I am eager to learn. I am eager to grow... But I know the *person* I was taught to be—and *that is* what I can offer you now, fully and without reservation."

I glanced at Kaizyn, and he gave me a reassuring smile and nod, so I kept going.

"I was taught to serve with honor—I will serve you the same. I was taught to value life—and I will value yours, no matter your station or role. I was taught to defend the weak, to stand up to those who would cause harm, and to never back down from what's right—and I promise, I will do the same for Teionyr, no matter what villains or evils we might face. But please..." A nervous laugh escaped me. "Feel free to call me King *Jordan*. I am honored to be Cathal-Reigar, son of Veilar, but I wish never to forget my roots. Though my blood may be royal, in my heart I am still an awkward, ordinary teenager trying to figure out how to tell a girl I like her while fighting secret Void monsters on the weekend."

A wave of low chuckles went up from the crowd.

"I am still learning our ways and our customs," I continued, "but I care about your concerns, and I vow to defend you and your lives. I have the support of the heir-prince to help me. I have a wise council to advise me. I have strong allies among the Earthside LeyGuards, who have an honorable history of protecting and serving our people, and who wish to continue that legacy. I have a powerful sear-bound dragon, Sorcha, who has vowed to use her magic and strength to defend our kingdom. And I have you—my people—whose cares and concerns I genuinely wish to hear, any time you choose to voice them."

From my peripheral, I saw Kaizyn draw the crown out of his cloak.

I focused on the people staring up at me. "I can't promise I will be the king my father was, at least not right away... but I will always strive to do what is right and honorable, and to put my people's needs—your needs—first. I will be your king as fully and wholeheartedly and selflessly as I can. That much, I *can* promise you."

I released my grip on the stone, and the last echoes of my words sank into the silence of the watchful crowd.

Kaizyn stepped forward, casting me a wide smile. "Long live the true king of Teionyr!" he shouted.

"Long live the true king of Teionyr!" the roaring crowd echoed as he placed the crown on my head.

And just like that, I was officially king.

King-of-mine, Sorcha's voice drifted into the bond. *Is it time, yet? I grow weary of hiding behind the palace.*

I returned Kaizyn's smile, then turned back to face my people. "So... who wants to meet a dragon?"

It was dark by the time the post-coronation celebration ended and our small group plodded back up the halls toward the royal suites, but my heart was buoyant with relief.

The people had welcomed Sorcha with a sense of awe rather than fear, Kurrum and the rest of the council had been pleased with my speech, and after personally greeting what must've been hundreds of families as they milled about the stalls of mouthwatering food at the outdoor festival the council had set up in the market of Teionyr, I felt fairly confident that my people didn't objectively hate my existence.

And apparently, Teionyrian food was delicious. I had no idea what the dish was called that Kaizyn and Callan had brought me when I finally sat down in a private tent at the corner of the marketplace to eat, but it resembled a pot-roast with vegetables. My mouth had been watering at the smell before I even took the first bite, and it even came with a steaming kettle of spiced tea with its own little cup, and a huge mug of cool, crisp water on the side.

All in all, the day had gone far better than I'd imagined it might... but I was ready for a good night's sleep.

As we reached our hallway, Kurrum directed Reina and her parents to the guest chambers he had set up for them, then pointed my parents' room out to them. Kaizyn already had chambers in the royal wing, and Callan's usual suite was adjacent to Kaizyn's, since he had been the prince's personal guard. And Champ, of course, would be staying with me.

"The palace staff are rapidly working to build Sorcha a massive barn on the hill beyond the palace," Kurrum told me, "so she will have a weather-safe place to rest should she wish for one."

I gave him a smile. "Thank you, Kurrum, but please tell them there is no rush. Sorcha insists she is perfectly comfortable sleeping up in the cliffs behind the palace while they work on her new lodgings."

Kurrum nodded. "Thank you. I will let them know, Your Highness."

I fought back a yawn, then turned to face the others as we reached our rows of doors.

"Thank you all so much," I said. "For everything."

My mom pulled me into a hug. "We're so proud of you."

She and my dad both gave me teary smiles.

"Okay, stop," I laughed. "Now you're going to make *me* cry."

"We really are proud of you, son," Dad said, ruffling my hair.

I smiled back at them. "Thanks." I fought back another yawn. "I'm going to call Ayla, and then I'm going to bed. It's been a long day."

They smiled at me, then bade me goodnight and headed toward their room.

Reina stopped outside of her door, her parents already heading inside. "You were awesome today, but we knew you would be." She gave me a weak smile. "Goodnight, Jordan." She turned and went inside.

"Goodnight!" I called to her back, but she was already shutting the door.

I tried not to read too much into that.

"She just needs sleep, I'm sure," Callan said, drifting up next to me.

Champ danced nervously at my side as Kaizyn and Vyrthil approached, too—Champ still wasn't sure what to make of the fire-cat.

Kaizyn smiled at me. "Father would have been proud of you today, Jordan." His eyes were sincere. "You will be a great king."

I drew a shaky breath. "I will do my best to be."

He smiled again. "I know. Goodnight, brother."

I held his gaze as his words sank in, and felt myself smile back. "Goodnight, Kaizyn."

He and Callan headed to their rooms, and I stumbled back to mine, seriously debating whether I had enough energy left to call Ayla, but I knew she'd be wondering how things had gone. I at least wanted to make a quick call, to hear her voice and tell her goodnight.

Champ flopped down on the fluffy rug the attendants had laid out for him—right next to a towering basket of treats and toys and the bowl of water and home-cooked dog food the palace chef had prepared for him after consulting me on his dietary needs—while I dragged myself to the changing room.

I kicked off my boots, then crossed to fetch the stone from my hanging clothes...

The clothes weren't there.

CHAPTER 36

LeyGuard Pants

Jordan

I rushed back through my chamber and out into the hallway, not bothering to put on my boots.

A guard turned to face me when I yanked the door open.

"Your Highness. Is something wrong?"

"The clothes I asked the laundress not to take—they're missing."

The guard's expression grew worried. "Perhaps she took them by mistake, or—"

"There was something very important in my pocket. I need to know where the clothes may have been taken."

"Of course, Your Highness." He hurried to a door beyond mine and knocked firmly. "Barthas! The king requires you—"

"No, no, please don't bother him," I said, but it was too late. The door was already opening.

"My king?" Barthas rushed out, fully dressed, with a look of concern.

By this time, the commotion had drawn a crowd. My parents, Reina and her parents, and Callan and Kaizyn had also joined us in the hall.

I drew a breath. "I'm sure it's fine, I just—my LeyGuard pants are missing."

Reina and Callan stared at me like I'd lost my mind, but I made eye contact with my parents.

"The ones with something *important* in the pocket," I told them, "the ones I asked Kurrum to make sure were not laundered yet."

"Oh," my mom said. She turned to Barthas. "Can you find out where the attendants may have taken the king's clothes?"

Reina stepped up next to me. "Jordan, what's going on? What was in those pants?"

I sighed, but now wasn't the time to keep more secrets from her. "A communication stone, for calling Earthside. Maddox Rogers gave it to me, but he told me to keep it a secret. I guess they're—uh—well, forbidden? Or... discontinued, I mean. Like, not used anymore."

Her eyes widened. "Oh. What happens if it's found by someone?"

"I don't know," I said. "Maybe nothing? But I still don't want to lose it."

"He uses it to call Ayla," my mom said, rather unhelpfully.

Reina stared at me.

"But it's also our best way to contact the Hub quickly if needed," my dad hurried to add. "Especially now that they're locked down. We really do need to find it."

"Okay," Kaizyn said, nodding, then turned to Callan. "You know the palace as well as I do. Let's check with the laundress, and if it's not there, we can split up and trace it back to whatever attendants may have cleaned Jordan's room. Barthas, you—Barthas?"

Kaizyn stopped, as my personal attendant Barthas was looking rather pale and shaken.

"I'm sorry, Your Highness," Barthas said, wringing his hands. "I fear this is my fault. Kurrum sent me to relay your message to the laundress, but she was out, so I left the message with her assistant. The girl is young, my king, an apprentice. She may have forgotten, or not relayed it correctly—please, if there's someone to take the blame, place it on me. I should have tracked down the laundress and told her directly."

I turned to him. "I could have done so, as well, if I wished to convey the importance more clearly, and if I hadn't been in such a hurry. I am not *blaming* anyone. I just need the stone to be found."

He nodded, brightening a bit. "Of course, Your Highness. I will go speak with Millia right now, to see who was sent to clean your room. Even if we have to search all night, we will find it."

The moment I nodded my agreement, he rushed off, already on his mission.

"The palace staff are honest people, Jordan," Callan said, clasping my shoulder. "I'm certain no one *took* the stone. It's probably still in your pocket in one of the bins down in the washrooms. We'll find it."

"Thanks," I said, but I couldn't shake the uneasy feeling of something important having gone missing. "I'd like to help look, too. Where should we start?"

Kaizyn shrugged. "My guess would be the laundry rooms."

The stone was not in my pants. We found *those* easily enough, because the laundress kept my clothes separate from the others she'd gathered to wash. Apparently she hadn't received the message, and my clothes had been carefully cleaned and hung to dry in the corner of the main washroom. The stone, however, was nowhere to be found.

My parents had gone to find Barthas, while Reina's parents had gone with the night-shift laundry attendant to retrace the steps the earlier attendant would've taken through the palace while bringing my clothes to the laundry area.

Meanwhile, Callan, Kaizyn, Reina, and I were all elbows-deep in various laundry bins, digging through soiled work clothes and unwashed linens in hopes the stone had fallen out somewhere.

My personal bin to search was one full of damp towels, musty enough to suggest they'd already sat in the bin longer than they should have. I removed my royal cloak and rolled my tunic sleeves up above my elbows so I could dig into the bin more easily.

When Barthas and my parents returned with the bleary-eyed head laundress in tow, the laundress let out a little yelp of horror.

"Your Highness!" She rushed forward, reaching as though to yank my arms out of the dirty laundry bin, but caught herself and jumped back before she actually touched me. "Those are *used towels*, Your Highness! From the attendants' chambers! They have not been washed yet!"

Dirty towels weren't a pleasant thing to be digging through, but given that I'd tried to choke a Selkblood with my bare hands, then held my girlfriend's bleeding body in the middle of a horrific battle, it also wasn't the most disturbing thing my hands had touched recently. I looked up at her. "I'm aware. Do you have any idea what might have happened to the contents of my pants pockets, earlier?"

Ayla still wasn't officially my girlfriend, I also realized. *Huh.* I supposed I would have to remedy that as soon as I found this stone.

The laundress stared at me. "There was nothing in your pockets when the pants arrived, Your Highness. I—"

"Aha!" Reina's dad let out a victorious yell as he and Reina's mom jogged back into the laundry room. "Look what we found in a random stairwell—*and* we found a couple of other things!" He held up my cell phone and my favorite ink pen in one hand, and the communication stone in the other.

I yanked my arms from the bin of damp towels with a sigh of relief. "Oh, thank goodness." I hurried over to him and grabbed the stone, realizing only afterward that I probably should have washed my hands first... but then something else grabbed my attention. "It's lit."

One rune on the stone was glowing—which meant Ayla had tried to call me.

I stepped back. "I'm sorry, I need to—" I looked up at all of them, and realized there was no need for secrecy at this point. They all already knew I had the stone. "Oh well." I shrugged, then pressed my thumb to the rune and whispered the activation word. "Ayla? Are you there?"

"Jordan?" Her voice was shrill, panicked. "Jordan! Thank goodness! I've been trying to call you for—*aah*!" She let out a brief scream as a loud bang sounded in the distance.

My whole body was immediately on high alert. "What is it? What's happening?"

Reina, Callan, Kaizyn and the others all rushed near me.

"Jordan!" I heard Doctor Harlowe's voice suddenly. "We need you to contact the Hub from the outside—the emergency line. Right away! Tell them we're in Archive Room Five."

I stared up at my parents in alarm. "Doctor Harlowe? Where's Ayla? What's—"

Ayla's voice came back on. "I'm here, I'm here. Jordan—please hurry! The Hub is under attack!"

The light on the stone flickered, then cut out. Why had it run out so quickly this time?

I reached to activate it again, but Kaizyn touched my arm. "You may need those runes later; I would save them—we know already what we need to do from here."

I wanted to argue, but he was right. If the Hub really *was* under attack, that stone might be my best and only way to contact Ayla for a while. I couldn't afford to waste it.

I drew a shaky breath. "We have to hurry. Is there a way to call the Hub from here? This stone is only paired to Ayla's."

Callan shook his head. "Regular phone calls can't cross the Veil. Usually, we'd send someone to the nearest Hub gate and wait for a LeyGuard to respond to our presence so we could relay the message, but that would take too long, even if the Hub hadn't shut down all the usual Gates. But I doubt they've shut down the one that empties near Maddox's cabin. We can get you there quickly. You can get through to Earthside that way, then call the Hub's emergency line directly with your cell phone—or go to the Gate yourself and try to get their attention. It's not far from the cabin."

"You have access to this private Gate?" I asked him.

"Kaizyn does," he said, glancing at the prince. "That cabin was where I stayed when I was Earthside, before."

Kaizyn slid a small, metal rod from beneath his tunic, hanging from a leather cord. "It was a favor from Maddox."

I huffed a sigh of relief. "Thank goodness." At the moment, I didn't care that a secret Gate was breaking a million LeyGuard rules, I just needed a way through. "I'll go. I'll call the Hub the moment I get Earthside, and then we'll go from there." I reached for the cord Kaizyn held, expecting him to hand it to me.

He hesitated.

"You cannot go, my king," he said, his eyes holding mine.

"What? Why in the world not?" I started to get defensive, then I realized—"*Oh.*" I was king, now. I couldn't just run off on a mission. My responsibility was *here.*

"Our people need you," Kaizyn said, "especially now. No matter what happens, you have to be here—and you have to be *focused.* You have to lead our people."

I nodded. "I know, but—" I stared at him. "I can't just sit here while Ayla is in danger and my friends at the Hub are under attack."

But I knew he was right. I also couldn't *go.*

My heart felt like it was ripping in two.

"My parents and I can go," Reina said. "We'll go quickly and report back the moment we know something."

Her parents nodded. "Yes," her dad said, sharing a glance with my dad. "We'll go. That way your parents can be here with you in case something happens here."

I drew a deep breath. "But—"

"Or I can go," Kaizyn's firm voice interrupted me.

"What?" I spun to look at him.

"I'll go instead of Reina," he repeated, his voice and gaze firm. "And Callan can join me, if he agrees."

Reina opened her mouth to protest, but Kaizyn was already explaining.

"Jordan, if your parents or any of your closest LeyGuard team suddenly vanish to go Earthside after all the preparations for their overnight stay, the palace staff will *know* something is wrong. Rumors will fly, and people may start to panic. But the people know I've been staying elsewhere, lately. Callan and I can slip in and out, and no one will think much of it. We can go Earthside and come right back with a report, so you can convene with your council on what needs to be done from here. If the situation looks urgent when we arrive, Callan and I will find a way in. We know Dark Fae, and how they fight. We'll make sure we get Ayla and her family out safely. You can trust us."

I stared at him. "But you—and Ayla..."

"I'm stronger now," he said. "I won't overwhelm the bond. I can do this, I know I can. Please let me do this for you."

I watched him for a moment, and I could see the resolve in his eyes, the need for action, the need to *go*—the same need I was feeling. Only *I* couldn't act on it.

"If you go, you'll be putting yourself in danger," I told him. "That would put you and Ayla *both* at risk."

"We'll stay low, get information, and get out," he said. "We'll only intervene if we have to, and if we have to move in, we'll be smart and careful. Callan and I are trained for this, Jordan. We can do this." He held my gaze with a look of utter confidence.

"He's right," Callan added. "*All* Teionyrian warriors are trained for this kind of mission, the prince included. But this is one area in which the prince exceeds even my own skill. There is no one more skilled than Kaizyn at stealth. It's how he survived so long in the Veil."

I studied them, considering. If anyone in the world would fight for Ayla's life as fiercely as I would, it would be Kaizyn—not only because he also cared about her, but because his own life depended on it.

I huffed a sigh. "Okay... You can go. But *please* be care—"

"I'm going with them," Reina interrupted.

When I turned to stare at her, her eyes were like steel. "I may not know Dark Fae tactics as well as Kaizyn and Callan, but I know the Hub and how to contact them. If they really are under attack and need help, I can ping the emergency access Gate and tell them to let me in. They're far more likely to respond to a LeyGuard than two Fae. I promise, I won't let anything happen to Ayla—or to him," she added, glancing at Kaizyn.

"What about the palace staff?" I asked her. "Kaizyn said it would draw too much attention for my LeyGuard guests to leave."

"That's what you have a council for, right?" Reina answered. "They can keep people calm. Plus, it's bed time. With any luck, we'll be back before anyone even realizes we're gone. But sending Kaizyn and Callan *alone* wouldn't be smart, and you know it. I need to go, too."

"I appreciate your concern," Kaizyn said, eyeing her strangely. "But I don't wish for you to risk—"

"I'm going," she said, crossing her arms and glaring at him.

Reina's mom glanced between them, then shared a look with Reina's dad which communicated something I couldn't quite interpret.

Reina's dad nodded. "Then we're going, too, of course," he said. "Your mother and I."

I wasn't surprised.

"Fine." Reina nodded, then turned her glare on me. "Looks like we've got a recon team. Do we have your leave to begin our mission?"

I stared at her. "Reina, this could be dangerous. You don't have to..."

Her eyes softened. "Let me do this, Jordan. For Ayla. Please. Let me help."

I glanced at my parents.

My mom raised an eyebrow, but then slowly nodded.

I sighed. "Okay. Go. But go quickly, and come right back—I need to know what's happening. And please, *please* be careful. I need you all safe."

Reina nodded at me. "I'll grab my stuff, then we'll leave right away. But Jordan—go get some rest. You're probably going to need it... plus, no offense, but you kind of look like crap." She smirked at me, but then her face turned serious. "We'll see you soon." She hurried out of the washroom, and her parents trailed behind her.

Kaizyn and Callan stared at me.

"I won't fail you, Jordan," Kaizyn said softly. "You can trust me."

I met his gaze. "And you can trust me with our kingdom. I'll be here, doing my best. But please hurry back. It will drive me insane not knowing what's happening out there."

Kaizyn clasped my shoulder. "That is because you have a warrior's heart—driven to action." He smiled. "In Teionyr, such has been the heart of our most legendary kings." He stepped back. "I'll see you soon, brother. But have your dragon keep a watchful eye around the city—just in case?"

I nodded. "I will."

"We'll see you soon, Jordan," Callan said.

The two of them hurried off.

Suddenly, I was no longer a LeyGuard in mission-planning mode—I was a shaken king with arms that smelled of damp, musty towels, standing in a washroom with my parents and two very startled-looking palace attendants.

"Please don't tell anyone what you just heard," I told the laundress and Barthas. "We will inform everyone of what's happening once we *know* what's happening, but I do not wish to incite an undue panic."

Barthas and the laundress both nodded.

"Of course, Your Highness," the laundress said. "I would not wish to incite panic, either, especially when it pertains to LeyGuard matters. Such things are not a palace attendant's concern. Our work is to care for *you*."

"I never speak of the king's private matters unless instructed to do so," Barthas added with an air of pride. "Discretion is one of the foremost qualifications for a royal steward."

I nodded. "Right. Okay. Thank you both."

My parents met my gaze. "Are you all right?" my dad asked.

I drew a long breath, and suddenly, even with my lingering panic over Ayla and what was happening at the Hub, I felt utterly exhausted. I could barely even think straight. I'd be no good to anyone, like this—and I needed to be sharp for whatever came next.

"I think I need a quick nap, if I can manage it," I told my parents, then wrinkled my nose as another whiff of the musty towels hit me. "And some soap for these arms."

My parents both chuckled.

Barthas gave me a kind smile. "Come, Your Highness. I'll have the attendants draw you a hot bath."

CHAPTER 37

OUT OF MY LEAGUE

Rory

A female voice drifted into the dark ocean of my sleep, pulling my consciousness to the surface.

"Dove?" I murmured, the memory of her singing me to sleep settling around me like a comforting fog.

But then awareness gripped me, and I froze. That was not Dove's voice. The fog burned away.

I peeled an eye open. I was no longer on my parents' couch. My body lay on the cold, dark surface of the Void.

"It's nearly time," the voice said. "Have you heard from the messenger?"

Miravel. I was sure of it. She sounded close enough to touch.

Adrenaline rushed through me but I bridled it, remaining still. I was back in an in-between place, but Miravel seemed to be talking to someone _else_. Maybe, like the first time, she hadn't yet realized I was here.

I knew Miravel had to be connected to the Dark Fae. Her magic was too—well, dark—to think otherwise. If our demented dark-magic bond went both ways, if this was me somehow stepping into Miravel's private conversation like she could step into my mind, then maybe I could use this to learn something about the Dark King's army.

Right now, _any_ new information could be useful, especially since Dove, Madison, and I were still unable to get ahold of the Hub. What if Arcvale had already been attacked? What if our friends needed us?

A male voice responded to Miravel. I couldn't make out his words, but the voice sounded eerily familiar.

I held my breath, trying to locate the sound in the darkness as my eyes slowly adjusted to the black Void.

There.

The bobbing lantern I'd seen the first time floated in the distance—farther than the voices had sounded. Its glow illuminated a hunched, shadowy form that I knew to be the hag I'd seen before. The light seemed stationary, as though the hag was standing still.

On the other side of the glow stood the tall, graceful form of Miravel. She wore a dark cloak with the hood pulled up, concealing most of her face.

Across from both of them, just on the edge of the lantern-light, stood a tall man—the source of the other voice.

My lungs burned with held breath. I released the air slowly, praying it didn't grab their attention as before—but apparently they were far enough away this time. I said a grateful prayer, then drew in another slow, careful breath as I listened.

"The Hub is in chaos." Miravel's satisfaction curled around the words like a purring cat.

The hag grunted. "Their system was more complex than anticipated. It won't take long for them to realize it's a false alarm."

Miravel waved a dismissive hand. "Long enough for our purposes." She turned back to the man. "We are on track. There's no cause for concern."

The man reached for her, trailing a finger down her face. "You've done well, my pet."

A chill spread through me. I was *sure* I'd heard that voice before...

"The prince should be coming into the Veil at any moment," Miravel said, shivering slightly at his touch—her voice sounded husky with desire, not fear. "The girl won't be a problem for you much longer."

"I knew I could rely on you, as always." The man stepped closer, giving Miravel the kind of smile I've seen women melt over as the light from the lantern spilled onto his face.

My chest turned to ice.

It was the man who had dated my sister. The man who, it turned out, was actually a monster—the man who had attacked Madison and killed her guard.

Sevryn. That was his true name, and he was Selkblood, a Dark Fae. I gasped.

Maybe this was one of Miravel's memories?

The man's gaze flicked in my direction, and I froze, holding my breath.

He'd heard my gasp, I was sure of it. This was no memory. At least he didn't seem like he'd spotted me.

But how was he here? He was supposed to be *dead.*

My mind raced. Miravel had said *the prince*—did they mean Kaizyn? Were they planning to ambush him in the Veil? And the girl—my heart sank as certainty settled in. *Ayla.*

Where was the escape hatch on this hell-hole? I needed out of this vision. I had to warn Kaizyn and Ayla. And fast.

But I forced myself to breathe slowly, listening for anything further about Sevryn's plans.

After a second, he turned back to Miravel, still holding his charming smile. His fingers trailed her jaw, then he pulled his hand away and stepped back. "It's too late to stop it. It's already in motion."

He flicked his pale face to me across the distance, and his gaze locked on mine. His eyes glinted ice-blue in the darkness.

Dread settled into my sternum as I realized those last words had been for me.

"I'm coming for *you* next, Rory Kane," he said with a chilling smirk.

A force sucked me backward, and the forms of Miravel, the hag, and the man blurred into the distance.

"Rory? *Rory!*"

I sat bolt upright, and almost smacked my head into Dove's panicked face.

She threw her arms around me. "Oh, I'm so sorry. I'm so sorry, Rory!"

My body slowly registered my new surroundings. I was back on my parents' couch, Dove half on a chair beside me and half on my chest from having thrown her arms around me. One of her hands gripped mine, the runed stone clutched between our joined palms, still warm to the touch.

Madison and my parents gaped at me from behind her, a mix of relief and fear on their faces.

Dove pulled back, staring at me with wide, panicked eyes, her brow pinched with worry. "I didn't catch it soon enough! I felt the darkness come for you, but by the time I got the stone out, I—"

I cupped her face with my free hand. "Dove, it's okay. I'm okay."

She sank back onto her chair and drew a shuddering breath. Her worried face softened a bit as she studied me. "Are you sure? Your skin was so strange, shifting between hot and cold, and your eyes—" She shivered, then peered at me more closely. "You still look unwell."

I swallowed, glancing up at my parents and sister. "Yeah, well—" I huffed an anxious breath. "I think I was actually *meant* to see this one, but..."

Madison's eyes locked on mine. "Rory," she said, her voice tense and wary. "What did you see?"

My stomach swooped to my feet, but this wasn't something I could keep from her.

"I think—I think Sevryn's alive."

Madison *and* my parents all gasped, but I pushed forward.

"He's working with the Dark King and the two women I saw before... and he's planning to ambush Kaizyn to kill Ayla."

Madison went bone-white. "*What?*"

My father's eyes widened in shock, then hardened with a rage I'd *never* seen on his face before. "That son-of-a—" Dad cut off, clenching his jaw. He reached for Madison, but I could see the fury still churning in his eyes.

"Could it have been someone who just *looked* like him?" Madison's voice quivered as she asked.

I drew a long breath, but in my core I knew the answer, had known it the moment he looked right at me. "No." At Madison's desperate expression, I softened the blow by instinct. "I mean—I don't think so."

"I will kill him. I will *kill* him if he touches you again," Dad muttered, stroking Madison's hair as my mom moved in to wrap her arms around both of them.

But Madison's eyes were locked on mine. We *both* knew Dad didn't stand a chance in a fight against monsters like these. He would only die trying. There was no way I could let that happen.

But I was only a human, too, no stronger than my dad. If these monsters attacked us, I would just end up bloodied and needing rescue, like before. A sense of failure swept over me again, followed by a pang of self-loathing. I couldn't protect my family, or Dove, or anyone else from threats like these. I was useless.

Fogarty jumped up on the edge of the couch, meowing and pacing, as Dove grabbed my arm.

I tore myself from my spiral of self-loathing long enough to look at her. She was *beautiful*—and completely, utterly not in need of me. Why had I ever entertained, even for a second, that this girl could have an interest in me?

"Rory, are you sure? Are you *absolutely* sure it was Sevryn?" she asked, her warm, dark eyes wide with the question.

I wished I could say no to that, but I nodded. "Yes."

Her whole body tensed. "That is *not* good news."

I wanted to pull her to me, to comfort her, but I held back. What possible comfort could I offer her? I was way out of my league—in my ability to fight these creatures, *and* with her.

Her eyes studied mine, but I tore my gaze away, focusing on a loose thread on the blanket still across my lap.

She drew a shaky breath. "What else did you see?"

I felt utterly defeated and helpless in front of her, but this wasn't just about me. I looked up at her. "They created some kind of false alarm at the

Hub—a distraction, maybe? I didn't hear enough to know for sure, but it sounded like they faked an attack."

Dove jumped up and raced toward the kitchen.

I threw off the blanket and followed, Madison and my parents trailing behind me.

Dove grabbed the landline phone and dialed—but after several tense moments, she placed the phone back into its cradle and shook her head. "Still no answer." She stared up at me with wide, scared eyes. Her lip quivered. "Do you think it's just the false alarm? That they think they're under attack? And what is it a distraction *for*? What are the Dark Fae trying to do?"

She looked so worried, it made my heart ache.

I shook my head. "I... I don't know." Yet another failure—I'd been so paralyzed with fear, I hadn't even thought to engage and ask questions of Sevryn once I knew he'd seen me. Maybe it would've accomplished nothing... or maybe I could've goaded him into telling me something more useful. I'd never know, because I had been too panicked to even try.

I was useless *and* a coward.

But useless or not, I still couldn't just sit here and do nothing.

I rushed for the couch, grabbing the sneakers I'd taken off before my nap.

Madison hurried toward me. "Where are you going?"

I glanced up at her as I crammed a foot into a sneaker. "The Hub. I don't care if the portals are all closed or whatever, there has to be *some* way to get in—and I cannot just sit here and let them ambush Kaizyn or Ayla."

Dove stepped into the room, watching me calmly. "I will come with you."

My heart lifted at the thought of having her with me—except for the part where I'd be putting her in danger. Sevryn knew I'd heard him talking to Miravel and the hag. Maybe he'd even *meant* for me to hear them; I couldn't be sure. Any actions we took from here could be walking right into his trap.

But I could tell from Dove's expression there was no use trying to convince her it would be safer for her to stay here. She would probably just throw her bear at me.

I shoved down the confusing whirlwind of pleasure and dread I felt about her joining me, and nodded. "Okay."

"We can return to the Gate we used to come here," she continued, "but—"

I looked up at her. "But what?"

"Not all Gates are watched closely, especially when they're locked down as they are now. Ordinarily, a LeyGuard can trigger a Gate and draw attention to let the Hub know they're there, even if the Gate is an obscure one. But I am not a LeyGuard. My runestone for Gate travel doesn't override a lockdown, and the nearest Gate isn't a commonly used one. If the Hub truly is under siege—even if it's a false alarm—they may not have anyone monitoring the lesser-used Gates. They may not even realize we're there."

Madison neared us as I tied my laces and shoved on my second shoe. "Is there no other way to get in? A Gate they might be watching more closely?" she asked Dove.

"There are other Gates," Dove answered, "but none very close. And if the Hub is dealing with a perceived attack, they may not be answering *any* of them."

"Then we'll try *all* of them," I said, standing. I turned to Mom and Dad, who were watching from the kitchen doorway. "I need to take one of the cars."

Dad wrapped his arm around Mom's shoulders and nodded. "Take mine. It's the fastest."

I hurried to the hall that led to our garage and grabbed my dad's keys from the hook on the wall.

Madison, Dove, and Fogarty followed.

I turned back to Madison. "Stay here. Please. I don't know what might happen, and if Sevryn—"

A flash of fear crossed her eyes at his name, but then she clenched her jaw. "They're my *friends*, Rory. I'm coming."

I studied her for a moment, and my heart softened a bit. "Dad's right, Mads. You really have become so brave. You've changed."

Tears swelled in her eyes as she smiled at me. "So have you."

Before I could ask what she meant, she turned to Mom and Dad, who were still standing near the entrance to the kitchen. "Can you two keep calling the Hub while we're gone? If you get through, you can tell them what Rory saw and that we're trying to get in."

I expected my parents to argue about us going without them—though I *really* hoped they wouldn't. They knew so little about the Fae they'd be walking in blind if they insisted on joining us, and my dad had already suffered enough at their hands.

Dad looked conflicted, but Mom gripped his arm and nodded. "If that's the best way for us to help, then that's what we'll do. Take your phone. If we get through, we'll call you—and you call us if anything changes. And *please*, be careful."

Madison nodded as she grabbed her backup cell phone from its charger on the kitchen counter and shoved it in her pocket, then hurried back toward me. "We will."

Dad held my gaze. "I'm proud of you, son."

I swallowed down the surge of emotion that brought, and nodded. "Thanks, Dad."

Madison, Dove, Foge, and I hurried into the garage.

Dove grabbed my arm. She stared up at me, seeming a little breathless. "Whatever we do from here, Rory, we do together. Okay?"

I wasn't sure if her concern was getting left behind, or me racing into danger like an idiot without her protection, but either way, with how her eyes were pleading with me, I wouldn't have been able to say no. I nodded. "Okay."

"The same goes for me," Madison said, giving me a pointed stare. "Don't you dare leave me behind. We're in this together."

I couldn't help but roll my eyes. "Of course. That's why we're all running into the garage... *together*. What did you think was happening?"

Madison huffed. "You knew what I meant, dork."

I smiled tensely at her, then pointed Dove and Foge toward my father's silver Jaguar. "That's the one."

I hit the unlock button on the keys as we all rushed toward the car, but when we reached the car doors, Madison and I both stopped and stared at each other.

"I don't think Dad has ever even let me *touch* this car before," Madison said.

"Me neither," I breathed.

Madison glanced at Foge with wide eyes. "We're about to put a *bear* in it."

That statement—and her bewildered expression as she said it—cracked right through the tension in my chest. A laugh burst out of me, and I grinned. "Think the insurance covers that?"

"Nope." Madison grinned back at me as she yanked open the door and slid into the backseat. To my surprise, Foge jumped in after her and settled himself on the other side of the backseat.

I turned to Dove. "You've got shotgun, I guess."

She tilted her head, a wrinkle of confusion between her perfect eyebrows as she stepped close, *very* close, peering up at me. "Shotgun?"

"Oh—uh—" I stammered, feeling my face heat. "I meant, you can ride up front next to me."

She stood on tiptoes—then grabbed my face and planted a gentle, lingering kiss on my cheek.

My whole body flamed as she stepped back and looked up at me. "I knew what it meant, Rory Kane." She grinned at me, and I swore my heart was about to flop right out of my chest. "I just like to tease you."

I gaped after her as she walked lightly around to her side of the car and got in, as though nothing had even happened.

I swallowed and hurried into the car, avoiding Madison's pointed and *extremely* amused stare in the rear-view mirror.

I cleared my throat, feeling Dove's gaze on me. "Which Gate first?" I asked as I started the car.

"The Gate we came through," Dove said, "and if that one doesn't work, there's another a few miles from there."

I nodded, hit the button on the visor to open the garage, and shifted into reverse. "Everybody buckle up. You know, safety first and all that—"

Dove's left hand settled on top of my right hand on the gearshift.

I startled and looked at her, but she was just facing forward with a subtle smile on her face.

A little thrill shot through me. This girl would probably be the death of me... but I suspected it would be a pleasant death.

I glanced in the rear-view mirror and saw a distinct smirk on Madison's face—and also Fogarty's narrowed feline glare, focused intently on me.

If Dove didn't become the death of me, Fogarty definitely would. Leave it to me to fall head-over-heels for a girl with magical powers and a *bear* sidekick.

And I *had* fallen head-over-heels. This girl had the power to crush my heart to powder like one of her magic flower petals. It didn't matter that it had happened crazy fast, I was a goner.

I just had to pray she'd go easy on me.

Madison leaned toward the back of my seat and whispered, "Save our friends first, *then* you can kiss her." I could hear the humor in her voice, but her words slapped me back to reality.

I cleared my throat, desperately hoping Dove hadn't heard what Madison said, and backed the car out of the garage.

As I turned the car around in the circular drive and sped down our long, private drive toward the outer gate of our property, my chest tightened. Whatever was happening between Dove and me was distracting in the best of ways, but even though Madison had been teasing, she was right—I couldn't afford to be distracted.

I pulled onto the road and sped toward the LeyGate we'd come through. While I drove, my mind spun with every possible contingency. Sevryn had said he was coming for *me*, next... a small fact I hadn't shared with the others but which now consumed my thoughts, because there was absolutely no way I was letting Sevryn near Madison again—*ever*. And though Dove and Foge could defend themselves, I hated the thought of that creep coming near Dove, either.

As useless as I might be compared to the Fae and LeyGuards, I did have *one* thing to offer: information. Sevryn knew I was having those visions. He knew I was a risk to whatever he had planned. I didn't have magic to protect my loved ones, and I couldn't compete with a Fae strength for strength. But I had something the enemy wanted—or wanted to get rid of. Either way, he was coming for me, and if I was smart, I could use that to my advantage.

I was determined to get my information to someone who could *do* something about it, even if I had to die trying—I'd already made that commitment between myself and my Maker. But Dove and Madison weren't a part of that arrangement, and if Sevryn was coming for me, then I needed to be far away from both of *them*.

I glanced over at Dove, and she squeezed my hand. I shifted my hand over hers and interlaced our fingers on the gearshift.

When she turned toward me with a smile, it stabbed like a stake into my heart—because even as I clutched her hand, I could already feel any possible future with her slipping away.

Certainty was driving itself deeper into my chest like a nail driven by a hammer: Despite my promise for us to stick together, I had to find a way to leave both Dove and Madison behind... even if they ended up hating me for it.

CHAPTER 38

DO IT OR SUFFER THE COST

Etcher/Varias

"Varias."

I shot upright on the mattress in Keyja's cottage, clutching my chest. The stabbing spasms in my heart and ribs were so intense I could hardly breathe.

I'd felt this before—the Dark King's hold. He wanted something.

"What?" I croaked it out, but it was enough. The spasms eased off, and I sucked a grateful breath through the residual pain. I hadn't ignored the Dark King's call and for now, that meant mercy enough to let me breathe.

The fact that I felt *grateful* to him for easing back his torment—even a little—made me despise myself. I was weak... but perhaps I always had been. Something, after all, had compelled me to bind myself to the Dark King in the first place. Even before I'd had a physical master, I'd been controlled by my own blind fears and desires. Now, I had a new fear: that I wouldn't live long enough to be *free*.

Freedom. It was the thing I wanted most—and the one thing I knew I could never have.

A vision of the grassy expanse near the eastern edge of the dome forced its way into my mind. He wanted me to go there, which meant there was almost certainly a messenger waiting there for me. I knew exactly whom he would have sent. Miravel. The Dark King loved jabbing his sword in and twisting it, and nobody could twist emotional weapons into a raw wound like she could.

I slid my legs over the edge of the bed and sighed. Keyja had left me here to rest. If she came back and I was missing, she would worry—but it would be worse if she saw me leaving to meet Miravel and followed. I would have to make sure Keyja was still out of sight before I headed to the barrier.

I was just heaving my sore body up from the bed when Keyja strode into the cottage.

"Oh! You're awake!" She crossed the room to set her small armful of herbs on the kitchen table, then turned to me with a smile. "Are you hungry?"

I was, but I shook my head. "I need to walk—to get some air."

Keyja removed the apron she'd been tying on and dropped it on the table. "May I join you?"

Her face was so full of affection and so *empty* of suspicion, it gutted me. She saw my expression shift, though I quickly tried to hide it.

"Varias—" She moved closer, mouth twisted in concern. "What is it?"

The truth burned like fire in my chest. I needed to tell her. I *wanted* to tell her. I stepped toward her. "Keyja, I—"

Lancing pain shot through my ribs, dropping me to my knees.

"Varias!" Keyja rushed toward me. "What's wrong?"

I couldn't even bring myself to look at her. I shoved to my knees and rushed out of the cottage.

Though I heard her yelling after me, she didn't follow… and I didn't stop running until I'd reached the eastern edge of the dome.

When I slowed, breathing heavily, I found Miravel smirking at me from the other side of the transparent barrier.

"What do you want?" I barked at her.

Her hand fluttered to her chest, and her smirk turned into an expression of mock hurt. "Varias! Is that how you would speak to an old friend? I am here on the king's business, with an important message!"

For all her games and manipulations, she *was* the Dark King's hench-woman. I had to proceed carefully. "Forgive me," I grunted out, not caring to make it sound genuine. We both knew it wasn't, but she still expected me to play the game. "What is the message?"

Her frown curled up into a grin. "They're coming, and there will be nothing you can do to save her." At her words, a dark cloud moved over the dome, dimming the sunlight.

"Varias!" Keyja's shriek sliced across the field.

I spun, and my heart stumbled in my chest.

Darklings covered the dome. Hundreds of them, clawing at the magical barrier in a frenzied mob. Several yelped and jerked back in pain—the wards Keyja had set were clearly affecting them—but more just surged in to take their place. The sound of their claws scrabbling against the dome's surface filled the air like a rush of wind through leaves.

Keyja's magic was tied to that barrier. Her strength–and Tofa's—was all that was preventing the darklings from swarming into Arcvale.

I spun back to Miravel. "Call them off!"

She tilted her head and grinned at me. "I'm afraid that's not in my power, Varias. This is in *your* hands, now."

"Keyja!" I shouted as I spun toward the cottage, suddenly desperate to find her. Where was she now? Had she run back inside?

A bolt of white-hot lightning shot up from the village courtyard in the distance, crashing into the barrier above—so she had made it there. That bolt was her and Tofa's attempt to ward off the assault.

Crackles of electricity surged over the barrier's surface, sending entire clusters of darklings flying with yelps of pain. But for every darkling that shrieked and pulled back from the dome's surface, two more flooded in.

Every claw to the dome, Keyja would *feel* it like claws down her own back. How was she even still standing?

My legs itched to run to her, but Miravel's voice pinned me to the spot. "Don't go running off yet, Varias. We still have terms to discuss."

The two LeyGuard men rushed out from the village, joining Keyja in the courtyard. One took aim with a pistol while the other called whips of flame, both ready to take down any darklings that breached when Keyja's magic failed. It wouldn't be enough.

It would never be enough.

Near the cottage, Mraugathal's branches flailed—I didn't have to hear him to see his panic.

I spun back to face Miravel. "Tell me what to do," I pleaded with her, pressing my hand to the barrier. "What does the Dark King *want* from me?"

"Your presence is required at the Hub," Miravel said, her dark eyes glinting. "The prince is heading for the Hub as we speak, and the girl is already there. They will ask you to do a ritual, and you will take things into your own hands. Understand?"

My heart turned to ash in my chest. "He wants me to kill them." If I did that even though Keyja had welcomed me in and vouched for me, even though I had reassured her that despite the LeyGuard girl's vision I intended no harm... if I betrayed Keyja like that, she would never forgive me. I would never forgive *myself*.

I straightened and clenched my jaw. "The LeyGuard are Arcvale's allies. And the young prince is Keyja's friend. I won't do it."

"You know the Dark King could kill you where you stand." Miravel's grin deepened. She was *enjoying* this.

I nodded once. "I know. Let him do it. I will not harm the prince."

Her face hardened. "Then Arcvale—and your *precious* Keyja—will fall."

My chest went cold. So *this* was the trick of the game. I was to lose, no matter what I chose.

I drew a breath. "No. There has to be another way. I'll come with you—I'll return to the Dark King. Or he can have my life, right now, if he wants. He can take it."

Miravel laughed, a cold, brittle sound. "Your life? *Obedience*, Varias. Your undying loyalty. *That* is what he wanted, and you have already failed him.

You betrayed him once before, and in your heart you have already betrayed him this second time. We both know it. Your life means little. He cares only what you can *do* for him." Her eyes narrowed into a glare. "He has told you what he requires. Do it, or suffer the cost of your betrayal."

I pressed my hands to the barrier. "Miravel, please. Is there no other way? Nothing else he wants? Why does he care so much for one fallen prince? He is no longer even Teionyr's ruler!"

Her expression hardened. "The prince and the girl must die, and *you* are the simplest way to accomplish that. But have no delusions—his desires *will* be achieved, whether through you or otherwise. You are saving no one in your refusal, only dooming that which you claim to love. Pleading does not suit you, Varias. *Do* what the Dark King has asked, or he will show no mercy here."

A cold, numb sensation flushed through me. How could I do this to Keyja, betray her in that way? But if I didn't—

"Varias!" Keyja screamed from the courtyard.

I spun toward the sound.

"What will it be, Varias?" Miravel called after me. "Whose blood will you have added to your conscience, when this night is through?"

"*Varias!*" Keyja shrieked again, her voice panicked.

I had lost the game already, but I still had one choice where Keyja could be spared.

I drew a shuddering breath, then turned back to Miravel and shoved my hand against the barrier.

As an ArcFae, the barrier responded to me, but Keyja's wards resisted me. I pressed harder, and the barrier flickered under my touch, then parted. The pain I had expected from the ward was barely a tingle, this time—Keyja's magic was already weakening. I forced myself through the rift and found myself inches from Miravel's smug face.

"A wise choice." She smiled, then flicked her wrist into the air.

The darklings launched up from the dome like a mob of frenzied vultures, then surged away into the night.

The air fell still.

"Better, my love?" Miravel cooed.

My stomach roiled as I glared at her. "If I do this, you will never speak to me again. You will leave me alone—*both* of you."

She sneered at me. "We have already made a deal, and you have yet to deliver your end. We promise no further bargains. Even *this* was a mercy you didn't deserve. Stop begging and go do what you've promised."

Rage seethed through me as I faced her. "I loathe you. I loathe you both!"

She smirked at me, eyes glinting. "More than you loathe yourself?"

I stormed away, but even once Miravel was out of sight, I could still feel her grin boring into my back... and her question boring into my heart.

CHAPTER 39

A FAE AT THE OUTER GATE

Ayla

The blaring alarm overhead finally silenced, and Doctor Harlowe ran for the archive room door. "It's responding again." He sighed in relief as the door slid open, then grabbed his tablet and tapped some buttons.

Chairman Hart's face appeared on the screen.

"We got stuck in an archive room and all the communications were blocked. What's going on out there, Meredith?" Doctor Harlowe asked her as my parents, Grandpa, and I all crowded around him to listen.

Chairman Hart looked weary and on edge. "All clear," she said, running a hand down her exhausted face. "It seems like a false alarm."

"Is that even possible?" Grandpa asked, edging closer to the tablet.

She shrugged. "Yes, but it would mean our system either malfunctioned or was hacked."

"Neither of which is good," I muttered.

"Or probable," Doctor Harlowe added, glancing at me. "We have layer upon layer of fail-safes to prevent hacks *and* malfunctions."

"Wait," I said. "Then what was all the banging? It sounded like someone was attacking the building."

Chairman Hart sighed. "Yes, well... several LeyGuards became trapped in rooms during the false alarm, and a few took it upon themselves to bust their way out."

I blinked at her face on the screen, imagining what a room would look like if a LeyGuard as strong as Brone or Striker had to break their way out of it. "Oh."

Chairman Hart sighed again. "No matter. Head to the main level, please, all of you. We're clearing all the other levels for damage inspections. Doctor Harlowe, once you've gotten them settled, please head to the meeting hall. I need to debrief all the Hub staff to see if we can figure out what caused this." Her face on the screen winked out.

Doctor Harlowe turned to the rest of us. "I'll show you to the cafeteria so you can eat while the rest of us meet. I'm sure you're all hungry."

"Thanks." I, for one, was definitely ready for some food. I was on edge and *exhausted*, and rapidly spiraling toward hangry.

Mom placed her hand on my shoulder, and we all followed Doctor Harlowe out of the archive room.

When we reached the main floor, the Hub had returned to a normal level of chaos, with busy-looking people rushing in all directions.

Doctor Harlowe pointed the way to the cafeteria. "Make yourselves comfortable. There are fountain drinks and water available, and I'll send one of the kitchen staff to set some food out for you before they head to the meeting." He turned and vanished into the mayhem.

Suddenly, I realized people *outside* the Hub might not know this was a false alarm. Jordan might still be worrying about me.

Mom, Dad, and Grandpa turned toward the cafeteria, but I waved at them to go ahead.

"I'll join you in a minute. I'm going to call Jordan and let him know we're okay."

They nodded and headed on without me.

I slipped into an out-of-sight, empty hallway, pulled out the stone, and spoke the word to activate the rune.

Jordan answered almost immediately after the rune lit up. "Ayla?" His voice was tight, worried. "What's going on? Are you safe?"

I sighed, half in relief and half in exhaustion. "Yes. Turns out it was just a false alarm."

There was a tiny pause. "A false alarm? That's... Are they sure?"

I nodded, remembering only afterward that he couldn't see me. "Yes. Chairman Hart seemed certain, though they're about to debrief everyone to figure out what caused the malfunction... or the hack. They aren't sure yet which it was."

"That's a relief," Jordan said, but his tone still sounded tense. "Listen, Ayla... When I thought you might be in danger, I wanted to come to you, I *really* did, but I—"

"It's okay," I interrupted him. "I understand. You have a kingdom, now. You're expected to be there. I'm not upset."

He breathed out a dry chuckle. "Yeah, well... I'm glad for that, but you might not be so happy when I tell you this next part."

My chest tightened. "Why? What did you do?" I tried to imagine him having a freak-out, trashing the palace in a panic, even screaming at people or something because he was stressed... but honestly, all of those were so *un*Jordan I could barely picture them.

"I... may have sent Kaizyn to come check on you," he said, sounding sheepish.

I paused. "Wait—you *what*? Kaizyn was there with you?"

Jordan laughed, a real one this time. "Oh! Yes. He and the others showed up to be there for my coronation, and... I guess we're kind of friends now. Really, Ayla, he was amazing. I couldn't have survived that ceremony without him."

A strange mix of joy and regret swirled in my chest. Jordan and Kaizyn had become friends, like I hoped. But Kaizyn—and Reina, I was guessing—had been there for Jordan's coronation, while I'd been stuck here under an attack that wasn't even a real threat. It felt like something had been robbed from me.

"Ayla?" Jordan's tone was laced with concern.

I drew a breath. "I'm sorry. I'm here. I'm really happy you and Kaizyn are becoming friends. I just wish I could have been there for you, too."

His answer was gentle. "You were the person I wanted there most. But I knew you couldn't be, just like I couldn't come to check on you when you called me. I don't blame you, Ayla. And I hope—"

"I don't blame you, either," I said quickly. Then I drew a breath. "So Kaizyn's coming *here*? How can he even get through with all the Gates locked down?"

"He's planning to use the hidden Gate by your grandfather's cabin."

"Oh." That made sense. But it was still embarrassing that an entire team of people were coming to check on me based on a panicked call I made over a *false alarm*. "Can't you catch him and tell him I'm okay? He doesn't have to come."

"He's already left, along with Callan, Reina, and Reina's parents. I won't have any way to reach him until they're through the Veil. But he'll be calling the Hub when he arrives. Their plan was to get intel before going in, just in case it *was* dangerous. I almost didn't even let him go, but I couldn't leave here, and I had to know you were okay. I made him promise not to risk his life unless you were in immediate danger, and he swore not to. Reina and the others went with him as backup. They should be contacting the Hub any minute, I'd guess."

I sucked a breath. "What about the feedback loop?" As much as I cared about Kaizyn, the thought of being stuck in that again filled me with dread.

"He says he has it under control now—enough to keep it from spiraling like before."

"And you believe him?" I felt guilty asking, but my trust in Kaizyn's control hadn't exactly been helped by our last encounter in the vault.

"I do," Jordan sounded confident. "I know it's weird, given our circumstances, but I trust him, Ayla." He chuckled again. "Besides, since it's a false alarm, maybe you can ask Chairman Hart to intercept their call when it comes in and make sure they know you're okay. He may not even have to come *to* the Hub. He can keep his distance, if it makes you feel better."

I paused. *Did* it make me feel better? I thought for a moment.

"Actually, I would kind of like to talk to Kaizyn. We have some things to clear up, after what happened before." I imagined that would be an awkward conversation, but a necessary one. "And I'd love to see Reina and Callan, too. In fact…" I paused as a tremor of anticipation settled in my chest. "Maybe I could come back *with* all of them, if the Gates are being reopened by then."

My heart sped just at the thought of that.

"Really?" I could hear the smile in Jordan's voice, which only made me more eager.

"Yes. I know we're still technically on high alert and on lockdown, but the Hub can't stay on lockdown much longer, right? When they start letting people in and out again, I'll be on the first bus out of here." I paused. "I mean—not *literally* on a bus, I don't think any buses go Faeside, but—"

Jordan laughed. "I knew what you meant. I can't even express how happy it would make me to have you here." His voice softened. "I miss you, Ayla."

I sighed, clutching the stone. "I miss you, too."

A strange alarm sounded from the speakers above, and I tensed. "Oh no. Another—"

"No," Jordan's voice said from the stone. "That's not an emergency alarm. It's the Gate access alert. Someone must be pinging one of the Gates, requesting access to get in."

"Oh. Maybe it's already Kaizyn?" Curiosity got the better of me. "Hold on a sec, I'm gonna sneak out there and see." I tucked the stone into my palm and slipped out of my quiet alcove, back into the main hall where I could see the courtyard.

Chairman Hart came rushing from another hall, her face tense. "Maddox!" she yelled. "Maddox Rogers!"

My heart lurched. Why was she calling for Grandpa?

She saw me and hurried in my direction. "Ayla, have you seen—"

Grandpa ran toward us from the direction of the cafeteria, his face tense and his gait stiff—he was still an old man, even with his powers returned. "What's wrong?"

Chairman Hart spun toward him. "There's a Fae at the outer Gate. He triggered the signal, somehow, even through the lockdown. He says he's here to help, and that you'll vouch for him."

"Kaizyn?" I asked, and they both stared at me. "I—I heard he might be coming. Or maybe Callan?"

Grandpa didn't bother to conceal his surprise at that, but Chairman Hart shook her head. "No, we would recognize either of them. This—" She took a breath. "I haven't seen one in person in years, but he looks like an ArcFae."

Grandpa and I shared a glance, then he turned back to Hart. "Show me."

Grandpa and I hurried after Chairman Hart as she led us to the security room that showed the Gate surveillance monitor.

"Yes," Grandpa breathed. "I know him. He's the ArcFae who held my secrets, the one who helped Jordan in the Teionyrian prison. We called him Etcher, though his true name is Varias."

I expected Chairman Hart to ask questions, but she only had one. "Can we trust him?"

Grandpa glanced at me. I knew we were both thinking about the ritual—and about the Dark King's possible hold on Varias.

Grandpa drew a long breath. "I believe so, though he might be... volatile."

Chairman Hart studied him for a moment. "Very well. Let's bring him in, see what he knows and how he means to help... but let's keep him in a warded room, just in case." She tapped something on her fancy watch, and one of the female Hub staff ran toward her from a nearby room.

"Yes, Chairman Hart?"

"Prepare a warded holding room and send me four armed LeyGuards," Hart said. "We have a... guest."

"Which wards?" the staff member asked.

"Every type of Fae magic."

The woman's eyes widened slightly, but she nodded and scurried off to carry out Hart's orders.

As Grandpa and Chairman Hart hurried toward the main floor where the Gate access would open, I slipped to the side of a quiet hall. "Jordan?" I whispered to the stone in my palm. But of course, when I glanced down, the rune had gone dark. Our time had run out. I tucked the stone in my pocket, planning to call Jordan back as soon as I knew for sure what was going on.

By the time the Gate was opened and Varias stepped through, enough word had spread of the unusual visitor that he had quite the audience... including my parents, who had joined Grandpa and me beside the opening Gate, Mom holding a wrapped sandwich she'd grabbed for me.

I took it from her, though my hunger was far from my mind now, and I mindlessly gripped the sandwich so tightly my fingers made dents in it.

A moment later, Varias was staring us down with an assessing glare. He was massively tall, at least a foot taller than any of the LeyGuard adults. He wore boots and loose trousers, but his torso was bare, revealing dusky skin and a muscular chest and arms. He had dark hair and dark eyes and a face that was handsome in an intimidating and not-quite-human way, kind of like Goliath from that *Gargoyles* cartoon show I'd watched as a kid. Dark wings arced from his shoulders down nearly to the floor.

Chairman Hart and her four armed LeyGuards—none of whom I recognized—intercepted him the moment the portal opened, before he could even step through.

"I do not mean to offend," Chairman Hart said, "but we have had some security concerns. We will be escorting you to a warded room the moment you enter, and you will stay there until we are certain you pose no threat. Do you object?"

Varias rolled his shoulders and glanced over Hart at the guards and the rest of the waiting crowd, many of whom were *also* LeyGuards, capable of interceding should he cause an issue. He shook his head. "I do not object. I will comply."

Hart's tense posture relaxed a bit. "Good. Then please, step inside, and we will escort you."

Varias had to stoop a little to step through the Gateway—and that was saying something, because even Striker came through those without having to stoop. He kept his long, dark wings tucked tight to his back when he straightened, which seemed like an effort in politeness, on his part, or maybe an attempt to avoid frightening us.

The four LeyGuards surrounded him on all four sides, and with Hart in the lead and myself, Grandpa, and my parents in the rear, our strange procession made its way across the courtyard and down an unfamiliar hall.

"This is the one," Chairman Hart said, opening a door toward the end of the hall.

From the doorway, the room looked a lot like the interrogation rooms they show on television, but with a plush sofa shoved against one wall and an end table with a Keurig in the corner in addition to the table and metal chairs in the middle.

Chairman Hart gestured for everyone to enter, and we all filed inside. The room became rather crowded.

Hart dismissed the guards, who shut the door behind themselves, then she settled herself down on the sofa while the rest of us stood awkwardly beside the metal table and the remaining, uncomfortable-looking chairs.

Varias' eyes swept over the room, swiftly assessing the environment. "There is no magic in this room?" he asked.

Chairman Hart nodded. "No *Fae* magic. LeyGuard magic still functions in this room."

I couldn't tell if her words were an explanation or a warning. Probably both.

Varias nodded in thought, then his gaze flicked to Grandpa. "Maddox." He tipped his head in respect. "Thank you for allowing me here."

"I vouched for you, but I didn't allow you," Grandpa said with a nod to Chairman Hart. "That was her."

Varias gave Hart the same respectful nod. "Thank you for allowing me to enter."

He turned to me. "And Ayla, it's good to see you looking so well." His voice was warm, and accompanied by a smile that seemed sincere.

"The last he saw you, you were... well, dying," Grandpa explained. "He tried to help."

"Thank you," I told him, sincerely. "For that and for what you did for Jordan and Madison." My memories of the battle in the square were *very* splotchy, but I'd heard the recount of most of what happened that day and while Jordan and Madison were imprisoned.

Varias held my gaze for a moment, still holding a friendly smile. "You're welcome." His smile faded, his expression suddenly all business. "There is a reason I have come."

"I would hope so," Grandpa muttered, but Varias ignored him, focused on me.

"I've actually come to speak with *you*, Ayla, and with the prince they call Kaizyn. Is he here?"

I paused, then shook my head. "Not yet."

Varias' gaze held mine. "So he is coming?"

I hesitated, but I couldn't think of a reason to deny it. "Yes. He should be here soon."

Varias sighed, and an expression crossed his face that almost looked like regret. "Yes—that is... that is good. I will need you both."

Chairman Hart shifted forward on the sofa. "You will need them both for *what*?"

Varias glanced at me again, then answered her. "The LeyGuard girl called Quinn informed me in Arcvale of a vision—she saw me harming the prince and Ayla."

Chairman Hart tensed and started to speak, but Grandpa gestured for her to wait.

She glared at him, but held her tongue as Varias continued.

"I believe, after hearing the description of what she saw, that I was actually performing an unbinding ritual." He looked at me. "You and the prince are bound by magic—are you not? An entwinement that equates to betrothal, according to his people's customs?"

I glanced at Grandpa, but he nodded for me to answer.

"Yes."

"And you wish to be unbound?"

That one, I answered without hesitation. "Yes."

Varias smiled. "If you can provide me with some basic Runing supplies, I can perform the ceremony this very day."

Chairman Hart glanced at Grandpa, then back to Varias. "I believe we could provide what you need."

Varias nodded. "Then we need only wait until the prince arrives."

Grandpa reached over and squeezed my hand. "Don't worry," he whispered. "I'll make sure it's all safe."

I squeezed his hand back.

Hart still looked wary, but as I fingered the communication stone in my pocket, a warm hope blossomed in my chest. With any luck, the next time I called Jordan, I would have some *amazing* news: that my bond to Kaizyn had finally been broken.

Chapter 40

A Viper Inside Your Refuge

Madison

Rory's hand hadn't left Dove's for more than a second at a time the whole last hour, though with the way Rory was clutching Dove's palm over the gear shift as he sped down the dirt road behind town now, I was sure both their hands had to be hurting.

"Up there, the woods on the right," Dove said.

The first three Gates we'd tried hadn't responded to us, and this was the last one within twenty miles.

Rory veered the car onto the grass, slinging me to the side as he took the sharp turn.

Thankfully, the seatbelt kept me from toppling into Fogarty in the backseat. He was glaring enough already.

The fact that we were off-roading in Dad's precious Jaguar wasn't lost on me, but that concern had been knocked down a few pegs from where it would usually have fallen on my worry list, landing somewhere between "Our friends might be in danger" and "I'm riding in the backseat with a glamoured Fae bear."

Rory skidded to a stop just shy of the line of trees.

I prayed my sore neck would survive the series of mild whiplashes it had sustained over the past sixty minutes.

Dove yanked her hand from Rory's and jumped out the moment the car stopped moving, then grabbed his hand again when Rory, Foge, and I joined her outside the car.

"It's right ahead," she said, pointing with her free hand at a shadowy place between the trees.

If I looked closely enough, I could see an arch-shaped section of the air shimmering—the Gate, glamoured to blend in with its surroundings.

Dove tugged Rory forward, then removed her runed stone from her pocket with her free hand and pressed it to the edge of the invisible Gate.

As we had at the previous three Gates, we held our breath and waited.

This time, the Gate surged to life after a few seconds, its edges solidifying into a stone archway. The air inside was still shimmering and translucent, showing the copse of trees behind it.

"Oh, thank goodness!" Dove dropped the stone back into her pocket and smiled at us. "They must still be monitoring this one. Now we just wait for them to respond."

A moment later, a male voice—young, like a teenager—spoke from seemingly nowhere.

"Dove?" His tone sounded as though he knew her, but it was also laced with concern. "What are you doing way out there?"

Dove stared into the archway, where I assumed they had some kind of hidden camera, or the magical equivalent. "We've been trying to contact the Hub, but no one was answering the emergency line and every Gate we tried closer to town was inactive. Please, let us in. We have an important warning—"

"If it's about an attack, we're fine. It was a false alarm," the voice answered.

Dove's face tensed. "I'm glad you're all right, but there's more. Please, Roinan. Just let us in. We need to speak with Chairman Hart."

"They told me not to—" the teen began to answer, but a woman's voice cut over his.

"Duvessa?"

Dove sighed in relief. "Chairman Hart. Yes, I'm here. Please let us in. I accompanied Rory and Madison to their home, but—"

"You were not supposed to leave the Hub. Any of you. The Hub is on *lockdown*." Her words were clipped, irritated.

Dove's brow pinched in worry. "Yes, I know, and I'll accept the consequences. But please, we need to speak with you right away. It's important."

Consequences? My stomach dropped at the thought that Dove would get in trouble because of us.

But Dove just stood, stoic in expression and bouncing slightly on her toes with impatience, waiting for Chairman Hart's decision.

"Very well," Chairman Hart said after a tense moment. "Roinan, open the Gate."

Air whooshed out at us from the archway, cold and salt-scented, then the Hub courtyard appeared through the opening. It was bustling with activity, with Chairman Hart standing just inside.

"Come in quickly. We need to seal this back," she said.

We all rushed through the Gate.

The moment it snapped shut beside us, Chairman Hart turned to Dove with an expression of concern, not the reprimanding fury I'd expected. "What is your news?"

From the way she said it, I took it that Dove didn't often cry wolf. She'd said there was a problem, and Chairman Hart was taking her seriously—thank goodness.

Dove dropped Rory's hand and wrung her fingers nervously. "Rory had a vision, one born of dark magic."

Chairman Hart glanced at him, eyebrows raised. "And?"

With what Dove had just stated, I'd expected a *much* worse response.

Rory blushed from Chairman Hart's sudden attention, but stammered out an explanation. "I—the dark magic from the Void seems to have connected me to the mind of some of the Dark King's minions. Or maybe to the Dark King himself? I—I don't understand how it works, I just—"

Chairman Hart stepped toward him, her expression turning gentle. "Sometimes none of us do. Dark magic can be tricky. It's okay, Rory. Just explain what you saw."

Her tender reaction to him honestly took me aback.

Rory drew a breath and plowed ahead. "I've been seeing two women. One's beautiful but obviously evil. The other's a squatty hag—long claws, very scary. She carries a lantern."

"That sounds like a Veil-witch, a female Veil-dearg,"a familiar voice said.

I spun to see Ayla standing to the side, gaping at us, with her grandfather close behind her.

"Ayla!" I rushed toward her, crushing her in a hug.

She laughed and returned it. "I'm okay."

When I pulled back, she smiled at me—and it was *so* good to see her looking normal again. I forced back a shudder at the memories of the battle, of what Sevryn had made me do to her. I wasn't sure I would *ever* get that out of my mind... or off my conscience. "Ayla, I'm so sorry. In Teionyr—"

She squeezed my hand. "It wasn't your fault, Madison. It's okay."

I sighed in relief, and nodded. "Thank you."

"Now, what's going on?" she asked, concerned.

Chairman Hart gestured for Rory to continue.

He drew a breath. "Anyway, I've been seeing these women in my mind—but it's like I'm really there with them, in the Void. Sometimes they see me, sometimes not, but I can watch their conversations. And this time..."

He paused as everyone stared at him in anticipation, but his eyes flicked to me. He couldn't bring himself to say it.

I met Ayla's stare. "He saw Sevryn with them." Just saying the name made my stomach clench with nausea. I swallowed it down.

Ayla gaped at me. "*What?*"

"It's true." Rory cut a worried glance at me, then turned to Ayla. "I saw him talking with the women. He's alive, I'm sure of it—he looked right at me. He knew me."

Ayla stared at him, at a loss for words.

"That's not even the worst part," Rory said. "They were talking about Kaizyn going into the Veil, that they were going to kill him. The Dark King saw me there. He told me it was already in motion, too late to stop it." He shuddered, then glanced at Chairman Hart, his expression desperate for reassurance. "But that's not possible, right? Kaizyn wouldn't be dumb enough to go back into the Veil right now. He's in Teionyr. Or maybe back in Arcvale?"

Ayla paled. "No," she said quietly. "He's on his way here... to check on me. Because I told Jordan the Hub was under attack."

Her grandfather wrapped his arms around her, pulling her close.

Ayla glanced at me, her face etched with worry. "Callan is with them. And Reina and her parents."

The pieces all crashed together in my mind, a perfect puzzle I'd never wanted assembled. "The false alarm—that must be why." I looked at Rory. "It was a trap, to bring Kaizyn here, because they knew if Ayla was in danger, he would come." My blood turned cold. "Sevryn could be waiting for Kaizyn in the Void. He could have a whole Dark Fae army, ready to ambush them."

And because of Callan's stupid, perfect, endearing loyalty, he would die before he ever let the prince be harmed. My heart plunged to my toes.

Ayla gaped at me, horror filling her eyes. "No, no, no. We have to find them. We have to warn them." She spun to look at her grandfather. "Please, we have to do something."

Chairman Hart turned to Maddox, her posture tense. "I'll assemble a—"

A beeping alarm sounded overhead.

"The Gate alert again," Chairman Hart said. She tapped something on the device on her wrist, then spoke into it. "Which Gate this time, Roinan, and who's there?"

"It's Brone and Striker!" the teen voice from before answered. "At the southeastern Gate. Quinn's with them. And a Fae woman. ArcFae, maybe? Like the other one."

"Keyja," Ayla breathed.

Her grandfather tensed, then turned to Chairman Hart. "If the Madame ArcFae *herself* is here, it can only be bad news… but I trust her completely. She poses us no threat."

Hart nodded. "Open the Gate, Roinan. Let them in."

A moment later, the brick wall behind us split open, and Brone, Striker, Quinn, and Keyja all rushed out into the Hub courtyard.

Brone turned to Chairman Hart immediately, his face somber. "We've got a problem, Meredith. A big one."

Chairman Hart gave Brone a curt nod, but turned to Keyja before answering him.

"'Dame Keyja," she said, tipping her head in respect. "You are welcome here—but please, allow me to skip the formalities." She glanced between Keyja, Brone, Striker, and Quinn. "What's going on?"

"It's about my vision—" Quinn started, at the same time Brone said, "Arcvale was attacked."

"*What?*" Ayla said, her voice climbing. "Is everyone okay?"

"We were the only ones still there," Quinn said.

"Arcvale still stands," Keyja said. "The darklings pulled back. However, the Eldervine Mraugathal witnessed something during the attack." She turned a wary stare on Chairman Hart. "Have you any other visitors here?"

"Yes," Chairman Hart said. "An ArcFae, the one called Varias. He's in a holding room."

The glowing orb in Keyja's chest crackled with electricity.

Chairman Hart flinched away.

Ayla and her grandfather exchanged a worried glance.

"You have brought a viper inside your refuge." Keyja's jaw clenched as she held Chairman Hart's gaze with a steely one. "Varias Burgild can no longer be trusted."

CHAPTER 41

THEN WHERE ARE THEY?

Madison

Everyone froze for a moment. Then Chairman Hart asked, her voice a little shaky, "Madame Keyja, what threat do you believe Varias poses to us?"

Keyja's expression shuttered. "I need to speak with him."

Chairman Hart sighed, but nodded. "Very well. I will take you to him." She started across the courtyard.

All the rest of us followed but Chairman Hart stopped, glancing at Ayla, Rory, Dove, Quinn, and me. "You six stay here."

I assumed the cat was the sixth, and from the way he glared at Hart from Dove's feet, he wasn't any more pleased with Hart's command than I was.

I opened my mouth to argue—the *last* thing I wanted right now was to be sidelined from any information that could affect Callan or my other friends—but Striker stepped forward.

"Hart, just let them come. At this point, you know they'll only get themselves into mischief if you shut them out of what's going on."

He made a really good point.

Chairman Hart glanced over us, chewing her lip, then sighed. "Fine. Come on."

She turned and led us—*all* of us, including Brone and Striker—across the courtyard and down a quiet hallway.

"This is the room here." Chairman Hart gestured to a door when we reached the far end of the hall.

This door was metal, like stainless steel, rather than the opaque glass-looking doors they'd had in the medical rooms. It had a metal doorknob and a security panel to one side.

"It's warded against Fae magic, but LeyGuard magic still works inside," Chairman Hart said.

I couldn't help but be reminded of the prison cells at Teionyr.

Keyja nodded thoughtfully, tracing her hand across the door. "*All* Fae magic, even dark magic?"

Chairman Hart studied her. "Yes."

"Good." Keyja reached for the door handle. "Is he restrained? Prevented from leaving, even if the door is opened?"

Now Chairman Hart seemed to be getting worried. "No—he's not a prisoner. Just a guest we treated with precaution."

Keyja's brow wrinkled. "That is fine. I will secure him myself. Is it unlocked?"

Chairman Hart tapped something on her wrist device, then nodded.

Keyja swung the door inward.

Varias jumped to his feet from the sofa against the far wall, but when he saw who had opened the door, he froze. "Keyja." His tone was pure terror. "You should not be here!"

Electricity snapped at the air around her chest as she stepped into the room. "Neither should *you*." Every word was stated like a slap to his face, and he reacted like he physically felt them.

His face and posture both drooped, his eyes full of sorrow. "Keyja, please, let me explain—"

But Keyja's gaze was already scanning the room, the walls, assessing something. She turned back to Hart. "I can feel the warding. When the door is closed, it seals out Fae magic completely?"

Chairman Hart nodded.

Keyja turned back to Varias. "Then I must leave Tofa in the hall. I will be vulnerable before you. Look me in the eyes, and admit you betrayed me. Admit what you have done and promise to bring no further harm to anyone here."

He glanced away.

"Are you a coward, Varias?" Keyja stepped toward him, her voice rising with anger. "Will you not own your sins, even when they are laid bare?"

When he looked back at her, his eyes were full of despair—a man truly broken. "I cannot, Keyja. I—" He stopped, his mouth gaping like a fish out of water for a moment. "I am..." Then his eyes widened. "I feel no pain. Even as I intend to speak, I feel no pain!" He spun, his gaze scanning over the walls, the floor—the door. "Come inside, close the door. Quickly, *all* of you!"

After a moment of hesitation, Keyja nodded at us, and we all crammed into the room.

"Do not move," Keyja told Varias. "I will be right back."

He nodded, looking slightly crazed.

I watched him warily, but Keyja seemed reassured.

She stepped out into the hall with the door still open, and I heard a small gasp from Chairman Hart as a bolt of lightning shot from Keyja's chest into the hallway, then rapidly expanded into a blazing, electrified bison that barely even fit in the hall.

"Stay here," Keyja told the blazing bison, then she slipped back into the room with us and shut the door.

Chairman Hart was still gaping, but she said nothing.

Keyja turned to Varias. "If you harm any—"

But Varias's crazed glare had melted, exchanged for a bright, innocent excitement. "His hold—I cannot feel it." He smiled at Keyja—actually grinning with joy. "I can speak, and he cannot stop me!"

Keyja stepped forward, studying him, while the rest of us lingered as close to the door as we could to give them space, though the room by this point was very crowded.

Keyja took his hands and peered into his eyes, her expression pleading. "Then confess your guilt, Varias, and be rid of it for good. Shed your dark secrets and be free."

He drew a shaky breath, and when his eyes locked on hers, they were full of hope. "I will tell you *everything*."

Varias talked for several minutes, hurriedly explaining his bond to the Dark King, his role in the first attack on Arcvale, his agreement with Maddox—which Ayla's grandfather himself confirmed while we all listened—his bargain with Miravel at the dome, and his agreement to kill Kaizyn and Ayla.

"I am truly sorry," he said as he finished.

We all just stared at him.

After a moment, Chairman Hart asked, "Then the Selkblood named Sevryn really is still alive?"

To my utter dismay, Varias nodded. "He is. Miravel serves him... or a form of him. As did I."

"So then *Sevryn* is the Dark King?" Rory asked.

"He is—and he is not. It is dark magic... a spell..." Varias hesitated, as though struggling to remember the name of it. "He has used it before, when orchestrating his plans from a distance. The Selkblood you know as Sevryn was perhaps several Selkbloods, operating under his control—and having taken his appearance—as the Dark King had need. Sevryn is one name he goes by, but there are others."

Ayla paled. "An avatar spell. He was controlling someone else's body."

"Yes." Varias brightened at her understanding. "It takes much power to sustain, but the Dark King *has* great power. When he knows he will be entering danger, he can use another in his place, and his own appearance transfers onto them unless he forces it otherwise. They become a…" He hesitated, looking for the words again. "… A *puppet.* That is your word for it, I believe. But the Dark King himself…" He shuddered. "He is not even a Selkblood, not fully. In his true form, he is something *other.*"

A shiver of terror shot down my spine. I'd faced Sevryn more than once, and nearly died every time. But if his true form made even this hulking ArcFae shudder…

I shoved the thought away. It was starting to make me panic.

Rory glanced over, seeming to notice, and gave my shoulder a reassuring squeeze.

Both Dove and Quinn, on Rory's other side, looked almost as unsettled as I felt.

Chairman Hart stepped forward. "And he can control *anyone,* at will?"

Varias shook his head. "No, they must agree. It requires a binding." He looked at Maddox. "I heard he used a similar spell on you, but he was not able to control you directly without your agreement, only to channel your consciousness into a form who *was* willing."

Maddox nodded.

Ayla shivered. "That form nearly killed me before it melted into goo."

Her grandfather wrapped his arm around her.

"Whatever form he takes, he has now set his sights on killing the prince," Keyja interrupted. "And *you* agreed to aid him."

Varias sighed and nodded. "I never wished to harm you," he said quickly, turning to Ayla, "or the prince. But between the choice of you, whom I hardly know, or my family—" He glanced at Keyja, regret in his eyes as she glared at him. "I am sorry. I know it was still wrong, but I am weak. Forgive me."

Tension fell over the room, then Ayla's grandfather spoke. "What of the prince himself? We have solid information saying Miravel and perhaps even the Dark King might be planning to ambush him in the Veil."

I noticed he didn't reveal Rory as his source—it would probably be awhile before *any* of us really trusted Varias again, if ever.

Varias' brow furrowed. "My instructions were to wait *here* for the prince, and to convince you to allow the ceremony. I know nothing of an ambush."

"That's good, right?" Rory asked, and I noticed he was holding Dove's hand again. "If there's no ambush, and you *aren't* planning to hurt Kaizyn and Ayla anymore... then everything will be fine, right?"

Ayla glanced at her grandfather, then at me. "Jordan said Kaizyn and the others were on the way here and should be contacting the Hub any minute... but that was over two hours ago."

"There's that weird time thing in the Veil, right?" I asked, desperately hoping for an explanation. "Maybe it's taking longer than—"

Chairman Hart shook her head. "With rifts, yes, but not with Gates. If they're using a LeyGate to come here, there should be no time distortion."

Ayla turned to her grandfather. "They were using the Gate behind your cabin. Does that have a distortion? I experienced one when the rift sucked me through near the cabin."

"You got pulled through a breach the first time, kid," Striker chimed in, leaning back against the wall. "The Gate's a different thing."

Maddox nodded. "The Gate behind my cabin is fully functional, albeit unauthorized."

Chairman Hart's gaze narrowed on Maddox. "What cabin are you all talking about?"

He gave Chairman Hart an apologetic wince. "I'll explain later."

Chairman Hart's eyes flashed with irritation, but she held her tongue.

Maddox turned back to Ayla. "Anyway, the answer is no. They shouldn't have experienced any time distortion." He glanced around at the rest of us. "Based on what Jordan said, they should be here by now, or at least have contacted us."

Another tense silence fell over the room.

My chest tightened. "Then where *are* they?"

CHAPTER 42

How Fast Can You Run?

[a couple hours earlier]

Callan

I glanced over at Kaizyn, who was striding silently through the Void beside me with Vyrthil on his other side. Kaizyn's gait was brisk, his muscles wound tight, his hand resting on his dagger as his gaze scanned the surrounding darkness.

"Expecting trouble?" I asked him.

"Always." He glanced at me, a weak smile appearing then slipping away just as quickly.

Reina and her parents followed close behind us, not saying a word.

We'd been in the Void for only a few minutes, but already it was getting to everyone. The purposeful determination we'd entered the Void with—bent on getting to the Hub as quickly as possible—was now overlaid with a strange sort of tight-wound tension.

Kaizyn and I had traversed the Void more times than I could count, and I'd never seen him this on edge. I suspected it had less to do with the Void around us and more with what was *ahead* of us—what we might find at the Hub.

My gut clenched with worry for Madison, again, but I shoved it back. To be honest, between my fear for Madison's safety and my eagerness to see her again, I was as much a mess of tension as Kaizyn was, I just seemed to be better at hiding it.

Kaizyn's tension, however, was likely also because of what we certainly *would* find at the Hub, even once the danger of an attack was past: Ayla.

Funny how our entire reason for coming was also the one thing that could make Kaizyn want to run away. I'd never seen him run from anything, until that moment in the vault with Jordan. My heart still ached for him just thinking about it... though he did seem to be doing better, now.

I couldn't help but wonder if that had something to do with Reina.

I had my doubts whether Kaizyn's control could prevent another mishap for him and Ayla once he was in close range again, and for all his stated confidence, I suspected he did too. But whatever happened, he would not be alone. Once we reached the Hub, Kaizyn would have more than enough skilled LeyGuards and resources on hand to counteract the effects of a feedback loop. The *awkwardness* created by the bond, on the other hand, no one could protect Kaizyn from—and in light of whatever was developing between him and Reina, I suspected that was a large factor in his tension.

I glanced over at Kaizyn again.

"Speak your mind, Callan," he said, cutting his eyes to me with a smirk. "I can feel your stare on the side of my head."

I couldn't voice what I'd been thinking, not with Reina right behind us, so I just smiled back. "Just analyzing your innermost thoughts, as usual. Have to be certain you aren't about to do something stupid."

At that, Kaizyn laughed. "Sometimes you're more like a worried parent than a guard my own age. I'm not a child, Callan. You can relax."

"Then why were you assigned *babysitters*?" Reina muttered from behind us.

Kaizyn's eyes widened, then narrowed as his good-humored expression flipped into a scowl.

I fought back a chuckle, but when I glanced back at Reina, her gaze was down on her boots.

Her parents met my eyes as I looked back, but said nothing.

We plodded ahead.

A few moments later, Kaizyn sighed and turned to me. "I know Madison is also at the Hub. I'm sure you're worried for her. Forgive me for making this all about Ayla and myself."

I opened my mouth to assure Kaizyn I'd taken no offense, but he continued.

"I know how much Madison means to you. We won't leave the Hub until we've confirmed her safety, too, Callan. You have my word."

I gave him a nod. "Thank you."

From the corner of my eye, I caught Reina studying Kaizyn's face intently, but when she noticed me looking, she glanced away.

Kaizyn retreated back into himself, and a tight silence settled back over us.

At this point, I almost would have welcomed an attack from a low-level Void-monster, just to break the tension.

"We're almost to the Gate that leads to the cabin," I said, mostly to fill the awkward silence. But as I said it, an unease filled me at how *quiet* things had been in the Void. We hadn't spotted a single creature, even though we'd made little attempt to be stealthy. I glanced at Kaizyn. "We should've encountered something by now."

Kaizyn met my glance, his expression wary. "You're right." His eyes skimmed the darkness, then he gestured to Vyrthil, who sidled up closer to him with ears perked and muscles taut. "The Dark Fae have seen us use this Gate before. There's a chance they're waiting for us near the opening." He glanced back at Reina and her parents. "Stay alert."

Reina cut him an annoyed glance. "We're *always* al—" She gasped. "Kaizyn, watch out!"

She lunged toward him just as a blinding light exploded the darkness.

A hot wave of energy knocked me backward, crashing me to the ground.

I shoved immediately back to my feet, but my vision was still splotched and blurry from the flash. My head throbbed. My ears were ringing.

A yowl of pain sliced through the Void. *Vyrthil.*

"Kaizyn!" I shouted, forcing my eyes to focus through the blur. "Kaizyn!"

There was no answer.

I spun, pulse racing. "Reina?"

"Callan." Her voice was breathy, weak—and coming from the ground. I dropped to my knees, finding her as my vision finally began to clear.

She was just trying to sit up, clutching her head. Blood trickled down through her fingers from a small gash on her forehead, though it seemed to be slowing already. There was more blood on a dark rock on the ground beside her, where she'd hit her head.

Her parents were pushing up from the ground nearby, where they'd obviously been knocked back, too.

"Are you okay?" I grabbed Reina's hand, helping her sit.

When she nodded, I drew a quick breath of relief.

"What happened?" I tried to keep my voice gentle as Reina wiped her bloody hands on her pants. "Where's Kaizyn?"

Then I spotted Vyrthil, his glow flickering as he lay on his side gasping heavy breaths on the ground a few paces away.

I rushed over to him and ran my hand down his heaving side. He yelped as my hand passed his ribs. Something was injured, possibly broken.

My panic mounted. "Kaizyn!" I yelled again, but he was nowhere in sight.

"We shouldn't stay here." Reina's dad hurried up beside me and carefully hefted Vyrthil up into his arms.

I winced as Vyrthil let out another whimper of pain.

Reina's dad swayed a bit under Vyrthil's weight as he stood—Vyrthil had to weigh close to two hundred pounds—but managed to keep him steady.

I spun to Reina as her mom helped her to her feet. "You said *watch out. What did you see? Where's Kaizyn?*"

Reina's dazed stare transformed into a scowl. "A crazy-looking Fae woman threw some kind of lightbomb at us and took him."

I stared at her, my anxiety mounting. "A *lightbomb?* Dark Fae can open rifts, but—"

"Okay, whatever, but she *took* him!" Reina flailed her hands, glaring at me.

Reina's jaw clenched as fear passed between our gazes.

Reina's mom moved close, placing a hand on her shoulder. "Don't worry, honey," she whispered. "We'll get him back."

Reina's arms wrapped tight around her stomach as she stared at me. "What do we do now? Where would the Dark Fae take him?"

I started to pace. "I—I don't—" My pulse raced. If they flashed into the Void like that, they could've flashed back out *anywhere.*

"Maybe we should continue to the Hub and get help," Reina's mom suggested.

"What help? They're under attack too!" Reina shouted.

But I was already shaking my head. "We have to act quickly. The Hub would take too—" My gaze caught on Vyrthil and I stopped. "They're bonded. Vyrthil can sense him."

Reina's mom glanced at the slumped animal her husband held. "He doesn't look up to that."

I hurried toward Vyrthil's face. "Kaizyn is the one best skilled to mend Vyrthil, too. He's a gifted healer. But if we don't find him…" I couldn't finish that statement, because the thought that we might already be too late wasn't something I could bear.

Vyrthil's large eyes flicked up to me, clouded with pain, but when they locked on mine, he surged bright for a moment.

I wasn't as skilled as Kaizyn at interpreting Vyrthil's thoughts, but I'd known the fire-cat for years and I could read the determination in his eyes.

I looked up at the others, clutching my small thread of hope. "Put him down. He can do it."

Reina's dad lowered Vyrthil gently, steadying him as all four paws hit the ground.

Vyrthil staggered and flinched, then took one cautious step—and then another. His steps evened out, his speed increasing as he paced the darkness, sniffing at the ground, though I could tell he was still in pain.

Reina ran up next to Vyrthil, watching his every move.

Vyrthil sniffed at the air, ears perked, then spun to the right. He glanced back at me, flaring bright again.

"We've got our direction," I said, moving to Vyrthil's other side. I turned to look at the others. "Get ready for a fight."

Reina's parents stepped up behind us. They still looked banged up, but Reina's mom was already dual-wielding a pair of glinting knives she'd pulled from somewhere. Reina's dad drew his sword from its sheath, flames crackling over his knuckles.

"Oh, we're ready," Reina's dad said.

Fury glinted in Reina's eyes as she clutched her dagger. "Let's go."

I drew out my own dagger, then turned to Vyrthil. "How fast can you run?"

Vyrthil flared bright and chuffed, then shot off into the darkness.

The four of us took off after him.

CHAPTER 43

A DEAD MAN

Kaizyn

I woke to a fierce throbbing in my head and leather bindings across my arms and legs, holding me to a table.

"He wakes," a female voice cooed.

I winced my eyes all the way open and found a woman staring at me—a breathtakingly beautiful one, if you ignored the glint of feverish evil in her eyes. Hers were the eyes of a woman about to inflict pain... and enjoy it.

I suppressed a shiver, trying to get my bearings. "Why did you bring me here?"

As she leaned in, I glanced around. We were still in the Void. The sheer, dark emptiness made that plain. But it wasn't a part I recognized, and the table I was strapped to seemed hastily constructed—the boards beneath me were uneven, the tops of half-hammered nails poking into my back and legs. I was relieved to find I was alone—that meant the others had likely escaped. At least, that's what I told myself. The other possibility was maddening.

The woman's face stopped inches from mine. "He *said* you would be trouble. The mighty Prince Kaizyn. We had plans upon plans to be sure we caught you." Her breath was warm on my face, and sweet, but with a bitter tinge beneath. Her full lips crept up into a grin. "In the end, though, you weren't much trouble at all."

"In the end of what?" I held her gaze as I flexed my wrists and ankles. There was no give—no way I was breaking out of these binds, unless I could burn them. I sent a surge of my power down through my wrists and ankles, but my magic fizzled the moment it touched the bindings. Were they *warded*? My pulse quickened. "What do you want from me?"

Her smile deepened. "Such a handsome, little pet." She trailed a cold finger down the side of my face, making my skin crawl. "It's almost a pity you got caught up in this. If it weren't for that girl and your bond, you may have survived this war." She frowned, seeming genuinely bothered. Then she pulled back and shrugged. "Ah, well. Fate has its way, and all that."

Understanding dawned on me. "You work for the Dark King."

She grinned at me, but there was a sinister edge to it. "What was your first clue?"

I wanted to say *the sadistic gleam in your eyes*, but I held my tongue. "Why does he want me? Is this about my kingdom?" Not that it was really *mine*, anymore—unless something had happened to Jordan. My stomach clenched.

She laughed. "Of course it is... in part. But we both already knew that, no?"

I held my voice even. "Why me? I'm not the king."

She stroked a piece of hair off my forehead, and I suppressed another shudder of revulsion. "Are you worried for him, the new king?" She pulled back and smirked at me, her eyes glinting with amusement. "How *precious*."

It was wildly disconcerting, how easily she seemed to read me. And all her answers were non-answers, not that I was surprised. I would have to be clever, goad her into answering my questions. Everyone wanted *something*—I just had to pinpoint her weakness, and leverage it.

"What's in this for you? Why are you doing this?"

Her mouth twitched with another smirk. "Does this usually work for you? This blunt manipulation?" She leaned in. "I am not a brainless beauty, my pet." Her breath was hot on my ear, and another shudder of revulsion raced down my spine. "*I* am the whole package."

She straightened suddenly, peering over my head. "Finally, my tools! I'd begun to think you abandoned me."

"I'm not your pack mule," a croaky voice snapped, then a squat, ugly Veil-witch came into view, one arm weighed down by the strap of a heavy satchel while the other held a lantern. "Next time, you bring your *own* tools." She scowled at the other woman, her warty eyebrows drawn down in irritation.

Tools. This was starting to sound very unpleasant.

My memories of the attack were fuzzy, but from what I remembered, she'd ambushed me through a breach. The dark magic implications of that were unsettling, but even more so... if this woman was breach-traveling in the Veil, there would be little way for Callan and the others to track me. I was on my own here—tied to a table without use of my magic, a crazy woman and a Veil-witch preparing to torture me or worse.

As bad days went, this one was rising to the top.

A movement to my left caught my attention—a glint from the darkness a few spans away, like from something metal... or someone holding a knife. Had someone found me, after all?

I forced my eyes away from it, hoping the woman hadn't noticed my glance.

She hadn't. She was too busy rolling her eyes at the Veil-witch, who had shuffled up next to her at the table.

"Just hand me the supplies so we can get started," the woman snapped. "We've waited long e—"

A flaming, snarling fire-cat smashed into the woman, toppling both her and the Veil-witch to the ground.

I'd never been so happy to see Vyrthil in my life.

"Hold still, I think I can cut these!" someone said, tugging on the bind across my left wrist.

I turned and found a pair of green eyes peering down at my arm.

My heart lurched. "Reina."

Callan flashed by the foot of the table, diving into the fray with Vyrthil.

The woman and the Veil-witch made some *very* unhappy noises from the ground, just out of my sight.

There was a hiss and a series of thumps.

A glance beyond my feet confirmed the shouting had attracted some kind of Void lizard, but Reina's parents were already making quick work of it a few yards away.

Reina yanked out a dagger, pulling my attention back to her. "Hold still. I'll have to slide the blade under the strap and pull."

"Reina." Now that I'd turned back to look at her, I couldn't seem to look away. "You came for me."

She rolled her eyes. "Of course we did—did you think we wouldn't?" Her gaze locked on mine for a moment, and when she saw that I'd honestly thought they wouldn't, she rolled her eyes again, though the corner of her mouth twitched up slightly. "Idiot."

She yanked her knife across the binding, and my wrist popped free. "Now the other ones."

I pulled my hand loose, flexing it, as she moved down to my feet.

When she'd freed my ankles, I sat up, angled awkwardly since my right wrist was still strapped to the table, and peered down.

Callan had the Veil-witch pinned to the ground.

She was snapping her teeth at him, trying to bite him, but he had one forearm pressed to her forehead, keeping her teeth out of range of the rest of him.

He glanced up at me. "You all right?"

I nodded, then yanked my spare knife from my ankle and cut my last binding as Reina moved around the table.

"Where'd that other woman go?" she asked as her parents joined us, wiping sticky black goo from their weapons.

I'd been wondering the same thing. But also—"Where's Vyrthil?" I knew he was nearby, but the bond felt muted. I couldn't pinpoint in which direction he had gone.

Reina paled. "He's hurt," she said. "He seemed okay on the way here, but if anything attac—"

A sharp yowl pierced the darkness in the distance. *Vyrthil.*

I was on my feet and running before I even realized what I was doing.

"Kaizyn!" Callan yelled. He ran after me, but though he was fast, I always had him beat in speed.

He caught up to me just as I rounded a large, black rock. "I was sure the sound came from—"

The shadows behind the rock roiled, then rose from the ground. Dozens of glinting yellow eyes flicked toward us in the darkness. *Darklings.* A small horde of them.

I spun to Callan. "Run!"

The mob rose in a frenzied flutter of wings and surged toward us.

We made it a dozen steps or so away before I glanced back... and caught a glint of orange flickering on the ground the mob had abandoned. My heart sank. *Vyrthil.*

I spun back. "Cover me!"

"Are you crazy?!" Callan yelled, but he dove in, slicing down the first few darklings, then shooting a stream of fire as more lunged toward us.

I dodged around the mob of darklings, who were now fully distracted by Callan's dramatic display—but I wasn't quick enough. A few of them glimpsed me and launched off from the rest, rocketing after me as I ran.

Ahead, Vyrthil's flame surged then flickered out again. Shadows swarmed over him. His flame surged again, then waned. He was trying to protect himself... but weakening.

I'm coming, I thought, pushing my legs faster.

A flash of red hair appeared beside me. "What are we doing?" Reina asked, already breathless from catching up to me.

"Vyrthil." I nodded ahead, then spun back to char a couple darklings just behind us.

Reina glanced in front of us, where dark shadows still roiled, lunging in at Vyrthil, lurching back each time his magic flared, then lunging in again.

She nodded, not even questioning. "Grab him. I'll cover you." Flames crackled from her hands as she drew daggers from sheaths at her hip and thigh, all without missing a step.

A strange fondness surged up in my chest, but I shoved it down—now wasn't the time for fancies.

I nodded back, then channeled my magic into churning bonfires in my palms. "I'm going in." I dove for the mob—

And smashed head-first into the woman from before.

"Uh-uh-uh," she chided, shaking her head as something invisible clamped around my throat, hauling me up until my feet dangled just above the ground.

Dark magic. It churned across my throat and raced down my arms, making my flames sputter and wane.

I struggled to breathe, and to make sense of the woman's sudden presence—she'd come out of nowhere.

Vyrthil still writhed on the ground behind her, guarded by a small group of darklings.

But—*Reina.* Where was she?

A flash of red hair dove across, knocking the woman to the ground.

The dark magic released me.

I rushed forward, shooting out a surge of flame to dispose of the last of the darklings around Vyrthil—just as Reina punched the woman square in the face, knocking her out cold.

Reina glanced up at me as she stood, and grinned. "I think I took her by surprise."

I pulled her toward me and pressed my lips to hers.

The world seemed to stop. A quick breath passed, and there was only *this*, this beautiful, brave woman in my arms, the press of her soft lips to mine, the feel of my hands in her hair—then I realized what I'd done.

I yanked back. "I'm sorry. I'm so, so sorry." Horror filled me as she backed away and stared at me, eyes wide, shock painting her face. "I'm *so* sorry. I didn't—I mean—I—"

I had no excuse. I'd kissed her. I'd *kissed* her—I could still feel the warmth of her lips.

Oh, heavens above, I'd kissed her. I was a dead man. If my life wasn't tied to her friend's, she'd probably have killed me already.

And yet—

She was still just staring at me.

I took a tentative step toward her. "Reina?"

Footsteps sounded, then Callan rushed up. "Are you all okay?" He glanced at the woman on the ground, then at Vyrthil, then back to the two of us. "You knocked her out?"

"Reina did," I said, still watching her.

"My parents had the Veil-witch. Have to go check," she said suddenly, then ran off.

Callan stared at me. "She's acting weird."

I drew a breath. "Yes."

I hurried past the unconscious woman, then scooped Vyrthil into my arms and stood.

Callan's eyes tracked me. "Are we going to talk about why?"

I shook my head. "No."

A sly smirk appeared on his face. "Right. Of course not." Then he neared Vyrthil, and his smirk slipped away. "Is he okay?"

I glanced down at Vyrthil. He was unconscious, breathing shallowly. Our bond was muted, but steady. My chest tightened. "I hope so. I need to get him somewhere safe so I can check further."

Callan nodded. "We passed the Gate as Vyrthil tracked you here. It isn't far." He glanced over at the unconscious woman. "Do you think we should try to take her for ques—"

She vanished right in front of us.

Callan turned back to me, eyes wide.

I shuddered, clutching Vyrthil tight. "I've officially had *enough* of the Void for one day. Let's get out of here."

CHAPTER 44

STUPID HORMONES

Reina

My parents glanced up from the unconscious Veil-witch as I approached. Mom scanned my face in concern.

"What happened? The prince—"

"He's fine." I waved off her worries. "He and Callan are with the other woman. I knocked her out." Even through the whirlwind happening in my mind, a smug smile tugged at my lips. It didn't last long, though, and my parents noticed.

Dad stepped closer. "Then why do you look so..." He trailed off, gesturing vaguely to my face.

I sighed. "He kissed me." I couldn't quite meet their eyes as I said it.

Mom let out a little gasp. "*Kaizyn?*"

"No, Mom, Callan." I rolled my eyes as her mouth dropped open. "I'm kidding. Of course it was Kaizyn. But—" I stopped, not sure what I had been meaning to say. Perhaps, *I thought he hated me?* Or *What kind of weirdo kisses someone when they've just punched an evil henchwoman out cold?*

"Reina," my dad said, lowering his voice. "Are you... okay with this? Did he do this against your will? Do I need to—"

"No, Dad." I hurried toward him, eyes wide. "*Please* don't confront him about anything. He was sweet—he even apologized. I mean, to be honest, I don't think he *meant* to kiss me." At my parents' confused stares,

I hurried to continue. "But it wasn't creepy or anything, it was actually kind of—well, I mean, it *might* have been kind of—if it wasn't right in the middle of—" I stuttered myself to a stop.

How *did* I feel about the kiss? Objectively, I should've been shocked, and I had been. But not exactly the *bad* kind of shock. Just... shocked. And, honestly, I'd kissed him *back*. I probably would've *kept* kissing him back, had he not pulled away.

...Not that I wanted to tell my parents that.

My dad's brow furrowed. "You're doing that half-sentence thing again. What exactly are you saying?"

I drew a deep breath. "Just—no. No, don't confront him. It was fine. The kiss was... fine."

Translation: I was kissed by a boy who was in love with my friend, and I'd kissed him back, and for a moment, I'd felt my heart soar as if it actually could *mean* something. For a moment, I'd been swept away. I'd let myself dream.

But I knew better than that. Dreams were dangerous.

My parents' silence drew my gaze back to them. "What?"

They were both just staring at me.

My mom's mouth slowly curved up into a smirk. "I don't mean to say I told you so..."

Dad's smile joined hers, and they shared a victorious side-glance. "He *was* flirting in Arcvale. We were right."

"Ugh." I groaned and dropped my head back in frustration.

Yes, Kaizyn was hot and sweet and basically every girl's ideal faerie-tale prince. Literally. But he was *also* a pain in my butt, seriously moody, and *in love with Ayla.* No way I could go down that path. I knew too well how much it hurt.

I straightened as footsteps approached. "Not a word about this in front of them. *Please,*" I hissed, glancing between my parents' faces.

My dad did that old-school *key locking his mouth* motion, and my mom just nodded.

"Of course, honey," she said. "Not a word." But the glint in her eyes was so intense it may as well have been a billboard screaming *Juicy Secrets Here.*

Please, don't let them humiliate me, I prayed as the footsteps drew closer.

Kaizyn and Callan appeared from around a dark boulder.

My heart did a nervous skip at the sight of Kaizyn, and I immediately chided myself. One kiss, and I was a stupid Disney princess wannabe. *Focus, Reina. You know better.*

But at the sight of Vyrthil draped limply in Kaizyn's arms, my angst about the kiss sank to the back of my mind.

"Oh, no. How is he?" I asked, hurrying toward them.

Kaizyn gave me a quick glance, then shifted his feet awkwardly and avoided eye contact, staring somewhere past my shoulder. "Okay, I hope. We need to get somewhere safe so I can examine him."

Callan was watching me closely, but his expression looked more confused and curious than anything else. Had Kaizyn not told him what happened?

And if not... was that because he regretted it?

The last little flicker of girlish hope I'd still been harboring in my chest curled in on itself like a wilting fern. Maybe Kaizyn had only kissed me out of relief that I'd freed him from that woman. Maybe he hadn't meant to kiss me at all, or hadn't really *wanted* to.

I'd known better—I'd *warned* myself! But being right still stung.

I sighed, looking away. "Okay. Let's hurry, then." I'd been ignoring the creep-factor of this place pretty well, but suddenly the darkness of the Void made my skin crawl, and I was eager to get out of it.

Callan nodded. "Follow me. The Gate isn't far."

Kaizyn fell silently into step behind my parents and me as Callan led the way to the Gate.

We emerged into the woods behind Maddox Rogers' cabin a few minutes later. The back of the cabin was blackened with soot, the plants and ground behind it all charred.

"What happened here?" I asked, but a sequence of shrugs and head shakes confirmed no one knew.

Callan glanced around, then turned to the rest of us. "You all stay here. Let me go make sure things are clear."

I started to argue, but my mission from Jordan was to protect Kaizyn, and he was burdened with an injured fire-cat, so I nodded. It was better for my parents and me to stay with our charge.

Callan slipped away, and a few moments later, came back looking relaxed. "All clear. We're only a half-mile from the nearest access point. Last I checked, the Hub was actively watching that one. Let's hope they still are."

"Let's hope they're still *standing*," I muttered.

"Reina!" my mom chided.

I cut a glance at her. "I mean, we're all thinking it, aren't we?" My chest clenched as the anxiety I'd driven to the background reared up in full force. It had been easy enough to forget my worries when we were rescuing Kaizyn—and when he was *kissing* me—but with those removed, the reality of what had brought us on this trip loomed over me like a menacing shadow. "We came here for a distress call. What if…"

My mom shook her head. "No *what ifs*. We'll get to the Gate, assess the situation, then decide from there, as we always do. No sense worrying about what hasn't happened yet."

"But Ayla was in trouble. And it took us *so long* to get here—" My panic was mounting now, hard to control.

"Reina." Kaizyn's calm voice stopped my downward spiral in its tracks. "Look at me."

I forced my eyes to his, and his gaze was steady—confident—and full of compassion in a way that made my heart twist.

Stupid heart. Focus.

Kaizyn held my gaze. "Ayla is okay, because *I'm* okay. If anything had happened to her, you would know it for sure." A humorless laugh escaped him. "Anyway, if she's fine, then the Hub is most likely fine, too. We just need to get there, and see how we can help. Okay?"

I drew a breath, feeling my face heat as my mind came down from its anxious ramp-up. "Right. Okay. I'm sorry. I don't usually do that. The freakout, I mean. It's just—"

"It's just that they're your friends, basically your extended family. We all understand. It's okay." Kaizyn's voice was gentle, and his gaze held mine intensely. *So* intensely that it became painful after a moment.

I tore my gaze away, pointedly not looking at him.

I heard Kaizyn draw a slow breath.

I was feeling *mega* awkward, but I knew he didn't deserve my snub... even if he *had* accidentally kissed me. I forced my eyes back to him. "Thanks," I muttered. "For understanding."

"You're welcome." His mouth ticked up into a half-smile, and my heart sped again.

Stupid hormones. I could reason that Kaizyn was bad news for me all day, but my chest still responded to his ridiculously charming face while he just stood there, looking all calm. How was that even fair?

I felt my face flush, and the others—including my *parents*—just stared at us, like we were a teenage soap opera and they were dying to see the rest of the episode.

Jerks.

I drew a sharp breath, shaking off the humiliation and the flood of stupid hormones that had that kiss replaying in my mind. "Shouldn't we take a minute for you to check Vyrthil?" I asked Kaizyn, my tone all business. Possibly *too* business, because as my mother's eyes widened, I realized how harsh my tone sounded against the caring one Kaizyn had just used with me.

Kaizyn didn't seem offended. He just shook his head. "I'd rather get him into the Hub, where I'm sure it's safe... if you think they'll let us in?" He addressed this last part to both my parents and me, glancing between us with a worried frown.

My mom smiled gently and moved closer, placing a hand on his shoulder. "Don't worry, Sweetheart. There may be a complicated history between the LeyGuard and the Fae, but Teionyr has always been our ally. It's the Dark Fae we're worried about. The Hub shouldn't have any issues letting you in. You're with us, plus they know who you are."

His eyes widened slightly. "They do?" Then he blushed. "Of course, they do. Callan would have told them about me, and my situation with Ayla—"

His eyes flicked to me when he said her name, then he stopped cold.

I waited for him to continue his sentence, but he just... didn't.

An awkward silence landed on us, and suddenly the air felt as grating as an itchy sweater.

When we all realized Kaizyn still wasn't going to finish his statement, Callan cleared his throat.

"Okay... right," Callan said. "I'll stay by Kaizyn, and you three lead the way. If the Hub surveillance team *doesn't* immediately recognize us, it'll be best for LeyGuards to be the first ones they spot, rather than a couple of Fae and a giant cat."

We reached the Hub Gate a few minutes later.

As soon as my mother activated it, the Hub responded.

"Recon Team 1—*thank goodness*!" The voice belonged to Roinan, a LeyGuard about my age who often worked the comms and surveillance rooms. His voice was tense, but he didn't give us a chance to ask about the status of things at the Hub. "Chairman Hart said to let you in immediately when you arrived. Opening the Gate now!"

My stomach clenched as I prepared to face whatever awaited us.

Chapter 45

The Dark King Dated My Sister

Reina

As soon as the Gate opened and the cool, salt-scented air of the Hub hit us, we could see things were business as usual. Or at least as *business as usual* as they could be with everyone surreptitiously staring at the Fae and fire-cat we'd brought with us.

We stepped inside, the Gate snapping shut behind us.

Chairman Hart came hurrying across the courtyard, Ayla and her parents and Maddox in tow.

I saw Kaizyn tense behind me, and felt a wave of sympathy for him. In addition to his awkward bond with Ayla, I was pretty sure he'd never been Earthside. This was all completely new to him, with no assurance yet of whom he could trust here or how he would be received. He probably felt as out of place as I had at first in Teionyr.

I turned to reassure him as Hart approached my parents, but Ayla forewent all the formalities and rushed toward me, wrapping me in a hug. "Jordan said you were coming, but when it took so long—I'm just *so* glad you're okay!"

Relief filled me. Despite all the weirdness between us, Ayla was still one of my two best friends in the world. It wasn't her fault the guys I liked kept falling for her, at least not entirely. It wasn't like she did it on purpose. She was Ayla—she would never hurt me *on purpose.*

I shoved all thoughts of guys away and hugged my friend tight, focusing on how very *Ayla* she smelled, a blend of lavender and mint. The Hub must've gotten her usual shampoo.

I, on the other hand, probably reeked of sweat and charred darklings, but Ayla said nothing of it. Because keeping insulting comments to herself was *also* so very Ayla. Jordan would've just told me I stank.

"And you're okay, too?" I pulled away from the hug to look at her. "The attack—you weren't hurt?"

"The attack was a false alarm," Chairman Hart interjected.

Ayla smiled at me, nodding, though she blushed a bit. "I'm sorry for startling everyone. We're still not sure what happened, but no one was injured. Well, maybe a door or two upstairs didn't survive, though. Apparently some LeyGuards got trapped in a room and busted out." She grinned as she said the last part, clearly amused. Then she glanced nervously at Kaizyn. "I'm glad you're okay, too."

"The same to you," he answered.

Their gazes lingered on each other.

Ayla's face grew puzzled for a moment, but then she shook it off and turned to Callan. "And you, as well. I'm glad you're all okay." She turned to my parents with a smile. "And you too, of course, Mr. and Mrs. Fisher. I'm just really glad you're *all* okay."

"Thank you, Ayla," my dad said, smiling. "So are we."

Ayla stiffened. "I realize what's bothering me now!" she said, turning to Kaizyn. "I still feel you, but it's different. It's not as..."

"Intense?" Kaizyn offered, meeting her gaze.

Ayla smiled. "Yes. It's muted. Does that mean—"

My parents, Maddox, and Hart were watching their exchange with interest.

Kaizyn shook his head. "We're still entwined. I've just... Well, to be honest, I couldn't know for sure that it would work until I got here, but I've been working on controlling my end of things, to prevent what happened last time. It seems to be working." The last phrase ticked up at the end, almost like a question.

Ayla gave him a warm smile. "Yes. It seems to be working." She fell silent for a moment, studying his face. "But, there's also—"

His eyes cut sharply to hers, his expression alarmed.

For a breath, their gazes locked, some kind of unspoken message passing between them.

Ayla's gaze flicked to me for a second, and I thought I saw Kaizyn give a minute shake of his head—but then in a blink, they were both back to normal, and I wondered if I'd just imagined it.

"Yes, it's working," Ayla repeated, smiling warmly.

Before I could ponder further what I'd just witnessed, Ayla rushed forward, bending over Vyrthil.

"I can feel your worry for him." She pulled back, looking at Kaizyn. "Is he okay? What happened?"

"He's..." Kaizyn's voice trailed off into uncertainty as he stared down at Vyrthil's face. "Honestly, I'm not sure. He hasn't woken since I picked him up."

Vyrthil was a large animal, and I was certain Kaizyn's arms must've been getting tired, but he still held him protectively, cradled close to his chest.

"We were attacked," Callan explained to Ayla and the others. "The prince was taken by Dark Fae"—there was a collective gasp at this—"and Vyrthil was injured. He managed to lead us to Kaizyn, but Kaizyn was being held by a Veil-witch and a woman who commanded a horde of darklings. The darklings attacked Vyrthil again while we were rescuing him."

"He's Kaizyn's sear-bind," I added, looking at Chairman Hart.

Chairman Hart's eyes widened, then she turned to Kaizyn. "What can we do to help? We don't have anyone qualified in his species, but whatever resources we do have, they're yours."

"Thank you," Kaizyn sighed, sounding immensely relieved. "I need to examine him. Is there a medical room I could use, or—"

Doctor Harlowe rushed up. "It really is a fire-cat," he breathed in awe, then his eyes snapped to Kaizyn's. "Absolutely. Come with me. I'll get you whatever you need."

"You can trust him," I heard Callan whisper near Kaizyn, though he kept his voice low enough that no one else could hear.

Kaizyn gave Doctor Harlowe a nod. "Yes, please. Thank you."

Kaizyn and Callan hurried off after Doctor Harlowe, but when I turned to follow them, Ayla grabbed my arm.

"We need to talk," she said softly.

I tensed, my first thought going to the kiss—but of course, it wasn't about that. She didn't even *know* about that.

Chairman Hart and Ayla's grandfather were both watching us, and neither of them looked surprised or even curious.

Whatever she had to say, they already knew it.

I glanced at my parents, then back to Ayla. "What is it?"

Ayla chewed her lip nervously. "Well, there's an ArcFae here who thinks he can break the bond between Kaizyn and me, the same one who was at the battle in Teionyr…"

"Etcher's here?" I smiled. "That's great! He was with us in Arcvale. He's Keyja's friend." My smile slipped as I noticed Ayla's expression. "You don't seem like it's great. Why is it not great?"

She winced. "He *might* also be working for the Dark King."

I stared at her. "What?"

"She means he's *definitely* been working for the Dark King, we just don't know yet if we can trust him now," Maddox clarified.

My parents and I all tensed, but Chairman Hart hurried to reassure us. "We currently have him held in a warded room, and he's also being supervised by the Madame ArcFae and her striniak."

"Keyja and Tofa are *here*?" I spat. "Why isn't she in Arcvale?" Unless the Hub's Fae Culture textbooks were very, very wrong, the striniak and the Madame ArcFae *never* strayed far from their domed village… or at least, they weren't supposed to.

Chairman Hart drew a sharp breath. "There was an incident in Arcvale. The darklings—"

My chest clenched. "Quinn was there. And Brone, and Striker."

"They're all right." Hart smiled, though it was brittle. "They are all unharmed, though the dome was severely damaged."

My heart sank. The dome. Keyja's *home*. "What will they do now?"

"They'll stay here until they can repair it," Maddox said, glancing at Hart. "Right?"

"Yes," Hart said. "They are our allies, and we will provide refuge for as long as they need it." Her tone was firm and reassuring, but there was an undercurrent of exhaustion behind it, not that I could blame her. It sounded like she'd been having a pretty intense day.

A guy's voice spoke from behind me. "So, about that woman and the hag you met in the Void…"

I turned to find Rory Kane staring at me, holding hands with *Dove*, of all people. When had *that* happened? I tried not to stare at their joined hands.

"Let me guess," Rory said. "The people who grabbed Kaizyn were a short, squatty hag ugly enough to scare the warts off a frog… and a dark-haired woman, very pretty, with absolute maniacal evil in her eyes."

I nodded. "Yeah, pretty much."

"Right, well, about that," Rory continued, giving me a wry smile. "They have a hall pass to my head."

I blinked at Rory. "*What*?"

"Yeah, they can link to my brain or something. They talk to me sometimes, or… sometimes I can see what they're doing." He shrugged. "It seems to go both ways, which would be great if I could just control it. *Not* controlling it is not so great. Oh, and sometimes I can see the Dark King, too." He winced. "But he can also see me, so… yeah… again, not so great."

He glanced down at Dove, and she gave him a sympathetic smile and squeezed his hand.

I gaped at him. "*What*?" There really wasn't a better word to capture my multitude of questions.

Dove shrugged, then smiled at me. "It's kind of good, though. It's how we knew about the Dark King's plan to ambush Kaizyn in the Void... not that we could *warn* you..." She trailed off, looking apologetic. "I mean, if we'd known sooner, we probably could have saved you all a lot of trouble. And helped Kaizyn's sear-bind..." Her large eyes filled with sympathy, then she turned to Rory. "Although, if it was *also* his plan to use Varias to kill Kaizyn and Ayla during the ceremony to break the bond like Varias said, then why did he even *need* an ambush?"

"He was going to use Varias to *what*?" I blurted.

Rory stared down at Dove in thought, ignoring my outburst. "Backup plan, maybe? Or maybe *this* was the backup. Oh, by the way," he said, looking up at me. "The Dark King was controlling Sevryn, or he *is* Sevryn... maybe? The Sevryn we knew was an avatar or something. It's confusing, honestly, but the main takeaway is that Sevryn's not, like, *dead* dead. And also, I'm pretty sure this means the Dark King dated my sister, which is—" He shuddered. "Yeah, let's just not think about that part too much."

My mouth dropped open, then closed with a snap. "Again... *what*?"

I looked at my parents, but they seemed just as shocked.

Seriously, what was going *on* in this place? I'd only been away from the Hub a few days and everything had devolved into chaos.

I turned my shocked stare on Chairman Hart.

Chairman Hart stared back at me, glanced at my parents who were also staring, then sighed. "Get something to eat, change, whatever you'd like to do, then meet me in my office in twenty minutes. We have a lot to discuss."

CHAPTER 46

PRIMARY TARGET

Ayla

Chairman Hart summoned us all to a group meeting in a conference room down the hall from her office. Doctor Harlowe, myself, my grandpa and parents, Reina and her parents, Kaizyn, Callan, Rory, Madison, and Dove were all there, sitting around a table very similar to the one where Callan had sat the day I'd learned he was Fae.

My heart squeezed at the memory of that meeting, of Jordan's tender protection of me when I still had so little clue what was going on... and of our first kiss, shared just moments afterward.

That had been the last time I'd seen him before he was taken by Sevryn at the docks, and although we'd gotten him back, it almost felt like we hadn't. Nothing had been the same, since. How could it? And it probably never would. Even if the chaos and danger eventually went away, I had magic now. Jordan was an honest-to-goodness king. Things would never go back to normal... but I still had hope that once all of this was over, Jordan and I would finally be able to figure out a *new* normal—together.

I looked around the room. I was seated about halfway down the length of the conference table. Grandpa had taken the chair across from me, while my parents had taken the seats on either side of me. The rest of the group had filled in around the table—Madison and Callan side by side at the far end, Rory and Dove to their left, Kaizyn to Callan's right, with Reina and her parents on Kaizyn's other side, an empty chair between him and Reina.

The fact that they'd sat beside each other, yet pointedly left a chair between, only made me more curious what was going on with them. But now obviously wasn't the time to ask.

The table was long enough that there were still a few chairs empty.

Chairman Hart shut the door, then took a seat at the head of the table, and Doctor Harlowe took the first seat to her left.

Hart gestured to Doctor Harlowe, who set a large tablet on a corner of the table, angled on a stand so we could all see it.

Keyja and Varias stared back at us from the screen of the tablet, joining the meeting virtually from the secured room where Varias was still being held.

Hart turned to face the rest of us. "Everyone has been apprised of the situation, so I see no need to beat around the bush. Ayla and Kaizyn wish to be unbound from one another, if possible"—she paused to glance at each of us, and we both nodded—"and doing so would remove significant risks for both of them as well as for Teionyr. However, given the situation with Varias and the Dark King, we have some significant safety concerns about the unbinding ceremony. While we appreciate Varias' recent candor with us, we cannot in good faith proceed with anything while there is a chance the Dark King might take hold of Varias. We cannot perform the ceremony in the warded room because he needs access to his magic to perform it... and we can't very well keep him contained in a room here forever, either. Having him here makes the Hub a potential target for the Dark King, even more than we already were. We need to decide how to proceed."

If Varias was offended at being talked about as though he wasn't even there, his face didn't show it.

Chairman Hart leaned forward, planting her hands on the table. "Generally, I have a council for these kinds of things. But since this situation has impacted—and could continue to impact—all of you in this room, in one form or another, let's discuss: What are our options? Is this ceremony even *worth* the risk to attempt, or is there a better way of securing Ayla and Kaizyn's safety?"

I stiffened. "Shouldn't it be *our* choice?" I glanced at Kaizyn, who met my gaze steadily. "Shouldn't Kaizyn and I get to decide whether we're willing to take the risk?"

"Technically," Hart said, "you are a minor, plus this is *my* facility and the safety of the other personnel and residents here is my responsibility, so no. It is not solely your decision to make."

As much as that rankled, I couldn't argue against her point. If the Dark King took control of Varias outside of that warded room, Kaizyn and I might not be the only ones in danger.

"I... have something unpleasant to add," Rory said in a low voice.

He suddenly had everyone's attention.

"When I saw the vision where the women were discussing the attack on the Hub, one of them told the Dark King, 'the girl won't be a problem for much longer.'" My chest clenched as his eyes locked on mine. "I'm pretty sure they were talking about Ayla. He saw her as a risk."

Beside me, my parents both tensed.

"Why would Ayla be a risk for him?" my mom asked. "I thought he just wanted her to hurt Kaizyn or get to Jordan."

But I saw Grandpa and Doctor Harlowe share a glance, and I knew the answer before Doctor Harlowe said it.

"He must know about your magic, Ayla." Doctor Harlowe's voice was steady, an anchor even while my pulse was skyrocketing. "He knows you are a threat to him."

"He could probably feel it, even before it manifested," Kaizyn added, his eyes locking on mine. "The same as I could. Even when he's using an avatar, he feels what they feel, sees what they see. The moment Sevryn first met you, he must have known."

From that very first moment he'd watched me in the parking lot of Gary's Café, before I even knew Fae existed, much less who he was... he'd known things about me that I didn't even know myself.

That was wholly, utterly disturbing.

"I should have seen this sooner," Doctor Harlowe said. "When he came after your grandfather, he attacked you—then he took Jordan as leverage to draw you out. We assumed it was all an attempt to harm Kaizyn, because of the bond, but maybe it was *always* about you."

I felt the weight of Kaizyn's shock blending with my own: his fear, his regret, his hurt, and then a flash of anger... and I instinctively knew why. Yet again, Kaizyn felt he wasn't important—was never important. This had all been about *me*.

Those last emotions were instantly drowned by a crash of guilt, but they'd been there.

All it took was a look at his eyes to confirm I was right about the cause.

"Stop it," I said, staring at him. "You *know* that's not true."

He stared back. "Isn't it?"

"No, it's not," I said firmly, then softened my voice. "But it's still okay to feel it."

Reina glanced between us, brows furrowed in concern. "Kaizyn?" she asked gently, eyes landing on him.

For a moment, he met her gaze, and I could see every emotion I knew he was feeling, laid bare for her to see.

She let out a tiny gasp—then I saw *and* felt Kaizyn slam the door to his heart shut.

"Kaizyn," I warned—not for me, but for *him*, because in that brief moment, I'd felt the full force of what he felt for her, and the fear he felt for feeling it... but I'd also seen how Reina looked at him. And I knew my friend well enough to *know*.

He met my stare, but shook his head. "Later, I promise. But I can't now. Understand?"

I could feel his focus and resolve settling in. He couldn't afford to *feel* now. He needed to strategize, to be the prince and soldier he was trained to be.

I drew a breath, then nodded. He was right. We needed to focus. But I *for sure* planned to bring this all back up later.

Varias cleared his throat. "I believe you could be right, about Ayla being a target—perhaps even a primary target. But not *the* primary one. I know the Dark King, for better or for worse, and he rarely has a one-dimensional plan. Odds are he's not after Ayla, or Kaizyn, or Jordan... he's after *all three*, because all three are potential obstacles. He doesn't take kindly to people getting in his way."

Chairman Hart nodded, processing that, then turned to Rory. "Have you had any further visions of the Dark King's plans?"

Rory shook his head, then looked at me. "No. I'm sorry. I wish I could help more, could see what they're up to. I really do. I just can't control it." His hands, resting on the table, were clenched in fists. He turned to Kaizyn. "I should've been able to warn you. I knew something was coming, just not in time. That put you *both* at risk." He glanced between Kaizyn and me.

"It's okay," I told him softly. Having the Dark King come and go in his mind at will was obviously *not* okay. Lots of things about this situation were not okay. But none of it was his fault.

From the other end of the table, Kaizyn echoed my sentiment. "We are all doing our best, Rory. What happened was not your fault."

Rory nodded, but his fists were still clenched.

Dove placed a hand on one of his.

Rory glanced at her, then relaxed, entwining his fingers with hers, and stared down at the table.

My chest warmed at the trust communicated in their silent exchange, but my heart also broke a little, watching Rory. Having someone tell you a thing wasn't your fault, even *knowing* it wasn't your fault, was not the same as *feeling* free of that guilt. I knew that from experience.

The Dark King sullied everything he touched, and his reach was only growing.

Hart drew a sharp breath, then returned to business. "Maddox, is there any other route to breaking this bond?"

Grandpa shook his head. "We've looked. This ceremony is the first real lead we've had."

"I know of nothing else besides the ceremony," Varias spoke, drawing all eyes toward the tablet screen. "But I might have a way to mitigate the risks."

Hart's gaze fixed on the screen like a hawk's. "Explain."

Varias hesitated, staring out at the room. "I will, but first, there is something else I believe you should know."

My stomach clenched, preparing for another blow, another admission of betrayal, but his next words were not what I expected.

"I have a theory for why the Dark King had Miravel intercept Kaizyn in the Void," he said.

Chairman Hart's eyebrows scrunched. "Something other than killing him?"

Varias nodded. "Yes. She could not have directly killed him herself—the Seal would have prevented it. But she could have used any number of creatures to do the job for her; the Void is full of things that would have gladly eaten him while he was tied up. All she had to do was walk away."

"She didn't," Kaizyn said.

"No," Varias agreed. He turned back to Chairman Hart. "At first, I assumed she just wanted to play with him before killing him—that is often her way."

He said that so calmly, like informing us of her favorite ice cream flavor.

He continued. "But when Keyja and I were discussing what happened, I realized there could be another reason."

He glanced at Keyja, and she nodded. "Yes. It's possible she may not have intended to kill him, but to drain him."

Drain him? A chill sped down my spine, and I felt the echoing surge of horror from Kaizyn in my chest.

"What do you mean?" Kaizyn asked sharply, and when I glanced at him, his eyes mirrored my fear.

Reina looked horrified as well. Her face had turned paler than usual, which for her complexion meant almost translucent.

Varias directed his gaze toward Kaizyn. "You bear the Teionyr Seal, but yours was sealed by magic alone, not by blood. It's possible if they drained your magic into something they could wield, they could use it to infiltrate Teionyr—to travel there instantly, as you are able to do."

This time, Kaizyn went pale—and so did half the people at the table.

"They can *do* that?" My voice shook.

"Yes, and many other things," Varias said, his gaze landing on me. "I believe I was sent here as a backup plan, in the event they failed to capture the prince."

My mind spun, twisting pieces into place like segments of a Rubik's cube. "So... are you saying the Dark King might try to use you and this ceremony to *drain* Kaizyn, not kill him?"

Varias shrugged. "It's possible, but that kind of magic is not my strength. I believe it's more likely that, in the event he escaped Miravel, the Dark King considered killing Kaizyn to be his next best option. Kaizyn is the heir to the throne, should anything happen to Jordan, but also, the new king's feelings for you are no secret to anyone, and killing Kaizyn would ensure your death as well." He stared intently at me. "Why destroy a king at the peak of his might, when you can bring him to his knees with grief and destroy him at his weakest?"

That phrase was like a shot of ice in my veins.

Kaizyn must've felt it, because he gave me a soft, empathetic grimace before turning back to Varias. "So he's looking to eliminate *all* the royals of Teionyr." It wasn't a question, more a statement of realization.

Varias turned his face toward Kaizyn. "He's looking to get power—and he will take it, as much as he can, in any way he can. Once he's set his mind on something he wants, he systematically destroys anything that stands in his way." Varias' jaw clenched. "He wants access to the magic and resources in the Teionyrian vault. And right now, you and Jordan are both in his way."

I turned to Kaizyn. "The Seal protects you and Jordan, though...right? That's why Sevryn couldn't kill you in the first place, why he cursed you to be stuck in the Veil instead. Even if he tried to kill Jordan, he would run into the same problems as he did with you... wouldn't he?"

Kaizyn studied my face while he thought. I desperately wanted him to say yes, but I could feel his caution, his trepidation at answering me, and I knew I wouldn't like his answer even before he spoke it. "In theory, yes. But as we saw with my father, there are ways around the Seal. A royal cannot be harmed directly, but an illness... or even collateral damage from an attack directed at another target..." A shadow passed over his eyes. "There are ways."

"But he still couldn't access the vault, right?" Madison interjected, glancing between Kaizyn and Callan. Her green eyes were wide, and she was clutching Callan's upper arm so hard her fingertips had turned white, though he gave no indication that he minded. "Even if... *something*... were to happen to Jordan and Kaizyn, the Dark King wouldn't be a royal. He wouldn't be able to open it."

Callan and Kaizyn shared a very concerning look.

Then Callan looked down at Madison. "There is a way," he said gently, then looked up at the rest of us. "If *all* the royals are removed, if there is no heir, another may be voted in by the people. Upon coronation, the new royal would inherit the full magic of Teionyr, and all the rights and privileges therein would belong to him, and to his lineage, from that point on."

"The people of Teionyr would never vote for Sevryn to take the rule!" I blurted, but then I saw Callan and Kaizyn's expressions, and my chest tightened.

"The people as a whole would not," Kaizyn said, his eyes locking onto mine. "But the ceremony requires only a majority vote of Teionyr's *living* citizens. And we know some Teionyrians helped Sevryn, when he tried to take my father's throne."

His words settled over the room.

"Then, you think..." I trailed off, unable to voice my thought.

"He plans to kill everyone," Varias answered, speaking the words I hadn't dared to. "Every single Teionyrian who might oppose him, until he's left with a majority who won't."

CHAPTER 47

DON'T PANIC

Ayla

He plans to kill everyone.

"I need to call Jordan," I said, my pulse racing. "I need to make sure he knows."

Hart nodded, and everyone stared as I pulled out the stone and activated it... but Jordan didn't answer. I left the stone on the table, so I could see and hear if he did. I tried not to panic about what it meant that he hadn't.

"He's a king," Reina said softly, her gaze steady when I looked up at her. "He could just be busy."

Kaizyn nodded, giving her an appreciative glance before looking back at me. "Yes. He absolutely could be."

Don't panic was implied. Kaizyn knew how much I needed to hear it, because he could feel I already was.

The tension in the room became suffocating. I stared across the table at my grandfather, while from either side of me, my parents each grabbed one of my hands. "What do we do?" I whispered.

Kaizyn glared at the table for a long moment, then stood, his jaw clenched with determination. "First, we remove every risk we can, every vulnerability the Dark King could use to his advantage." He turned to Hart. "We remove the bond."

"I'm not sure that's—"

"Varias said he had a way to mitigate risk," Kaizyn continued. "Right?" He addressed his last question to Varias, who nodded.

"Yes."

All eyes turned to the tablet.

"I can unbind you," Varias said, "but not inside this warded room, and we all know it's likely the Dark King will try to take control of me the moment I leave it. However, it takes no magic to *etch* the runes, only to test or wield them. I could etch them here, in the room, and have someone else wield them."

A sliver of eagerness passed over Hart's usually impassive face. "You would do that for us?"

"Yes," he said, looking at Keyja. "I know I can never balance the list of wrongs I've done, but I will not die a slave to the Dark King. I choose to do whatever good I can, even if he will strike me down for it the moment I step outside these walls. I will die a *free* man."

A look of tenderness passed between him and Keyja, then he turned back to look at Hart.

"You will need someone very powerful to wield these runes. The magic doesn't fall into one of the LeyGuard divisions, or even the divisions typically seen among the Fae. This spell requires a channeling of all *four* magical properties." He glanced at Keyja again, regret etching his face. "It requires an ArcFae."

"I will do it," Keyja said, without a moment's hesitation.

"It will drain you," Varias said, his voice and expression tense. "Even with your immense power and the aid of Tofa, it will take weeks for you to return to full strength. Perhaps *months*. If the Dark King attacks again when he finds out what we've done, you will be unable to fight back. You will be *vulnerable*." It almost sounded like he was trying to talk her out of helping us, but then I realized it was just concern. *He loves her.*

"If even someone as powerful as Keyja will be that drained," Reina asked him, "wouldn't it have been worse for you? Would you even have *survived* it?"

Varias fell silent, and the realization swept over us all at once. He hadn't intended to survive it. If the Dark King hadn't killed him, the ceremony may have. He had never planned to walk out of here alive.

Keyja turned to face him, showing us her profile. "Kaizyn and the Ley-Guard are our allies, and both have proven their friendship several times over. I accept the risk, Varias, and I will do it." Her tone left no room for argument. Then she turned to look at Chairman Hart. "But I would like to ask a favor in return."

She waited until Hart nodded, then continued. "I ask ongoing protection for Varias. Let him stay here, as your guest."

"Keyja," Varias warned, "I do not wish to—"

But Keyja silenced him with a scathing look. "You owe me this, Varias. Give me this one request." She turned back to Hart. "Let him stay here, in a warded room, until the Dark King is no longer a threat. Until it is safe for him to leave these walls."

"Done," Hart said immediately, "so long as he will agree to remain in the room. We will ensure he is well-treated, and that he is made comfortable, but he must remain within the wards."

Varias drew a breath, then nodded, acquiescing to Keyja's glare. "I will stay."

Keyja gave him a tender smile.

Varias returned it, briefly, then looked back at Hart. "I will need a table brought in here, a wooden table, large enough for both Ayla and Kaizyn to lie on. I will need tools brought in so I can etch the runes into the wood, and when I am done, the finished table can be taken out for Keyja to use."

"We can arrange that," Hart said, "but we may need to clear out the other furniture in your holding room to make space."

Varias nodded. "That is fine. I am used to making do with very little."

While Hart sent some attendants to commandeer a picnic table for our use, I slipped out and into a quiet hall to try to call Jordan again. The light from before was still lit—he had never responded. Even so, I lit another one, watching it glow blue beside its neighbor.

Two charges used... and still no reply.

"You're worried," a deep voice said gently, and I turned to find Kaizyn watching me. "About the ceremony?" Then he saw the stone in my hand. "Ah. He still hasn't answered."

"I know there are a million possible reasons—"

"Perhaps not a million, but plenty, yes." Kaizyn nodded.

"But I still can't help worrying—"

He stepped forward and took my hands, the stone still closed in one of them. "When has worrying ever changed a single thing?"

I stared at him. "There's a Bible verse that says basically that same thing."

Kaizyn smiled at me. "I know. I've studied it." He let go of my hands and slid his into his pockets.

Our eyes locked, something almost tangible passing between us. Not romantic, but soul-deep all the same. "You believe in the Bible? In God?" I asked him, genuinely wondering. Jordan studied the Bible, attended church, believed in God... but he'd been raised human. I'd never heard a Fae mention the Bible.

Kaizyn studied my face. "Do you?"

"Yes," I said, tilting my head. "But I asked you first."

"I do," he said, eyes not leaving mine. "It's not a common belief, where I'm from, but I do." The ends of his mouth curved up ever so slightly. "When a person has seen as many miracles as I have the past few weeks, how could they not? Among other reasons, of course."

I nodded.

He stepped closer. "You are one of those miracles, Ayla."

The intensity of his gaze, the closeness of him, would normally have made me panic—but he had stopped within a respectable distance, plus I could *feel* the meaning of his words, and they weren't romantic. They were just utterly, entirely sincere.

"I love you, Ayla, but it's changed," he said. "Actually, I think now I really *do* love you, whereas before I thought I did, but it was... something else." A tinge of embarrassment crossed his face.

"You were lonely, and hurting. I understood. You really just needed more friends."

He nodded, thoughtful. "Yes. That doesn't completely remove my mortification, but at least I learned from it, right?" He gave me a sheepish smirk.

I laughed. "Yes."

"But what I feel for you now, you can feel it?"

"Yes," I said, nodding slowly. "It feels... like mine." Like what I felt for him, but he already knew that. "Like family."

He smiled, seeming relieved. "Yes. Family." His smile grew, then slipped away. "I never had much family, and then Sevryn took almost all of what little I had. Callan was my only remaining family, closer even than blood. But now..." He looked down at the stone I held. "You are family. Jordan is family."

"And Reina?"

As his face snapped up to look at me, I felt his flash of alarm—and also enough beyond that to answer my question.

"I won't tell her." I laughed, then softened my tone. "But you should."

He glanced away, and the muscle in his jaw ticked. Then he looked back at me. "I will. When it's the right time." He glanced down at the stone again and drew a breath. "As much as I want to tell you Jordan is just busy and it's nothing..."

"Something doesn't feel right," I finished, my voice barely audible. "I know. I feel it, too."

Our eyes locked on each other. Kaizyn swallowed. "As soon as we finish here—"

Chairman Hart shouted our names.

I jumped, turning just in time to see her striding toward us, heels clacking on the tile.

"The table is ready, and Etcher has already applied the runes," she said. "It's time to do your ceremony."

The table had been set up in a big, empty room that looked like an abandoned gymnasium. The bleachers were folded up, pressed back against the walls, revealing an empty stretch of polished floors. The ceiling was high, arched with metal beams. The room vaguely smelled of feet, which was comforting in its own way. The gym at my high school had always smelled like feet, too.

The group from the meeting earlier, plus Brone and Striker and Quinn, had all joined us in the gym.

Keyja directed everyone else to stand back, near the edge of the room, then led Kaizyn and me to the table. "Lie down next to each other, but facing opposite directions. Ayla, your head will go here," she said, pointing at a swirling symbol charred into the table. "Kaizyn, yours will go there." She indicated an angular symbol at the opposite end of the table.

Kaizyn and I shared a glance, then both climbed onto the table.

We'd decided against restraints—partly because, in my mind, avoiding the restraints was yet another way of ensuring we didn't fulfill Quinn's vision—but Brone and Striker were both ready to intervene and hold us down if necessary. Varias had assured them they could approach the table during the ceremony without harming themselves or us, so long as they didn't interject their magic with Keyja's or allow us to move off of the runes etched beneath us.

Somebody neared, and I glanced over to see Doctor Harlowe, holding up a tablet with Varias on the screen.

"It will take a few moments for the magic to activate once you begin," Varias told Keyja. "Just continue channeling your magic into the runes. You mustn't pull back, once you've started, until it's complete."

Keyja listened carefully, then nodded. She turned back toward Kaizyn and me. "You cannot move once I begin. Just stay calm and let the magic work. Are you ready?"

A sudden fear gripped me.

I glanced over and saw my grandpa and parents and everyone else watching us.

My dad met my gaze. "We're all here. You can do this."

I swallowed, tears prickling at my eyes, then nodded and turned my head back to stare up at the ceiling.

I felt Kaizyn's hand touch mine, and I gripped his fingers and squeezed.

He squeezed back. I could feel his fear, a thin string tangling with my thicker one, but I could also feel his courage, a peaceful resolve far stronger than the fear. I gripped onto that for dear life, using it to fuel my own.

"This is going to hurt," Keyja said, her voice gentle. She placed a hand on each of us.

I felt her magic begin to seep into me, warm and bright—

Every nerve in my body exploded with sharp, searing pain.

CHAPTER 48

ALL I HAVE LEFT IN THE WORLD

Callan

As soon as Keyja's magic for the ceremony took effect, I knew something was wrong. I could just *feel* it, like gnats tingling my skin.

"Kaizyn?" I stepped away from the wall of the gymnasium, toward the table.

Both he and Ayla were stiff, heads thrown back, eyes wide open, bodies quivering... not making a sound.

Streams of electric-blue magic spun between them and around each of them, intersecting with another loop of fast-moving magic spinning between Keyja and the table. She wasn't speaking, either.

"Maybe they can't speak while the ceremony is going?" Madison was next to me, her voice trembling as she neared the table. "Ayla?"

Chairman Hart hurried over, her mouth drawn tight and her face pale as she studied Kaizyn, Ayla, and Keyja's faces. "Is this normal?" she asked Doctor Harlowe. "Should they be non-responsive?"

Behind us, I felt everyone tense, watching us—we could *all* tell something wasn't right.

But he just shook his head, eyes wide with concern. "I don't know. I've never—"

Reina was at my side in a moment, checking on both Ayla and Kaizyn. "I don't think they can hear us." She turned to me, her lips trembling. "Something's not right, Callan, I can feel it."

So could I.

"Show me," Varias said from the tablet, sounding concerned.

Doctor Harlowe angled the tablet.

"The ceremony appears normal... but you said they're not responding?" Varias' question was directed to me, but before I could answer, he called out. "Keyja? Can you hear me?"

I spun to look at Keyja, but her eyes had gone glassy, even while streams of power still flowed from her.

"She should be able to respond," Varias said, his voice growing more tense. "Hold the screen over the prince and Ayla," he told Doctor Harlowe. "Let me see the table."

"The runes are correct, and the power is flowing as it should..." Varias commented as Doctor Harlowe swept the tablet slowly over the table. "Get me closer to the runes?"

While Doctor Harlowe complied, Striker moved up beside me.

"I'm with Reina; this doesn't feel right," Striker said, his face tense. "My skin's crawling like I'm in the Void." He glanced at Brone with a look of concern.

My heart lurched—he was right.

"Dark magic," Rory breathed, suddenly beside me with Dove, speaking the very words I'd just been thinking. "Look at their eyes." His voice was tight with alarm. "They're turning black."

"It's seeping from Kaizyn," Dove said, her eyes wide. "I can feel it. He's the source."

My blood went cold. Miravel must have done something to him, before he'd woken.

"She set a trap," Rory whispered. "A trap inside him," yet again echoing my thoughts.

"Show me Keyja's eyes. Quickly!" Varias snapped.

Doctor Harlowe raised the tablet level with Keyja's face, and I heard Varias gasp.

Her eyes were blown wide open now, and a dark shadow was creeping into them, the same as with Ayla and Kaizyn. Dark threads were also spiderwebbing across the bright orb in Keyja's chest, slowing only when bright lightning snapped out every few seconds, chasing the dark threads back. It was like dark magic was trying to strangle out Tofa.

The sight sent a shiver all the way to my toes.

"Stop the ceremony," I said, a thread of panic in my tone. I spun toward the tablet. "Varias, tell me how to—"

"You can't," Varias said, his tone unreadable. "If it's interrupted or stopped improperly, the loop will continue to siphon energy from them. They could die."

Startled gasps echoed around the room, then Ayla's family rushed to her side.

Reina covered a sob with a shaky hand, and her parents wrapped their arms around her.

"What can we do?" Maddox asked, eyes pleading with Varias while his son and his wife clutched Ayla's trembling hands. "There has to be *something*."

"Can we move them to the warded room?" Reina asked, pulling away from her parents to stare at Varias. "The magic would stop, and—"

"That would take too long." Varias' voice hardened. "Let me out," he commanded, his eyes flicking to Chairman Hart. "*Please*. I have to intersect Keyja's magic with my own. Another ArcFae is the only way to stop the ceremony safely. I don't know what Miravel may have done to the prince, but I assure you, we don't want to find out. If I don't stop this ceremony immediately, all *three* of them could die."

"But the Dark King—" Chairman Hart began, but Varias interrupted her.

"I know. And I know you don't trust me. But *please*—" His eyes were desperate, his voice trembling. "Keyja is all I have left in the world, the only good I have. *Please* let me save her. You have some version of warding cuffs, yes? Put them on me until I get to the table. I only need a few moments, and I can hold out on his pull that long. I can save all three of them. Please. I can do this."

"Will warding cuffs block the Dark King, or just your own magic?" Hart asked.

"I'm not sure," Varias said. "But you have to let me try."

Chairman Hart drew a shaky breath, her eyes falling closed for a moment—then she snapped them open and jabbed a button on her wrist device. "Put warding cuffs on Varias and bring him to Gym Four. Now."

"The Arc—" a shocked voice answered, but she cut him off.

"Yes, the ArcFae! And hurry!"

We all crowded around the table, watching helplessly.

"What if he can't hold out? Or if the Dark King has already taken over?" Brone asked quietly.

"Ready your magic," Hart said, "and your weapons. If the worst comes, we cannot allow anyone who has been compromised by the Dark King to leave this room."

Madison clutched my arm, her wide, frightened eyes staring up at me.

I squeezed her hand, then slid my other hand to my dagger.

We all stood silently, waiting for the ArcFae who could either be our hero or our doom.

A startled-looking young LeyGuard jogged into the gym a few moments later, a ward-cuffed Varias right behind him.

Varias rushed directly to the table. His gaze swept over Kaizyn and Ayla, then landed on Keyja with a look of devastation before his expression shuttered into resolve.

"Remove my cuffs," he told Chairman Hart.

There was no time for second thoughts.

Hart tapped her wrist device with a shaky finger, and the cuffs popped open, clattering to the floor.

"Stand back," Varias told the rest of us, then he shoved his arms into the swirling current.

Keyja immediately screamed.

I rushed toward her. "Keyja! Can you hear me?"

"I—can't—," she gasped, eyes flicking toward me, breathing heavily. "Something's wrong."

I met her panicked stare. "We know. Varias—"

Keyja screamed again, then her head swung toward Varias. "*No!*"

Their eyes met in a look of mirrored devastation.

"Varias," Keyja gasped. "You can't!"

"Let go, Keyja. I can feel him pulling," Varias said, his eyes locking on hers. "I can't hold this much longer. You have to let go."

"I can feel him!" Keyja cried. "If I pull my magic back, he'll kill you." Her voice shook.

"If you don't, all *three* of you will die." His voice was completely calm as he responded. "When I release this, if he takes me over—you know what you must do." His gaze was steady on hers.

Keyja glanced down at Kaizyn and Ayla, then drew a sobbing breath. "Don't make me do this, Varias," she whispered.

"I was already a dead man, Keyja." Through the torrent of magic, his eyes held hers with a look of pure devotion. "There is no other way." His voice grew firm. "Pull back, Keyja. Now."

Keyja stared at him a moment longer, then thrust her arms forward.

Streams of dark magic shot out from the swirling loops, slinging themselves around her arms like ropes.

Keyja screamed, arms shaking with effort as she thrust them upward, then a surge of bright magic crackled from her chest, flaring in intensity until—with a deafening *crack* like lightning—she broke free and stumbled backward, Tofa snapping into physical form beside her.

The swirling loops of magic around the table instantly winked out.

"Varias!" Keyja rushed toward him as Brone, Striker, and I rushed toward the table.

I heaved an unconscious Kaizyn up into my arms, then hurried back a few steps and laid him carefully on the ground. Striker did the same with Ayla.

The others huddled around them, but my attention snapped back to Varias and Keyja.

"Varias?" Keyja asked again.

Varias was heaving deep breaths, standing stiffly, his eyes fluttering between open and closed.

"Get behind me," I said quietly to Madison, and she huddled behind my back.

Varias' eyes snapped open.

They were pure black.

CHAPTER 49

ANOTHER VISION

Callan

I grabbed my dagger.

A surge of power shot out of Varias, pure black streams of darkness from both hands, aimed right at Keyja.

Tofa rushed forward with a deafening bellow, intercepting the dark magic. It flickered through her, a flutter of shadows amid her blinding light, then vanished.

I lunged forward, ready to do what I had to if Keyja wouldn't.

But with a cry of utter devastation, Keyja sent a blinding, white-hot stream of power at Varias' chest.

A guttural howl of pain burst from him—then his eyes flicked to Keyja's, whole and *his*, for just one moment.

"Thank you," he whispered.

He crumpled to the ground.

Keyja rushed over to him, felt for his pulse, then dropped to her knees, sobbing.

Chairman Hart and Doctor Harlowe exchanged stares as a tense, silent moment settled over the room.

Then Kaizyn and Ayla stirred.

I shoved my dagger into its sheath and rushed to Kaizyn's side, next to Reina.

"Kaizyn?" Reina brushed a piece of hair back from his forehead.

He moaned lightly, then his eyes fluttered open.

I drew a breath of relief to see they had returned to normal.

"Reina?" he muttered, pushing slowly up onto his elbows. "What—"

"Ayla!" her parents leaned in over her a few feet away and helped her sit up. "Are you—"

I lost track of that conversation as Reina yanked Kaizyn's shirt to close the few inches between them, and pressed her lips to his.

Well.

I caught Madison's shocked stare from over near Ayla, and a chuckle burst out of me.

Reina and Kaizyn immediately separated. Reina scooted back a full foot, her face flushed red. Kaizyn looked dazed.

Reina drew a sharp breath, then turned back toward Kaizyn. "I'm sorry! I—"

"Don't be," Kaizyn said, his eyes locking on hers with an intensity that made me feel suddenly unwelcome.

"I'll... just..." I said, scooting back.

Kaizyn didn't even glance at me as I made my rapid escape. His attention was entirely on Reina.

Madison hurried over to me. "That—" She stopped, losing her words.

"Was a long time coming," I finished for her, my mouth pulling up into a smile. "Anyway, he seems fine. How's Ayla?" I glanced over, but Ayla looked fine, too. Her parents were taking care of her.

I breathed a sigh of relief, then turned to the woman still kneeling on the ground by Varias. "Keyja?"

She pulled her hand back from Varias' unmoving chest and looked up at me as I approached. Though tears streaked her face, her expression was calm. "He just wanted to be free," she said quietly.

I met her eyes. "He saved three lives. He fought the darkness until the very last moment. His choice to do that, even knowing what would happen—in that moment, he *was* free."

Something shifted in her eyes, then she nodded. "I did what I had to, and so did he." She glanced over at him. "He died with honor."

"Yes, he did." Chairman Hart stepped up beside us, then placed a sympathetic hand on Keyja's shoulder. "I know this cost you greatly—both of you. I am very sorry."

Keyja glanced up at her, then swiped her eyes of tears. A resolve settled over her face. "He must be buried in the ways of my people. Buried with honor, in Arcvale."

"Of course," Hart said. "As soon as we know it's safe to return to Arcvale, we will help you. Whatever you need, just let us know."

Tofa stepped toward Varias, sniffed him, then pressed her massive snout to his chest. A glittering substance sped out from both sides of where she touched, faceted like crystal, wrapping over and encasing him.

"He will be preserved until it is time," Keyja said by way of explanation, then she and Tofa simply strode out of the room.

I turned back toward the others, and found Kaizyn and Ayla both standing up, everyone crowded around them, with Reina and her parents hanging back, watching but not quite part of the crowd.

"It's broken," Kaizyn told me, smiling as I approached. "The bond is gone."

I grabbed him in a quick hug, then pulled back to look at him. "That's amazing." I'd worried that losing the bond would be bittersweet for him, but he seemed genuinely happy. "And you're both okay?" I asked, glancing at Ayla.

"Yes." He nodded, and Ayla did too.

Madison moved in and hugged Ayla, then came to stand beside me.

I reached down for her hand. She looked up at me and smiled, and my heart sped a little. I squeezed her fingers, so glad to have her back at my side.

Madison returned my smile and leaned into me, then looked at Ayla. "You're sure you're all right?"

"Yeah," Ayla said, then shuddered. "But that was horrifying." Her eyes glanced off as she remembered. "It was like I'd been dropped down a deep, dark hole, with walls pressed against me on all sides. I couldn't see or hear anything. I couldn't move."

Kaizyn put a hand on her arm, and her eyes refocused. They exchanged a look of understanding, then Kaizyn dropped his hand and stepped back.

Ayla drew a deep breath. "I'm just glad it's over. They explained what happened. Where's Keyja? I need to thank her... and tell her I'm sorry."

"She left," I said, and everyone looked at me. "I think she just needs some time alone."

Ayla nodded.

Her mom wrapped an arm around her shoulder, pulling her close.

Meanwhile, I eyed Kaizyn, noting how he and Reina had subtly shifted closer to one another while the rest of us listened to Ayla... even though they were still an arm's length from each other and were pointedly *not* looking at each other.

He caught me watching him, but at my hinting glance between him and Reina, he quickly shook his head and looked away, a blush flooding his face.

If the girl randomly grabbing him and kissing him hadn't been his green light to make his move, he might be more hopeless at romance than I thought. But he had almost died. Maybe it just wasn't the right time.

I kind of wished I'd stuck around to hear what they'd said to each other after that kiss.

"Chairman Hart," Ayla called suddenly.

Hart turned from a whispered conversation with Doctor Harlowe a few feet away and looked at Ayla.

"We need to check on Jordan. I tried to call him twice with the stone, but he never answered. Kaizyn and I both got the feeling that something isn't right."

Hart mulled that over a moment, then nodded. "I'll dispatch one of our discreet messengers immediately, and see what we can find out. But the rest of you"—her eyes flicked over all of us, as though daring us to argue—"are temporarily removed from duty."

"*What?*" Ayla said, among a chorus of complaints from the others as well.

"Just for an hour," Hart said, her expression softening. "I know you all have things to do, and I *know* I can't keep you benched, as much as the break might help you. But you all *have* to rest. Go eat. Take a nap. Do *something* for at least an hour other than fighting and recon and worrying. That's an order."

Kaizyn and I didn't take orders from Hart, and strictly speaking, neither did Madison or Rory. But none of us argued. We all realized the wisdom in her command.

Finally, Kaizyn nodded. "I have to admit, I'm tired... and hungry." He glanced at Reina. "Maybe we could go get some food?"

Reina met his eyes warily, then slowly, she smiled. "Okay."

He smiled back.

"Let me just go make sure my parents are okay, first, then we'll head to the cafeteria." Reina hurried over to where her parents were speaking with Maddox.

I tried to catch Kaizyn's attention, wanting to subtly let him know that we were *definitely* going to talk about him and Reina later... but then Madison's fingers dug into my arm.

"Callan." Madison called my name, and I looked down to see her beautiful eyes staring straight up into mine.

I turned to face her, then pulled her close, wrapping my arms around her. She melted into me, returning my embrace.

"Will all this danger ever be over?"

Her words would have barely been audible, if not for my Fae hearing. I pulled back slightly and tipped her chin up so I could meet her eyes. "Yes," I told her with all the confidence I could muster. "One day, it will."

"When?" She looked *and* sounded utterly exhausted, not that I could blame her.

"I don't know." I couldn't lie to her, so instead I pulled her close again, breathing in the scent of her hair. She had used a citrus shampoo, maybe grapefruit, but I could smell her natural scent beneath it, and it was far more intoxicating than the shampoo. "Let's go somewhere," I whispered into her hair. "Just you and me, for this hour."

She pulled back to look up at me, eyes hopeful.

I tucked a strand of her blonde hair behind her ear. "Let's go to the cafeteria, stack a tray high with all the best foods the Hub has to offer and whatever drinks your heart desires, then slip away to the upper level. There's a brilliant view of the woods from one of Hart's spare conference rooms off the medical wing. I discovered it when I was here before. You can tell me about anything you want—anything at all that doesn't involve Dark Fae or any of *this*. Tell me about your favorite games as a girl, or your dreams for your future, or anything you want. I just want to *exist* with you, Madison, just for a bit. Just the two of us, together."

As she stared up at me, my heart pounded, waiting for her response.

Then she gave me a brilliant smile that sent my pulse racing, wrapped her arms around my waist and leaned her head onto my chest. "That sounds perfect."

I held her for a moment longer, until suddenly she pulled back and grabbed my arm, her fingernails digging into my skin.

I looked down at her, worried I'd somehow upset her, but she was staring across the room.

"Rory," she said sharply. "He looks—"

I glanced over just in time to see Rory Kane collapse to the floor.

Madison ran toward him, and I followed.

Dove knelt beside Rory, her eyes wide and worried as she clutched one of Rory's hands. "Another vision."

Rory flinched and moaned, eyes flicking back and forth between his closed eyelids as though he was trapped in some kind of nightmare.

Dove's gaze flicked up to Madison. "I gave him the stone the moment it happened. I can feel the darkness pulling back. He should be about to come out of it."

As if on cue, Rory gasped, and his eyes flung open.

"Teionyr," he said, and the entire room fell silent.

Rory sat up, his gaze sweeping across the rest of us. "We have to get to Teionyr, *now*. Miravel is there, just outside the walls. She was talking about a traitor—someone she sent to open the breaches in the tunnels by the vault."

His eyes landed on Ayla and Kaizyn, who were both watching him in horror.

"An ambush," Kaizyn said, his voice deadly. He spun toward me, and our eyes locked.

"Call Jordan again," he said as he turned toward Ayla, but she was already holding the stone.

"He's still not answering." She looked up at us, her eyes panicked.

Chairman Hart stiffened. "Ready the team," she said, unable to keep the tremor from her voice. "Immediately."

Striker and Brone jogged for the door, along with Reina's parents.

Reina glanced at Kaizyn, then turned and hurried after them.

"You and I have to get to Teionyr *now*," I said, meeting Kaizyn's eyes. "Before they breach the palace."

Kaizyn nodded, striding toward me. "As soon as we're across the Veil, I can transport us in. If we hurry, maybe we can warn them."

"She was praising the traitor to the Dark King." Rory's shaky voice cut through our conversation as Madison helped him to his feet. "She spoke of the darklings as though they were *already* sneaking through."

Kaizyn and I turned to look at him.

He stared at us, eyes full of regret. "Even if you leave right now, I think you're already too late to warn Jordan or anyone else."

Ayla hurried toward us, eyes full of fire. "Then we go to *help* them. Quickly. All of us—together."

Brone and Striker hurried back in.

"Of course we do," Striker said, dumping an armful of supplies on the floor. "Gear up. The others are already grabbing their equipment. In five minutes, we're opening the secret Gate, the one Maddox used inside the palace."

He glanced at Brone, then pulled a fresh match from his belt.

"I helped train Jordan," Striker said, looking up at us. "He's smart and resourceful, and we all know he's powerful. Even if the Dark Fae have made it into the palace, I'm sure he can hold his own." Striker rolled the match between his fingers, then his eyes grew hard. "But anyone who's tried to harm that boy will have to answer to *me*."

CHAPTER 50

THE DARK FAE ARE COMING

[about an hour earlier]

Jordan

I leaned back on the couch in my sitting room and turned the runed stone over and over in my hand, trying not to worry. Ayla had confirmed the initial attack was a false alarm, but then someone had triggered the access alert at the Hub, and our call had cut out just after she had gone to see who it was. That had been ten minutes ago. I couldn't afford to waste any of the stone's charges just for my own impatience. Surely if there were trouble, Ayla would have called me right back. The alert had probably been Kaizyn and the others, and she just hadn't had the chance to call me back yet.

That's what I was telling myself.

"Your highness?" Barthas knocked on the outer door to my chambers, then peeked his head in.

I slipped the stone back into my pocket, then straightened and forced a smile. "Come in."

He shoved the door open and stumbled in holding a large basket of... dog toys?

Champ looked up from his position at my feet, stretched, then trotted happily over to greet Barthas.

"I hope you do not mind," Barthas said as he set the basket on the floor. "I took the liberty of having some of the staff recreate the items you described to me." He pulled a length of knotted rope from the bucket, then a hand-sewn stuffed rabbit, followed by a stitched ball made of a leather-like substance, but dyed bright green to resemble a tennis ball.

The basket was *full* of things like that, all custom-made replicas of Champ's favorite toys.

Barthas glanced sheepishly at me. "I know they aren't the same as what Champ had Earthside, but—"

I stood and smiled at him, genuinely this time. "They're perfect, Barthas. Thank you."

Barthas beamed. "I am so glad, Your Highness!" He knelt and set the rope, rabbit, and ball in front of Champ.

Champ grabbed the ball, tail wagging, and dropped to the floor to gnaw on it.

Barthas laughed and rubbed Champ's head, then straightened. "Let me know if you need anything else, Your Highness. I'll be right down the hall." He bowed, then left the room.

The moment the door closed behind him, my anxious fidgeting returned.

My parents had slipped away to rest in their guest chambers for an hour or so, and I was in an odd limbo state, waiting to hear back from either Ayla or from Callan and Kaizyn and the others.

Fifteen more minutes, I told myself. If I hadn't heard from anyone by then, I would call Ayla back.

I'd never been good at waiting in limbo.

I glanced down at Champ. "How about we take some of those toys outside for a few minutes?"

He looked up at me, tail thumping.

I reached into my mind, where I could feel Sorcha circling above the palace.

Yes, King-of-mine? she answered warmly.

I did my best to send her a mental image of Champ and me, playing fetch on a sunny stretch of grass. *Do you want to join us on the hill outside the—*

The door to my chambers burst open.

"Your Highness, forgive me!" Barthas burst in, eyes wide and wild. "There's something wrong in the tunnels. The maids—"

"Show me," I said, instantly on my feet. I grabbed my sword and ran after him into the hall.

Trouble had erupted somewhere beyond this hall—I could hear sobbing, screaming, sounds of chaos.

My parents' door flung open as we passed.

"What's happening?" Dad asked as he and Mom caught up to us. He had brought his bow and quiver, and Mom was gripping her dagger.

"I don't know," I said. "I—"

Maxim Warwick came sprinting down the hallway, faster than I would've imagined the old man could run.

"My king," he said briskly. "Hurry! We have to get you to safety!"

I jogged up to him, then stopped. "What's going on?"

"The breaches in the tunnels have reopened somehow. The darklings—"

I darted around him and dashed for the hall that led to the tunnels.

Champ raced up beside my parents and me, catching up to my pace.

"Your Highness!" Maxim screamed after me. "You can't! It isn't safe!"

I ignored him. The palace attendants, whoever may have been down near the tunnels, were my people now. Teionyrian royals were famous for fighting alongside their people, but even if they hadn't been, LeyGuards were fighters. And I was both. If the darklings were breaching in the tunnels, then the tunnels were where I needed to be.

I shouted to Sorcha. *We've got trouble! Meet me at the tunnels.*

Her response was immediate. *I'm coming.*

My parents, Champ, and I sprinted toward the tunnel corridors.

"What's our plan?" my mother asked, keeping pace just behind me.

"I don't know," I said honestly. "I'm not sure how bad it is."

I summoned my magic, flames dancing over my fingers, and on either side of me, I saw my parents' magic flare up, too.

My dad readied his bow as we ran. "You take point," he said, glancing at me. "You're the king."

I'm the king. That settled over me with a new kind of weight. I was the king. And this was *my* palace.

If the Dark Fae really were in those tunnels, I was going to make sure their assault on this palace ended there. If they made it out of the tunnels, they would have to go through me.

My parents and I took the corridors to the ground level as fast as we could go, Champ racing at my side. The halls sloped downward in a series of turns and adjoining passages, but I could see by the large windows spaced along the halls that we had nearly reached the ground level. Outside, all seemed peaceful... but inside was another story.

As my parents and I rounded the final turn before the tunnels, a handful of panicked-looking palace attendants rushed past us, going the opposite direction.

"What's happening?" I shouted to one of them, but most of them didn't stop.

One actually noticed me, and he staggered, then gave a hurried bow. "Your Highness!" His voice shook. "The tunnels—Dark Fae—"

From up ahead, I could hear screeching, clawing—the sounds of darklings.

"How many?" I asked, my voice tense.

His eyes were blown wide with panic. "The tunnels are overrun."

Alarm flashed through me. I glanced at my parents, then turned back to the attendant.

"Run," I told him, meeting his stare. "Run, and get everyone away from these halls."

He ran.

There was a cacophony of shattering glass just around the corner ahead, then a *thump*, and a moment later, Sorcha's massive, red-scaled body came into sight. She barely fit into the hall.

Window was the fastest way, she said, her gaze locking on me, then, *Darklings ahead. I can feel them. Let me go first; I can clear the way.*

I nodded and shifted back so I could protect her flank, with Champ still at my heels.

My parents did the same on her other side.

We rounded the final corner to the tunnel entrance. There were so many darklings filling the hallway, we couldn't even see the tunnel opening.

Their eyes flicked up to us, all at once... then they pounced.

They flooded Sorcha like a swarm of ants, before I could even take down my first row of them.

Sorcha blasted out a stream of fire, frying every darkling in her path, several rows deep.

More came.

I summoned my fire, blasting back an entire group of them, but their numbers seemed endless. They just kept coming. I seared as many with fire as I could, stabbing at the ones the fire missed, dodging their teeth and claws.

I heard my parents on Sorcha's other side, doing the same.

Even Champ dove in, snarling and tearing at them.

But already, exhaustion pulled at me. It was too much—none of us would be able to hold this up for long. There were just too many darklings.

I felt my bond with Sorcha flare bright with pain, and I glanced up—the darklings were tearing and biting at her, digging their claws and teeth in between her scales. Streams of silvery blood ran down her sides—dragon blood.

I felt her magic flicker and wane.

"Sorcha!" I screamed, then reached deep inward to summon more magic.

I had done this, in the market—the blaze of heat, the fire-blast that took them all out at once. I could do this. I *had* to do this.

But I hadn't *meant* to do it then. And I wasn't exactly sure *how* I had done it.

I summoned everything I could, blasted my fire around her and into the hall and tunnel as far as I could—

Every darkling in sight burst into clouds of ash.

I sank forward, resting my hands on my knees, then glanced up at the others. "Everyone okay?"

I am wounded, Sorcha replied, her voice breathy in my mind, *but I will live.*

Champ was cut up and bleeding, and my parents were not much better off—but we were all still standing. We were all breathing hard and exhausted, but we'd done it. We'd gotten rid of them.

A scrabbling sound came from the tunnel, followed by the sound of screeches.

A whole new slew of darklings came pouring toward the mouth of the tunnel.

For a brief moment, I almost wanted to give up.

Then I summoned my fire and sent it blazing into the tunnel.

Sorcha sent a flickering blaze of white-hot flame that joined mine. Our joint flame crashed into the tunnel opening, destroying the closest darklings.

Then Sorcha flicked her blazing stream upward, sweeping it across the arch of the tunnel opening.

The archway cracked, then crumbled in on itself, blocking the darklings into the tunnel.

I could hear them shrieking on the other side of the rubble.

It won't hold long, but at least the vault beneath is secured without a royal to open it. We must only worry about them getting out. She flicked her face toward me. *You must go.*

Our bond was still waning, flickering. Something wasn't right.

"You're hurt," I said aloud.

I can feel the darkness seeping. The bites. Dark magic and dragons do not mix well. Her eyes met mine. *You must go, King-of-mine. Clear the palace. Get your people out of the city.*

"I'm not leaving you," I said firmly.

Her stare bored into me, but I felt the moment she realized my stubbornness matched hers. She acquiesced.

Fine. Then we must all go. Quickly.

I turned to my parents. "Help me spread the word. We have to evacuate the city." My voice broke on the last words as it hit me how badly I had failed—what this could mean for Teionyr. For my people.

My dad placed his hand on my shoulder, then nodded.

We hurried back up the twisting corridors, Mom and Dad and I in the lead with Champ and Sorcha behind us.

Champ hung near Sorcha protectively, as though he could sense she was injured.

When we reached the landing where the tunnel halls joined the rest of the palace, we found my council awaiting us, surrounded by a cluster of terrified attendants.

"What news of the tunnels?" Kurrum asked tensely.

I met his gaze with all the courage I could muster. "The darklings have completely swarmed them. I don't know if this *is* the attack, or just a diversion. We should be ready for either. The tunnel opening is blocked by rubble now, but it won't hold long. We need to get everyone out." I glanced across them, then stopped. "Where's Orvyx?"

Maxim stepped toward me, his face somber. "In the prison. We caught him outside the city, trying to sneak back in. He confessed to tampering with the warding on a section of tunnels."

Orvyx had been one of the original council members, supposedly loyal to my father. I blinked, then shook off the betrayal. "It doesn't matter now. We have to get everyone out of the city. Where can the people go that will be safe?""

Kurrum spun to the others. "Tell everyone to—to—" He stopped, panic overtaking his expression as he looked at me. "Usually we use the *palace tunnels* as our emergency escape."

Maxim drew a breath, then turned to me. "Tell everyone to get to the citadel in the market square."

I turned to him. "The citadel?"

"There's a secret tunnel there, the one Maddox Rogers used to get your father to safety in the last war. It leads to the woods just outside the western walls. It will be safe. Not even a royal can open it, without the king's personal key."

I stared at him. "Then how will we—"

He lifted a chain from around his neck. On it dangled a small, ancient-looking key, etched over its full length with complex Fae runes. "I have the only copy. Your father himself entrusted it to me, before his death."

I gaped at him, then nodded. "Okay, everyone. Divide up. A third of you spread out through the palace, the rest to the city. Get every last person to the citadel, and get them there *now*. Tell them there's no time to pack—that their king commands immediate evacuation." I stared at them, dread settling on my chest. "Tell them the Dark Fae are coming."

Everyone scattered in various directions, except my parents.

I turned to them. "Please get to the citadel. Help Maxim oversee the evacuation. Take Champ with you."

"Where will you be?" my mom asked.

There was no way I could send all my people into the woods without checking the area around the kingdom, first—without making sure there wasn't another ambush awaiting us... or on its way.

I glanced at Sorcha. *Can you fly?* I sent her a mental image of what I was planning.

Yes, she answered. Her voice in my mind was steady, but weak. *For a bit, at least.*

I turned back to my parents. "I'll be on a dragon, protecting my kingdom from the air."

CHAPTER 51

SILENT AS A TOMB

Jordan

Climbing onto Sorcha's back was easy enough, once she flattened herself to the ground, but nothing could've prepared me for the sensation of flying on a dragon.

I wrapped my arms wide around the back of Sorcha's neck and gripped tight as she launched herself from the hilltop.

The palace quickly grew small, the air thin, the wind biting. It was terrifying and exhilarating all at once, and the view—it was breathtaking.

But Sorcha was already trembling. She was weakened more than she'd wanted to let on, and carrying my weight wasn't making things any easier.

Sorcha? I sent the question to her through our bond.

I am fine, she insisted, though I could tell she was anything but fine. *We will make a wide circle to look for approaching enemies.*

Her wings shot out wide, catching a current, and I leaned into the turn as she banked away from the city to do a sweep over the surrounding woods and fields.

Nothing looked amiss—no sign of any armies. Yet. But that didn't mean they weren't coming. I was sure they were; it just might mean they weren't coming *out here.*

Let's head back, I told Sorcha. I could feel her breaths getting heavier, like every stroke of her wings took more effort than the last. *Sweep low over the woods west of the city on the way. That's where the people are headed. Let's be sure it's clear.*

She did as I requested, circling wide across the western woods and then back toward the city, bringing us so low we nearly brushed the tops of the trees.

I peered down into the forested area. The woods weren't especially dense there, and I could see enough through the gaps between leaves to feel confident nothing unexpected was awaiting us in the woods.

But I didn't see the *expected,* either: no sign of the people who should've been emerging from whatever hidden tunnel existed and into the woods by now, if nothing had gone awry inside the city. There must have been a delay.

We need to check on the evacuation, I told Sorcha.

She angled us back toward the city.

As we neared the skies above Teionyr, I expected to see rows of people filing from their homes down into the market square, where the citadel—and the secret tunnel—were, or at the very least, a chaotic mob of panicked Teionyrians, haphazardly *running* toward the citadel.

The streets were empty. The marketplace, with its crowds of colorful, tented booths, was abandoned. The city was silent as a tomb.

Sorcha felt my alarm and mirrored it. *Maybe they are in the palace.*

She soared past the empty city, toward the hilltop above it where the palace sat, and landed us outside the palace.

I slid off her back, then rushed forward and threw the palace doors open, not sure what to expect.

Silence greeted me there, too.

A chill snaked down my spine.

The evacuation was happening from the citadel, right? Get back on, Sorcha told me. *I'll land as close to the citadel as I can.*

I clambered onto her back again, and she launched toward the city below. When we reached the market square, Sorcha swooped lower and tucked her wings tight, landing us—and stumbling forward several steps as the momentum carried us—within sight of the citadel gate.

The massive gate, usually flanked by guards, was empty... and open.

I slid off Sorcha, my boots thudding to the dusty ground.

Sorcha swayed.

Sorcha? I spun back. I didn't need to ask how she was—I could see the fatigue in her eyes. I could *feel* it.

Go, she told me. *I'm right behind you.*

The citadel gate spread before us, dark and foreboding, and I couldn't shake the feeling I was about to walk into the mouth of something evil. Into a trap. My instincts screamed at me, screamed against going in.

The problem was, my people—and my parents—might already be in there. I had no choice but to look.

I stepped through the yawning gateway.

Sorcha followed me, ducking low to avoid hitting the top of the gate.

The inside of the citadel was dark, the only light coming from the open gateway behind me.

As my eyes adjusted to the dimness, I found a large, open room with stone floors and walls and a heavy, metal-barred gate on the other end, opening into a long corridor lined with rows of holding cells.

I couldn't see very far past the barred gate to the corridor, but I could see the first several prison cells. They were filled with Teionyrian people, men and women of all ages. Even children. Dozens of them, packed into the cells like cattle held for slaughter—and those were only the ones I could see from the front gate. Their eyes were wide with fear.

When they saw me, many of them rushed to the bars of their cells, reaching out toward me, trying to speak to me. Their faces were afraid, and their mouths were open, screaming, as if they were yelling words—but I could hear none of what they said. It was like there was an invisible, soundproof wall between us.

I rushed toward them.

The outer gate slammed shut, trapping Sorcha and me inside.

For a moment, it was too dark to see.

Then someone lit a torch on the far wall, setting off a series of flames that lit rows of matching torches on both sides of the room, and a figure stepped toward me.

I sucked in a shallow breath as he came into view. "Maxim." My chest tightened, my stomach plunging as I glanced between his sneering face and the terrified people in the cells behind him. "What have you done?" I asked him, my voice turning hard. "Why are the people in cells?" My pulse increased. "Where are my parents?"

His eyes locked on me, his expression cold with hatred. "*You* were supposed to die in the tunnels." He rushed toward me with inhuman speed.

Before I could even react, his wiry fingers were around my throat.

I knew how to break a throat-hold, it was basic defense training, but *this*—it was like he'd grabbed my whole body with that one hand, somehow. My arms and legs would barely move.

Sorcha lunged toward us, but he slung his gaze toward her, his eyes flashing black.

She reared back like she'd been struck.

She *had* been struck—I could feel the pain and alarm flash through her.

"Stop it!" I yelled at him, the words scraping out with my strangled breaths.

Dark magic. I hadn't seen him wield it, but Sorcha's response meant he must have.

She swayed, barely keeping her feet. Her eyes turned glassy.

I called for her in my mind, but her answer was dazed, weak, more a jumble of confusion and pain than any coherent words. That plunged a pit of dread into my stomach like nothing else could have.

"Leave her alone," I growled at Maxim. I fought the magic enough to raise my hands and grab his wrists—even that took effort—but he was unnaturally strong for an old man. His grip was like iron.

I summoned my flames, but he squeezed my throat harder, almost entirely cutting off my breath.

"Don't," he said simply. "Or I kill them all."

I froze. Was he bluffing? I didn't dare tear my eyes from his to look at the cells, to see if there were any obvious traps. He *could* have been bluffing. Or... he might not have been.

He relaxed his grip slightly, only enough to allow me to breathe, but his hold was unyielding.

Behind me, I felt Sorcha rally slightly, her thoughts clearing, though I could still feel a fog of pain and weariness over them.

Stand down, I sent to her. *Don't do anything, yet.*

I couldn't risk provoking Maxim any further, not until I was sure what we were dealing with. I couldn't let *Sorcha* risk it. She didn't have it in her for more than one attempt at turning this situation around. I had to make sure it was the right one.

My whole body and mind fell instantly, incredibly still. I could feel the pool of my magic, churning just beneath my reach—but I didn't grasp it. I just met Maxim's stare. "*Why*?" I squeezed the word out, barely able to draw a breath. "Why are you doing this?"

"Decades of work—thwarted." His glare tore into me, seething with hatred. "The *wrong prince*. All these years." His breathing grew heavy, his words heated. "Do you know how much *work* you caused me? What it *cost* me, to have gotten that *wrong*?"

I stared at him, the pieces slowly settling into place. "He knew. My father. He started to suspect you worked for the Dark King. *That's* why you left the palace before the end of his rule. He didn't trust you anymore."

His fingers tightened on my throat again. His eyes narrowed. "He had reason not to."

I sucked a desperate, shallow breath as I stared into his eyes. The truth crystallized for me, as suddenly as if someone had flipped a switch. "*You* poisoned my father. The illness—getting Sevryn into the palace." I felt my magic churning, mounting. Certainty settled in more with every word. "The traitor wasn't the king's brother." *My uncle.* "It was never Beirthyr. It was you."

His mouth pulled up into a smirk. "Guilty as charged."

My magic exploded into an inferno.

His magic slammed back, smacking against mine like a dark, solid wall.

Maxim dropped his hold on my throat and stepped away, my magic still struggling against his. "We've learned some things, since your last fight," he said, grinning confidently. Dark tendrils snaked up from his fingertips as he spread his arms wide. "It turns out, dark magic *does* have an answer to fire-Fae magic, if you know how to construct it. Fire, after all, needs fuel. And your magic—"

—Is not the only magic he has, Sorcha said.

A rush of pure, bright energy surged through me, past me, and slammed into Maxim.

He flew backwards, airborne for a moment, then crashed back-first into the barred gate in front of the holding cells.

I tensed, waiting for him to get up, but he didn't.

He slumped to the floor.

The soundproof barrier vanished. The panicked shouts of my people filled the room.

"Your Highness! King Jordan! The king is here!" Their sobs and cries and shouts all blended together.

I hurried toward the barred gate and hauled Maxim's unconscious body aside. I yanked the gate, but it was locked shut. "How do I open it?"

"The key," a voice said, and I turned to see my dad shoving through the crowds in one of the cells with Mom just behind him. "On the wall, over there."

I grabbed the key and unlocked the gate, then fumbled through the rest of the keys until I found one that opened the first cell.

My parents rushed out toward me, and I shoved the key ring at the first adult Teionyrian I reached.

He was wearing a guard uniform, one of the usual citadel guards.

"Unlock the other cells, quickly," I told him.

He turned wide eyes on me, then nodded and grabbed the keys, rushing toward the next cell in the row.

King-of-mine.

I spun, panic flooding me at the tone in Sorcha's voice, at the rush of pain and fear she projected into my mind.

She swayed once, stumbling, then her legs buckled, and her whole, massive body thumped to the ground.

"Sorcha!" I screamed, running toward her.

Her presence in my mind winked out, a sudden, gaping hole... then slowly eased back in, so weak it felt like a flickering candle the faintest breath might extinguish.

Claws of panic clenched tight around my chest.

"Ma—" I started to call for Maxim, the only person I knew who knew about dragons, but caught myself. Terror and revulsion flooded in anew. I spun toward my parents, who had hurried up behind me. "Who else on the council is here? Were any of them also—"

"Traitors? No," my mom said. "They fought him. They tried to stop him, like we did. He put them in a cell."

I jumped to my feet, rushing back into the hall of prison cells, which was now a chaotic, nervous mass of milling people finding their loved ones.

"Kurrum!" I shouted. "Kurrum!"

Barthas and Champ rushed out to greet me from the crowd.

"Down there!" Barthas yelled, pointing ahead.

"Here, Your Highness!" Kurrum's voice yelled from the end of the hall.

The man with the keys caught sight of our exchange and rushed to open the cell.

As soon as Kurrum was freed, I grabbed his arm. "Come, hurry."

He stumbled behind me, not daring to question why his king was dragging him, but the moment he laid eyes on Sorcha, he pulled up short.

"Your Highness," he breathed, then dropped to his knees beside her. He placed a hand on her massive side. "Dark magic," he whispered.

I knew that much already. "How do we *fix* it?" I asked him.

Barthas and Champ caught up to us. Barthas hovered back, while Champ slowed, approaching Sorcha with a whimper.

Kurrum stared up at me from Sorcha's side. "We cannot."

I gaped at him. "No. There—"

He shook his head, cutting me off. "There is no way for *us* to heal her, not here. She needs *pure* air. *Dragon* air, free from all taint of dark magic, like they have in their mountain realm beyond the Wilds. She must return to her own, to the other dragons. If anyone can save her, it will be them."

I glanced at Sorcha, hulking and lifeless on the citadel floor. "*How*? She can't fly right now. She's not even awake!"

Champ nosed her, whimpered again, then came to my side.

"The other dragons will not be able to heal her while she is bound to your magic," Kurrum said quickly. "The magic of a sear-bind augments the bonded Fae, but the bond, unlike a Fae-to-Fae entanglement, flows mostly one way. As your sear-bind, Sorcha can feel your strains, your injuries, your weaknesses. You, as the Fae royal, are somewhat shielded. You have access to the sear-bind's magic, but a sear-bind's wounds do not become your own, not like yours become hers."

His eyes were on me but unfocused, as though he was thinking through the logistics out loud.

"You are injured and weary, and she was already weakened by the dark magic, even without your ails compounding it." His gaze slid to mine, focused again. "Your weakness is only draining her further. You must free her from the bond and let her go."

My pulse sped. "There's a way to do that?"

Kurrum nodded, his face growing grave. "When a sear-bind is on the brink of death, then, and only then... yes. The magic will allow the royal's bond to be transferred to a different sear-bind."

Dread settled in around my heart again as Kurrum's words sank in. "Then, she's..." Sorcha was *dying*?

He held my gaze, his eyes sorrowful. "We must act swiftly. I don't believe she has much longer."

CHAPTER 52

THE FEARSOME THING

Jordan

The other three council members broke away from the crowd, clustering silently behind Kurrum.

Sorcha was dying, and her bond to me was only making things worse. I needed to set her free, the very thing I'd promised her I would do... and I wanted to. I just hadn't expected it to happen like *this*.

"We need to transfer your bond to some other creature, and quickly," Kurrum said.

I drew a sharp breath. "But how? We can't go back into the vault. Sorcha might not have the time that would take, even if it were safe in the tunnels. And I can't—" I stopped. I didn't *want* to bind any other creature against its will. There was no way of knowing what the pool might call up for me the second time, but Sorcha had called the bond *enslavement*. "Are you sure I *have* to bind something else? We can't just dissolve the bond and free her?"

Kurrum shook his head. "We cannot."

I looked up at him. "What if the magic summons some other sentient creature whose life I destroy by binding it to me? At least Sorcha *wanted* to help me. If I somehow catch another dragon..."

Champ nosed me, huffed, then nosed me again.

I stared down at him.

"Your Highness," Kurrum said slowly, drawing my eyes to him. "It does not need to be a *magical* creature." His gaze cut to Champ. "It would be unconventional, and it would mean no access to augmented magic, but..."

Champ's trusting, dark eyes peered up at me.

"No," I said. "I can't." I couldn't do that to Champ, couldn't bind him to me like he was just an object to be used. Not when he couldn't tell me whether he was *okay* with it, and not now that I knew more of how the bond worked—that if I got hurt, it would hurt him, too.

But if I didn't...

Champ pawed the ground, snorted, then stared up at me again.

"I think he *wants* you to," Barthas said softly.

I glanced at Barthas. He looked entirely serious.

I stared up at my parents.

My mom's eyes locked on mine. "Do it, Jordan. That dog has never left your side by choice a single moment since you've had him. Just do it."

I looked at Kurrum. "Can we even do this here, without the pool?"

Kurrum nodded. "Yes. It's a different process. It doesn't require initiating a new bond, only transferring the current one. My own magic will suffice."

I hesitated, studying Kurrum's face. I was wary of trusting anyone, anymore, but what I saw in his gaze put me at ease. *Lord, please let this man be trustworthy.*

I dropped to my knees, gripping Champ's face. "Forgive me, if you don't want this," I whispered to him, then looked up at Kurrum. "Tell me what to do."

"A hand on Sorcha, a hand on Champ," he told me, then placed one of his own hands over mine on each. "Hold steady."

I felt a warm hum flow through both of my arms as Kurrum tipped his head forward and closed his eyes.

King-of-mine.

My heart lurched as Sorcha's voice drifted into my mind like a faint breeze, so weak.

I felt her presence, just barely, like a mist... and then I felt *Champ*, all warmth and loyalty and boundless energy, slide into my mind.

His presence wasn't verbal, like Sorcha's, but it was unmistakable. And it came with a knowing, a blunted comprehension. He didn't fully understand what we were doing, but he knew it helped me. He *wanted* to help me. He didn't care if he was now bound to me—I had already been his *pack*, his family.

He peered up at me, bouncing slightly, wagging his tail.

I couldn't hear his thoughts, really, but I could *feel* him. He was content. He was, even, a little *excited* by his ability to understand me more.

Relief filled me as I adjusted to the new sensation, then I startled as I felt Sorcha's presence peel away, sliding out from underneath Champ's.

Sorcha! I called to her in my mind, but the link was already fading.

One final thought surged through the bond, then dissolved as soon as I'd grasped it: *You kept your promise.*

I had set her free.

The sensation I'd known as Sorcha vanished completely from my mind.

Even with Champ's now there, glowing brightly, her absence in my mind was like a gaping hole.

I turned to Kurrum. "It's done. Is she okay?"

He dropped down level with her snout, then nodded. "Puffs of breath. Shallow but there."

I exhaled in relief, then stood and faced him. "There's no way she can fly like this, though. What do we do?"

Orvyx—the supposed traitor that Maxim had tried to blame for his own sins—stepped toward me. "Magic runs through dragons like blood." His eyes flicked to Kurrum, then landed back on me. "She needs fresh magic, untainted, to regain some of her strength. It wouldn't last long, and it wouldn't be *dragon* magic, but it might be enough."

I met his gaze. "Like a transfusion."

Orvyx's brow wrinkled in confusion.

"A transfer," I said quickly. "Of magic from someone else."

He nodded, his expression brightening. "Yes."

"I'll do it," I told both him and Kurrum. "Tell me how."

Kurrum opened his mouth, then closed it and swallowed. He stepped toward me. "You would simply push your magic into her until you feel it take hold... but Your Highness, I—" He glanced at the rest of the council, still huddling behind him. "It would drain you too much," he said softly. "Enough magic for her to fly beyond the Wilds? To fly for *hours*, until she reaches home? Such a transfer would drain you immensely. You are the most powerful of all of us, even without the dragon's bolstering. You are *the king*, tied to the magic of Teionyr itself. The Dark Fae are coming, any time now—any moment. Your magic is all we have left to protect us, to protect our kingdom. If you are weakened..."

Arval, one of the council members who had remained silent until now, stepped forward. "Dragons are sacred, Kurrum," he said, his voice low and firm. His jaw was tense. "Sometimes, the right thing is the hard thing—the fearsome thing." He looked up at me, his gaze confident as it held mine. "We are not a helpless people. We will stand with our king, no matter what he chooses. But sometimes, doing what's right requires stepping into the fear. Sometimes it requires *faith*."

I stared at him, my eyes studying his. I'd never heard the Teionyrians speak much about faith. From my studies, I knew they weren't a very religious people, on the whole. Their worldview tended more toward agnostic. But the way he said the word *faith*, the intensity in his eyes—whatever faith he meant, he *believed* it.

I nodded, and a smile crept onto my face. "Yes. Sometimes it does."

I tore my eyes from his and looked over at Sorcha.

"This was never her battle," I said, mostly to myself. "She was coming, even *before* the bond caught her. She *chose* to help us. To help me." Resolve settled in my chest. I knew what I had to do.

I turned back to the council. "Is there truly a tunnel here that leads out to the woods?"

Kurrum raised an eyebrow at my sudden change of topic, but nodded. "We checked it, before Maxim ambushed us. It was clear and untouched."

I drew a breath. "Maxim knew about it, which means the Dark Fae might, too."

Kurrum, Arval, Orvyx, and Thorim all exchanged glances.

"There is another here in the citadel, too," Thorim said, turning to me. "One only the former king's *council* knew of. Your father had it constructed after the last war, since in the wake of the stories and legends of his escape, the other tunnel was too well known. It leads to the *southern* woods, just outside the wall."

I exhaled in relief. "Take the people there, quickly, and hide them. We don't know how much longer we have until the Dark Fae flood the palace tunnels, or march on the city, or come in through Maxim's tunnel or something else. Get the people to safety."

His eyes narrowed. "And you?"

I turned back to Sorcha. "This was never her battle, but she put her life on the line for *us*. For me. I have to help her. Get the people out, and get them to safety. If things go wrong, keep running."

I yanked off my boot, slid out the runed coin I'd had there since I first came Faeside, and handed it to Kurrum. "There's a LeyGate hidden in the southwestern edge of those woods... one that leads Earthside. This coin is runed with LeyGuard magic. If you get close enough with this coin, you should be able to see the Gate shimmering. Hide the people in the southern woods if it's safe, and wait for me—but if you sense danger, use the coin to open the Gate and ask the Hub for refuge. Tell them Jordan Peters asks sanctuary for his people."

Kurrum clutched the coin and nodded.

I turned toward the people, who were watching from the corridor, and raised my voice. "The council will take you through another tunnel, to the southern woods. If you must, you will flee through a Gate to the LeyGuard refuge, the Hub. You will be safe there. The LeyGuard are our allies."

I tried not to imagine how alarmed Chairman Hart would be when *hundreds* of Fae came knocking on her door, asking for safe lodging. But the Hub had the space, in its wings and levels. It had been *built* for worst-case scenarios like this.

I leaned toward Kurrum and locked my eyes on his. "Get the people to safety, Kurrum. Whatever comes next here, it's *my* problem to handle, not theirs."

I spun and planted both my hands on Sorcha's side, starting to channel my magic into her while she still had time.

I felt it flow into her, at first like a stream of water sailing over a cliff into an empty abyss, but then something caught it and pooled it, and suddenly it felt more like filling a bucket. A very, very large bucket—in need of a *lot* to fill it—but contained, rather than bottomless.

My parents hurried up to either side of me and planted their hands on Sorcha next to mine, adding their power into mine, amplifying the rush of magic like turning up the flow on a faucet.

I could feel the dark magic inside Sorcha like a thick shadow, dancing toward my magic, my parents' magic, then retreating further as our magic filled up more space.

Exhaustion tugged at me almost immediately, but I forced it away. Sorcha needed more magic; it wasn't nearly enough yet.

Champ pressed in against my legs, bolstering me the only way he knew how—with his presence.

I smiled down at him. If I could have, I would've ruffled the fur on his head.

Kurrum strode over to the crowd of people huddled in the corridor, then handed the runed coin to the guard I'd given the keys to earlier. "You heard the king," Kurrum said. "There's a loose stone halfway up the far wall in the cell at the end on the left. Push it until it clicks, and a passage will open. Take the people through the tunnel, as quickly and quietly as you can, and wait for us in the woods. Put the women and children in the center. Have the men of fighting age make a barrier around them. Keep a sharp eye."

He locked eyes with the guard. "I'm putting you in charge. If the woods become unsafe, use the LeyGate as the king commanded."

The guard nodded, then shoved through the crowds, hurrying down the hall between the cells. The mass of people in the corridor churned, falling into rows and following after the guard as quickly as the width of the corridor would allow.

Kurrum hurried back over, peering at me across my father, who stood on that side of me.

I glanced at Kurrum and raised my eyebrows. "I told *you* to take them."

He planted his hands beside my father's on Sorcha's scaled side. "You said what comes next was *your* problem to handle. With all due respect, Your Highness, I am the head of your council and your father was my *friend*, so right now, *you* are *my* problem to handle." I felt his magic churn into Sorcha and merge with mine, the flow increasing. He cut a glare at me, but there was a fondness in it, and the ends of his lips hinted at a smile. "He would have been quite proud of you."

His words stirred a strange feeling in my chest.

I gave him a nod, swallowing back the surge of emotion. Then my gaze caught on my dad's, next to me, and the feeling doubled. I could see it, in his eyes—he was proud of me, too.

Arval, Thorim, and Orvyx stepped up next to Kurrum, placing their hands on Sorcha, too. Their magic crashed into the flow and melded with it.

Then Barthas rushed up, adding his hand to the crowd. His magic joined ours, a faint trickle compared to the others.

Though I was fighting exhaustion more and more by the moment, I smiled at Barthas, grateful. His magic might not be strong, but he was willing to give it, and that meant more to me than I could express.

He met my eyes and nodded.

Together, our little group poured our magic and energy into Sorcha, chasing the darkness back as much and as fervently as we could, while behind us, the people of Teionyr rushed to safety.

Eventually, the citadel grew quiet. The last of the people had gone.

Barthas swayed, then slumped forward against Sorcha. "I'm sorry, Your Highness. I—" He sagged to the floor.

I stiffened in alarm, but Kurrum reassured me. "He's unconscious. His body would not have allowed him to drain beyond its own limits. Self-protection: a person faints before they drain too far, unless something else intervenes." He drew a breath. "The body—it is intelligent." I could hear the weariness in his own voice. His words were slightly slurred.

A moment later, he slumped, then sank to the ground, draped against Sorcha's side. His eyes drooped closed.

Next to drop was Arval, then Orvyx.

"Jordan."

I cut my gaze to my mom. Her face was pale, her eyes unfocused.

"It's okay, Mom," I whispered. "I've got this. You can let go."

She shook her head, but her hand slid off of Sorcha of its own accord, her body slumping backward.

My dad lunged around me to catch her. I felt his magic break off as he dropped with her to the ground, cushioning her fall. He lowered her gently to the stone, then pushed up onto his knees and pressed a shaking hand against Sorcha's side again.

I turned to him. "It's okay, Dad. Rest."

His eyes flicked to mine, defiant, then rolled back as his eyelids sank shut. He slumped to the ground next to my mom.

Champ whimpered, nosed them both, then hurried back to my side.

I turned back to Sorcha, intent on my task. I couldn't feel her presence anymore, not like when we were bonded, but I knew she was there. I could feel her magic flickering, steadily growing stronger. The gaping hole the dark magic had made in her was no longer empty. Not *full*—maybe halfway, three-quarters, at most—but no longer just dregs in an empty barrel.

I could still feel the shadow of dark magic inside her, too, though. I got the sense that it was cowering, like a scared animal, but also watching—waiting for its moment to drain her again.

Pure exhaustion suddenly hit me like a sledgehammer. My knees buckled, and I leaned into Sorcha's side to keep myself upright. Dark spots pushed in at the corners of my vision, but I forced them back. I removed one trembling hand from Sorcha and drew the communication stone from my pocket. I pressed my thumb to one of the runes and whispered the word to activate it. My hand shook.

A moment later, Ayla's voice broke through. "Jordan!"

"I'm here," I said, my voice weaker than I'd expected.

"Where?" Her voice was high, worried. "Are you okay? Where are you?"

"Citadel," I whispered. "The people—hiding. Southern woods." The stone slipped from my numb fingers and clattered to the stone.

"Jordan? Jordan!" I heard Ayla yell. She drew a sharp breath. "I'm coming. Just hold on. We're coming!" The call cut out.

The darkness pulled at my eyes, my body trembled, my legs weakened. The hole inside Sorcha still wasn't full... but it would have to be enough. I leaned into Sorcha a moment longer, forcing the last of my magic into her until my body sagged of its own accord, then the room tilted sideways and I felt my side hit the ground.

My eyes were too heavy to open, sleep yanking at me like gravity, my consciousness dangling by slipping fingers from a ledge.

Beside me, something big moved.

There were heavy steps, the scuffle of claws on stone. I felt a warm burst of light, then a chuff of charred-wood smoke filled my lungs.

Sorcha, I thought, though I could no longer hear her voice.

I heard an excited bark—Champ's—then something scraped near the citadel gate.

There was a pulsing breeze, and a strange, unrecognizable sound. A churn of dust from outside danced over my face.

I placed the sound, just as I sank into darkness—*beating wings*, fading into the distance.

CHAPTER 53

WE FIGHT

Ayla

I lowered the communication stone, then looked up at the others. Words failed me, but I didn't need to say anything. We'd *all* heard Jordan's call. Something was wrong—very wrong. My chest felt hollowed out, my hands cold.

"I'll go tell Hart," Dove said, then rushed out of the room with Fogarty on her heels.

We were all prepped to leave. Brone and Striker had gone to grab the last of our supplies and to get Vyrthil from the med rooms. Kaizyn had gone with them. Reina, Callan, Madison, Rory, Grandpa, my parents, and I were huddled near one of the unopened Hub Gates in an empty room, waiting for them all to return.

We'd be leaving as soon as they were back, jumping straight into the palace at Teionyr. Rationally, I knew I couldn't speed the process, that it would only be minutes longer before I'd be there, before I could find him.

But after that call—my entire body itched to go *now*.

"We'll be leaving any moment," my mom said, her hand coming to rest on my shoulder. "We *are* coming to help him, like you told him. Just breathe."

I drew a breath, then paced away from the group. I couldn't stand still a moment longer, and if I couldn't leave yet, the energy had to go *somewhere*.

Reina jogged after me. "Ayla!"

She fell into rhythm beside me, pacing with me—back and forth, back and forth along the wall of the room.

"He loves you," she said after a few moments. "Jordan."

I stopped pacing and spun to look at her.

"He loves you," she said again. "You love him, too."

I nodded. And to my surprise, staring into her eyes, I saw that she was *okay* with that.

She grabbed my hands in both of hers and squeezed. "We'll get to Teionyr in time," she said, her voice firm. "He'll be fine."

I could hear the subtext, the same one I was feeling: *He has to be.*

I almost asked, *What if he isn't?* but I couldn't even bring myself to utter the words. Instead, I said, "You and Kaizyn?"

Reina's eyes widened. "I—" She dropped her hands and glanced away. "There's something, I think?" Her eyes flicked back to me, vulnerable. "But we're stepping back. Only for now. There's so much going on, and I didn't want this to be a heat-of-the-moment thing. When something more happens between us, *if* it does, I want—I *need*—it to be real. We both do."

I studied her face, then nodded. "What he feels for you *is* real." The words flew out before I could second-guess them. "He cares deeply for you. I felt it before the bond broke." I owed her that much, that reassurance.

Her gaze locked on mine with a glint of hope.

"Ready the Gate!" Chairman Hart called out, rushing into the room.

Brone and Striker ran in right behind her, both wearing supply packs, along with Kaizyn and Vyrthil, then Dove and Fogarty. Vyrthil looked stable, much better than before.

A dozen other adult LeyGuards I'd never seen before hurried in after the others, armed and looking ready for battle.

Doctor Harlowe jogged in next, clutching his tablet and looking flustered.

Reina and I rushed back over to the others, near our parents.

Kaizyn stepped near Reina immediately, then glanced at me and nodded.

Callan slid his hand into Madison's—she'd resolutely refused to stay behind, this time, and so had Rory. Because of that, Dove was going, too. She and Fogarty were already at Rory's side.

We were *all* going, for better or worse, our whole little group.

Grandpa glanced over at me, then reached across my parents and squeezed my hand.

Madison caught my eye, a nervous look on her face.

It was crazy to think that only a while ago, Madison and I weren't friends, I didn't know Callan, Rory was some guy whose life I thought I'd ruined, and Jordan and Reina were just friends I hung out with at school. I didn't even know Fae or LeyGuards *existed*. And now—

I swallowed back the knot of emotion in my throat. What we were about to walk into could change everything.

Please, God, keep them all safe.

Hart turned to address our whole group. "I wish I could come with you, but I'm needed here." Her eyes landed on Striker and Brone. "This is *your* mission. You're in charge." She handed Brone a runed communication stone. "When you get there, whatever you find, whatever you need—tell us, and if we can, we'll send it."

Brone slipped the stone into his pocket.

A nervous energy settled over the room as Hart turned to the rest of the group. "That boy is ours—one of our own. Normally I'd say *bring him home*, but he belongs on that throne. So I'll say the next best thing: *keep him safe.*" Her face hardened. "And take the Dark King down."

A chill spread through me at her expression, then the Gate flew open.

I could see a room of the Teionyrian palace through the opening, the same room Grandpa and I had used to come here for my training.

Brone and Striker stepped through the Gate, followed by the other LeyGuards.

The rest of us lined up, filing through the Gate as quickly as possible.

As I neared the Gate, Doctor Harlowe grabbed my arm. "Your magic is our best weapon, and the Dark King knows it." His ice-blue eyes locked on mine, his jaw firm. "Be careful, but don't hold back." He dropped my arm.

I swallowed, meeting his gaze. "I won't."

I stepped through the Gate.

The moment my feet hit the palace floor, Brone caught my attention, signaling silence. I huddled with the others in the small room.

The Gate snapped shut as soon as we were all through.

Brone pressed flat against the doorframe, peering into the hall. "It's quiet," he whispered. "Too quiet. Be alert."

He signaled the other LeyGuards to move to the rear, then he and Striker led our group out into the hall.

As we hurried down the abandoned corridors, the eerie silence made my skin prickle.

We reached the bottom floor, then the foyer, and Brone moved toward the palace doors. "Team A with me to the southern woods," he said, his words firm and confident even in a whisper. He tossed Striker a runed stone, smaller than the one Hart had given him. "Team B with Striker to the citadel."

The LeyGuards I didn't recognize all peeled off with Brone. Team A slipped through the doors and hurried down the hilltop toward the southern wall, crouched low but moving quickly.

Team B was apparently the rest of us.

Striker turned, his face solemn as he scanned over us. He nodded. "I got the better team." A smirk flashed up, then vanished. His jaw clenched. "Let's go get our boy."

We moved down the hill and into the city as quietly and quickly as possible, keeping to the shadows of the buildings, rushing toward the market square—and citadel—at the city's center.

By the time the citadel came into sight, my heart was in my throat. I shoved back thoughts of what I might find there and focused on running, step after step, until we reached the citadel's open gate. It was dark within, nothing visible.

Reina glanced at me, her mouth pulled into a thin line. Her eyes were worried. "It's quiet here, too," she whispered.

Striker nodded, then moved in front. "Behind me."

We all obeyed, clustering behind his massive form in front of the darkened doorway.

Reina's parents took up the rear of the group, weapons at the ready, eyes scanning our surroundings. Sometimes I forgot they'd been trained for this, that they were soldiers. But right now, they looked every bit the part.

A shadow barrelled toward Reina from within.

"Reina, watch out!" I whisper-yelled, heart lurching.

She tensed and Kaizyn leapt in front of her, drawing his dagger in one smooth motion.

Then Reina yelled, "No, wait!"

Kaizyn froze, still tense, as Reina dropped to her knees.

The thing crashed into her, a blur of white in the sun.

"Champ!" she whispered, clutching him as his whole body wagged.

Reina stood, and Champ bounded up to the shadowed doorway, then bounced impatiently and stared back at us.

We all exchanged tense glances... then we followed Champ into the dark room.

Striker's eyes adjusted first. I heard his sharp intake of breath, then he rushed forward and knelt down by a bunch of dark shapes.

My eyes adjusted a moment later, and my pulse skittered—bodies. My heart stopped beating as I saw who Striker hovered over. *Jordan.*

I rushed toward him and dropped down beside him.

"He's breathing. Unconscious," Striker said.

I pressed my hand to Jordan's face, needing to confirm Striker's statement for myself. Jordan's skin was warm. I could feel his breath, see the tiny pulse flicking in his neck. *Alive.* My heart resumed beating. I sucked in a shaky breath.

Striker moved quickly to the next crumpled person.

Kaizyn rushed up beside him, along with Callan, checking the people.

"They're all alive," Striker said, once Callan and Kaizyn had nodded to confirm the others were also breathing.

I glanced around. The crumpled bodies beside Jordan were Jordan's parents and some Teionyrians I didn't recognize.

"What's wrong with them?" Madison asked from behind me, her voice shaky.

Callan knelt and swiped his finger on the stone floor. He held up his hand, his face somber. A silvery liquid shimmered on his fingers. "Dragon blood."

My heart sank as I met Callan's stare. "Where's Sorcha?" I looked at the scene—bodies crumpled in a semicircle, as though they'd been gathered around something large.

Kaizyn pressed his hand to one of the Teionyrian's foreheads, then the man's chest. His mouth tightened, then he moved to the next person, doing the same. "They're drained."

Kaizyn rushed toward me and pressed his hands to Jordan's chest. Kaizyn's fingers flashed golden-red, and I felt a hum rush through Jordan's body. *Magic.*

Jordan flinched and gasped, though his eyes were still closed.

I pieced together what *drained* meant, then, but I didn't like it... or my guesses as to what might have caused it.

A moment later, Kaizyn jumped up and moved to the Fae man next to Jordan, channeling magic into him as well.

On the other side of the semi-circle, Callan did the same to one of the others.

My grandpa and Reina joined in, channeling magic into Jordan's parents.

A low moan came from Jordan. I spun back, placing my hands on his face. "I'm here," I whispered. "You're okay. You're safe."

Champ rushed up next to me, dancing impatiently as Jordan came to.

Noises and motion from the others signaled they were waking up, as well, but I couldn't tear my attention from Jordan.

Jordan blinked his eyes open, unfocused at first, then he saw me. "Ayla." He said my name in an exhale, like a prayer, scanning my face like he thought I might be a dream.

Then he reached up, buried his hands in my hair, pulled my face down to his, and kissed me like he needed it more than his next breath.

I kissed him back.

It was brief, but when he released me a moment later and stared into my eyes, there was no question of what he felt for me.

He sat up and pulled me to his chest, smoothing my hair gently, just for one breath.

Then he stiffened. "My parents. The council."

He shoved to his feet, swaying a little, then grasped my hands and pulled me up with him. Relief flashed over his face as he saw that his parents and the others were waking up and standing, and that the rest of us were there, but it was brief.

"Sorcha's gone," he said, turning back to me. "I had to free her—the dark magic poisoned her. Our magic was barely enough to help her. She nearly died." His voice faltered on the last word.

I grabbed his hand, squeezing it tight. I knew what Sorcha had meant to him, and I also knew him well enough to know that if she'd been hurt, he was likely blaming himself.

We also *all* knew what it meant for his magic—and for Teionyr's—that Sorcha was gone. I could tell he was exhausted and weakened. Without the dragon to bolster him, and now having drained himself to save her...

My chest tightened. Why now, when the Dark King's army could be attacking any moment? This was *horrible* timing for Jordan to be drained, but that was probably the Dark King's intent.

Jordan turned to the rest of the group, his posture tense. "Have you heard anything from the people? Are they safe?"

"We came in from the palace," I told him. "It was empty. But Brone has a team, too. They're on their way to the southern woods now."

Just then, as if on cue, Striker stiffened. "The stone." He pulled it from his pocket and pressed his thumb to the glowing rune.

"The people are all here, hiding like Jordan told us," Brone's voice said, briskly and quietly. "You?"

"We've got Jordan," Striker replied to the stone, "and his dog and parents and some Teionyrians. They're all alive, but drained. Dragon's gone—she was wounded. Jordan and the others channeled their magic to save her, then set her free."

Brone let out a sharp exhale. "Copy that. What's our next move?"

I glanced around at the others. Our group from the Hub was a mixture of scared and ready. The council members, Jordan's parents, and Barthas all looked tense and weary.

Striker stepped forward. His gaze landed steadily on Jordan. "Hart put me in charge, kid, but you're the king." He held up the stone, so Brone would be able to hear, too. "What do you need? What's our next move?"

Jordan glanced across our motley group. The muscle in his jaw ticked. "If the Dark Fae haven't flooded the palace, yet, and they haven't come in here… then they're probably planning to attack *out there*. Or maybe from all directions at once." He paused, looking at the stone. "Brone, can you get the people to safety?"

There was a silent moment, then Brone answered. "I'm telling you right now, some of the men won't agree to go. They want to fight alongside their king."

Jordan and Kaizyn exchanged a long glance.

"We are a peaceful people, not all trained in war," Kaizyn said softly, "but many of the men are strong in magic, and Teionyrians have never lacked courage in their conviction. This is their home, and you are their king. If they have chosen to fight, you will be hard-pressed to stop them."

"You cannot protect them from every harm, Jordan," Callan added gently. "Nor would they want you to."

Jordan drew a breath, his eyes falling closed, but when they reopened, he looked calm. "Keep anyone who wants to fight with you," he told Brone, "and we'll meet up with you when we can. Can you get the rest to the Hub? Anyone who can't or doesn't want to fight?"

There was no judgment in Jordan's tone, only concern. He didn't condemn the people who chose to flee rather than fight. He just wanted them all safe.

Brone grunted an agreement. "Yes. But there must be close to three hundred people here. Maybe more." His voice ticked up at the end, like he was amused. He let out a dry chuckle. "Meredith is going to *love* this." His voice returned to all-business. "I've got this, but it could take a while to get everyone through. Call me if something changes."

The stone went dark.

Striker slid it back into his pocket, then focused on Jordan. "What's *our* next move?"

Across the group, Jordan locked eyes with Kaizyn again. "We don't know the Dark King's numbers. We could be leading our people to a slaughter." Jordan's voice was flat, just stating the obvious, but I knew he was looking for feedback, for anything he might have missed.

"He wants Teionyr. He wants control of the vault," Kaizyn said quietly. "If we don't confront him *now*, if we run, our people won't ever be safe. We'll be looking over our shoulders the rest of our lives, waiting for him to strike again."

Jordan nodded, his expression tight. His gaze slid across the rest of us, then glanced off.

I knew that look, now. His *strategy* look.

"Then we don't run," Jordan said, turning back toward Kaizyn. "We fight. But first, we need a plan."

CHAPTER 54

MISDIRECTION

Ayla

"We can't just go barreling in outnumbered and expect to survive this, much less *win* this. We need a plan, something they wouldn't expect." Jordan glanced off again, thinking, while the rest of us watched in tense silence.

Finally, his gaze flicked back to Striker. "How many LeyGuards are with Brone?"

"Twelve," Striker answered. He didn't interject any further; just waited patiently with an expression somewhere between appraisal and pride.

I didn't often think about the fact Striker had once been Jordan's trainer and mentor, but I could see it, then, in the way Striker watched him.

The rest of the group watched, too, even Jordan's parents. I could see their pride in him, and their concern, but also their respect.

What would it be like for your teenage son to suddenly become a *king*? Then again, my parents were here, as well, concerned but lingering back, ready to help but letting me do what I'd been called to do, even though they knew it would be dangerous. How hard must this be, for them? To be out of their element, out of their own *world*, knowing that I needed to do this, but helpless to protect me?

I glanced over at them, where they were engaged in a whispered conversation with my grandpa.

My mom caught me watching and gave me a warm smile. I could see in her eyes she was afraid, but that smile—it was complete trust. Trust in me, and knowing my mom, also trust in God that if He'd called me to this, then He'd be with me in whatever was to come. My mom's faith had always been her anchor, and by watching her, I'd learned how to find my own.

I smiled back at her, and it struck me, right then, that Jordan and I must have won the parent and grandparent lottery. And Reina, too. All our families were amazing.

Maybe this was just what love looked like.

Jordan turned to me. "Are there any new developments from while you were at the Hub? Any information we should know?"

By *we*, I assumed he meant himself, his parents, and his council—the ones who had been in Teionyr.

I met his gaze. "My bond with Kaizyn is broken."

Jordan's eyes widened as he glanced between Kaizyn and me. "It is? How?"

I looked back at Kaizyn, who gave me a nod of support then turned to Jordan.

"Keyja and Etcher," Kaizyn said. "It's a long story, but... Etcher died to make sure the bond was broken, and to keep us both safe."

Jordan's jaw tensed, and he swallowed. "I owe him much, then." His eyes were heavy with emotion as he squeezed my hands.

I squeezed them back, then continued. "My magic is stronger, now, and I can control it... for the most part." I swallowed down my fear that maybe I hadn't learned enough, that maybe I couldn't control my magic *enough*, and shook my head. "I don't know what else—" I stopped and glanced at Rory. "Have you seen or heard anything new?"

Jordan turned to face Rory, one eyebrow raised in question.

"Rory had a vision just before we came here," Dove said softly. Her eyes were on Jordan, but she grasped Rory's hand. "He saw the Dark King, talking with the woman who works for him. That's how we knew the tunnels were under attack. We were already preparing to come here when you called. It wasn't the first time Rory has had a vision of them."

Jordan's eyes widened again.

"I can feel the dark magic hovering at the edge of my mind," Rory said warily, glancing between me and Jordan. "It's still there, for sure. But no, no new visions. It feels *dormant*, right now, like a lingering shadow. And I'm pretty sure they can't see me right now, either. I can feel it, when they do."

Now Jordan's eyes were *very* wide. "The visions go both ways?"

"Yes," Rory said, looking a little sick to his stomach.

Dove leaned into him, gently rubbing his arm.

Jordan glanced away for a few breaths, thinking.

I wanted to slide my hand into his, but didn't want to distract him. Instead, I stepped closer, watching but letting him think.

I saw the exact moment the idea hit him, the moment his features flipped from concentrating and distant to tense with urgency.

He spun back toward Rory. "You said the magic is hovering at the edge of your mind, dormant. Do you think you could make it *un*dormant?"

We weren't sure the plan would work, but Rory was willing to try it.

We contacted Brone, and he sent half his LeyGuards to meet us at the palace. The rest were still funneling Teionyrians through the Gate to the Hub.

The palace was still eerily quiet and empty. Our steps echoed on the polished floors as we entered the foyer.

Jordan gathered the LeyGuards, his council, and all the rest of us over to one side of the foyer, then dragged a chair over and stood on it, facing us, like he was about to address the small crowd.

Rory and Dove hovered near the back of our group, Fogarty near Dove's feet with his tail flicking anxiously. If I had to guess, the bear-cat wasn't the biggest fan of this plan, but it was the only one we had.

Jordan met Rory's eyes across the crowd. "You sure you'll be okay?" No matter his desperation for this to work, or his lack of other plans, he would never have forced Rory to do this.

Rory nodded. "I'm ready."

Dove clutched his hand in one of hers, the runed stone to control the dark magic gripped in her other palm.

Jordan nodded, then looked at the rest of us and drew a breath. "You all know what to do." He glanced at Rory. "On Rory's cue."

Rory and Dove stepped away from the crowd, just far enough into a side corridor to make it plausible that the rest of us couldn't see Rory even though he could see us—that he wasn't part of our assembly and had gone off on his own.

Rory closed his eyes, probing his own mind. Then he stiffened and collapsed to the floor.

Madison was standing next to me. Her hand shot out and grabbed mine.

I squeezed her hand back as we both locked our eyes on Jordan, pretending we didn't know Rory was there at all, didn't know he was convulsing, didn't know the Dark King or Miravel could be probing his mind that very moment.

Madison's fingers trembled, digging into the back of my hand.

Jordan began talking, his voice loud and confident. "It's a risk, but we can't abandon the vault. It's too important. We need to get back into the tunnels. With any luck, the darklings will already be gone from them. We're short on soldiers but we also can't abandon the people. They can't all fit in the palace, but many can. And if we barricade the rest of the city—"

"It's done," Dove's gentle voice called from the shadows of the alcove. "He's waking up."

I exhaled in relief, and Madison dropped my hand.

We all rushed toward the corridor.

Rory was sitting upright, but pale. His eyes flicked up and locked on Jordan's. "I could still hear you when Miravel spotted me—drawing the darkness on purpose gave me more control, like we'd hoped. Like I was only halfway in. Miravel was alone, in the woods somewhere. I couldn't see much else. She told me I was a fool to think they wouldn't notice me spying, and that I wouldn't get any information from them. Then she stared off, listening. When she looked back at me, she had a sadistic smirk. She said *he* was coming for me. Then I let go." He shuddered, then smiled. "I think it worked."

Misdirection. Making the Dark King think we were centering our efforts inside the city to protect the vault was the best we could do, our only hope at having an advantage. Well, that and a boatload of magical traps in the palace and the city. Apparently, the Teionyrian council was good at those. Maxim hadn't been the only one who knew some scary tricks.

Kurrum gave Jordan a quick nod, then he, Orvyx, Arval, and Thorim hurried off to set their traps. When we were planning, Jordan had worried Kurrum and the others were still too drained from helping him bolster Sorcha, but they'd insisted they had magic enough for this.

Jordan grabbed Rory's arm, helping him to his feet. "Thank you," he told Rory, then he turned to the rest of us. "Now we get to the woods and hope the Dark King takes our bait."

When we made it to the southern woods, Brone and the rest of the LeyGuards were waiting for us under cover of the trees, along with a small crowd of Teionyrian men. Brone had chosen a dense part of the forest, and the people were spread out, hovering in the shadows of the trees. If we hadn't known where to look for them, we may not have even seen them.

The Teionyrians were talking softly among themselves, and a few were conversing with Brone and the other LeyGuards.

Before we'd made it far enough into the trees for them to notice us, Keyja intercepted us.

Jordan stepped up next to me protectively, and I was reminded he didn't know Keyja well, didn't know if we could trust her. But he relaxed slightly when I smiled at her.

"You came." I was stating the obvious, but she'd taken me by surprise.

Keyja nodded. "I want to help. I went to Arcvale first—and before you ask it, yes, I knew the risks. That Chairman woman made sure I heard an earful of them. But I needed to check on Mraugathal. He could not flee as we did."

I tensed. "Was he okay?"

Keyja smiled. "He was, indeed. He can be a crafty plant, when he wishes to be."

She didn't elaborate, and I didn't have time to ask more.

"His cousins are watching the army," Keyja continued quickly. "The Dark Fae appeared not long ago, inside the southern border of Upper Faeside. They are headed in our direction."

Kaizyn came toward her from the rear of our group. "*Inside* the southern border?"

"Yes." Keyja's expression was grave. "They have already crossed the Dual Mountains boundary, somehow. And their army is large, as Mraugathal had seen before."

"How large?" Jordan asked, his voice tense.

Keyja met his eyes. "Three squadrons that we've seen so far. Each one has five Selkblood commanders, each with twenty or more wind-Fae marching under their command, and each squadron also has a small horde of darklings circling above it. It's an organized march—though the darklings will frenzy into chaos when they begin to attack. They always do."

I did the math. Five Selkbloods per squadron, each commanding twenty wind-Fae and a group of darklings. I wasn't the best at mental math, but that meant a hundred wind-Fae soldiers per squadron. With three squadrons total... that was fifteen Selkbloods and *three hundred* soldiers. And that wasn't even counting the hordes of flying darklings they had in tow. Even *one* Selkblood was formidable enough, with the way some of them could control minds and manipulate emotions. But this...

My chest tightened, my breaths quickening.

Jordan glanced over at me, then took my hand and pulled me close, wrapping an arm around my shoulders. Somehow, he always knew when I was starting to panic. Even in the middle of *all this*, he'd noticed and known I needed him. His heart beat, fast but steady, as I leaned against his chest.

"Mraugathal will have his cousins warn us when the army is near," Keyja continued. "The squadrons are moving quickly—perhaps an hour or two out, at most."

Our group followed Keyja deeper into the trees.

Brone was the first to notice us, and when his gaze snapped in our direction, the rest of the men looked our way, too.

This was the first good look I'd gotten at the Teionyrians who had chosen to stay. There were maybe three dozen of them, no more than forty total, and they were men of varying ages from young adulthood to middle age, but all looked fit and healthy. They held an assortment of weapons—swords, knives, spears, shields. I assumed the Hub had provided the weapons, but to my surprise, most of the Teionyrians looked comfortable holding them.

"Are the rest of the people safe?" Jordan asked as we neared. He kept his voice low. There was no sign of the enemy nearby, yet, but we still needed to be careful.

As soon as Jordan came into sight, the dozens of Teionyrians dropped into kneeling bows. "Your Highness." Their chorus of statements came almost in unison.

Reina and I shared an amused glance from where she stood near the other side of the group.

Brone turned to answer Jordan's question. "Yes. Hart sealed the Gate behind them. The Hub has gone back on lockdown, as a precaution. She will send whatever we need, but she cannot put the Hub at risk, and most of the personnel are busy with accommodating so many people."

The Teionyrians stayed in their bows, waiting for Jordan to address them.

The other LeyGuards who had been conversing with the Teionyrians remained standing, glancing between Jordan and the men bowing to him with expressions varying from surprise to respect. Jordan wasn't their king—he was a kid they'd probably seen training, and not even a full LeyGuard yet.

Now, he was in charge.

The rest of our group moved in closer.

Reina's parents stood beside her, and Madison, Callan, Dove, Fogarty, and Rory clustered near them. Striker had made his way over near Brone with the other LeyGuards. My parents and grandpa stood near me and Jordan, with Champ not far behind. Kaizyn stood on Jordan's other side. Vyrthil stood at seeming ease beside Kaizyn, though his scorpion-like tail twitched every few seconds, and his eyes were sharp and alert.

Hundreds of Dark Fae were on their way this moment, and this was it—this was our army: my friends and family, a few LeyGuards, one ArcFae and her striniak, a dog, a bear, a fire-cat... and three dozen Teionyrian men.

CHAPTER 55

WE FIGHT AS EQUALS

Ayla

Jordan turned toward the kneeling Teionyrians, whose heads were still tipped in bows. He clenched his jaw, and I could see him fighting back a wave of emotion. He cleared his throat. "You do not have to do this. You can go to safety, with your families." His voice was steady and compassionate.

One of the men looked up, his brown eyes sharp with conviction. "Our families are why we stay, Your Highness."

Kaizyn stepped forward.

Jordan drew a breath as Kaizyn placed a hand on his shoulder. They exchanged a glance, then Jordan nodded.

Kaizyn met the kneeling man's gaze. "You have all trained with these kinds of weapons?"

The other men looked up from their bows as the first man replied, though they all remained kneeling. "Yes, Your Highness. From the moment King Veilar was slain, and you vanished, a group of us began to train."

I noticed that the man addressed Jordan and Kaizyn both the same—*Your Highness*. I wasn't sure of the usual titles in Teionyr, but so far I'd only heard Your Highness used when addressing the king. The way the man had used the term for Kaizyn didn't seem a disrespect to Jordan's place as king... but it *did* seem an honoring of Kaizyn's place as the prince and heir. As the king who might have been.

The man's mouth pulled into a frown. "We never believed you had killed your father. We felt trouble coming, and we did the only thing we knew how, to prepare. We didn't know which guards we could trust, so we found or made what weapons we could and started training in my shop, after dark. Our skills are not as polished as yours, Your Highness, but we can hold our own. We did the best we could."

Kaizyn smiled and placed his hand on the man's shoulder. "You did well."

Jordan stepped toward the men. "Please, stand. If we fight together, we fight as equals."

The men exchanged surprised looks, but they stood.

There was a rustling in the trees, and we all stiffened—but it was only Kurrum, Thorim, Arval, and Orvyx, rejoining us.

"It is done," Kurrum said, out of breath and flushed. His council robes had sweat stains at the armpits. The other council members were in similar states.

"Thank you," Jordan told him. Then he stepped back, addressing the whole group in a voice low in volume, but tight with intensity. "I need you all to know—my magic is weakened. The dragon is gone. To save her life, we had to break the binding."

The men who hadn't known that made noises of surprise, but did not interrupt.

Reina's gaze met mine over the crowd, wary.

Jordan continued. "The Dark King's army is strong and large—maybe several hundred wind-Fae with more than a dozen Selkbloods and a horde of darklings. We do not have a large army. But we have magic, we have weapons, we have surveillance on the enemy, and with any luck, we may also have the element of surprise. We should all pray, and pray hard, that it will be enough."

He paused, letting that sink in.

"We have led the enemy to think we are barricaded inside the city," he continued. "When the enemy nears the city walls, we will ambush them from behind. It's a simple plan, but the only one we've got. The councilmen have laid wards around and inside the city, but those wards cannot trap a whole army. They will catch a few at a time, at best, mostly if the Dark Fae happen to breach the already warded outer walls or attempt to send another group in through the palace. The rest will be up to us, out here." He drew a breath. "Take a few moments, do whatever you need to get ready. We may have only an hour."

He turned and strode away from the crowd, clearly needing a moment alone.

I hesitated, debating whether to follow—but in the end, it was never really a question. My feet were moving after him before I'd even officially decided.

He stopped just inside the next row of trees and leaned his hands on the trunk of one of them, letting his forehead rest against its rough bark.

"Jordan?"

He tilted his face just enough to look at me. "Am I making a massive mistake?" His eyes were full of worry, his voice barely above a whisper. "I'm supposed to be Teionyr's best protection, but Sorcha is gone, we've had to abandon the city, and my magic is still so drained it's barely a flicker. What if we can't do this? These people—even *you*—could all..." His jaw clenched, and he trailed off, unable to say it out loud.

I drew a long breath, then crossed the distance between us and wrapped my arms around his waist. "We could. We *all* could. But that has always been true. Any day, any moment, a car accident, cancer—Jordan, life has *never* been guaranteed."

He shifted, leaning his back against the tree, and pulled me to his chest. His face buried in my hair. "Today is different odds," he muttered, his voice scraping.

Worse odds. But we already knew that. I tightened my arms around him.

He drew a shaky breath, then pressed a kiss to the top of my head. "I know we can't run. If we do, none of us will ever be safe. This might be our only chance to confront the Dark King head-on, when we *know* where and how he will strike. But to fight... like *this*? With so few of us? I don't know what else to do now but to pray for a miracle."

I thought of my magic, of his, of everything we'd been through and how far we'd all come. I tipped my head back to look up at him. "Then we pray."

His anguished eyes searched mine, then he pulled me close again, and leaned his forehead against mine.

Together, in the shadows of the trees, we prayed desperately for every single person standing with us in those woods, and whatever was about to come.

A little while later, Kaizyn came running toward us. "Look at the trees."

Jordan and I both looked up. The leaves were waving back and forth, like the wind couldn't decide which direction to blow them.

There was no wind.

Jordan and I hurried behind Kaizyn, toward the others.

"Mraugathal's cousins are warning us," Keyja said, glancing up. "The army is almost here."

The trees suddenly went still.

Jordan clenched my hand tight as the group of us moved as quietly as possible toward the edge of the forest.

The sky over a hilltop in the distance grew dark, a heavy cloud moving in, then the ground began to tremble.

The heavy cloud was churning... made of darklings.

A moment later, a mass of Fae soldiers poured over the distant hill.

The Selkbloods were easy to spot, even at a distance. They were unarmored, and compared to the ordered march of the rows of armored Fae behind them, they almost seemed to saunter. Arrogance poured off of them, even from far away, and I wondered which one was Sevryn—if *any* of them were. It was too far to see faces. But this was the Dark King's parade, and the marching rows oozed of theatrics, of intimidation and a show of power. He'd been building to this, this final act, and I knew Sevryn's mind well enough, by now, to know that he wouldn't have wanted to miss his own performance. If Miravel and the Dark King weren't marching with the army, they were sure to be close by.

Jordan turned toward our group, instantly in king-and-soldier mode.

Champ moved close to him.

Our entire group was tense, mouths drawn tight.

"Mr. and Mrs. Rogers," Jordan said, addressing my parents, "please stay with Madison and Rory in the trees. The four of you will keep watch for any more approaching armies, but keep clear of the fight. Brone, Striker, make sure they have communication stones to reach the two of you if they see anything important, or if Rory has any other visions. We can't afford an ambush." He glanced at each person in turn. "Dove, you and Fogarty stay here to protect them. Don't engage with the main battle unless you have to."

Dove nodded, eyes wide, and gripped Rory's hand.

Jordan addressed the council members next. "I will not tell you whether to stay here in the woods or come with the rest of us to fight. You have already done much to help our attempts today, and in saving Sorcha before that. I know you are tired. If you stay here, please be ready to help protect the others if necessary. Ayla's parents, Rory, and Madison are human civilians—they are not soldiers, and they do not have magic."

Kurrum and the other council members nodded.

I wasn't sure what they would choose, but they had already exerted themselves laying the traps, and before that they'd drained their magic for Sorcha, just as Jordan had. Jordan was right; they'd already done their part for our mission. I hoped they would stay hidden, if it was what they needed. I didn't wish for any of them to die.

Jordan turned to me.

"Ayla—" Jordan looked at me, and for a moment I thought he was going to tell me to stay in the woods, too, but he knew I couldn't. My magic was needed in the fight. "Stay close to me, *please*," he said. "Don't leave my side unless it's to run to safety." He glanced across the remaining people. "Kaizyn, Callan, Reina, Maddox, Mom, Dad, and Mr. and Mrs. Fisher, you're with us. Our team will be going straight for the Selkbloods. We have no real plan other than to kill as many of them as we can, and keep everyone on *our* side alive."

Callan nodded, smirking slightly. "I like that plan." His eyes cut nervously to Madison, and I could see that it was hurting him not to be able to stay near her and protect her, but he had a king and a prince to protect, and he had his orders. He was a soldier. He would obey.

Jordan turned to Striker and Brone. "The rest of the men are under your command. Engage the wind-Fae and darklings however you see fit. I hate to take Fae lives, but—"

"But if we must, we must," Kaizyn said, giving Jordan a reassuring nod. "If these are under the Dark King's control... I mean, look how they're marching." He gestured to the hilltop, where the Fae marched with unnaturally rigid, perfectly timed movements.

The way they moved, so mechanically and precisely, while the Selkbloods sauntered in front of them... there was something eerie about it, more than just a well-organized, well-trained army.

"They may not even *be* normal Fae anymore," Kaizyn continued. "But even if they are, they've made their choice... unless..." He trailed off, brows lowering in concern.

Jordan drew a breath. "Striker, Brone... change of plans. You and your men take out the darklings, as quickly as you can."

Striker grinned at Brone. "Mass slaughter of dark, hideous things is our specialty."

"As for the wind-Fae soldiers," Jordan continued, "keep them at bay, but try not to kill them. I'd prefer to take out the Selkbloods, first... just in case."

In case the soldiers were being puppeted against their will, I realized. The thought sent a chill down my spine.

Brone and Striker both nodded, catching Jordan's meaning.

Jordan drew a breath. "Everyone to your places."

That meant those who weren't fighting were supposed to fall back, to stay hidden in the shelter of the trees, while the rest of us readied to move out.

I hurried over to my parents and hugged them both.

There were tears in my mom's eyes when I pulled away. She smoothed my hair. "I would tell you to be safe—" She stopped, biting her lip.

My dad pulled us both back into a hug. "Just be careful, Ayla," he whispered. "Be smart and trust your instincts. In training, you always knew what to do when the time came, if you didn't overthink it."

I knew it was killing him to let me do this, to watch me walk out into danger.

I hugged them both tight. "I love you both. So much."

Grandpa came up beside me. "Come on, Peanut. We need to get into position." He hugged each of my parents quickly.

"Be careful, Dad," my father said as they separated.

Grandpa smiled. "Careful is for tottering old men." Then his face grew serious as he turned to me. "Let's go."

My parents moved further back into the trees with Madison and Rory and Dove.

I found Jordan where he was crouched, waiting near the treeline with the others.

The ground quivered beneath my feet as Dark Fae soldiers, hundreds, marched toward the city with a frenzied mass of darklings circling overhead. The dark army was making quick progress, spreading over the field and now broaching the hill nearest the palace. The closest side of that hill was only a few yards from where we hid. They would be near us soon.

Our army huddled down, unmoving. I scarcely dared to breathe.

The marching rows seemed endless. Maxim had tried to ambush us, maybe to kill Jordan or maybe just to weaken him, thinking we couldn't take the army without the full strength of Jordan's magic... and he had been right. We could never have overpowered this army directly, not with

Jordan weakened as he was. There were way too many of them. I hoped our last-ditch plan would work. But if it didn't...

If we failed here, if the Dark King won, he would only get stronger. He would probably go after the Hub next, and the Teionyrians who sheltered there. He wouldn't stop until he had control of the vault, of the power inside it—until all of Upper Faeside cowered beneath him like Lower Faeside already did. Would he even stop there? Would it be enough? Or would he come for Earthside next?

I thought of the Hub, of Gary's Café, of all the places the Dark King had *already* touched when he was playing there as Sevryn, and his attention hadn't even been on conquering Earthside, at that point. Would there be *anywhere* safe, by the time this evil psychopath was done?

Even if there was, everything that mattered most to me was *here,* on this battlefield.

I couldn't bear to think what it would mean if we didn't win.

Jordan clenched my hand, then tugged me deeper into the shelter of the trees.

Behind us, our own small army waited, hidden in the shadows.

My magic tingled at my fingertips, ready to protect Jordan if needed, because if I knew one thing in all this craziness, it was that I could *not* lose him. Not again.

Jordan glanced through the branches toward the sky. Any minute, the clouds of darklings would be passing right over us, the army nearing the city—and it would be time to move.

Beside me, the others fidgeted, waiting for his signal.

Please let our traps and this ambush be enough.

Days of planning and preparation, and all the weeks of chaos and heartache before that, had brought us to this one moment. The Dark King's army was marching for Teionyr—and the fate of Upper Faeside depended on whether we had done enough to stop them.

CHAPTER 56

THE FINAL BATTLE, PART I: JORDAN

Jordan

The first of the traps went off when the front squadron was almost to the city walls. A column of flame shot high, searing through rows of wind-Fae and Selkbloods, and singeing some darklings overhead. Screams of pain cut through the air.

Beside me, Ayla winced. "What if the wind-Fae *are* being controlled?"

I gripped her hand, trailing my thumb over her knuckles. "We're doing what we can to protect them." That trap may have maimed or injured the ones it caught, but I doubted it had killed anyone. It had been just a quick flash. These traps were an inconvenience and would slow the Dark Fae, but they wouldn't be enough to stop their advance.

The army continued marching steadily toward the city walls—hundreds of wind-Fae, rolling toward the city like an unstoppable machine.

My stomach clenched. The wards on the city walls were tied to royal magic—to *my* magic. Would they hold, now that I was weakened? Now that I had no dragon to bolster them? Suddenly, this whole plan seemed like a massive risk. Kaizyn's magic was also tied to the city, though more weakly than mine, since our father had made him an heir ceremonially. If we both fell in battle, the city's magic would falter, and the Dark Fae would pour right in. The Dark King could destroy our entire kingdom in a blink, leave our people with nothing to come home to... and that was only part of the risk, the part assuming he didn't figure out a way around the wards on the vault. If he did *that*, he'd have access to the Teionyrian magic itself, and all of Upper Faeside would be doomed.

I glanced at Kaizyn. He looked worried, too.

We had abandoned Teionyr, and I'd gotten the people to safety. It had seemed like the right move, the *only* move—but what if it wasn't enough? What if we should've stayed and fought?

Another trap went off, another segment of wind-Fae and darklings charred. The army kept moving.

Keyja moved up beside me, magic crackling from an orb on her chest.

A lightning bolt snapped out from the orb, then flashed into form next to her as a massive, glowing bison.

So *that* was the striniak the textbooks referenced, the creature the Madame ArcFae was guardian of. I had to admit, a crackling bison unfolding from a hole in her sternum was not what I had expected.

It blinked slowly at me with large, dark cow eyes.

I tried not to gawk.

"The council chose to remain here with Ayla's parents and the other non-magical humans," Keyja said, and I forced my eyes back to her. "I've moved them all further back into the trees."

I nodded. "That's good. The council members are exhausted already, and we'll need them after all this to help rebuild. The people trust them."

"I will help as much as I can in the battle," Keyja said, "but Tofa and I are still drained from the ceremony at the Hub. We must not expend everything before we face the Dark King and Miravel. The rest is a game to them. They *enjoy* watching us scramble, watching us hurt. But when we face them directly…" Her expression hardened. "We cannot fail. They must not leave this battlefield alive."

Her meaning was clear: we couldn't count on a massive show of magic from her or her crackling bison in this battle, at least not until the grand finale. And even that would be a fraction of what she could normally do.

Not that I really *knew* what she could normally do—all the Hub books described the Madame ArcFae's abilities vaguely and mysteriously—but I knew she was usually quite powerful.

The third trap went off, and suddenly the entire dark army halted.

We all tensed, staring out at the field.

The darklings fluttered in a restless mob above, hovering in place, while the wind-Fae and their Selkblood squadron leaders stood still as statues.

A dark figure emerged, walking through the center of the rows. The Dark King. *Sevryn*.

His head flicked toward the woods, toward *us*.

Even across the distance, I could see the eerie blue glow of his eyes as he scanned the trees. And I *felt* them when they locked on me.

Dread pooled in my stomach as his lips pulled slowly up into a smile.

His whisper carried across the field: "Attack."

The front half of the army resumed their march on the city. The back half spun on their heels and charged directly at us.

A raging wall of wind from the wind-Fae slammed into the trees, sending leaves flying and whipping the branches. The wind-Fae weren't advancing into the woods, but they wouldn't have to if they brought the trees down *on top* of us.

"Get back!" I yelled, dragging Ayla further into the cover of the woods.

The others followed us, but the wind was only ramping up.

Maddox rushed forward, shoving a wall of his wind magic back against their onslaught.

It helped a little, at first, but then his current got swept up in theirs, churning within it rather than holding them back. One LeyGuard's wind magic was no match for an entire army of wind-Fae. It was a wonder he'd been able to push back at all.

Ayla yanked her hand from mine and ran up to help Maddox, blasting the nearest wind-Fae with bursts of ice. It surprised them and slowed them for a moment, but not enough. The wind lagged only for a moment before resurging.

I glanced around, scrambling for a plan.

A chorus of angry shrieks sounded above.

I looked up. Mobs of darklings came hurtling in, hovering above the worst of the wind, then dive-bombing toward the trees and tearing at the overhead branches. Tearing an opening to get to us.

"Form up!" I yelled.

Brone and Striker rushed toward me.

"Still the same plan?" Brone yelled over the rushing wind. "Us on the darklings, you on the Selkbloods?"

"Yes!" I shouted back as the others rushed up around us. Champ slid to my flank, ready to protect me, as always.

Brone aimed his pistol upward, dropping darklings one after the other like ducks from the *Duck Hunt* game I played as a kid. Striker shot two columns of flame from his hands, charring a whole cluster of them. The darklings shrieked, and several dropped, but the rest rallied and resumed swooping at the trees.

My parents and Reina stepped up next to me, scanning the field.

"Take down the Selkbloods if you can, but try to avoid the wind-Fae—no lethal force on them, not yet," I called out.

My dad loosed an arrow toward a Selkblood he could see through a gap behind several rows of wind-Fae, but the breeze caught the arrow. It curved wide, then cartwheeled uselessly in the wind until it hit a tree and fell to the ground.

We all exchanged glances. We were trying not to harm the wind-Fae in case they were innocent, but aiming through their wind was useless. The Selkbloods were at the rear of the assault, probably puppeting the wind-Fae, but we'd never get to them without going *through* the wind-Fae first.

The wind ramped up.

The tree branches whipped so violently, we had to move or else get bludgeoned by them.

I grabbed Ayla's hand, and Maddox, Keyja, Reina, Kaizyn, Vyrthil, and Callan rushed up next to us, along with my parents and Reina's. Our group skirted back, further into the trees, ducking to keep from getting hit by waving branches as we tried to regroup. Brone and Striker and the Teionyrians fell back to join us, hunkering around us in the shelter of the trees.

The group of the others—Dove, Fogarty, Madison, Rory, Ayla's parents, Barthas, and the council—huddled just behind us all, staring up at the trees in alarm.

I glanced around and saw the hatch to the tunnel near the base of a tree, the tunnel the people had used to come up from the citadel.

"Get everyone who isn't fighting into the tunnel!" I yelled to Keyja, nodding to the hatch.

She hurried over toward Madison, Ayla's parents, Rory, and the council members, herding them all toward the hatch.

"I will keep an eye on things from up here," I heard Dove say—probably to Rory. I heard him try to argue, but it was pointless. "Stay safe, Rory Kane. Please!" Dove urged him toward the hatch.

"Barthas, please take Champ with you!" I called to him.

Barthas grabbed Champ's collar and tugged him toward the tunnel. Champ didn't want to go, but he wasn't a bear or fire-cat, and he didn't have magic. I couldn't risk him getting hurt.

As Keyja ushered them all into the safety of the tunnel, I huddled down with the remaining group near the edge of the forest, and really *looked* at the wind-Fae nearest me, at their faces. Their eyes were glassy and unfocused, their movements almost in unison as they swept their arms wide, directing the wind. We were right. They *were* being puppeted. Which meant they could be innocent.

Frustration churned in my chest. In the big picture, it was *good* if the Selkbloods were running the show. That narrowed our targets from hundreds to barely more than a dozen. But right now, we couldn't *get* to those targets.

When Keyja rejoined us, I spun to the others. "Okay, new plan. Brone, Striker, and Keyja, stay on the darklings. The rest of us are going to charge the wind-Fae. Knock the wind-Fae out however you can, but don't kill any if you don't have to. We just need them down so we can get to the Selkbloods."

The wind whipped higher, and the branches overhead groaned and cracked. "Move, now!" I yelled.

We ran for the open field. The last of our group, one of the Teionyrians, dove out of the woods just in time as a large branch crashed down where we'd been.

We all jumped to our feet quickly—but now we were exposed.

The wind-Fae pivoted in unison, facing us. The wind spiraled into a cyclone.

One poor Teionyrian close to the edge of our group got sucked up, screaming as the wind slammed him into the trunk of a tree. He sank to the ground, eyes glassy—dead.

My heart clenched. I gritted my teeth. "Knock out as many as you can!"

We rushed toward the mob of wind-Fae.

The darklings surged toward us, swooping as close as they could get in the wind.

Callan, Ayla, Maddox, Kaizyn, Reina, her parents, and my parents rushed into the fray beside me. We clobbered the dazed wind-Fae with the blunt ends of our weapons, taking down as many as we could.

They didn't fight back, didn't come to each other's rescue or even defend themselves. As some dropped, the rest just stepped over them, regrouping, and intensified their efforts with the wind.

Even as they dropped, the wind grew stronger. I had to lean into it just to keep my footing, and more than once, I reached out to steady Ayla as she stumbled from its force.

Then the Dark King raised a hand, and the *other* half of the army rushed toward us, abandoning the city to dive into the fray.

I bit back a groan of frustration as the whole new onslaught of wind-Fae surged up and fell in behind the others. The wind swept up, tossing dirt and leaves. Behind us, branches flopped and cracked, pieces breaking off and tumbling into the air.

Overhead, the massive cloud of darklings churned, looking for any gap in the wind to strike at us.

Brone and Striker aimed high again, taking down swaths of darklings, but at least half of their shots swung wide from the wind.

Tofa burst free from Keyja's chest again, she and Keyja shooting crackling streaks of electricity up into the roiling mob, dropping darklings by the dozen.

But there were just so *many* of them—the darklings *and* the wind-Fae. And we still couldn't reach the Selkbloods. Taking down enough wind-Fae to get to them now seemed nearly impossible.

"I have an idea!" Ayla yelled, clutching my arm. "Move everyone back!" She rushed off, grabbing her grandfather and pulling him aside to say something into his ear.

I wanted to ask what the plan was, but there wasn't time. I just had to trust her.

"Fall back!" I yelled at the others.

They glanced at me in surprise, but did as I said. We fell back, toward the edge of the battered, swaying trees.

Then Ayla and Maddox rushed forward.

I tensed, hating how exposed Ayla was, itching to run to protect her, but not wanting to be in the way of whatever she was about to do.

Maddox threw his hands wide, calling his wind into a whipping frenzy, then circled his hands, spiraling it into a growing cyclone that then duplicated itself and spread wider and wider, into a churning wall of wind and dust and stray leaves.

Ayla planted herself next to him, face scrunched in concentration, hands curled in front of her like she was holding something invisible.

The temperature of the air dropped suddenly, a cold gust sweeping over us like a winter chill.

"Now!" Ayla screamed.

Maddox thrust his arms forward, and shoved his wall of wind toward the army.

And Ayla—*my* Ayla, who had battled anxiety at every judging glare from a classmate, who never seemed to see her own strength, who constantly worried she wasn't good enough or strong enough or brave enough to take on the world—

She flung her arms wide with a cry of fury, and summoned a full-blown hailstorm.

CHAPTER 57

THE FINAL BATTLE, PART II: AYLA

Ayla

"It's working!" I shouted, grinning at Grandpa.

I'd thrown all the ice magic I could muster into the air at once, chilling whatever moisture I could siphon, clustering it into chunks, making golf ball-sized hail... then shoved the whole mess into Grandpa's cyclone wall.

The result was instant—golf-ball-sized hail, slamming into wind-Fae's foreheads. The whole front row swayed and dropped, knocked out cold.

Grandpa was moderating the wind-force, as I'd asked him to, doing his best to keep it at a knockout velocity and not a lethal one.

He glanced at me with a joyous grin, then turned back toward his wind. "Keep it coming, Peanut. We've got this!" His voice shook a little—this was taking a lot of effort from him—but his magic held strong. He was shockingly powerful, every bit the legend the Fae books painted him as.

And I was fighting *with* him.

A warm surge of pride flowed into my chest.

I gathered more droplets, channeled more ice, and funneled more hail into Grandpa's storm. He shoved the wall of wind forward. Another row of wind-Fae fell.

From somewhere beyond the wind-Fae, I heard an angry howl. Probably the Selkbloods, annoyed we were downing their puppets, but that just meant my plan was working. It was already draining my energy, though, and I knew it must be draining Grandpa even more. We wouldn't be able to do this for long, but we could sustain it long enough to take out most of the rows of wind-Fae—I hoped.

Jordan rushed up beside me, hand up, blocking his face from the raging wind. "You're doing amazing!"

My hair whipped out, smacking him in the face, I was sure, but he didn't seem to mind. I could only spare a glance at him, but it was rewarded with a beaming grin of pride.

"Thank you," I choked out, then sent another wave of hail into Grandpa's storm.

Our people rushed forward, on the move.

It wasn't safe for them to run into the fray, not with all the hailstones, but they did what they could from the sidelines.

Jordan angled himself defensively in front of Grandpa and me, protecting us in case any wind-Fae or Selkbloods broke through.

Jordan's parents aimed arrows at the wind-Fae's boots, maiming a few but also effectively tripping them and interrupting their magic.

Reina and her parents shot small streams of flame between the rows, singeing the wind-Fae's legs.

Dove and her bear stood on either side of Reina and both sets of parents, guarding them.

Kaizyn and Callan sheathed their daggers and took up stray branches and fallen hailstones instead, chucking them at the wind-Fae with startling accuracy while Vyrthil snarled and paced behind them.

And all the while, Brone and Striker and Keyja and Tofa flambeed the darklings out of the air above us, their winged bodies thumping down into the growing mass of unconscious or downed and moaning wind-Fae.

Each time we took out a row of wind-Fae, our entire group moved forward, making slow progress across the field.

It was a haphazard, ridiculous attack, and most of these wind-Fae would definitely have injuries, but it was working.

It was *working*.

Grandpa and I were exhausted by the time we reached the last row of wind-Fae, far now from the clump of woods where we'd started, but at least now their wind wasn't much of a resistance. We moved through it, past it, knocking them all down—then, finally, we were face to face with the cluster of Selkblood commanders behind them.

The Selkbloods must've been exhausted from puppeting so many wind-Fae. I felt their magic claw weakly at my mind, a flimsy attempt at control, little more than an annoying tickle—then our hailstorm slammed into them, too.

All fifteen of them fell like toy soldiers, knocked out cold.

The rest of our group rushed forward, some of the Teionyrians making sure the Selkbloods *wouldn't* be waking up—but I turned away. I knew these Selkbloods were evil, but I still couldn't bear to watch them get stabbed and charred.

While they did that, Brone and Striker sent surges of flame upward, joined by electricity from Keyja and Tofa, downing the last of the shrieking darklings.

The battlefield fell quiet.

Grandpa smiled at me, then leaned forward, resting his hands on his knees. He was spent, his legs and arms trembling.

We had done it. We had really done it.

Jordan tugged my shoulder, turning me toward him as the others regrouped around us.

"The Selkbloods are all down," he said quickly. "We got them all, but—"

He didn't get to finish his statement.

A gorgeous, dark-haired woman with cold, calculating eyes appeared right in front of us, out of thin air.

Vyrthil let out a low growl.

"Miravel," I heard Kaizyn whisper.

She was smiling in a way that summoned dread deep in my gut.

"The Selkbloods were puppeting the wind-Fae," she said, her voice like thick syrup. "But *who* was puppeting the Selkbloods?"

Sevryn appeared suddenly, in the mess of all the fallen wind-Fae, and I couldn't help but wonder if he'd apparated like in *Harry Potter*, or if he'd been there all along, just cloaked somehow. He grinned, then nodded at Miravel.

She flicked a hand, and like an army of robot soldiers, the wind-Fae all popped back onto their feet around the Dark King, hiding him from view.

I shuddered at the sheer creepiness of it, then a second rush of fear hit me.

Some of the wind-Fae were bleeding from their heads, some from other places, but it didn't seem to matter. In unison, their eyes flicked open. They hurried into rows and thrust their hands forward, summoning their magic in a steadily building breeze.

Grandpa and I exchanged a despairing look. We were already exhausted—and now, the wind-Fae were all back in the fight.

From the sideline, Miravel's dark eyes flashed a shocking ice-blue. She turned to us, and her mouth flipped into a scowl. "I'm done playing your little games."

The sky darkened with a distant cacophony like a chorus of bats.

I looked up in horror.

Another cloud of darklings hurtled in from the distance, already frenzied and shrieking, this time diving headlong into the burgeoning wind.

The wind-Fae's magic was more dangerous if we were near trees or projectiles, but if we stayed out in the open with that many darklings incoming, they would flay us alive.

"Get back under the trees!" Jordan yelled, and we all dashed for the woods.

As soon as we hit the treeline, Jordan spun, shoved me behind him into the shelter of the trees, and gripped his dagger. Brone and Striker and the Teionyrian fighters rushed up next to us, eyes on the sky, ready to fry any darklings who came close. Keyja and Tofa came with them. The others fell into position around us, too, as the wind whipped up again, tossing the branches overhead.

The wind-Fae marched steadily toward us, an advancing column of wind-wielding zombie Fae with the Dark King at its center and Miravel at the outer edge.

Somewhere behind me, Vyrthil let out another low growl.

The darklings barrelled toward the woods overhead, then circled wide around the wind, readying to swoop down on us.

"That is not good," Striker said, eyes on the sky. He turned to Jordan, yelling against the building wind. "What's the plan?"

Jordan stared at the wind-Fae, and I knew he was debating, trying to think of a way he wouldn't have to kill them, wouldn't have to take innocent lives.

My heart ached and my mind scrambled, but I was coming up empty, this time, too. No more brilliant ideas.

Jordan ran a hand through his hair. "I—we—" He drew a breath, then turned back to face us. "We'll take on the wind-Fae again, and knock out as many as we can," Jordan yelled. "This time, the Dark King himself is using them as a shield, so be careful. Don't kill them unless you have to, but do what you have to do to protect yourself. Brone and Striker and Keyja, stay on the darklings." He glanced over the group. "If *any* of you can get to Miravel or the Dark King, do it, but don't go alone. We fight in pairs or groups. Retreat or yell for backup if you need it. I don't want to lose *any* of you today. Understand?"

Everyone nodded. Those who had blunt weapons readied them. Everyone else grabbed rocks or branches or whatever they could find. I summoned the biggest hailstone I could muster from the air, about the size of a softball, and clutched it ice-cold between my palms. I glanced at Grandpa, who nodded and grabbed a downed branch.

Jordan squeezed my shoulder. "Stay close," he said.

We all charged back into the wind.

CHAPTER 58

THE FINAL BATTLE, PART III: RORY

Rory

I was supposed to be in the tunnel. But Dove was out there, with… whatever was making those horrible sounds. And so was Callan—a fact Madison was reminding me of every two seconds. Incessantly.

So, of course, Madison and I weren't _strictly_ staying in the tunnel. Actually, we weren't in the tunnel at all. We were pressed to the ground, in the shadow of the waving trees, trying to see what was going on.

"Rory! Madison!" Ayla's mom hissed at us from the lifted tunnel hatch. "This isn't safe. Please, come back inside!"

I glanced back at her. Her face looked so worried, so reminiscent of my own mother, that my heart squeezed. I _was_ being unsafe right now. And if anything happened to Madison on my watch…

I sighed. "Come on, Mads. She's right. We shouldn't be—"

A flash of dark hair and pale skin suddenly appeared at the treeline, stealing my breath.

Miravel.

She stalked along the treeline, seeming not to see us, slinking along the shadowy edges.

Then she blinked out of sight… and reappeared a few feet further away.

My chest clenched. What was she doing? Did the others even know she was here? Whatever she was up to, it couldn't be good.

"Rory?" Madison whispered. "What's—"

"Get inside, Mads," I whispered back, waving her toward the tunnel.

She started to argue, then saw the alarm on my face. She nodded and moved back toward the hatch, where Ayla's mom was still peering out at us.

I pushed up into a crouch.

"Rory!" Ayla's mom whispered after me. "Where are you going?"

But I ignored her, because Miravel had vanished again.

I crept forward through the trees to get a better look, keeping my back pressed against the trees and using the shadows to conceal myself, my gaze locked on where I'd last seen her.

There. Miravel popped into sight again, right behind a Teionyrian fighter near the treeline. She grabbed him from behind, stabbed him in the back with a knife, then dropped him and winked out of sight again.

My stomach roiled. I rushed toward him.

He was still alive, gasping. I grabbed his legs and dragged him into the shadow of the jostling trees.

Madison was waiting for me there, wide-eyed. "Rory! What—"

"Get help," I whispered.

She raced back to the hatch, and a moment later, came back with some of the council.

They hunched over the man, doing what they could—which didn't seem to be much. None of them were healers.

I crept back toward the field, dread churning in my gut.

What I saw on the field only made me feel worse. It was mass chaos. Wind was whipping everywhere. It was hard to make out what was happening, but it looked like *our* people were darting in and out of the rows of wind-Fae, knocking them in the heads and slashing at their legs. Clearly, they were trying not to *kill* them, but it was a really inefficient way to fight. To make things even worse, darklings swarmed overhead, swooping down every few seconds, despite the fire and electricity being shot up at them.

Behind me, Madison gasped.

I spun around. "Mads! You were supposed to be—"

She pointed a shaking finger, interrupting me. "Rory—Dove!"

I spun back around, and my heart stopped.

Dove and Fogarty were fighting a cluster of wind-Fae at the edge of the fight... and Miravel had just reappeared a few yards behind them.

I took off running.

"Rory!" Madison yelled after me, but my own shouts drowned her out.

"Dove!" I yelled, shoving through the onslaught of wind, jumping over downed wind-Fae. "Dove!" I was almost there, but she couldn't hear me over the chaos. I shouted again with everything I had. "Dove!"

Miravel turned first, saw me, and sneered... then spun back toward Dove.

I leaped.

I wasn't sure I would be close enough, but I smashed into Miravel just before I hit the ground, knocking her legs out from under her.

Dove spun with a gasp.

Miravel let out a snarl of anger as we hit the ground, then flipped over on top of me, driving her knife at my chest.

I threw up my hands—

Fogarty crashed into us with a furious roar, knocking Miravel off of me.

Her knife slashed down, her arm brushing my side, as she and the bear both tumbled to the ground beside me.

Miravel rolled out from under Fogarty and leaped to her feet.

He spun to pursue her, but a mass of darklings crashed into him before he could get to her. He roared again and tore at them, tossing them off of him, still trying to get to Miravel where she crouched, catching her breath.

"Rory!" Dove rushed toward me.

Miravel vanished.

Then she reappeared right behind Dove, knife already on its way to Dove's back.

"No!" I yelled, grabbing for Dove.

Something glinted through the air, then smashed into Miravel's chest, knocking her sideways before her knife could hit its target.

I grabbed Dove and shoved her behind me, then lurched to my feet, my heart still pounding.

Miravel was on her side on the ground, gasping, an *icicle* impaled in her chest. Blood pooled out around her, her eyes shut and her lips pale.

Fogarty roared, then leaped over the downed darklings to Miravel.

I turned to Dove, holding her as Foge did what was necessary to make sure Miravel wouldn't be vanishing again.

"Are you okay?" I whispered to Dove.

She nodded, arms tight around me. I could feel her heart pounding in her chest.

I spotted Ayla standing between us and the trees. Maddox stood near her, concentrating on a funnel of wind.

Ayla met my gaze across the chaos, looking shaky and pale.

The icicle, I realized. It had come from *her*.

The wind around us faltered, then gusted up again, twice as furious.

Dove and I were just on the edge of the wind and chaos. I glanced toward the center of the wind-Fae army, and my blood ran cold.

The Dark King stood a few yards away from us, arms wide, eyes flaming blue.

His gaze locked on Miravel's body, then on Fogarty near her, and his face contorted in rage. He vanished from sight, swallowed into his army of wind-Fae minions.

A chill snaked down my spine.

In the distance, our friends continued to dive in, knocking wind-Fae down one by one, as quickly as they could without killing them.

Dove grabbed my arm, pulling my attention back to her. "You saved me." She looked over at Ayla, then back at me. "So did she, but I would've been dead already the first time if it weren't for you. Thank you." She threw her arms around my chest in a quick hug.

I pulled her tight and pressed a kiss to her forehead. "I'm so glad you're okay."

She pulled back, smiled, then tugged my shirt near my waist, drawing me further from the battle. "The same for you, but you shouldn't be out here, Rory. It isn't safe." She pulled her hand back and gasped. It had come back bloody. "Oh! You're hurt!"

I looked down, and *ow*. There was a growing splotch of blood on my shirt, and now that the panic and adrenaline of saving Dove (and almost dying) was fading, the searing pain rushed in at me. I carefully lifted my shirt. There was a gash down my side, several inches long. Miravel must have caught me with her knife, after all. It wasn't deep, thank goodness, but it did hurt, and it was trickling blood.

"Come, Rory, we have to get you out of here." Dove tugged my arm.

I let her take me, but I halted as we passed Ayla. "Are you okay?"

"I–I think so," she said, her eyes wide as they met mine. Then she saw the blood. "Are *you* okay?"

I nodded. "Just a gash. I'll be fine."

Dove placed a hand on Ayla's arm as Fogarty moved up beside us. "Thank you, Ayla," she said sincerely.

Ayla nodded, still looking shaken, then her gaze caught on something beyond us and she stiffened.

Dove glanced back, then turned to Ayla. "Foge and I will get Rory to safety. Go."

Ayla nodded again, squeezed my arm, then darted back off into the chaos.

Chapter 59

The Final Battle, Part IV: Ayla

Ayla

I just took a life. That thought kept repeating as I ran back toward the mob to help Grandpa knock out the next section of wind-Fae he was struggling against. He seemed tired, weakening. I rushed toward him, leaning into the wind, stepping over unconscious wind-Fae. *I took a life.* I took a life to *save* a life, but still... I took a life. Fogarty had finished Miravel off, but that was just a technicality—it was my icicle that had sealed her fate.

I wasn't sad she was gone... it was just *heavy*, the thing I'd done, even though I had to do it. Heavier than I'd thought it would be.

I was halfway to Grandpa, forcing my way through the battering wind, when someone appeared right in front of me.

I nearly crashed into him before I processed his face. His eyes.

Sevryn. The Dark King.

"Hello, Ayla," he sneered. He looked happy to see me, in the most frightening way possible.

This version of Sevryn had strange symbols tattooed up and down his forearms. His face was the same as the ones I'd stared into so many times before, but his blue eyes glowed eerily, like the blue part of a flame close to the wick. His lips pulled up slowly into a grin, and a chill shot straight down my spine.

Then his gaze flicked past me, to Miravel's body. To the icicle still melting in her chest. And the glint in his eyes flipped to absolute fury.

"What... did... you... *do*?" He spat the words at me, his glare burning straight into me, his fists clenched and shaking. "It wasn't that blasted bear—it was *you*!"

From his fury, I almost thought he'd actually *cared* for Miravel—that I'd taken someone he loved. Maybe I had... but he hadn't really left me a choice, and I couldn't bring myself to feel bad for him. Not with everything he'd done.

I did feel *afraid*, though, as he stepped closer, his furious glare still searing into me. Very, very afraid.

I took a trembling step backward.

"Ayla!" Jordan shouted.

I glanced up, equal parts relieved and terrified to see him running toward me.

I reached for my magic. At first it fumbled, made slippery by my fear, but I reached again, grasped it, and clung to it for dear life. Jordan was coming for me, *without* the use of his magic—and there was no way I was letting Sevryn hurt him. Not now, not ever again.

Jordan was almost to us, shoving his way through the battle.

I raised my hands as Sevryn took another step toward me.

He glanced back at Jordan, then shouted in fury and flung his arms upward.

A roaring cyclone burst straight up from the ground, knocking away everything around us.

I staggered back, throwing up a hand to shield my face against an onslaught of dust and wind.

"Ayla!" I heard Jordan shout, in a drifting, fading-off way.

Then the world went eerily gray, all outside light muted, all sounds drowned in the roar of rushing wind, though around me the air fell perfectly still.

I dropped my hand. My heart stuttered.

I could see nothing but blurred shapes outside the whooshing circle of wind and debris around us, hear nothing beyond garbled noise. Even above us, there was nothing but rapidly swirling clouds and an eerie, grayish-green sky. But around us, it was utterly, chillingly calm.

It was just the Dark King and me, staring at each other—standing in the eye of his own personal tornado.

Chapter 60

The Final Battle, Part V: Callan

Callan

Rory rushed past me in the chaos, injured and bleeding, Dove and Fogarty at his side.

I spotted Madison bouncing at the edge of the woods, waiting for him. It took everything in me not to run over, to tell her to go hide in the tunnel, to make sure she and Rory were both okay. But Dove was helping Rory, and Madison was smart; she would get to safety.

That's what I told myself, over and over, because my duty right now was here, beside Kaizyn and Jordan—beside my prince and my king.

The wind-Fae were battering us with debris.

We were taking them down as quickly as we could, trying not to kill them, but there were just so many of them, and the wind, though lessening bit by bit as they fell, was intense.

Were these men conscious beneath the Dark King's control? I wondered as I dodged a rogue rock. Could they feel the pain when we hit them? I drove the blunt end of a branch into another one's head, knocking him out cold.

Then suddenly I flew backwards, thrown by a gust of wind far fiercer than any so far.

My spine smacked into the hard ground.

"Kaizyn!" I was on my feet in a moment, ignoring the pain that shot down my back when I stood. "Jordan?"

Kaizyn and Vyrthil staggered to their feet beside me, but Jordan was already up and running—toward a massive cyclone that hadn't been there a moment before.

"He's got Ayla!" He lunged at the cyclone, was thrown back, then lunged in again. He spun toward me as Kaizyn and I rushed up. "Ayla's in there, with the Dark King! I can't get in!"

I stared into the wind. I couldn't see much, just blurred shapes—two figures, the taller one stalking toward the smaller. But it could be her. It looked like her. My heart lurched. "We have to get in there."

The three of us raced in a wide loop around the tornado, but it was solid, a spiraling, circular column of air, reaching straight up to the sky.

Above us, a new chorus of shrieks broke out—more darklings, appearing from somewhere.

A few yards away, Brone reloaded his pistol and resumed firing upward at the darklings, while Striker sent up flames, charring any darklings that tried to swoop down into the people.

It was a never-ending loop, darklings breaking off from the mob, swooping down, getting charred, more swooping down to take their place. The Dark Fae had to run out of darklings eventually, but they certainly had a *lot* of them to waste.

The remaining wind-Fae still raged around the cyclone, whipping wind in every direction, a bit less coordinated than before.

I couldn't see the rest of our group. They were, presumably, somewhere in the chaos.

Kaizyn, Jordan, and I exchanged glances. "Okay," I said. "Let's think. There's got to be—"

Kaizyn's eyes flashed wide, then he dove at my chest, tackling me to the ground.

A blade glinted, sailing right over us. If I'd been standing, it would've buried itself in my chest.

Kaizyn rolled off of me, and I hurried to sit up.

Some of the wind-Fae were now drawing their previously unused weapons, throwing knives at the Teionyrian soldiers or slashing at them with swords.

They were no longer fighting with just wind.

Kaizyn dropped into a crouch, then gestured for me to stay low, too. Vyrthil slunk up next to us, eyes alert, body tense.

I turned to Kaizyn. "You aren't supposed to risk your life for mine. I'm supposed to be protecting *you*."

Kaizyn clasped my shoulder. "I will always protect my family."

This was the man I fought for, whom I would die for. Prince or not, king or not, he was a leader worth following, worth risking everything for—he always had been.

I clasped his shoulder in return. "Thank you, brother."

Jordan hurried toward us, still in a crouch. His eyes were on the cyclone, his mouth pulled into a tight line. It was killing him, being out here while Ayla was trapped in there. "Look," he said, pointing at the storm.

A shadowy figure was forcing its way into the cyclone from the other side.

I squinted. "Is that Maddox?" His wind magic may have made it possible for him to breach the storm, but he was already weakened even before that—he would be meager protection for Ayla now, if any.

The figure broke into the center, then stumbled. The figure I took to be Ayla rushed toward him, then spun back toward the taller figure, who advanced toward them.

Jordan stiffened. "We have to get inside that windstorm."

Reina, her parents, and Jordan's parents rushed up, all dirty and bloodied, though I wasn't sure if any of the blood was theirs.

"Ayla and Maddox are in there," Reina said, pointing at the storm with her dagger. "We tried, but we can't get in."

Jordan met her stare. "Neither could we."

A chorus of shrieks and screams broke out overhead. A mob of darklings barrelled down from behind the cyclone, then careened toward Brone at the edge of the field.

Brone shouted something, unloading his pistol into the mob. Darklings dropped one after the other, but not quickly enough.

Striker spun and dove in front of Brone, sweeping an arc of flame through the darkling mob—but the remainder regrouped and crashed right into him.

Striker howled in pain as the darklings knocked him to his knees, swarming over him with shrieks and flailing claws.

Brone crashed in, knocking them off of Striker with the blunt end of his pistol.

We all rushed toward them.

Striker surged up into flame. The darklings shrieked and recoiled, then dove in again. His flames sputtered.

Kaizyn and I drew our daggers, but we didn't dare toss them—even our aim couldn't overpower the gusting wind, and we couldn't risk hitting Brone or Striker.

We were almost to them when Striker flamed up once more, and the last of the darklings burst to ash.

Striker swayed and sank backward. Deep gashes bled from his arms, his thighs, the top of his head—even on his chest through his vest.

Brone was already at Striker's side by the time we made it there.

There was blood. A *lot* of blood.

"Go," Striker rasped, staring right at Jordan. "I'll be fine. Go get Ayla."

Jordan's parents rushed up behind us.

Jordan and his parents exchanged a glance, then Jordan's mom dropped to her knees, tore off part of her shirt, and started binding a large gash on Striker's leg.

Jordan met Striker's glassy gaze. "I'll be back. Just hang on." He took off back toward the cyclone.

I dashed after him, the others close behind.

"Okay," Jordan said, staring up at the storm. "Let's circle it again. Maybe there's a weak spot, or—"

Keyja ran up with Tofa right behind her, crackling like a living ball of lightning. Keyja glanced up, taking in the storm, then turned to Jordan. "I think I know a way."

CHAPTER 61

THE FINAL BATTLE, PART VI: MADISON

Madison

Rory and I huddled in the tunnel where Dove had deposited us, which was lit only by flickering torches on the wall. Rory leaned against the wall near the darker part of the tunnel, the part that led toward the city. The council and Ayla's parents sat against the wall on my other side, waiting with us.

Basically, Rory and I had been dropped off with the babysitters while our friends went to fight a battle.

I could hear rushing wind outside, shouts, darklings shrieking—a whole slew of things trying to murder our friends. Trying to murder *Callan*.

The anxiety was driving me insane.

A roaring scream like someone in pain cut through the wind, driving chills down my spine. "What was that? Something's not right."

From the other end of people, Champ whimpered. Barthas whispered to him and patted his head.

"It's a battle. People scream." Ayla's mom reached across her husband and grabbed my hand. "Breathe, Honey." Her eyes were tired and stressed as they met mine, but she offered me a smile. "Do you want me to pray with you?"

I'd been praying this whole time. Right now, my anxious body needed to *move*. I shook my head and stood. "Thank you, but no. I just need to walk."

She looked up at me. "Stay in sight, okay?"

That meant I could pace a total of about ten steps, but I nodded. "Oka—wait, where's Rory?"

Ayla's mom stiffened as we glanced around.

Ayla's dad and some of the council got to their feet.

"He didn't go up; we'd have seen him," Ayla's dad said. "He must've gone—"

Jogging footsteps neared from the dark tunnel, and I sighed in relief as Rory came back into sight, holding a wrapped bundle.

It clanged as he threw it on the ground, then spilled open.

Knives, a couple swords, a sharpened shovel, and three long, cylindrical things, each with a fuse on the end, toppled out.

"Weapons." I glanced up at him. "Where did you get these?"

He shrugged. "Found a stash back there. I'm guessing they're backups the Teionyrians brought."

One of the council members stepped toward us, pointing toward the cylinders. "Those are explosives... cannons, I believe you call them? A form of them, at least."

Rory slid his gaze to me, eyes widening, and picked one up.

"No," I said. "Rory, no. We don't even know *how* to—"

"I'm pretty sure we just aim it and light that fuse," Ayla's dad said, lifting another of the cylindrical weapons and examining it. He glanced at the council member. "Right?"

I stared. Ayla's dad was as crazy as my brother.

Her mom, however, seemed to have retained some sense. "How do we know it won't just blow *us* up in here?" she asked, her voice rising.

Another horrific shout sounded from above, another chorus of shrieks.

She and I exchanged looks, then I dove for the third cylinder.

It was heavy and awkward to wield, but I followed Rory's lead, bracing its weight against my shoulder and supporting the end with my other hand.

"We'll need fire to light them," Ayla's dad said. He turned to the torch.

"Leave that there," the oldest council member said, stepping forward. He snapped his fingers, and a flame surged up from his thumb. "I can do it more safely."

We carried our weapons up the dirt ramp.

The hatch for the tunnel was huge, basically like a heavy wooden gate, wide enough for several people to walk through at once. It took three councilmen to shove it up. As soon as it lifted halfway, the wind caught it, slamming it wide open with a *bang*.

The branches above us were whipping like crazy.

Above them, darklings swarmed and shrieked in angry clouds.

Out on the field, LeyGuards and Fae were leaning their weight against gusts of wind, their hair and clothes whipping about as they darted into the rows of sword-slashing wind-Fae.

I couldn't make out who was who from this distance, but people in LeyGuard gear were slamming things into the wind-Fae's heads, stomachs, whatever they could reach. wind-Fae were dropping to the ground, but more kept getting back up and surging in to replace them.

Streams of fire and arcs of lightning surged up from the ground where a mass of Teionyrians stood, along with Keyja and Tofa, battering clusters of the darkling mob overhead.

And in the middle of it all stood another cluster of LeyGuards, and two Fae who looked like Callan and Kaizyn, staring up at a freaking *cyclone* that was swirling straight up into the sky.

In other words, things had gone utterly, flipping crazy.

"Maybe we can help with the darklings?" Ayla's dad suggested, staring up at the churning mob overhead, visible even through the canopy of branches.

Rory and I exchanged glances with Ayla's dad.

"Spread out," her dad said. "We shouldn't go above ground, not with the wind as crazy as it is. We'll just have to aim from here."

We spread out in the hatch opening as much as we could, then shouldered our cannons, aiming them at the darkling mob beyond the overhead branches.

"Here's hoping we don't die," Rory said—then the council member lit the fuses.

He had barely made it back down the ramp when all three cannons went off in rapid succession.

The force of mine sent me tumbling backward down the dirt ramp, but Ayla's mom caught me.

She helped me stand back up, and I rushed back to the opening to survey the damage.

We'd blown a big, smoldering hole straight through the branches overhead—and through a section of the darklings. The rest of the mob had scattered away, shrieking furiously.

Rory let out a *whoop* and aimed again.

The darklings regrouped into a dense cluster, then flicked their heads toward us... and dive-bombed right for us through the hole we'd just made in the tree cover.

Rory dropped his cannon. "Close the hatch! Close the hatch!"

Rory and I frantically yanked at the hatch door, but it was too heavy to pull from our angle. Ayla's dad leaped up to the surface, staggering in the wind, and shoved his arms under the door. Rory jumped up to help, and together they got it upright, then braced against it to hold it up as they pivoted it around it to climb inside. It nearly slammed shut on them, but they dove inside just before it closed—and just in time. The darklings slammed into the closed hatch with a series of thuds, shrieking angrily as they clawed at it, trying to get in.

Below, Ayla's dad hung from the metal handle on the underside of the hatch, using his weight to make sure it stayed shut.

We all exchanged glances, panting.

The old council member had a stern, worried look on his face. The others simply looked anxious.

Rory stared at me. "Well, that was—"

A rumble trembled through the ground above us.

"Was that thunder?" Ayla's mom asked.

There was another roar, kind of like a whooshing sound.

Ayla's dad yelped and dropped his hand from the hatch, shaking out his palm. "It's hot," he said, glancing at his wife.

"A lightning strike, maybe?" she asked, eyes wide.

There was suddenly an eerie silence outside.

"The darklings have gone quiet." I said. "Do you think they left?"

Another boom of thunder echoed above.

I rushed up the dirt ramp, shoving at the hatch.

The hatch door was heavy, and the wind prevented me from shoving it open more than a few inches, even with my full strength.

Rory and Ayla's dad ran up beside me and helped, and together we edged it open enough to peek out.

Charred darklings littered the ground in a ring of singed grass and tree bark. The hole we'd blasted in the trees was even bigger now, with jagged and broken branches all around its edges, like something massive had crashed down through it.

Something huge and red shifted in the trees a few yards away.

I gasped. "Sorcha."

She flicked her snout toward me, then launched off, sailing up through the hole in the trees.

Rory shoved up beside me. "Madison..." His voice shook. "Please tell me you also just saw an honest-to-goodness *dragon*?"

"*Jordan's* dragon, or she was." I nodded, then pointed up. "Rory, look, she's coming back."

Sorcha sailed back over the trees, and my breath caught.

It wasn't just Sorcha. It was a flying V of *seven* dragons, each a different color, like a deadly rainbow, with Sorcha in the lead. They slammed into the mob of darklings, shooting arcs of flame at some and snatching at others, crushing them and flinging them to the ground.

"Not just one dragon," I said, excitement growing deep inside my ribs as I turned to look at Rory. "*Dragons!*"

Rory blinked at me, then rubbed a hand over his hair, looking like he was questioning his entire life. "I tripped and hit my head or something," he muttered. "I'm trapped in some kind of weird Dungeons and Dragons coma-dream."

The oldest council member rushed up next to us, staring skyward, then gasped.

I grabbed Rory's arm, a grin growing on my face. "Rory—we have *dragons* in this fight!"

He stared blankly at me. "It makes sense now. First, I got an amazing Fae girlfriend, and now *dragons* fly in to save us. Yeah, I'm definitely unconscious."

"This isn't a dream, son. It's a rescue." The council member dropped back from the hatch and turned to look at us, his stern expression now transformed into wide-eyed wonder. "With their help, we may actually *win.*"

CHAPTER 62

THE FINAL BATTLE, PART VII: AYLA

Ayla

The cyclone had just closed in around us, trapping me alone... with *him*.

A series of booms in the distance distracted me for a moment—was someone bombing the city?

But my attention quickly snapped back to the Dark King in front of me.

He was glaring at me, fists clenched and breathing heavily. The effort of channeling the cyclone *and* controlling the wind-Fae was obviously taking its toll, but he was still dangerously strong, and the venom in his murderous glare hadn't lessened in the slightest.

He took a step toward me. "You will pay for that, for Miravel."

So he *did* care for her.

My pulse thudded in my ears. My heart felt like it was about to beat out of my chest. I took a step back. "I didn't want to hurt anyone. You didn't leave me a choice." My voice cracked on the last word, betraying my fear.

"Ayla!" Grandpa's voice broke through the wind, then *he* stumbled in, staggering as the cyclone snapped shut behind him. His eyes flicked to mine. "Ayla."

I moved toward him.

The Dark King flung a hand outward.

Grandpa went sailing backward.

"Grandpa!" I rushed toward him as he crashed into the ground, then slumped.

No no no! His eyes were shut, and his arm flopped as I turned him over. I pressed my fingers to his throat.

He had a pulse. A weak one, but he was alive. I heaved a sigh of relief.

Then I flicked my face up toward Sevryn, who was watching us with a sneer.

"You," I growled—and suddenly I was furious. I shot to my feet, fists clenched and trembling at my sides.

I didn't usually get angry. Anger was an unsafe emotion, an *out-of-control* emotion, and as a rule, Ayla Rogers didn't lose control.

But right then, I *was* the anger.

"*You.*" The word tore from my throat like a snarl. My fury mounted, coursing through me, churning my magic within me like a swirling, raging blizzard. "I am *done* with you hurting the people I love!"

His gaze locked on mine, his eyes glinting blue. He sneered. "Oh, *are* you?"

A wall of dark, writhing magic slammed into my mind.

The Selkblood control. I could feel it, like claws trying to dig into my brain.

My magic sputtered and slid from my grasp.

"Stop it," I grunted, fighting back his hold with everything I had. "Get out of my head!"

He was strong—*so* strong, even with his attention divided by the cyclone and the wind-Fae outside. The dark claws of his magic pulled at my mind, tearing, a building pressure like fingers ripping my skull open from the inside out.

My magic slipped further away, drowned in a surge of pure, raw pain.

A scream tore from my throat as I dropped to my knees, clutching my head. "Get *out*!"

I felt my body slump sideways and hit the ground, but the pain consumed everything; I couldn't see anything outside the pain, anymore. I was *pain*, now; the anger was gone.

Then a tiny voice whispered, breaking through the screaming noise: *He can only control you if a part of you lets him.* It felt like it came from inside me and outside me at once, speaking directly to my heart.

Sevryn's dark claws were like a screaming pressure, tearing at my mind... but his hands weren't *really* in my brain. Selkbloods worked by manipulating emotion. That's what this pain was—manipulation. This pain was a lie. The control was a lie. My fear had let them in.

Kaizyn had been able to block our feedback loop, when he finally closed off his mind to what I was feeling. Selkblood control wasn't so different, really—a projection of thought and emotions. Did that mean I could block this?

I drew a shaking breath. "He can't control me unless a part of me lets him," I whispered to myself, the realization taking hold. Heaven knew I had a hard enough time letting people into my life, into my heart, into my mind—and suddenly, the thought that Sevryn had shoved his way in by force made me utterly, seething *mad* again.

I forced myself upright, arms shaking, vision blurry with pain, and turned to him. "Get out—of my—head!" I pictured those slimy, dark claws, and *shoved*.

His hold snapped loose, dark claws retreating.

He howled in anger and dove at me.

I lunged to my feet and dodged, but he caught my waist, knocking me back to the ground.

I landed, breath knocked out of me, just inches from Grandpa.

Grandpa moaned lightly, but didn't rise.

Sevryn flipped me onto my back, trapping my hands beneath me, pinning my legs with his weight. He pressed my shoulders to the ground with two powerful, wiry-muscled hands, leaning into me.

I couldn't move.

"You think you're high and mighty?" he snarled. His glare bored into me, spittle flying in my face. "Some special weapon, made to destroy me? You're *weak*. You're nothing. You've always *been* nothing, just riding on the power of those around you." He shook my shoulders, slamming my head against the ground. "The prince's spell, your grandfather, your precious *king*—Where are they now? What are *you*, now, without them all to prop you up? You're *nothing*. Look at them!" He gestured to the whirlwind, to the darkling shadows mobbing outside, to the chaotic battle happening outside our little storm. "They're dying—barely holding on, themselves. *Who* will save you now?"

I wrenched my hands free from beneath me and shot spears of ice at his face, but he dodged them, then pinned down my wrists.

I summoned more magic, trying to form hail, more ice, anything—but my magic was exhausted. *I* was exhausted. Fighting his hold in my mind had sapped my strength more than I'd realized.

The rage seeped away, and I stared up at him. This could be it. This could be how I died.

I was suddenly terrified.

He reared one hand back, a ball of dark magic churning in it, then leaned close.

I turned my face to the side.

"No one will save you now," he whispered, his breath hot against my cheek. "You will die the most excruciating death I can envision, Ayla Rogers. You will die *today*, and you will die *alone*."

Lightning crashed into a wall of the cyclone.

"One problem," a voice said. "She's *not* alone."

We both flipped our faces toward the sound, and my heart soared. "Reina!"

She stood inside the wall of the storm like a raging goddess, red ponytail whipping in the wind. Behind her stood Tofa, blazing like a pure white inferno. A straining dome of magic churned up from Tofa's back, holding an archway open in the tornado.

Keyja stepped up to Reina's side, electricity crackling over her fingers, and Dove moved up on Reina's other side, large eyes dark with fury, flanked by a very angry, very impatient-looking bear.

Behind them, outside the arch, the others—Jordan, Kaizyn, Callan, Jordan's parents, Reina's parents, Brone with a battered-looking Striker on the ground behind him, and a whole group of Teionyrians—had formed a semicircle behind Tofa's archway, keeping the wind-Fae at bay.

My heart lurched at seeing Striker on the ground, bloodied, rather than fighting—he was alert, but clearly hurt. I'd never seen him sit something out.

But they had come for me. *Every single one of them* had come for me.

Charred darklings were dropping to the ground like rain outside the cyclone. Something glinted in the sky beyond the archway, and I gasped. Were those *dragons*?

Jordan glanced back and saw Sevryn pinning me. He shouted something to the others and broke free, rushing toward us with a look of pure fury.

Reina drew a sword as her glare locked on Sevryn. "You have two seconds to get off my friend, or your head's gonna be on the ground."

CHAPTER 63

The Final Battle, Part VIII: Reina

Reina

Jordan rushed into the whirlwind. "Now!"

Electricity exploded across the cyclone, crackling down its sides. Dove ran in, throwing handfuls of something from her pouch, and vines shot straight up from the earth toward Sevryn. Fogarty charged in, raging, tearing the Dark King right off of Ayla and throwing him to the ground.

Dove's vines snaked up over him where he landed, trapping him as soon as he hit the earth.

Jordan rushed toward Ayla.

For a moment, I thought we'd done it.

Then Sevryn slammed a bolt of dark magic into the bear and burst straight through the vines.

Fogarty reared back with a howl.

Dove screamed and rushed for Fogarty as Sevryn rolled and sprung to his feet.

Jordan and I leaped for the Dark King at the same time.

Sevryn swung his arm wide, and I felt a wall of pure *evil* slam into me—dark, slithering, and cold.

I hit the ground, gasping. It choked me, grabbing at my throat. It felt like it was writhing *inside* of me.

Jordan hit the ground beside me, then groaned, clutching his head.

"You can fight it; don't let him in!" Ayla told him, then dropped to her knees beside me. "Fight it, Reina. He can't get a hold on you if you don't let him. You have to fight it!"

Fight it. I could *feel* where his tendrils had grabbed hold of my mind—it was almost tangible. I could do this. I drew a breath, then forcibly, slowly, and with a monumental effort, I pried Sevryn's sleazy, black claws from my mind. The pressure slipped out of my chest. I felt the dark magic recoil and retreat, and a second later, I could breathe again.

I sucked a couple of desperate breaths, then rolled to my feet.

Beside me Jordan moaned, shoved to his feet, too, and charged back at Sevryn.

Electricity crackled as Keyja battered Sevryn's cyclone again, coming at him through his own magic.

Sevryn rushed forward and backhanded Keyja in the face, an audible *smack* that made me gasp and sent her sprawling.

Tofa flared up in the archway, letting out a bellow of fury as Keyja staggered to her feet.

Ayla helped me to my feet—just in time to see Jordan go flying backward.

"Jordan!" Ayla yelled.

Jordan crashed to the ground near Maddox, and Dove rushed over to help him up.

Sevryn spun toward Ayla and me, his eyes raging with blue flames.

"You—will—die—*today*!" he snarled, then lunged at her.

I pushed Ayla to the ground and threw my body over hers, bracing for the hit.

It never came. Something else sailed over me first, crashing right into him.

I hurried to my feet, and found Kaizyn staring down at Sevryn, hands flaming, one boot planted firmly on the Dark King's throat.

Sevryn was sucking strained, rasping breaths. The cyclone around us was flickering—his magic finally failing. Outside, wind-Fae staggered and dropped as his hold on them slipped.

Kaizyn drew a dagger and leaned down close to Sevryn's face. "This is for my father," he whispered. Then his hand came down.

I turned away, clinging to Ayla as Sevryn's guttural scream gurgled to an end.

The cyclone fell.

CHAPTER 64

THE FINAL BATTLE, PART IX: KAIZYN

Kaizyn

I'd seen the Dark King send Jordan flying, then lunge at Reina, and the rest had been blind rage.

But I was staring down, now, and... it was done.

I glanced up and met Jordan's stare, where Dove had just helped him to his feet. He gave me a sober nod.

It was actually *done.* The Dark King was dead.

I spun around. "Reina?"

For a split second, I was terrified I'd been too late, that he'd hurt her—but she was there, whole and unharmed, one arm still wrapped around Ayla as they clung to one another.

They both stared up at me, then Reina glanced past me, at Sevryn.

"He's finally dead," Reina said. She seemed just as shocked as I was.

I wanted to rush toward her, and I started to... then I remembered she'd said she wanted space, wanted to put things on hold. I stopped mid-step, stumbling awkwardly, as our eyes locked.

She jumped to her feet and rushed toward me.

I met her halfway, our bodies colliding, and wrapped my arms tightly around her.

She trembled, clutching the back of my shirt in her fists.

She was shaking. The after-battle adrenaline plunge—shock setting in. I knew it well. "You're okay," I whispered, holding her tight. "We're all okay."

Over her shoulder, I saw Jordan drop to his knees beside Ayla, wrapping her in his arms.

All around us, wind-Fae lay unconscious across the field. And not only wind-Fae were down. Striker lay, bleeding—hurt, but alive. A few of the Teionyrians were injured, too, but others had not been so lucky. Several of them had fallen in the battle, men who had believed in me when no one else did, who had trained in secret, running solely on the belief that I wasn't a traitor, that I hadn't killed my father, that something worse was brewing. They'd prepared for a battle like this one, but my heart still ached that they'd had to die in it.

I glanced across the surviving Teionyrian fighters, who had gathered loosely around us when the cyclone fell. "Thank you," I told them, though I knew the words could never suffice.

Callan glanced over the group, making sure we were all okay, then rushed off toward the woods to get Madison and the others.

Maddox stirred, then moaned lightly as Jordan and Ayla helped him sit up.

Sorcha thumped to the ground near us, and a series of thumps followed as the other dragons landed behind her. Seven of them, each a different color. They stared at us silently as we all gaped back.

I glanced up—the darklings were gone. Killed by the dragons, or felled with Sevryn's death, it didn't really matter. They were gone. The battle was over.

And up above us, the sun was peeking out of the clouds.

Jordan turned to me with a smile. "We did it."

I smiled back. "We did."

"Kaizyn!" Callan shouted from the woods. "I need help!"

CHAPTER 65

THE FINAL BATTLE, PART X: AYLA

Ayla

Everyone who could move rushed toward the woods at Callan's call—except for Brone, who stayed with Striker.

I stopped to help Grandpa stand, but he waved for me to go ahead without him. "I'll be fine; go see what Callan needs."

When I caught up to the others, they were trying to open the hatch. A tree had fallen across the door, blocking it.

A massive, golden dragon lumbered over to us and made quick work of shoving the tree aside.

When we yanked open the hatch, we found everyone safe—and more than eager to get out of the tunnel.

As they all climbed out, Champ dashed past them all, rushing to prance around Jordan's legs.

"Hey, boy." Jordan bent down to pet him, then stood and wrapped his arms around me, resting his face against the top of my head.

My parents rushed out, burying both me and Jordan in their group hug, while Jordan's parents watched nearby with exhausted smiles.

Rory and Madison emerged from the ground, and Dove and Callan both ran forward to meet them.

From the safety of Jordan's and my parents' arms, I watched Dove crash into Rory and Callan crash into Madison, watched them cling to each other... and I couldn't help but grin.

We were alive. We were *alive*. But not without a cost.

"Where's your grandpa?" my dad asked as we pulled back from the hug, his face etched with worry.

"Over there." I pointed to where Grandpa was sitting, staring in our direction. "He's hurt, but I think he'll be okay."

My dad let out a relieved breath.

"You should've seen him, Mr. Rogers," Jordan said, his eyes wide with awe. "He was incredible." He turned to me with a tender smile. "They *both* were."

A flutter of pride stirred in my chest. "Thank you," I said, squeezing his hand, "but it wasn't just us; it was *everyone*." And I meant that. Grandpa and I had fought like our lives depended on it—because they had—but without *everyone else* also fighting with everything they had, things would have gone very differently.

Near the hatch, Kaizyn slipped his hand out of Reina's and turned to Kurrum. "Are the packs we brought from the Hub still down there with you?"

Kurrum nodded, and Kaizyn dashed down the ramp. He came back with a bulging satchel of supplies. "I'll bind the rest of Striker's wounds as best as I can, but we need to get him to the Hub for treatment."

Jordan glanced back at the field, at the waiting dragons. "Wait. I might have a faster way."

J ordan could no longer hear Sorcha's voice in his mind, but that didn't mean she couldn't understand him.

Striker winced as we laid him flat on a cleared section of ground. "I'm fine," he insisted again. "Check for others who are injured." His pale face and blood-soaked clothes said something different.

"Stop whining," Brone said, leaning over him with a smirk. "Lie back and let the dragon do her thing."

Striker groaned. "Fine."

Sorcha leaned in, pressing her massive nose to his chest.

Striker's entire torso lit up with a glow, and he sighed. "Ah, okay, yeah—you're right, that does feel much better."

A moment later, Sorcha pulled back.

Jordan rushed forward, throwing his arms around her massive nose. "Thank you."

Her eyes closed as she leaned into him. Then they both pulled back.

Jordan glanced over the field. "Could you—"

Sorcha turned to the other dragons, letting out a rumbling roar.

The sound was frankly terrifying—I literally felt the ground tremble—but I guess among dragons it passed for language.

The other dragons flicked their massive heads in acknowledgment, then wove their way into the mass of bodies strewn across the battlefield. They moved gingerly for their massive sizes, taking care not to step on anyone and stopping every so often to press their snouts to those who needed healing.

They treated the Teionyrians first—those who could be saved.

When they were all clustered near us, we looked back out over the field of unconscious wind-Fae.

"Whatever the Dark King did to them, it was more than us just knocking them out," Jordan said. "When his hold fell away, they just collapsed, like marionettes whose strings had been cut." He swallowed. "Part of me worries they're beyond waking up—that maybe we're too late to help them. But we have to try."

"There are hundreds of them," I said, a nervous pinch working its way into my chest. "What if they *aren't* innocent? What if they were working *with* him?"

Jordan glanced at me. "We won't know until we wake them up."

Kaizyn stepped up next to him. "I agree."

We gathered everyone from *our* side behind the dragons, then Jordan turned to Sorcha. "Can you remove any dark magic still in them? Or can you try?"

She and her clan turned back toward the battlefield and let out a massive, earth-trembling roar.

A wave of light surged out with it, rushing across the bodies.

I gasped. I hadn't even known they could *do* magic like that.

The wind-Fae stirred, waking up.

There was a long, tense moment as row after row of them sat up, blinked, and glanced around, looking confused.

Then they noticed the dragons.

The whole field went eerily quiet and still.

Dove stepped up next to Jordan. "I don't sense any dark magic in them," she said softly. "I think they're just scared."

Jordan stepped forward next to Sorcha at the center of the row of dragons, projecting his voice. "I am King Jordan of Teionyr. Who are *you* and why have you come?"

A murmur broke out across the field, mounting into a loud chatter.

Finally, a man a few rows back stood up. "We are wind-Fae of the Mountain Kingdom, Your Highness," he called out. "We—" he glanced around at his fellow Fae, then turned back to Jordan. "We were prisoners in the Mountain palace. I... I am not sure how we got here."

Murmurs of agreement sounded from the crowd.

"Who imprisoned you?" Jordan called out, his voice cutting through the noise.

Another man stood up from the left side of the crowd. "A Fae named Sevryn imprisoned our families *and* our queen and usurped her throne." His voice hardened. "He calls himself the *Dark King*."

Jordan let out his breath in a whoosh. "If that is true, then you have nothing to fear from us," he called back. "The Dark King—"

But before he could say anything further, a man near the edge of the crowd let out a loud cry.

"The Dark King! He is dead! He is dead!"

Everyone turned to stare where he pointed—at Sevryn's fallen corpse.

"We have seen these tricks before," I heard someone say, but most of the crowd jumped to their feet, rushing toward Sevryn's body.

"It's truly him. Look! His runes, the tattoos," one of them yelled. "The Dark King truly is dead!"

A stunned silence fell over the crowd, then they worked back up into an excited chatter as more groups of them rushed over to see Sevryn's body, to confirm the truth for themselves.

A man toward the front of the crowd, near us, swept his eyes over us, across the dragons. Then his gaze locked on Jordan. "Thank you," he said softly. "We prayed for months on end, and today, He sent you as our answer."

Then he dropped to his knees. "Praise God above," he called out, bowing his head and raising his arms upward. "The Dark King has fallen. We are free! Praise God! We are free!"

First a few at a time, then in large clusters, the wind-Fae dropped to their knees, bowed their heads, and raised their hands skyward. Their voices joined the first man's, staggered at first, then surging up into a resounding chant that made my eyes flood with tears.

Jordan moved back, wrapping his arms around me, as their shouts echoed across the field.

"We are free! Praise God! We are free!"

Epilogue, Part I: Jordan

Jordan

I slipped into fresh clothes, glad to be rid of the battle grime, and also grateful for the herbal concoctions the attendants had poured into the bath to soothe my many bruises.

It had been a very long day, even after the battle. We had fed all the battle-weary wind-Fae from the palace supplies, made sure their wounds were healed, and even offered them shelter... but they were eager to get back to their families, and to spread word of their kingdom's regained freedom.

In our brief talks with them, I'd learned their former king had been killed in the Dark King's assault, much like my father had been. Their queen and the teenage princess hadn't been seen in some time. It was suspected they were hostages within the palace, which the Dark King had taken over. The wind-Fae who had been at this battle were mostly from the royal army. The council and I drafted a missive to send with them which offered their queen an alliance between our kingdoms and opened the conversation for peaceful trade between Upper and Lower Faeside. We hoped they would find their queen alive and well, and that peace could finally be an option between the two realms.

We also learned that even though Sevryn—who was half-Selkblood himself—had used Selkbloods for many of his conquering missions and for commanding his army, not everyone from Morrowen had agreed with Sevryn's obsession for conquests. There were many Selkbloods who had *opposed* the Dark King, good people who had been forced into hiding across Lower Faeside because they were no longer safe in their city. Hopefully, now, they could all return home.

Sorcha and I had said our goodbyes, with the other dragons watching. It was strange, not hearing her in my mind, but she understood me well enough. She and the other dragons took off at the same time as the wind-Fae, watching over them as they marched toward the southern border into Lower Faeside. We'd learned there was a working Gate still there they could use to cross the Dual Mountains barrier, probably the one Sevryn had used to bring his army through. Knowing Sorcha, she wouldn't leave the wind-Fae until she knew they were safely back in the Mountain Kingdom. And then... well, I supposed she had business of her own to tend to. Now that she was free of our bond, she could rule her clan, like she'd always been meant to do.

I peered at myself in the mirror. My partially buttoned tunic only concealed *some* of my bruises, and the dark circles under my eyes were evidence of how exhausted I was. But we'd survived, and we had *won*—the worst was finally over. There could still be some of the Dark King's allies in hiding, and it might take some time to rout them all out, and to be sure both Upper Faeside and Lower Faeside were safe. But we'd cut off the head of the beast. For the first time in decades, there could be peace in Teionyr—peace in Upper Faeside.

And I, for the first time in a *long* time, could relax without my loved ones in danger.

A gentle knock sounded on my door.

Champ perked up from his nap on the pillow by my bed, his ears tilting, then stretched and bounded over to me.

I finished buttoning my tunic—the king's tunics had way more buttons than any clothes I'd ever worn Earthside, a seriously ridiculous amount of buttons—then strode over to the door. The king's crown—*my* crown—glinted at me from a table next to the door as I pulled it open.

"Jordan." Ayla smiled at me from the doorway, and my heart immediately warmed.

Barthas hovered behind her in the hall, wringing his hands. "It is not appropriate for a young miss to be alone in the king's chambers," he mumbled.

"You can join us, then." I laughed, then tugged Ayla inside my room.

Barthas came in, too, hovering near the closed door.

Champ ran over to greet him.

I opened my arms to Ayla. "Come here."

She melted into my embrace, tucking her arms around my back and resting her head against my chest. She smelled good, like herbal soap. Her hair was still damp from her bath.

After a moment, she pulled back, smiling up at me. "Your people are all home. Hart just sent the last group of Teionyrians through the Gate. The council is gathering them on the hillside like you asked."

I smiled back down at her. "I suppose I should get ready for a speech, then." I tucked a strand of her damp hair behind her ear. "Have you seen Kaizyn?"

"Are you sure you—" She stopped, cutting a glance at Barthas.

He immediately busied himself playing with Champ. "I assure you, I am of the utmost discretion," he said. "Just speak as though I'm not even here."

Ayla turned back to me, lowering her voice. "Are you sure you want to do this?" Her eyes peered up at me, full of love and acceptance... and concern.

I pulled her close, pressing a gentle kiss to her forehead. "I've never been more sure of anything in my life—except you."

She smiled.

Another knock sounded on the door.

"That must be him," Ayla said.

Barthas hurried to open the door.

Kaizyn stepped in, a glint of curiosity in his gaze as he spotted me. "You sent for me. Is something wrong? It's almost time to start the assembly. The people are already gathering."

"That's what I wanted to talk to you about." I squeezed Ayla's hand, and she smiled at me, squeezed Kaizyn's shoulder, then slipped out into the hall, shutting the door quietly behind her.

Kaizyn's gaze followed her, then locked on me, wary. "What's this about?"

I lifted the crown from the table and held it out to him.

His hands came up by instinct, like most people's do when you shove something at them, but then he tensed. "What are you doing?" His gaze flicked between the crown and my face.

I pressed the crown into his hands. "I know what I am, Kaizyn. I may have been born to be a king, but I was *raised* to be a LeyGuard. *You* are the son our father raised to rule this kingdom."

Kaizyn yanked his hands away, leaving the crown in my grip. "No, Jordan. I—"

"Just listen, please," I said, then waited until his eyes landed back on my face. "If you don't *want* this crown, I will stay. I won't leave our people without a ruler. But honestly, in my heart of hearts—" I paused, swallowing, then sighed. "In my heart, I am more LeyGuard than king. I was made for recon missions, not royalty."

"You're wrong," Kaizyn said, his expression fierce. "The people love you. They trust you."

"And they love and trust *you*. They've always trusted you. You were their prince before they even knew who I was. Those Teionyrians who fought with us? They trained all those nights for battle, in secret, because of their belief in *you*, not me." I stepped toward him, placing the crown back into his hands.

This time, he didn't pull away.

"Our father established *you* as the heir to the throne, Kaizyn. Had I never been found, or if something had happened to me, it would always have been you. No one but our father would've even known I existed." I closed his hands over the crown and slid mine away. "I've already spoken to the council, and the laws exist to make this happen. One simple ceremony before the people, and you become the rightful king. I will become the heir-prince, until you one day have heirs of your own."

His gaze met mine. "This is why you called the assembly."

I nodded. "Tell me you don't want it, that in your heart you don't feel the responsibility of leading these people, that you won't feel it *every single day*, for the rest of your life, whether you wear this crown or not. Tell me—honestly—that you don't want to be the king, that you don't believe deep down our father always *meant* for it to be you... and if you can say those words and mean them, then I will march right out there and make up some grand speech about the battle and pretend like this conversation never happened."

Kaizyn opened his mouth, shut it, then stared down at the crown in his hands.

I smiled. "That's what I thought."

He tore his gaze from the crown and looked up at me. "But what will *you* do? You'll just leave? What if something happens to me? You're the blood heir. What if the people need you?"

I put my hand on his shoulder. "If our people need me—if *you* need me—I will always come."

Kaizyn's fingers tightened on the crown, then he threw his arms around me. "You had better come more often than that," he said. "We're brothers, now."

I hugged him tight, then we both pulled back. "I'll visit," I said, smiling. "And yes, we are."

I glanced over toward Barthas. He had completely abandoned all pretense of playing with Champ and was beaming at us, his eyes full of tears.

Kaizyn drew a breath, then held the crown back out to me. "If we're going to do this, let's do it right. I presented this crown to you before the people. Now, will you present it to me?"

I took the crown and grinned. "It would be my honor."

Epilogue, Part II: Kaizyn

Kaizyn

I am king. I was still adjusting to that, rolling the phrase around in my mind, even an hour after the ceremony when I returned to my chambers. I peeled off my ceremonial robe, hung it over the back of a nearby chair, and sank back against my closed door.

I'm king.

Father's face surged up in my mind, and I swallowed back the wave of grief that came with it. I wished he could've been there to celebrate this. But then, he never would've been. Me becoming king would *always* have been in the wake of his loss. I'd envisioned that going much, much differently than it had, but I couldn't resent what had happened—not really. Not when it brought my father's other son back to his kingdom. Not when it had brought my brother to me.

And the people hadn't been disappointed in Jordan's decision, as I'd feared they would. They had cheered.

Jordan's speech, though I only remembered half of it due to my nerves, was eloquent and moving. And afterwards, as I greeted everyone, as was always the custom after a coronation, the people's words were all grateful—to all of us, for defending Teionyr and for protecting them. To Jordan, for doing what he felt was best for the people, even if it meant losing the throne. And to me, for my willingness to accept the throne in his place.

Not that I ever could have chosen differently.

As much as I'd wanted to tell Jordan he was wrong when he offered me the crown, he wasn't wrong about my heart. I would have felt a responsibility to look after my people, throne or no throne, every day for the rest of my life. Now, thanks to my new brother, it was also officially my duty. I just hoped he didn't regret it—that his decision brought him the same sense of freedom, of *rightness*, that it had brought me.

A knock sounded on my door.

Vyrthil chuffed from his spot near the wall, but I waved for him to stay. Then I spun and pulled the door open.

"Callan."

He smiled at me, then swept his arm dramatically and dropped into a low bow. "My king."

I rolled my eyes. "Enough. Stand up."

He straightened, grinning at me, then stepped inside my chambers.

I shut the door behind him, but by the time I turned around, that familiar sense of dread had settled into my chest. "Callan... do you think I did the right thing?"

He tilted his head, studying my face. "Accepting the throne, you mean?"

I nodded. I trusted him—with my life, and to be honest with me, even if it stung.

But he just smiled. "Without a single doubt. And if you'll still have me as a royal guard—"

I held up a hand, stopping him. "Callan, you know I would make you the head of my entire security and advisory council, wholeheartedly and without a second thought. But what about Madison?"

Callan glanced away.

I stepped toward him. "Don't pretend you don't long for a life beyond guarding me, now. I know you too well."

He sighed, forcing his eyes back to mine. "I do—but I also cannot leave my kingdom. I cannot leave my *family*."

That word hung between us, and I nodded.

"Which is why..." He drew a breath. "Which is why I have a favor to ask you." He stepped around me and pulled open the door. "More to the point, *she* has a favor to ask you."

I turned, and there stood Madison, chewing her lip nervously, hands clasped tight together. "Um—hey, Kaizyn." She stiffened. "I mean, Your Highness." She dropped into a curtsy.

I sighed. Would *everyone* be awkward around me now? "Please, Kaizyn is fine," I told her. She straightened, and I studied her face. "Please, come inside."

She stepped in, leaving the door partly open behind her and still looking nervous.

Callan moved next to her, taking one of her hands in his. She clenched it tight, like a drowning woman gripping a rope someone had thrown to her.

I met her nervous stare. "Callan is like a brother to me, Madison, and you are his... well... whatever it is you two are." I cleared my throat. That had come out more awkwardly than I'd intended. I gentled my voice, wanting to put her at ease. "What favor do you need?"

She drew a breath, then her words came out in a rush. "I would like a job here at the palace."

I stared at her. "A... job?"

"Yes." She nodded emphatically. "I'll earn my keep. I only had one more year of high school, anyway, and the Hub said they can arrange for me to do distance studies from here. I talked to my parents, and they would like to come, too. I'll do whatever is needed, to earn room and board for all three of us here at the palace, if you'll just please give me the chance."

I blinked at her. "Madison, you are my friend. Before all this, I had precious few of those. I do not take them lightly. You are *welcome* here. All of you. And we have plenty of space. There's no need for you to *earn* anything, though keeping Callan in check will probably be a full-time job of its own." I grinned at her, and her mouth slowly pulled up into a smile.

"Thank you," she breathed, relaxing.

I turned to Callan. "I assume this means you're staying, too?" He nodded, and I smiled and crossed my arms. "Then there's no favor involved here. I get the best possible head advisor I could've wished for, *and* I don't have to watch you mope around, miserable and heartsick, filling the palace halls with your tears."

He and Madison both laughed, then Callan put his arm around her, pulling her close.

I looked at them, at how happy they looked together, and something ached deep in my chest.

I cleared my throat, forcing a smile back on. "Yes." I nodded. "This is a win all around, from where I stand." And I meant it. I was happy for both of them, and would be thrilled to have them here. I turned to Madison. "You mentioned your parents, but what about Rory? Is he not staying, too?"

She shook her head. "Oh, no, he has other plans. Chairman Hart has agreed to let him train as a LeyGuard, especially with the dark magic interaction he had. The Dark King is gone, but the magic, his ability to glimpse into the Void, might *not* be entirely gone. They want to teach him how to control it, and *he* wants to learn how to fight." She smiled. "Plus... I kind of think he wanted to be near a certain Fae girl who lives at the Hub."

I smiled back and nodded. "Right. Of course."

We fell into silence for a moment.

A knock sounded on the door frame, from behind the slightly closed door. "Are you decent?" Reina's voice asked.

Are you decent? My heart shot straight up into my throat at the familiar phrase—the one from Quinn's vision.

Callan stared at me, noticing my sudden alarm.

"Ye–ugh—" I hacked, clearing my throat. "Yes!"

Reina poked her head into my room, then drew back in surprise. "Oh! I'm sorry. I didn't realize you guys were in here. I can come back."

"No!" I shouted, lunging forward.

Everyone froze and stared at me.

"I mean—uh—it's fine. Come in."

Reina glanced at the others, then at me. "Okay." She stepped inside.

Callan gripped Madison's hand. "We've got a—a thing." He dragged Madison out the doorway and away down the hall.

Reina stared after them, then turned back to me. "Why is everyone being weird?"

I opened my mouth, but before I could concoct an excuse, she drew a breath, then shook her head.

"Nevermind, it doesn't matter. I came here to say something and I need to say it. Do you have a minute to talk?"

I stared at her, my heart thumping hard against my ribs. "Yes, of course." I started to offer for her to sit on my sofa, then I remembered that in the vision Quinn described, we'd been standing. Would changing the scenario keep the vision from happening? I froze, hand halfway outstretched toward the sofa, then dropped my arm. "Um... go on?"

Reina chewed her lip in thought, which was torturously distracting and not at all helping my frazzled brain, then she drew a breath and crossed straight toward me.

She stopped within arm's reach and stared up at me. "Before, after your bond broke at the Hub... I pushed you away out of fear. I realize that, now. But I don't want to be *afraid*, anymore, Kaizyn," she said, her eyes suddenly wide-open and vulnerable. "I just—"

I stepped toward her, taking her hands in mine. "You don't want to be hurt again," I guessed, my eyes searching hers.

She nodded, then glanced away, though she left her hands in my hold.

I sucked in a breath. "I'm king now." The words just flew out, heaven help me. I wasn't even sure why I said them.

Reina stiffened, looking down at our joined hands. "I know. So then we—*us*—"

"No." I shook my head quickly. "That's—that's not what I meant to say." I huffed in frustration at myself, then raised one of my hands, hers still clasped inside it, and nudged her chin up to look at me. "Reina, do you want to know the reason it was so easy for me to control the bond when we went back to the Hub, even *before* the entanglement was broken?"

She stared at me, and I forged ahead, for better or worse.

"It was you. I could barely even feel Ayla, anymore, because even with you just standing near me in the room, my mind was full of *you*."

She gaped at me, eyes wide, scarcely breathing. I was pretty sure she didn't believe me.

I squeezed her hands in mine. "Reina, you are fierce and courageous. You might be the bravest woman I've ever met. But you are also gentle, and so full of compassion. You speak your mind with boldness, but you also put others before yourself, even when it hurts you to do so. You love with a fire I've never seen in anyone else." I shifted our clasped hands, tracing the back of my knuckles along her face. "And you are so, so beautiful."

She pulled one of her hands from mine and pressed it to my chest.

I leaned my face down over hers. She didn't stop me, but I paused just before my lips touched hers. Her breath danced warm on my lips and I hovered there, torturously close, but waiting—searching her eyes. My heart was hammering so hard I suspected she could feel it.

"Reina?" I whispered.

"Yes," she said, gripping my shirt and pulling me toward her. "Yes. Kiss me."

I closed the distance, tangling my hands in her hair, and pressed my lips to hers.

Our kiss was gentle at first, then it flashed as hot as fire. I pulled away a moment later, but we were both already breathing heavily.

My heart was about to race out of my chest.

We stared at each other, then she smiled, looking a little dazed. "Wow."

I pulled her close and pressed a gentle kiss to her forehead—not realizing until I'd done it that *this* was it—Quinn's exact vision.

Reina tightened her arms around my waist, leaning into my embrace.

After a moment, I pulled back to look at her, taking her hands in mine again. "I would never expect you to stay here with me. I know you have a life at the Hub, a life back home. I shouldn't even ask it. If I were a better man, I'd just figure it out, figure out a way to do this long-distance without you sacrificing anything, but—" I huffed out a breath. "I'm sorry; I at least have to ask. Stay here in Teionyr? Please? It doesn't have to be forever. Even just for a while would be better than no time at all, even though I'd happily make you my queen, in a heartbeat—a betrothal, I mean, not the actual *marriage* in a heartbeat, because of course we're still young, and—" I gasped, my mind catching up with my words.

Reina was just staring at me, utterly startled and speechless.

"Oh, heavens," I said, dropping her hands and stepping back. "I didn't mean to say that part out loud. I just couldn't watch you walk away, not when—this—" I drew a shaky breath as she stared at me. "I'm so sorry. I wouldn't blame you if you ran screaming from my chambers right this instant and never spoke to me again."

Finally, *finally*, my brain got control of my mouth. I stopped talking and just stood there, gaping at her, my cheeks flaming, my whole heart flayed open at her feet.

"Kaizyn," she said, stepping toward me again. "You really want me to stay?" Her gaze searched my face. She didn't look mad, or even freaked out. Her voice actually sounded... *hopeful.* She placed her hand back on my chest.

I looked down at it, then back at her face, trying to parse this latest development. "You're not... I mean... You actually *want* to? Even after I said... all that?"

"Yes," she said softly. "More than I've ever wanted anything."

I stared at her. "Oh." *Oh?* This was not the best day for my brain function, obviously, but I was honestly a bit confused. I placed my hand over hers, clutching it to my chest. "Are you... sure?"

She laughed. "Yes. I'm sure. At least for a while. I just—I just want to give this a chance. To give *us* a chance." She peered up at me, studying my face, then she sighed softly. "I feel safe with you, Kaizyn." She shifted her hand, placing it over my heart, then placed her other hand over her own heart. "I feel safe *here*. Unlike I ever have with anyone."

My heart was absolutely pounding, and this time I *knew* she could feel it.

She smiled up at me. "Ironically, feeling safe like this is actually kind of terrifying. I've never known anyone like you, Kaizyn. I've never felt *understood* like I feel with you." Suddenly she stiffened and rolled her eyes. "Oh, my parents are never going to let me live this one down. I will *never* hear the end of the *I told you so*'s." She lifted her empty hand to the side of my face, toying with a piece of hair near my ear, then shrugged. "But they were right, and I'm not mad about it."

I was pretty sure I was following this conversation, but half of me still worried I'd misunderstood her. I raised both hands to cup her face, my heart racing. "So you'll stay? At least for a little while?"

She raised an eyebrow, her eyes sparking. "My parents can stay too, right? They like you, but I doubt they'd agree to just leave me here alone with a dashing Fae king."

"Of course!" I said quickly. "You can bring the entire Hub with you, I don't even care. Bring a whole menagerie, with elephants, if you want. I'll build you a barn for them. Just... stay. Please, stay."

She nodded, and I pulled her close, letting out a slow sigh of relief. Her in my arms, like this... it hardly felt real.

"Quinn predicted this," I whispered, then pulled back to look at her. I didn't want to alarm her any further—I felt unbelievably lucky she was still standing here with me, and not running away screaming—but I also didn't want us to have secrets from each other.

She tilted her head. "Quinn predicted *what*?"

"This." I gestured between us. "And this." I pressed another kiss to her forehead, then pulled back to meet her eyes. "I didn't believe her."

Reina's mouth slowly curled into a smile—and it was full of mischief. "I wouldn't have, either. I guess we've got another person who'll be saying *I told you so*."

I laughed, pulling her close. "Let them all say it. I don't care in the least."

She tilted back, gently tugging my face down, and recaptured my lips with hers.

Epilogue, Part III: Rory

Rory

I sat on a bench in the hall outside Callan's chambers, waiting for Madison to come back out. She and Callan were supposedly discussing the logistics of Madison and my parents' impending stay here. We'd left the door open, and I'd been posted as an "escort" at the insistence of Jordan's strange assistant, Barthas, who had loudly decreed that young ladies were not allowed in young men's chambers unaccompanied. It wasn't a bad policy, all things considered, but Madison and Callan had been talking in hushed voices inside for a long time, and I'd heard more than enough sentimental things to have staunchly committed to *not* eavesdropping.

Basically, I'd been just sitting in this dim, lantern-lit hall forever with my fingers in my ears, trying to ignore how my butt was going numb from the bench, and I was really, really bored.

That was, until Dove came striding up the hallway. Suddenly, the hall felt a lot brighter.

I dropped my fingers from my ears and grinned at her. Her long, dark hair was damp, and she was wearing a simple blue dress I'd never seen before, tied with a sash around her slim waist. As she neared, I noticed Fogarty behind her. He was back in cat form, his fur was wet and sticking up in clumps, and he looked rather disgruntled about all of it.

I chuckled. "I guess you couldn't find a tub big enough to bathe a bear?"

Dove's musical laugh felt like sunshine beaming straight through my chest.

"No," she said, smiling at me. "Besides, the palace staff find him less alarming this way." She glanced down at him, and he flicked his tail angrily. "I'm sorry, Foge." She shrugged. "It's true."

She stepped close to me, close enough I noticed she smelled of roses rather than her usual honeysuckles, then she reached up and gently trailed her fingers down my face.

My eyes slipped closed, almost of their own accord. When I blinked them back open, she was peering up at me, her dark eyes searching my face with concern.

"I can still feel a hint of dark magic in you... faint, like a residue. Can you feel it?"

I sighed. "A bit. Only if I focus on it." A knot of worry tensed deep in my stomach. "What do you think it means?"

She pursed her lips in thought, then shook her head. "I don't know. Perhaps a part of you will always be connected, now, to the goings-on in the Void. Perhaps it means nothing. But I know it doesn't mean what you *fear* it means."

I stared back down at her. "And what do you think I *fear* it means?"

She took my hands in hers, though her eyes never left mine. "That you are broken. That you are tainted. That you are not useful, or even worse, a threat."

My chest clenched, and I glanced away. How did she *do* that? See straight through me like that? Her words pierced right to the place that hurt most.

I drew a shaky breath. "You can't know for sure that I'm not."

She drew one hand out of mine and placed her cool fingers back on my face, turning me back to look at her. "My love, have you heard the story of how I became bonded to Fogarty?"

My heart raced at her calling me *my love*, even as I willed it not to. I locked my eyes on hers. "No, I haven't."

"Fogarty was my father's bear," she said quietly. Her dark lashes dusted her cheeks as she glanced down in thought. "His bonded one. They fought side by side, always. Until the day the Dark King attacked our village... and my father commanded Fogarty to leave him. To leave him and take *me* to safety." She looked up at me. "Fogarty carried me Earthside, even though parting from my father caused Fogarty literal, physical pain. I begged him to go back, but he wouldn't. *I promised, little Dove,* he said. *I promised to keep you safe, and I will not break it.*"

She glanced down, drawing a breath, and I decided now was not the time to ask about the bear *talking* to her, even though I really, really wanted to. I also felt a wave of gratitude for that grumpy cat-bear, and for what he'd done to make sure Dove was safe.

She looked back up at me, continuing, "By the time I convinced him to go back, it was too late. My father had been hurt. He was dying. We found him, and I tried to save him." She stopped, her eyes tearing up. "We were too late."

The tears in her eyes, and the expression on her face, nearly broke my heart. I pulled her to me. "I'm sorry. I'm so sorry."

"Fogarty is mine, now," she said against my shirt. "The bond transferred to me when my father died. Foge insisted we go Earthside, into hiding, and eventually we made it to the Hub, where we've been ever since." She pulled back, then placed a hand on my chest. "The Hub has never truly felt like home," she said softly, staring up at me. "I haven't felt *home* in a long time... except for when I'm with you."

My heart was pounding from the way she was looking at me, but I tried to keep it together. I couldn't just grab her and kiss her. That would probably be... inadvisable. Instead, I placed a hand on her cheek and traced her jaw with my thumb. She shivered, and I smiled. "I feel the same way about you."

She stared up at me. "We both have scars and shadows, Rory, but yours do not scare me. We both fight them with light. You and I, we are more alike than you realize. The truth is, I am a little broken, too. But with you, Rory Kane... I feel whole."

Now my heart was beating double-time. I thought I might legitimately be about to have a heart attack. "Dove," I whispered, "I—"

She smiled up at me. "I think you're supposed to kiss me now."

I pulled her close with her hand on my chest, my fingers on her jaw, then pressed my lips tenderly to hers... and kissed her.

It felt like home.

Epilogue, Part IV: Ayla

Ayla

I knocked on the guest chambers where Grandpa was staying, and my mom pulled open the door. She was wearing a simple cream tunic and brown breeches, nothing like I'd ever seen her wear before, but it looked comfortable. Her hair, though, was normal—dark, slightly frizzy like mine, and piled into a messy bun on her head. Somehow, she always made that hairstyle look far more glamorous than I ever could.

"Ayla." She smiled when she saw me, and pulled me into a hug. "Come in!"

I stepped inside, and Mom shut the door behind us.

Dad was sitting on a sofa in Grandpa's room, holding a piece of charcoal and something that looked like a handmade notebook with parchment pages. He looked up and smiled as I entered. "Hey, Peanut. Barthas brought me some stuff to keep my mind occupied until we head back. After everything we saw here, I thought I'd try capturing—well, anyway, how does it look?" He held the page out toward me.

I gasped, then hurried over to him. "Dad, that looks amazing!" He had sketched a tiny replica of the battlefield, but with everything happening at once: the wind-Fae in rows, the churning cyclone, arcs of fire and lightning shooting up into the sky, darklings with a swarm of dragons swooping overhead, even a hole blown in the trees over to the side, three small figures pointing cannons up from a hatch in the ground. Everything was so detailed, and he had captured the dragons perfectly—all but their colors since he was using charcoal. I stared at him. "I didn't even know you could draw!"

He blushed slightly, but grinned. "I used to, when I was younger. I'm a little rusty, but it's coming back to me."

I beamed at him. If *that* was rusty, I could hardly wait to see what he'd do when his skills fully kicked back in.

"Your grandpa taught me," he added, then glanced over at the bed. The mood in the room shifted.

The covers were pulled up nearly to Grandpa's chin in the tall bed, with the bed-curtains open. I could see his chest rising and falling beneath the blankets as he breathed, but with all the pillows piled up around him, I couldn't see his face. "How is he feeling?" I asked, more quietly.

"I'm trying to sleep, that's how I am," came a grumpy voice from the bed.

I hurried over toward him. "I'm sorry, Grandpa."

He pulled his arms out of the covers and flopped them on the blanket with a huff, then looked up at me. "It's all right, Ayla." He smiled, though his eyes were droopy from exhaustion, with dark circles underneath.

Grandpa had come through the battle okay, especially once Sorcha had healed his injuries, but using his magic so intensely had taken a lot out of him. He was still regaining his strength. He looked old, lying there in the bed, but—he *was* old. And honestly, he still looked worlds better than he'd looked before all this, when his mind was failing him. His eyes now, though exhausted, still held a sharp, perceptive glint.

"Don't look so worried," he grumbled. "I'm not dying, I'm just tired. And hungry." He glanced over at my dad and grinned.

My dad laughed. "Okay, Dad," he told Grandpa. "I'll see what the kitchen can whip up for you."

He set his sketchbook down and headed out into the hall.

Mom moved up behind me. "Do you need anything else?" she asked Grandpa.

"I need to be left alone so I can sleep without an entire room of people hovering over me," he grumped as he shifted his pillows to sit up, but his eyes were glinting with amusement.

"Okay," Mom chuckled. "I'll be just across the hall if you need anything—either of you." She kissed the top of my head, then slipped out.

"I'll let you sleep," I told Grandpa, then turned to go.

"Wait, Ayla," he said.

I stepped back toward the bed. "Yes?"

Grandpa reached out and gripped one of my hands in his weathered fingers. He stared up at me. "In all my years as a LeyGuard, even in my time here in Teionyr, I have *never* seen anything like what you did on that battlefield. It was... incredible."

I blushed and glanced away. I'd never been good at receiving compliments. "Thanks," I muttered. "I just—I mean, I did what I needed to, I guess. I didn't really think about it."

Grandpa squeezed my hand. "Ayla, look at me."

I did. His warm, brown eyes were sharply focused, despite his exhaustion, and brimming with pride and love.

"I know the weight of battle, Ayla," he said. "I know you may replay those moments in your head, again and again, wondering if you should've done something differently, remembering how close we came to losing it all, every pivotal moment. Those moments will revisit you, sometimes when you least expect it—bursting into your waking thoughts, haunting your nightmares. When we're back at the Hub, and training, it won't mean you'll escape what happened here. Maybe never. But you can learn to *use* it, to process it and let it fuel you. I can help teach you that."

I swallowed and nodded.

"But listen, Ayla, and really *hear* me." His thumb traced my hand, his eyes intense on mine. "I know you were scared—that you're often scared. And you'll be scared again. But what you did out there, what you've done these past couple of weeks—I've watched you unfold into the woman I always *believed* you could become." His eyes moistened as they bored into me. "Your potential isn't hiding behind that fear anymore, Ayla. It's on full display... and it's *breathtaking*."

My chest clenched, my throat aching with a withheld sob. I blinked back tears. "Grandpa, I—"

He smiled at me, cupping the side of my face with his other hand. "The fact that we're here, that my mind is back, that my magic is back, that I'm once again the man I was, that Jordan and Kaizyn are both alive, that we're *all* alive right now—that's in a huge part, if not entirely, because of *you*, Ayla. And I am so, so proud of you."

My tears spilled over, and I threw my arms around him. "I love you, Grandpa." I hugged him tight. "I couldn't have done any of this without you. You were amazing, too. I had no idea how powerful you are."

He pulled back to look at me, then smoothed my hair and smirked. "Where did you think you got it from, Peanut?"

Barthas greeted me in the hall outside Jordan's chambers, where Jordan had gone to take care of a few documents and final logistics after Kaizyn's impromptu coronation ceremony.

"Are you going in, miss?" Barthas asked.

"Yes," I said, knowing that would mean he'd follow me inside. Whenever our parents weren't around, Barthas took his chaperone duties seriously. Not that I really minded. It was kind of refreshing, actually, that he paid attention to that and cared.

He hovered beside me as I knocked on Jordan's door.

"Come in," Jordan answered, and I pushed the door open.

He smiled at me from his desk by the window, then stood. "Ayla."

We met in the middle of the room, and he drew me into a hug.

"How are you feeling about everything?" I asked gently when we pulled apart. "Do you regret your decision to leave here?"

He sighed, wrapping his arms loosely around my waist. "No—but I will miss it here. And the people *staying* here."

My heart clenched just thinking about leaving some of our friends behind. "So will I, but at least you and I will finally be together at the Hub. And we can come back here to visit as often as we're able."

He stared down at me, a fog of worry appearing in his golden eyes.

"What's wrong?"

He smiled. "You know me too well."

I laughed. "That one goes both ways. Seriously, though—what is it?"

He took his time answering, filling the space by raising a hand up to play with a piece of my hair. When his eyes finally met mine, I saw a hint of fear in them. "Are you sure you won't think less of me? Now that I'm not a king?"

I blinked up at him. *That* was what he was worried about? I moved my hand up to his face, resting my fingers on his cheek. "Jordan... I was already falling for you the day you walked me home, moping about how Callan was a black belt and you weren't."

He chuckled, glancing off, but I pressed my fingers gently against his jaw, drawing his gaze back to me.

"I'm serious, Jordan. I was already falling for you then, and every day it seems I learn something new about you that only makes me love you more."

His eyes darted between mine, scanning them, then he asked softly, "And today, you learned...?"

"Today I learned that your heart is every bit as selfless and caring, now that you know you're a royal, as it was when you carried my books in the hallway or came crashing through my bedroom window. I don't care about your *titles*, Jordan. I never did. I just want *you*."

His face lit up in a half-smile that made my breath catch, then he placed his hands on either side of my face, leaned down, and kissed me.

A moment later, he tensed and pulled back. "I just realized something," he said, looking genuinely worried.

My heart thumped. "What?"

"I never officially asked you to be my girlfriend."

I laughed, staring up at him. "Well, then... ask me."

He smiled, then cleared his throat. "Ayla, will you be my—"

I grabbed his face, pulling him back into a kiss. "Yes," I whispered against his lips. "Always yes."

He wrapped his arms around my waist and kissed me again, then smiled. "I like that answer."

READ MORE LEYWARD STONES!

T hank you so much for reading this series!

This marks THE END of Book 3.... and of Trilogy 1 of The Leyward Stones...

But if you want more Leyward Stones, don't worry! There *are* more stories available to read in this world, starting with my ongoing Leyward Stones serial, *Fate Rising*!

When Lena befriends the mysterious new boy next door, she discovers a terrifying folklore creature is targeting her father. To save him, Lena must dive into a dangerous world of Fae, magic, secrets, & a war she never knew existed. What she learns could change her life—and the LeyGuards—forever.

Featuring cameos from Season 1/Trilogy 1, but in a brand new storyline with new characters, new romances, new conflicts... and of course, more Fae & LeyGuards. Get ready for a whole new adventure!

This story is currently posting in serial format—visit **the Leyward Stones page on my website** for the latest info on posting schedules and where to find it!

Be sure to also subscribe to my newsletter at **http://ccrawfordwriting.com/subscribe** to receive updates on future Leyward Stones stories! You even get a bonus Leyward Stones short story for subscribing!

ACKNOWLEDGEMENTS

Yet again, thank you to my husband and kids, who are always so supportive of my writing, and to M.J., my editor Christy, the Alphas (including Lydia), Candice, the Wulf Pack, my Patreon and PirateCat subscribers, my Vella readers and Vella author friends who supported the early version of this book, and all my subscribers and readers who hung in there with me for the long months and years of working on this series. And especially to God, from whom all blessings flow—and without whom, my writing would not exist. I pray that, first and foremost, my writing always brings Him glory.

Want to see more from me, outside my published books? Come find me where I hang out online!

If you love **clean young adult fiction** and want a portal where you can read a bunch of my clean YA content, interact with me and other readers, and help me build a community around clean YA fiction, **check out my Story Subscribers portal on my website!** Find out more on the next page, or at **http://ccrawfordwriting.com/storysubscriberscontent**.

If you'd like to receive updates on future releases, behind-the-scenes info on my writing, and personal updates, subscribe to my monthly email newsletter at **http://ccrawfordwriting.com/subscribe**. I never spam my email subscribers—you can expect one email per month, with occasional bonus emails if I have a new release, sale, or something important to share. And you'll even get free story downloads for subscribing!

I'm also on social media! You can find me at:

Website: **http://ccrawfordwriting.com**

Blog: **http://ccrawfordwriting.com/blog**

Facebook: **http://facebook.com/ccrawfordwriting**

Instagram: **http://instagram.com/ccrawfordwriting**

YouTube: **http://youtube.com/ccrawfordwriting**

Or contact me directly through email at **ccrawford@ccrawfordwrit ing.com**. I'd love to see your comments and respond to any questions you might have.

Thank you so much for reading!

Then check out my Story Subscribers portal!

It's a special section of my website where you'll find a collection of stories from me right there online & ready to binge-read! Some of the stories in there are free, and others are behind a small paywall... right now (as of May 2026), that paywall is only $1.99/month to access ALL of my Story Subscribers content. This small fee helps keep my business running... plus my Story Subscribers get access to some *exclusive* content not available anywhere else, like my ongoing serials and bonus side stories set in some of my published story worlds.

Also, EVERYTHING in my Story Subscribers portal is clean and either YA or YA-appropriate in content. **What do I mean by "clean"?** For me, that means:

PG-13 or less for violence (battle violence in the fantasy/sci-fi but no gratuitous gore).

Sweet/wholesome romance (when romance is present) that focuses on relationship and never goes beyond a chaste kiss.

NO profanity (but with an occasional mild euphemism like "dang" or similar, and occasional in-world, made-up "swear" words).

I write from a Biblical worldview (though much of my content is not explicitly religious), and do my best to portray healthy relationship dynamics, especially in parent-child relationships and romantic relationships, which I've found are often quite *unhealthy* in much of the mainstream YA fiction. My characters are not perfect, and do not always make the right choices, but their mistakes are always used for growth. There will always be a clear concept of good versus evil in my stories (especially fantasy!), and they'll always end with either a hard-fought happy ending, or at least a note of hope.

If this sounds like your cup of tea, I'm thrilled you found me—and I hope you'll check out my Story Subscribers content!

Just visit my Story Subscribers page at **http://ccrawfordwriting.com /storysubscriberscontent**to join or find out more!

Crystal Crawford writes clean YA fantasy and clean YA romance (and a smattering of other genres) in Florida, where every natural body of water hides something that could eat you, and if they don't get you, the weather might. She lives with her husband, five kids, two cats, one doofusy dog, and two live-in grandparents, who have all supported her dream of writing and drinking far too much coffee. Her imagination is her happy place! (But a deserted beach is nice, too.) When she isn't writing, she enjoys reading, napping, watching shows with her family, working in the garden, and homeschooling the kids, though most days you'll also find her doing laundry.

The Leyward Stones

Macchiatos, Faerie Princes, and Other Things That Happen at Midnight
LeyGuards, Faespells, and Other Things That Breach the Veil
Fae Curses, Dark Kings, and Other Things That Must Fall
and more books to come!

The Lex Chronicles (Legends of Arameth)

The Edge of Nothing
The Path to Paradox
The Ends of Exile
and more books to come!

Aubrey Lance, S.S. (Supernatural Sleuth)

Season 1: The Vanishings, now available to read in serial format in the forum on my website: http://ccrawfordwriting.com/forum/aubreylance -season1

Secret Messages Sweet YA Romance Series

I'm Not a Stalker
The Five Suspects
and more books to come!

Love and Aliens

The Extraordinary, Extraterrestrial Love Lives of Doppelgangers
and another book to come!

Published Short Stories

- "Our Kind" (a Leyward Stones short story published in DreamForge Magazine) — available to read free at https://dreamforge.mywebportal.app/dreamforge/stories/show/our-kind-crystal-crawford

- "One Shot at Aeden" (a Leyward Stones short story published in DreamForge Magazine) — available to read free at https://dreamforge.mywebportal.app/dreamforge/stories/show/one-shot-at-aeden-crystal-crawford

- "Cheer Hawks and a Side of Murder" (a short story originally published in the Murderbirds anthology by Mike Jack Stoumbos)

- plus loads of other Leyward Stones, Legends of Arameth, and assorted short stories available inside PirateCat!

Nonfiction

- The Unspoken Language: An Animal Trainer's Memoir

- Slap Him with a Fish: a Crash-Course in Fiction Writing

- Put Some Pants on That Kid: a Writing Handbook for High School and Beyond (Student Book and Parent/Teacher's Guide)

- The Other Side of the Law (a co-written lawyer's memoir)

- Unbreaking: How Giving Up Saved Our Marriage (a raw, real marriage memoir)

**Find the purchase links to many of the above books all in one place
at**
http://ccrawfordwriting.com/books

www.ingramcontent.com/pod-product-compliance
Lightning Source LLC
Chambersburg PA
CBHW022016300726
48970CB00003B/908